DIVINE DESCENDANTS

THE COMPLETE SERIES

USA TODAY BESTSELLING AUTHOR
ALICIA RADES

Published by Crystallite Publishing LLC.
Cover design by Rebecca Frank.

aliciarades.com

DIVINE DESCENDANTS

Concealing Magic
Exposing Magic

ALSO BY ALICIA RADES

HIDDEN LEGENDS: ACADEMY OF MAGICAL CREATURES

The Fire Prophecy

The Water Legacy

The Earth Legend

The Air Omen

The Elemental War

The Soul Sacrifice

HIDDEN LEGENDS: COLLEGE OF WITCHCRAFT

The Coven's Secret

The Reaper's Shadow

The Cauldron's Curse

The Demon's Spell

The Warlock's Trial

The Witch's Fate

HIDDEN LEGENDS: PRISON FOR SUPERNATURAL OFFENDERS

The Villain Institute

The Criminal Lair

The Infernal Underground

The Assassin's Destiny

The Devil's City

The Elven Gate

The Phoenix Dawning

DIVINE FATE TRILOGY

Chosen by Grace

Touched by Grace

Awakened by Grace

SEA OF MERMAID SECRETS

Deep Waters

Rising Tides

Crashing Waves

VENGEANCE AND VAMPIRES

Ravenite

Resilience

Resolute

Retribute

CRYSTAL FROST

Fire in Frost

Desire in Frost

Inspired by Frost

Fading Frost

STANDALONES

Murder at the Magic Academy

Distant Dreams

Dreaming With Frost

The Lost Sphinx

Aura, Aura

Where the Darkness Ends

Split

To you.

CONCEALING MAGIC

DIVINE DESCENDANTS BOOK ONE

1

*E*very supernatural being lives by one single rule: Never let a human see you as your true self. No wings. No essence. For all intents and purposes, when you're around a human, you are human.

But I wasn't human. I was a Davina—or an angel, as some stories went, though the stories were way off—and I wasn't going to let my powers go to waste. That's why I was attending the academy. It was a Davina's best chance at making a difference in a world where our essence—our magic—was otherwise kept a secret. And come hell or high water, I would make a difference.

The thick stone walls surrounding Harris Academy came into view, and already my heart was pounding in exhilaration. I leaned forward between my mom's and dad's seats, trying to take in the wonder of the structure. The wall was made of a beautiful white brick that looked like it belonged in a sacred temple. Bright sunlight reflected off the surface, making it look more beautiful and glorious than I remembered from the times we drove by it when I was a kid. It stretched two stories high and surrounded fifty acres, enclosing the small campus inside.

The campus would be my home for the next two years. Its perimeter wall kept out prying eyes and allowed us to study as ourselves—wings, magic, and all. I'd had that freedom back home at Galen High School, but somehow, this felt different. It was my stepping stone toward bigger and better things.

In the distance, tall buildings reached twenty stories high. All around us, the streets bustled with traffic as a thousand other eager freshman like me flooded onto campus from all over the country. Celia, Minnesota wasn't a huge city, but it felt like it compared to Eagle Valley, the small town I grew up in. And it was *amazing*.

"Nervous, Cora?" Dad asked from the driver's seat.

"Me? Nervous?" I feigned. Of course I was nervous. But my nerves couldn't mask my excitement. I'd been waiting for this day my whole life. "You should be the ones who are nervous."

I was grateful Mom and Dad made the trip with me. Otherwise, all eyes would be on me. With them here, I doubt anyone would even notice me.

Dad pulled up behind a long line of cars at the front gate. I craned my neck, trying to catch a glimpse of the buildings inside. I could just barely make out the Academy Center straight in front of us past the parking lot. It was four stories high and made of red brick, with various peaks in its roof that reminded me of the Galen High mansion. Rising up from the center of the building was a pointed bell tower. It was like a beacon welcoming me to my new home.

"I can't wait to check out campus," I said. "I heard they just made an addition to the Activities Center and added a new rock-climbing wall. Plus, they're working on building an obstacle course for training. Doesn't that sound cool? Oh! And I want to see the Winged Fountain and check out the bar on the lower level of the dining center."

Mom turned in her seat and frowned. She wore her brown hair up, with loose tendrils framing her face. Normally, Mom was dressed in an apron and covered in flour, but today she'd worn a sleek black dress with three-quarter length sleeves and low heels, a real business-style look. "You're only eighteen. You're not going to a bar."

"I don't have to *drink*. I hear they play live music and have standup comedians come in all the time. It sounds fun, doesn't it?" I bounced a little in my seat.

Mom smiled, but it didn't reach her eyes. "You know you don't have to do this. You can always stay home and work at the restaurant."

I sighed. This was the third time Mom had said that today. And yes, I was counting. It wasn't that she didn't want me to become an emergency responder. She knew this was everything I wanted in life and more. The look in her eyes told me it was because she wasn't ready to let me go yet.

"I'll come to visit," I told her. "I promise."

Mom's eyes brightened. "We don't have any plans this weekend."

"Slow down, Ryn," Dad said with a laugh. "You're suffocating the poor girl."

Mom gaped at him, then looked back to me. "Am I suffocating you?"

"A little," I admitted, crinkling my nose.

Mom scrunched her face up at me, but she couldn't hold the expression for long. A moment later, she was smiling. She reached back and poked me playfully between the eyebrows. "What are mothers for?"

I pushed her hand away, laughing. "Why can't you be more like Grandma Gloria? Go find yourself a rich guy like Calvin and explore the world. Let me study my powers in peace."

Mom reached over and brushed her fingers through Dad's dark hair. "I'd rather have a nice man over a rich guy any day."

Dad tilted his head toward hers and gazed into her eyes.

Even after twenty years of marriage, they still looked at each other like they were on their honeymoon.

I couldn't help it. I started making gagging noises from the back seat.

"Keep that up and you're grounded," Dad teased. The man had never grounded me a day in my life.

The traffic started moving again. By the time we reached the front gates, I was sitting so close to the edge of my seat that I was practically leaning over the middle console between my parents.

A campus security officer holding a tablet approached Dad's open window. "ID, please?"

Dad pulled out his driver's license and the paperwork the school had given us with our passes onto campus. The guy glanced at the names, then stared at my parents in shock.

"James and Kathryn Marek?" he asked in disbelief.

"That's us," Dad said with a smile. He leaned an elbow against the open window, where a soft, pleasant breeze drifted into the car.

The guy opened his mouth and then closed it again, like he couldn't find the words. Then he stuck his hand out in my father's direction. "Wow, sir. It's a real pleasure."

Yep. I was a legacy. *The legacy.* Twenty-five years ago, my parents discovered that the Davina and the Aedes—angels and demons— were more powerful *together.* They were responsible for ending the age-old war between them and bringing our races to peace. It was only because of them that the academy even existed. Before I was born, Aedes and Davina tried to kill each other. Now we were allies revolutionizing the law enforcement and medical fields. Most people chalked it up to science, to medical advance-ments. They still had no idea angels and demons were behind it all.

The security guard quickly scrambled back toward his papers and pressed his tablet a few times, then handed the papers back to Dad. "You're all set to go. You'll want to go straight ahead into the parking lot. Your daughter can pick up her information packet and student ID from the Academy Center. Just follow everyone else; you can't miss it. Orientation starts in three hours, so you have plenty of time."

"Thank you, sir," my dad said.

"My pleasure." The guy waved to us as Dad started inching forward. Traffic was slow, so we moved at a snail's pace.

"Wow, this place is packed," I glanced toward the parking lot, which was almost full by now. Soon, people would start having to park on the streets outside campus. "Guess it's good we got here early. You know, I think I'd still benefit from my own car. What do you guys think?"

"No," my parents answered in unison.

"Come on," I complained. "This city's huge. What if I want to go shopping or something? Will you at least consider a moped? Hey, Dad, maybe I can borrow your motorcycle for the semester."

"You can take the bus. Besides, we offered to bring your bicycle," Mom pointed out.

I crinkled up my nose. "That rusty old thing?"

Mom shrugged.

"Grandma gave me some money for my birthday," I said. "Maybe I'll—"

"You can't do this! This is police brutality!" someone yelled outside the car.

I instantly cut off and sat back in my seat to get a better look out the window. Two security guards were dragging a guy out the front gate right next to our car. He looked older than me, at least mid-twenties, with blond hair and a strong jawline. If he weren't kicking and screaming like a little girl, I might've said he was cute. But there was something about him that repulsed me. There was a sense of entitlement in his perfect hair and dark blue blazer, like he thought the world should be bowing at his feet just because he'd been born.

"No ID, no entry," one of the guards told him sternly.

"You can't just refuse people entry!" he screamed.

He kicked his legs out, struggling out of their hold. Somehow, he managed to slip his arm out of his blazer sleeve and free it. He ducked out of the guard's reach, then twisted around until his other arm broke free. He sprinted back inside the wall, but he only took a few paces before a guard jumped him from behind. The two of them went flying straight into my window with a *thud*.

My heart leapt into my throat, and I jumped back, pushing across the bench seat all the way to the other side of the car. My pulse didn't slow as the guard pressed the guy's face up against the window, squishing it flat.

"How would you like to add another trespassing charge to your record, *Colt Walter*?" the guard threatened.

"Ooh, I'm so scared," Colt replied flatly.

"Yeah, yeah," the guard said. "Daddy's not going to bail you out every time."

The guard handcuffed him and pulled him away from the window. Finally, my heart rate began to slow. Then the trespasser turned his gaze inside our vehicle, and his dark brown eyes met mine. They were hooded in so much anger and resentment that it sent a chill over my skin. He couldn't look away from me soon enough. Finally, the guard dragged him around the side of the security wall, and I felt like I could breathe again.

"Sorry about that!" the second guard called to us.

Mom just waved back to him like it was no problem.

I finally sat up straight in my seat again. "What the hell was that?"

Dad took a long breath. "My guess? A curious human."

"What?" I asked in disbelief. "People actually try to sneak into the school?"

"Don't worry," Dad replied, not really answering my question. "The school is perfectly safe. If I know the founder Casey Harris well—and I do—she wouldn't accept anything less than the best. The best facilities. The best security. You name it."

Then how'd he get in? I wanted to say, but I didn't. Instead, I said, "What do you think would happen? If humans found out about us, I mean."

"I'm sure he doesn't know anything," Mom said. "If he did, the Alliance would deal with him. There are procedures for this kind of thing."

"Okay, but that doesn't answer my question."

Dad sighed and glanced at me in the rear-view mirror. "There's a reason we've kept the Davina and the Aedes a secret for so long. When you've been keeping a secret for Millennia, there's not really a good time to come out with the truth."

"Yeah, but people would know we help them, that we heal them and stuff. It's not like they would shun us, right?" I bit my lower lip.

Mom and Dad exchanged a glance, then Mom turned to look at me. "People believe what they want to believe. Sometimes, they don't want to hear the truth."

"Uh, okay..." I said, feeling like my parents were downplaying the whole thing.

I guess they had one good point. Some things were just better kept secret.

2

"Wow, this place is amazing." I couldn't take my eyes off it all.

We'd already gone through the registration process, and I had my picture taken for my student ID. Now I was strolling alongside my parents on a wide sidewalk with a thick folder in my hand and my full backpack on my shoulders, trusting them to be my eyes as I looked all over campus. Mom rolled my suitcase behind her, and Dad carried a laundry basket full of odds and ends. The Academy Center was behind us, and a wide-open courtyard stood in front of us, where groups of parents and students roamed. At least half of them had shifted into their supernatural form, displaying their white or black wings for everyone to see.

It was so strange. Back home, we were only ever allowed to have our wings out at school. I guess that was the case here, too, but the campus was so much larger than I was used to. It was like its own mini village where we didn't have to worry about being seen. We could just be ourselves.

Tall maples and oaks shaded the walkway, until we reached a sunny clearing. In the middle of a grassy courtyard, glowing

10

white balls of essence the size of my fist whizzed through the air. Freshman laughed and dodged out of the way to avoid getting stunned by the magic in a game of essence dodgeball.

Further down the walkway in the center of campus stood a large fountain.

"Look!" I shouted, pointing. "It's the Winged Fountain. I've heard so much about it."

The Winged Fountain was a symbol of campus, much like the bell tower at our backs. The way people back in Eagle Valley talked about it, it was like its waters contained essence itself. Aunt Allie claimed it was magical—but that was only because it was where Uncle Kyle had proposed to her.

I quickened my pace, leaving my parents behind me, and rushed up to the fountain. The pool at the bottom was huge, at least twenty feet across. Three tiers of white marble rose up from the center. At the very top was a carving of open wings bigger than my own. I quickly dug into my pocket and pulled out a penny, which I'd brought along for this very occasion. I stood at the edge of the fountain with my eyes closed, clutching on to the penny like it was my very life force.

What to wish for... What to wish for...

I could wish that Kaylee was with me. My best friend from Galen High decided she had better things to do than spend the year rooming with me at the best place on the planet. Instead, she was spending the year traveling Europe on her parents' dime. Which was cool, I guess, but it wasn't Harris Academy.

I wish... I wish Harris Academy is everything I dreamed it would be.

I tossed my penny into the fountain and heard it land with a *slosh*. Smiling, I turned back toward my parents—and promptly smacked into two-hundred pounds of solid muscle. I looked up to find myself staring into a pair of dreamy blue eyes. The guy was my age, with tousled dark blond hair and the most gorgeous cheekbones. He smiled down at me. Oh, lord. He had dimples.

"S-sorry," I stammered, stepping around him.

"My bad," he said at the same time. His voice was so smooth.

He tossed a coin into the fountain, but I was already headed in the other direction. I glanced back to catch another glimpse of him and saw that he was watching me. My cheeks went beet red under his gaze, and I clutched my folder tighter to my chest.

"Who's that?" my mom asked when I reached her.

"Who?" I asked innocently, knowing exactly who she was talking about. "Oh, that guy? I don't know."

"He's cute," Mom said.

"Oh, God." I hooked my folder under my elbow and covered my ears for show. "Don't ever let me hear you say that again."

"Ew." Mom crinkled her nose. "I meant for you."

Ugh. Don't tell me she was going to start hounding me for grandchildren already.

"I'm not here to meet guys," I assured her, which my father looked more than happy to hear. "I'm just here to study."

But as my parents and I started away from the fountain toward the dorms, I couldn't help but steal a glance back at the blond cutie. I hadn't dated in over a year. A date or two wouldn't hurt anything, right?

I barely noticed the eyes on my parents and the whispers as people recognized them. I couldn't take my gaze off the architecture around campus as we walked. Everywhere I looked, I saw Harris Academy's emblem. In color, the emblem sported one black wing and one white. Where it was etched into surfaces, like the lamps lining the sidewalk, one wing popped outward and the other was carved inward.

Campus wasn't very big. There were four co-ed dorm halls, two main class buildings—the Elemental Building and the Science Building—and the Academy Center, where most of the professor's offices were, along with the administrative departments. Close to the dorms sat the dining hall and Activities Center, which boasted three full-sized gymnasiums and an Olympic-sized pool, along with a rock-climbing wall, a gym with top-of-the-line workout equipment, and outdoor tennis courts.

We arrived at Clark Hall, and I found my room on the second floor. The door was already propped open. Inside, a girl my age sat on one of the beds, and her parents stood beside her. She was petite, with dark brown hair that fell in waves to her shoulders. She wore a cute floral-printed dress with a belt around the middle. My roommate gave a sweet smile when she saw me standing in the doorway.

"Hi!" I squealed in excitement. We'd already talked online to coordinate who was bringing what, but I hadn't had a chance to get to know her yet. "You must be Laura."

I stepped into the room and held my hand out to her.

"Cora!" She shot to her feet and bounced over to me. Instead of taking my hand, she pulled me into a tight hug. I could smell the fresh scent of her shampoo, and I felt warm in her embrace.

"Cora and Laura," I heard my mom whisper to my dad. "How cute."

Laura drew away. "Oh my gosh. It's so great to meet you. This semester is going to rock."

"Damn straight," I said with a chuckle.

"Hi," Mom said kindly, reaching out a hand to Laura's parents. "I'm Ryn, and this is my husband, James."

Laura's mom took my mom's hand, but she stared agape at my parents.

Laura elbowed her in the side. "Jesus, Mom. They're just people."

She quickly composed herself. "Of course. Where are my manners? It's just such a pleasure to meet you. If it weren't for you, Sam and I never would've met. I'm Briana."

My dad set my laundry basket beside my bed and shook Sam's hand.

"What do you mean?" I asked, glancing between my new roommate's parents.

"Oh, Laura didn't tell you?" Briana asked. "I'm an Aedes, and Sam's a Davina."

My eyebrows rose involuntarily. Mixed families had become more common in the last decade, but it almost never happened in my parents' generation. Back then, there was still so much stigma. I'd never met someone my age with mixed powers.

"That's amazing," I said, turning to Laura.

She breathed a sigh of relief, like she'd been holding her breath. Had she been afraid I'd judge her?

Briana and Sam started talking to my parents, while Laura and I spoke amongst ourselves.

"So, you can perform Aedes and Davina magic?" I asked her.

Laura bit her lower lip. "Yes."

"Wow," I said. "That must make you super powerful. Can you draw your own essence to enhance your element?"

Laura shook her head. "Unfortunately, it doesn't work that way. I still need a partner."

"But you could have an Aedes or a Davina partner, right?" I asked.

The mechanics fascinated me. Davina were more powerful than Aedes. Our essence could control the elements as well as heal, but we couldn't do it without the Aedes. They were the only ones who could access another being's essence and draw it out of them. They acted as a sort of battery, charging up our essence and helping us pull more from the earth so that we could perform these amazing acts. Without them, our essence was nothing more than a party trick.

"I'm a jack of all trades," Laura said proudly. "Except air, water, and fire." She ticked each one off on her fingers and chuckled.

"So your element is earth?" I asked.

Laura began unpacking one of her suitcases into her dresser. "Yep. I do trees, grass, rocks, you name it."

I felt a little awkward standing around, so I pulled my sheets out of the laundry basket and started making the bed. "Sounds cool. Do you know what you'll major in?"

Laura wrinkled her nose. "I could go the earthquake cleanup route, but I've also thought about focusing on my Aedes side so I could work anywhere."

I fluffed my pillow on the bed. "That sounds like a good idea. My element is fire, so I'm studying to become an emergency response technician specializing in fires and burns."

"So a firefighter?" Laura asked.

"Medical firefighter, I guess," I said as I started organizing my antiques collection on my desk. I collected anything with a story—including the Davina Blade Uncle Kyle had given me that I kept in my boot at all times. "I intend to graduate top of my class."

Not only that, but I intended to win the Chancellor's Award. It was an honor given to the top performing team in each program their first semester. It opened doors for advanced classes and future job opportunities. And it was mine.

"I'm sure you'll hit the top. You sound pretty determined." Laura finished with her clothes and turned to the large suitcase on her bed. When she opened it, I was shocked to see it was filled entirely with shoes. Heels, boots, flats, sneakers, you name it. There were shoes for every occasion.

My eyebrows shot up. "Whoa."

She laughed. "First thing you need to know about me, I *love* shoes. What do you think of these?"

She twisted her foot to display a pair of fashionable black flats with faux straps that crisscrossed near the toes.

"Cute," I said honestly.

"Second thing you should know about me, I'm a California girl and absolutely *terrified* of your winters." Laura laughed.

"Look on the bright side. The snow's a good excuse to go shopping for a new pair of boots," I pointed out.

Laura beamed. "You totally get me. I think we're going to get along well."

"I hope so," I said.

An hour later, we'd finished unpacking and had gotten lunch at the dining hall with our parents, and one thing was very clear. Laura and I were already getting along great. She was smart, determined, and had graduated top of her high school class like I had. She'd make an equally good study partner as she would a friend. Kaylee would've liked her, too.

On our way to the Academy Center from the dining hall, I caught sight of a girl with a dark pixie cut and legs that went for miles standing in the grassy courtyard. Her white wings were on display, and she was surrounded by people, both Aedes and Davina alike. They all watched in awe as she manipulated fire in her hand, twisting it into a mini tornado and then shaping her flames into the shape of a dragon. She directed her essence so it looked like the dragon was flying. It flew straight toward a guy's face but fizzled out before it hit him. He ducked, then clapped when he realized he wasn't in any danger.

The girl doubled over in laughter, and I finally got a good look at the guy she was laughing at. He was the blond cutie from earlier, the one with the dimples. And he was *laughing* with the show-off.

I couldn't explain the pang of jealousy that hit me just then. She must've been in the four-year program—and a senior. I couldn't manipulate my element like that.

I hadn't realized I'd stopped to watch them until Laura stepped up beside me. "Um... it looks like you might have competition."

I scoffed. "Competition? No way. She can't be in our class."

Laura frowned. "I think she is. I saw her at registration."

My breath grew hot. The blond cutie composed himself, and he caught my eye across the grass. My stomach flipped in my abdomen. He held my gaze a few seconds longer, then turned back to the Davina girl in front of him. His eyes sparkled when he looked at her.

"I guess you're right," I said to Laura. "I do have some competition."

3

I shook off the encounter in the courtyard as we entered the auditorium for orientation. I gazed around in wonder. It was even more beautiful than I'd imagined. The room was bathed in dark wooden tones and soft lighting. A high ceiling stretched up two stories, and there was a balcony with extra seating high above us. Beautiful designs were carved into the balcony banister. Matching ornate carvings outlined the large stage at the front and were brushed in golden paint. I loved it.

Laura leaned over to me as we sat down. "Rumor has it, there's a stone from the site of the Malum portal buried beneath stage."

"It's true," I told her, sharing in her enthusiasm. "Casey Harris said so in an interview."

Laura and I continued to speak in hushed whispers until the auditorium filled and the lights dimmed. The room slowly quieted until it went completely silent. The only sound came from the click of heels across the stage as a blonde woman my parents' age came to stand behind the podium.

Laura straightened in her chair. "Oh my God," she hissed under her breath. "It's her. It's Chancellor Harris."

Chancellor Harris raised her arms in a welcoming gesture. "Welcome, First Years, to Harris Academy."

Applause filled the auditorium. Laura and I screeched beside each other in excitement.

Chancellor Harris beamed behind the microphone until the applause died down. "At Harris Academy, we strive to prepare our students for a better tomorrow in every way possible. Our history is long rooted in the segregation of our differences. Even before the creation of man, the Divinities and Sanctities separated themselves."

We all knew the stories. My dad had been telling me about them since I was a kid. I didn't have to listen to follow along.

Before humankind ever walked the earth, the earth belonged to the gods. The higher gods, the Divinities, began to have children, who became the Davina. They created a new realm, a paradise, called Vehena, which they gifted to their children. They forbade the lesser gods, the Sanctities, from producing children, because they didn't want the power of the gods diluted. But the Sanctities went behind their backs anyway and birthed a race called the Aedes.

When the Divinities learned of their children, they took away the Aedes' immortality and marked them with darkness. They banished them to a dark realm called Malum. But the connection between the realms was unstable, and the Aedes returned.

To punish the Sanctities for going against their wishes, the Divinities cast another curse, one that would prevent the Aedes from interacting with their parents or the earthly realm. They could only walk the earth as ghosts.

This sparked the Great War between the Sanctities and Divinities, and they eventually killed each other until there were no gods left. To show the Aedes they were nothing like their forefathers, the Davina brought life out of what remained of the Sanctities' ashes. This was the beginning of humans. This new race did not have the gods' powers, and like the Sanctities, they could not see, hear, or touch the Aedes.

At this time, the Originals—the first generation of Davina—realized that the realms were tearing each other apart. They pushed the Aedes back to Malum and sealed off the realm. By the time the last sixteen Originals made it to the portal to Vehena, they found that their realm was already on the brink of collapse. And so they had to say goodbye to their home and seal the portal for good. Vehena died.

Meanwhile, a few Aedes had managed to stay behind. As they and their children roamed a realm they could not interact with, the only way for them to grow and stay alive was to feed off the energy of humans, sucking their essence and life energy away from them in order to survive. But at the time, the Davina didn't understand their true motives, and they were at war for thousands of years.

Twenty-five years ago, everything changed. Malum collided with earth, forming a portal that had the potential to destroy our realm. My parents teamed up with the Aedes and found a way to seal off the portal before both realms were destroyed. When Malum fell, so did the curse keeping the Aedes from interacting with the earth. The Alliance was formed to facilitate peace among the three races—Davina, Aedes, and human.

Davina in government helped the Aedes assimilate into society, granting them citizenship and other necessities to give them a home on earth. It was because of my parents that we discovered the Davina and the Aedes are stronger together, that the Aedes can help us unlock the powers of the gods, including earth-creating powers like fire, water, earth, and air.

But there was one more power that wasn't discovered until months later—healing. The government—who were the only humans who knew about us—wanted to study this power and turn us into soldiers, but we refused. They knew a war would break out if they forced us—a war they wouldn't win—so they made a compromise.

We agreed to serve in the medical field and became doctors and emergency responders. Everyone thinks medicine has changed because of recent medical advancements, but that's not true. It's because of the Aedes and Davina. The Alliance thought it was best to keep our races a secret due to fear of mass panic on both sides. Casey Harris started the academy, and we've been learning how to heal ever since.

No one outside our community knows the stories of the gods anymore—not the ones that actually existed, anyway. And that whole angels and demons stuff? So not us, but we were where the stories came from. I mean, humans with the wings of a giant eagle? How much more specific can you get? No, we weren't angels or demons, but we were still pretty badass.

Chancellor Harris told a condensed version of the story, then concluded with, "And that is why here at Harris Academy, we embrace our differences. Because our differences are what make us stronger. We stand together as one."

"We stand together as one." The crowd repeated the academy's motto.

Chancellor Harris waved to the crowd, then exited the stage. Another man came to the podium after her. He looked the same age, with black hair and a thick beard.

"Let's have another round of applause for my wife," the man said.

I inhaled a sharp breath and leaned over to Laura. "That's her husband, Kane Harris! Did you know they were the first Davina-Aedes couple to get married?"

Laura beamed as she clapped wildly. "I know! Did *you* know that he took her name because he admired her so much and thought she deserved all the recognition?"

I sighed. "Swoon. You know he teaches advanced-level Aedes Essence? Maybe you'll have a class with him."

"I hope so," she said. "He's a hottie."

I giggled. "Careful. He's married."

She shrugged. "What? I can't at least *look*?"

Kane went on to give us the rundown of campus, safety regulations, and more. He warned us of protestors outside campus but assured us that we were safe and just had to steer clear of them. When he finished, we were given fifteen minutes until we had to be outside in the courtyard with the rest of our class for full campus tours and icebreaker games.

"I guess it's time for us to go," Mom said in a sad tone as we stood outside the auditorium in the wide hallway.

"I'm gonna miss you guys," I said. At the same time, I was excited to be on my own.

"You call us anytime," Dad told me. He pulled me into a hug, and I squeezed him back.

Mom looked like she was about to cry when she embraced me. "You have lots of fun. Study hard."

I chuckled as she drew away. "You know me. You don't have to worry."

"I know," she said. "But I'm your mom. It's what I do."

"I love you guys," I told them honestly.

Far too soon, they were gone, and I was being ushered outside to the courtyard. Laura had said goodbye to her parents as well and stood beside me. We were told to find the group leaders with our color of lanyard that we'd gotten at registration.

I looked to Laura. She wore a yellow lanyard, while I wore a dark purple one. "Dang it, we're not on the same team."

She frowned. "I guess we'll meet back at the Winged Fountain?"

My shoulders fell. "Yeah, I'll see you."

She hurried off to a group of yellow lanyards, while I

continued to search the courtyard for my group. I passed by at least a dozen groups before I finally saw a guy a few years older than me standing on the edge of the fountain. He had dark hair and a shadow of a beard lining his jaw.

"Purple group!" he shouted out into the crowd, with his hands cupped around his mouth. "This way to the purple group!"

I hurried over to them, but I stopped dead when I saw Blond Cutie standing in the center of the group. He had his arms crossed and was glancing around, like he didn't know anyone else. Good. I wouldn't be the only one.

"Okay, how many people do we have?" our group leader said, counting our group members. He mumbled numbers under his breath, then spoke out loud. "Fifteen. Perfect."

He jumped down from the edge of the fountain, then grabbed a clipboard and a hula-hoop that had been sitting at his feet. He twirled it around his arm a few times, then looped it over his shoulder.

"Hello, purple team!" he said enthusiastically. "I'm Kumar, and I'll be your team leader for the day."

A girl near the front raised her hand.

"Yes?" Kumar said.

"What's the hula-hoop for?" she asked.

He winked at her. "I'll get to that. Any other questions?" He glanced around, but our team stayed quiet. "No questions? Great. So, we'll be starting with some ice breakers, then moving on to our campus tour."

I noticed Laura's team was already headed off toward the Science Building. It looked like her group was starting with the tour.

"Why don't we all take a seat in the grass?" Kumar suggested.

We formed a circle facing each other. I was directly opposite from Blond Cutie. He caught me looking at him once, and I quickly turned my gaze away, blushing.

"Let's all go around and say our name, ability, and one interesting thing about ourselves," Kumar suggested. "I'll start. I'm Kumar Combs, and I'm a fourth-year Aedes majoring in surgical studies. An interesting thing about me is that I spent last summer studying abroad in India."

He looked to the girl next to him, and she dove into her introduction. My mind was racing with what I would use as my interesting fact that I barely heard what everyone else had said. When it got to Blond Cutie, though, I immediately took interest.

"I'm, uh, Kellan Greene," he said in that smooth voice. "I'm an Aedes majoring in emergency response."

My program, I thought. *Maybe we'll be teamed up.*

"An interesting thing about me..." Kellan hesitated. "My father was Ronan Greene."

Ronan Greene! So Kellan was a bit of a legacy himself. His father was a member of the Alliance. He'd been instrumental in helping the Alliance understand the Davina's healing powers and how the Aedes could help refine them.

Introductions continued around the circle before I could really process what Kellan had just said. Eventually, it reached me.

"I'm Cora Marek," I said with a smile. "I'm a Davina majoring in emergency response with an emphasis on firefighting. An interesting fact about me is that my parents are Ryn and James Marek."

Gasps traveled around the group. Kumar leaned forward in interest. "You're kidding. Your parents closed the portal to Malum!"

I beamed. "I know."

"Your parents broke the Aedes' curse!" a girl across from me exclaimed.

"Yep. Davina power, right?" I chuckled and threw a fist up into the air.

All eyes were on me, and everyone looked amazed—everyone except Kellan. When I stole a glance at him, the look in his eyes was cold. What the hell? He could brag about his legacy status, but I couldn't? It felt like a stab to the gut, and I didn't even know the guy yet.

I barely heard the last few introductions. I was still stealing glances at Kellan, trying to figure this guy out.

"Okay," Kumar said, standing. "Let's move on to a little team-building exercise."

He set his clipboard in the grass and held his hula-hoop out in front of him. He kept it at chest level and parallel to the ground. "We call this the Floating Hoop. You'll stand in a circle and each place an index finger straight out. The hoop will rest on top of all your fingers. The object is for your team to lower the hoop to the ground without anyone losing contact with it. You lose contact, and your team has to start over again. Only your index finger can touch the hoop, and you must keep your finger straight. No 'hooking' allowed."

Kumar demonstrated by wrapping a finger around the hoop. "Easy enough, right?"

I smirked. This was going to be simple.

We formed a close circle, so tight that I had to turn my shoulders to squeeze in.

"Fingers out," Kumar instructed. He placed the hula-hoop in the center of our circle. "And go!"

Before I could even think about lowering the hoop to the ground, it started to rise, like someone was pulling on it with a string. I lifted my finger to keep contact with it, but it just kept going up and up and up…

"What the hell?" the girl beside me asked in disbelief, the same time two people from the other side of the circle remarked on the strange phenomenon.

"Who's doing that?" I demanded.

The hoop reached so high that I had to stand on my toes to

try to keep contact. It floated up until I couldn't touch it anymore. Several of us lost contact at once.

Kumar stepped in and took the hoop. "Looks like a few of you lost contact. You'll have to start over."

He held it at chest level again, and we all stuck our fingers out to touch the bottom of it.

"And go," Kumar said as he stepped back.

Again, the hoop began to rise, and I had to raise my finger to avoid losing contact.

"Someone's using their air power to make it float," I accused. "It's not funny."

Kumar chuckled. "I assure you, no one's using their air power. You must all work together."

I gritted my teeth. Was this some sort of joke?

Several people started talking at once, all trying to throw theories around for what might work.

"Everyone just stay still," the guy on my right said when we resituated the hoop back at our chests again.

We all tried not to move, but the hoop started floating again.

"Who's doing that?" I asked, but so many people were talking that I didn't think anyone heard me.

Then Kellan's voice came across the circle. "Blaming each other isn't going to help."

I caught his eye, and I knew the statement was directed at me.

"This exercise is about teamwork," Kellan said confidently. When he spoke, the whole team listened. "We need to trust each other if this is going to work."

We started over again, but no matter what kind of pep talk Kellan gave the team, we couldn't manage to work together. When people tried to keep their fingers steady, others pushed up on the hoop to keep contact, and we had to start all over again. It was clear from the onset: Nobody trusted each other to get this task done.

"Guys, we have to move together," I said above the other chatter. I was getting more frustrated with each passing second. No one was listening to each other. I didn't even think they were listening to me.

"Let's forget about keeping contact with the hoop for a second," Kellan said. Of course, the group quieted to listen to *him*. "If we fail, we can start over. Let's start with keeping our fingers steady. Don't worry about the hoop moving. Consider it a sacrifice for the team."

Everyone stilled as we set the hoop back in place. I tried not to move, and it was starting to work. The hoop wasn't floating.

"Okay, good," Kellan said. "Now everyone start to lower together. Ready?"

I could feel the hoop start to rise off my finger. Panicked, I followed it with my finger, and it started to rise again.

Kellan caught the look on my face, and his eyebrows knitted together. It was like he thought *I* was the problem. He held my gaze for a second longer. Whatever fluttering feeling I'd felt before when I'd caught his eye was gone. My guts started to feel heavy in my stomach.

I glanced around just to break his gaze and noticed all the other teams that had started on the courtyard were gone. They must've already finished their challenge.

We started over... *again.* And just like all the times before, the hoop began to rise.

"Everyone needs to stop lifting the hoop," I said.

Kellan was quick to shoot back at me. "I just watched *you* lift the hoop. Maybe focus a little more on yourself and a little less on what everyone else is doing."

The whole group went silent as Kellan and I held each other's gazes. I was starting to realize he was a serious jackass.

"Okay," Kumar said quickly, pulling our attention away from each other. "It looks like it's time to start our tour."

Our group stepped back, and Kumar took the hoop. "This is

something you might want to try another time. If there's one thing you need to learn while here at Harris Academy, it's how to work well with others."

Kumar's eyes darted between Kellan and me.

"Let's get going." Kumar started leading us toward the Science Building.

I crossed my arms and followed behind, feeling absolutely let down that we hadn't completed the challenge.

"That was way harder than I thought," the girl beside me said.

"It was impossible," I muttered back.

An hour passed before we finished our tour. When I returned to the courtyard, I found Laura sitting on the edge of the Winged Fountain.

"How'd your tour go?" she asked as she stood and fell into step beside me.

"The tour was amazing. I love campus. But the team-building exercise... Not so much," I admitted.

"Oh, really? I thought it was fun," she said.

I frowned. "My team failed. I got that cute guy's name, though. Kellan Greene. But now..." I scrunched up my nose.

"What?" she prodded.

"I don't know, he seemed kind of arrogant," I told her. "And rude."

Laura shrugged. "There are plenty of other guys. Oh, by the way, that girl from earlier—the one with the pixie cut—she was in my group. Turns out she *is* a freshman. Her name's Celina Dyer. She's actually kind of cool."

"Oh," I said dryly, remembering the display she'd put on earlier.

"You can meet her later," Laura said enthusiastically as we entered our dorm hall. "She lives in our dorm."

We were passing by the rec room when I heard my name. I

grabbed Laura's elbow and stopped dead in the hall. We paused to listen.

"You met Cora Marek?" a girl said. "She's supposed to be really good, right? Like her parents."

A guy scoffed. I peeked around the corner to see Celina twisting a piece of chalk around the end of a pool cue. She was talking to Kellan, who was arranging the balls on the table.

"I haven't seen her essence yet," he said, "but…"

"But what?" Celina pressed.

Kellan shrugged. "After our team-building exercise earlier, I'm not sure she has what it takes for the academy."

My fists clenched at my sides. Who did this guy think he was? He didn't even know me!

"If she's anything like that in class," he said, "she's not going to pass."

What a prick! I'd graduated top of my class at Galen High. I was a damn good Davina.

Gonna give me shit, Kellan Greene? Fine. Two can play at that game.

4

Classes started two days later, on Monday. Laura and I woke early for our Art of Healing I class. Her heels clicked against the tile as we headed down the hall of the Essence Building and to our lecture hall. We both had our wings on full display. Mine were all white, with hints of blue and purple that shone in the light at different angles.

Laura's were much cooler. Her feathers were white at the top of her wings, but the further down they went, the more they gradually turned black, creating a seamless gradient. The white feathers at the top shone sky blue in the light, and the black ones at the bottom shimmered a midnight blue. It was gorgeous.

"This is weird," Laura said, clutching her messenger bag to her chest as we walked down the hall. A few people took notice to her unusual wings, but most didn't seem to care.

"What's weird?" I asked curiously.

"Having my wings out," she admitted. "I don't usually do this. People stare."

I glanced up and down the hall to the passing students, who also had their wings out. There was an even mix of students with black wings and white wings, but no one had both like Laura. I loved that hers made her unique.

"No one's staring," I assured her. "Remember what Chancellor Harris said at orientation? Here at Harris Academy, we embrace our differences. Own it, girl."

Laura offered a shy smile. "You're right. I shouldn't worry."

"Your shoes are cute, by the way," I told her, glancing down at the four-inch blue heels.

"I know, right?" She stopped outside the classroom door and twisted her ankle at various angles to show them off.

"They match your dress perfectly," I said.

"Thank you," she replied in a chipper tone.

She curtsied for show, then we entered the room. The lecture hall was set up like a movie theater, with endless rows of chairs that descended into the room. Long tables stretched out along each row, and there was a large desk and projector screen at the front of the room.

The class was already buzzing with conversation as other freshman filed into the room. I noticed Kellan and Celina at the front, chatting with each other. Kellan's dark wings shimmered green, while Celina's White wings had a red tint to them.

Laura and I claimed seats in the middle of the room. Since the academy was built for supernaturals, we didn't have to put our wings away. There was enough room on either side of us to spread our wings out without disturbing the students seated behind us. I pulled out my laptop to take notes on.

There were four words displayed on the projector at the front of the room: body, life force, consciousness, and essence. They were the four energies that make up a person—basic information all supernaturals knew from a young age. Your body was your physical self, and your life energy was the energy that kept you alive. Consciousness referred to the energy of your thought processes.

And then there was essence—your soul energy that was

stored inside the earth. Everyone had it. It was just that Aedes and Davina could access it physically when humans couldn't. But we could only access so much at a time. Because of Aedes' unique ability to borrow essence from another being, they could help Davina access more—and in exchange, they got physically stronger and healthier, too. It was easier for them to borrow essence from another being than to pull it from the earth. Which meant we needed each other.

All four energies were interconnected to create balance within an individual. When life force is severed, essence energy returns to the earth to be used by later generations. It was the only thing that survived after death.

I typed the words into my computer, even though I knew them by heart.

Moments later, our professor strolled into the classroom from a door at the front. She seemed young but was probably in her forties, with tight brown curls and a friendly smile. She wore an olive-green turtleneck that had slits in the back for her white wings.

She adjusted the microphone clipped to her shirt, then looked out at all hundred of our faces. "Hello, and welcome to the Art of Healing I. I'm Professor Kovski. I'll be co-teaching this class with Professor Sanders, whom you'll meet during your lab hours. Shall we get started?"

Professor Kovski clicked a button, and the screen zoomed in on the word *essence*, where her notes were outlined on the screen. "We all know the basics behind essence energy. Alone, you are virtually powerless, apart from stunning your classmates in a game of essence dodgeball." She chuckled. "But when the Aedes and Davina team up, we are capable of so much more."

She paced at the front of the room. "You've all experienced this in high school. An Aedes member draws essence from their Davina partner to open their essence channel wider. These effects last up to three days if the team forges a strong bond, but they wane when the team is separated. We all know that any Davina and Aedes team is capable of manipulating the elements."

She clicked another button, and the screen switched to a slide highlighting the power of healing. I hurried to copy down her notes.

Professor Kovski continued. "The concept is the same with healing, but you can't do it with just anyone. Healing power is so advanced that it takes specific teams to heal. The connection between a healing team must be so strong that it creates the strongest channel to essence energy. With a strong enough connection, you can even perform channeling, a very advanced healing technique."

I barely wrote down the word *channeling* before she continued.

"Because it takes a special connection to perform healing magic, we will be testing you to see who you will work best with," Professor Kovski explained. "These pairing tests will begin next week, after we've covered healing theory."

Whispers started to spread around the room. I heard one girl a few chairs down from me whisper to her friend that this was going to be easy and they were going to be paired up for sure. Another guy got a horrified look on his face and glanced around the room, like he feared he was never going to be paired up.

"Do you want to be paired with an Aedes or Davina?" I asked Laura in a low whisper.

She shrugged. "Whoever I work best with, I guess. I don't care which type of magic I'm doing as long as my team is healing."

I smiled. "I hope we're paired up."

Our professor waited for the room to quiet, then said, "Now, don't worry if you aren't teamed up right away. It sometimes takes weeks for assignments to fill. That said, let's get started on healing theory."

She changed the slide, and a diagram showing the flow of essence from one being to another came up on screen. "When healing, essence flows in two directions. The first is from the earth, through the Davina, and to the Aedes partner. This expands the channel so that the Davina member can access enough energy to direct the flow of essence into the injured party."

I scrambled to write down every word she said, but she spoke so fast that I couldn't get it all down. It became clear very quickly that I was going to have to pick and choose which points to take notes on.

Professor Kovski continued. "When healing, a Davina will have to visualize their essence differently than when they perform elemental magic. Elemental magic is forged on strong emotions, while healing magic requires a sense of calmness and trust between you and your partner."

She continued the lecture, covering techniques behind accessing your healing power. An hour passed before the lecture finished. Laura and I followed the rest of the class out of the room.

"What class do you have next?" she asked.

"I have an hour until Introduction to Firefighting," I told her.

She frowned. "I have Aedes Essence in an hour. Do you want to grab some breakfast before then?"

"Sure," I said, and we started toward the dining hall. "That lecture was pretty cool. I had no idea healing was so involved. I thought it was just like elemental magic, but with a special partner."

"Are you nervous?" she asked. "About the tests next week and getting your partner assignment?"

"No," I told her honestly. "I'm sure whoever they find for me will be a great fit."

Laura bit her lower lip. "I've heard that some people never get paired up. Like, they just don't have it in them to heal or something."

My stomach sank. "Don't tell me that."

She chuckled. "Why not?"

"Because *now* I'm worried," I admitted.

I'd find someone to heal with… wouldn't I?

5

he following week of testing arrived, and I was more excited than ever. Laura and I sat beside each other in our Art of Healing lab. This classroom was different than the lecture hall and had fewer students. Each table sat two people. I noticed Celina and Kellan in the back beside each other. I already knew that if they ended up together, they'd be top contenders for the best team.

Professor Kovski and Professor Sanders entered the room wearing lab coats. Professor Sanders was an older guy of at least sixty, with black wings and salt and pepper hair. He pushed a cart into the room, which had surgical trays on top.

"Oh my God," I whispered to Laura. "Are those *rats* on that cart?"

She craned her neck to get a better look. "I suppose we need *something* to practice healing on."

"Welcome!" Professor Kovski said from the front of the room. "Who's excited to start healing?"

Most of us responded with enthusiastic cheers. I couldn't believe I might actually heal something today.

"Professor Sanders is going to go around the room and hand out your rats," Kovski explained. "They are each under anesthesia. Please don't touch them until you're instructed to. Now, these rats have just come from the physiology department, where upper-class students have just performed spays on them. The incision sites have been stitched up, but it will be your job to heal the wound. Keep in mind that we are only performing a surface-level healing. You are not ready to try healing internal wounds yet. We will be rotating partners, so don't worry if you don't get it right away. Also be aware that just because you complete the task does not mean you'll be paired up with that person. Assignments won't start until at least the end of the week, so just relax and do your best."

After we received our rats, our professors stood in front of the room to demonstrate healing their own rat. They had a camera set up above their workstation, which projected onto a large screen.

Professor Sanders placed a hand on Professor Kovski's shoulder to draw her essence into himself. We couldn't see it happening, but it was obvious by the way Sanders's skin seemed to brighten with color and his eyes looked less tired.

Kovski explained everything as they performed the procedure. "Since the animal is so small, I will place only two fingers over the wound. As I feel my essence channel widen, I will direct my powers into the wound. Now, focus only on the incision site. If you try to heal the rat as a whole, you may overwhelm its body and unbalance its four energies. This can cause it to go into cardiac arrest."

We'd learned all about it during her lectures earlier that week, so all of this was just a reminder.

The ends of Professor Kovski's fingers glowed a bright white. When she drew her fingers away, the incision site was completely healed. The class broke out into a round of applause.

Kovski turned toward the class. "You may begin."

My heart pounded nervously as I stood over the rat. I reached a finger outward, but pulled back at the last second.

"What's wrong?" Laura asked.

I shrugged, but inside, I was screaming. I had to make this work. "I don't know the best angle to place my fingers."

Professor Sanders heard me and walked over to our table. "Don't worry so much," he encouraged. "Focus on your essence, and the rest will come naturally."

I nodded. "Okay, I think I'm ready to give it a shot."

Laura reached out and placed a hand on my shoulder. Tingles spread through my body as I felt her pulling my essence into herself. My magic became more and more intense the more she drew from me and the wider my channel opened.

I placed two fingers to the incision site and guided my essence down my arm and to the tips of my fingers. I expected my hand to glow like Professor Kovski's had, but nothing happened. My essence stopped at the ends of my fingers, like there was a wall blocking me from sending it toward the rat.

I pushed against that wall, guiding more and more essence toward it. My essence broke through in a single burst, and flames at least six inches long shot out of my fingers. I gasped and drew back instantly to avoid burning the rat, but I'd already singed some of its hair off. Several other people turned to look at me, but I was relieved to see they all looked like they were struggling as well.

"I-I'm sorry," I stammered, looking over to Professor Sanders.

"It's okay," he said gently. "This isn't the first time it's happened, and it won't be the last. Just relax and try again."

"You've got this," Laura said encouragingly.

"Okay," I replied with a sigh.

I placed my hands on the rat again. This time when I hit that wall, I tried not to push too much essence all at once. Instead, I waited for it to flow on its own, but it never did.

"We did it!" Celina exclaimed from the back of the room.

Kellan and her exchanged a high-five. I couldn't help the scowl that crossed my face. How'd she manage it on her first try?

Several people stopped to watch as Professor Kovski and Professor Sanders went over to inspect their work. Kovski placed a hand over the rat's abdomen and closed her eyes. Her entire hand glowed a soft white, but not as much as when she'd been healing the rat earlier. It looked as if she was using her power to inspect its body for internal injuries, rather than healing it.

Kovski sighed and opened her eyes. "You've done a great job of healing the incision site, but unfortunately, you overdid it. Its internal organs have suffered some damage."

Celina gaped at her, and Kellan dropped his shoulders. The two looked devastated.

"No," Celina said quickly, looking over the rat. "No, that can't be right."

"Don't worry," Kovski told her. "The damage is reversible. We'll heal the rat."

"But I did it," Celina snapped. "I healed it. How could I have hurt it?"

Laura and I exchanged a glance. It felt like we shouldn't be listening in, but everyone could hear her. There was no looking away.

"It's very common," Sanders assured Celina. "But I think it's time we rotate partners."

I frowned and turned back to Laura. "I'm sorry it didn't work."

"It's okay," she said hopefully. "There are a lot of other tests this week, so we can still be paired up."

Laura waved as she headed off to the next table. Another Aedes came up beside me, and I tried to work with him to heal, but I could already feel that it wasn't going to work. He was a complete stranger, and it felt awkward when he placed his hand on my shoulder to draw my essence. I could barely feel enough energy to conjure a fireball.

Two other teams made headway on our first rotation, but neither of them had healed the incision completely.

"It's a good start," Professor Kovski had told them.

I went through three other partners as class went on, and my rat wasn't any closer to being healed. A girl named Shaylene approached on our next rotation. She was pretty, with pale skin and dark curls. I thought I felt something with her. I'd gotten my fingers to glow, but the incision hadn't healed.

"Well, it was worth a shot," Shaylene said as she moved on to the next table. "It was nice to meet you."

"You too," I said with a smile.

My smile instantly faded when I saw who came up beside me next. *Kellan.*

He had a smirk on his face, like he thought this was going to be an interesting experiment.

Well, this is going to be a total bust, I thought. He already made it clear he didn't like me. There was zero trust here.

"What's wrong?" he asked, noticing my fallen face.

"Nothing," I lied.

"Are you ready?" His voice was kind, like he hadn't said those things about me in the rec room.

"Yeah, let's do this," I said without a hint of enthusiasm.

Kellan reached out for my shoulder, and I swore I felt tingles spread across my skin before he even touched me. His hand was warm, but everything else about him was unexpected. Essence whipped through me, and my whole body came alive with energy. It sizzled down to my toes, then back up to my head again. It felt so powerful that I wondered if anyone else could see it. With the other Aedes, I'd felt enough power that I could sustain fire for maybe a day, but with Kellan, it was different. I felt like I was charged up to go for a month straight.

I stumbled back a step and grabbed on to Kellan's other arm for support. For a second, I was so overwhelmed that I forgot Kellan was my partner. Then I looked up into his eyes, and it hit me.

We're compatible.

He had the same look of shock in his eyes, like he'd felt it, too.

That doesn't seem right.

The sensation only lasted a second before my essence channel slammed shut again. Kellan seemed to sense it.

"Relax, Cora," he said as I found my balance again.

My cheeks flamed red, and I couldn't meet his gaze. I was still trying to process the sensation I'd just felt. It was the same as always… but different, too. Stronger. A helluva lot stronger. How was this possible for the two of us?

I kept my eyes on my rat and said, "I can't."

It was true. If that channel opened up the same way again, there's no way I could relax. It was just too much stimulation at once.

"Why not?" he asked, dropping his hand to his side. I couldn't read his tone.

"Because I don't think we can work together," I admitted.

Kellan looked totally taken aback, then started laughing lightly. All the other teams were chatting, so nobody but me heard him.

"You don't want to work with me?" he asked in amusement.

I finally looked him in the eyes. He was smirking at me, like this whole thing was a game to him. I couldn't work with someone who didn't take this class seriously.

"I know you don't like me," I snapped.

His laughter died. "What gave you that impression?"

I crossed my arms. "I heard what you said about me. You don't think I have what it takes to pass."

Kellan shrugged. "Why do you care what I say?"

I opened my mouth to say something, but then his question truly hit me. I stood there with my mouth agape, unanswering. Why *did* I care?

I shook it off. "Whatever. I don't."

"Really?" he asked. "Because you sound like you do."

I was starting to get irritated. "Look, you don't know me. So if you could just leave me alone and let me study in peace, that'd be great."

He held his hands up in surrender, but he looked like he was enjoying this more than anything. "Agreed. I'll leave you alone— after we finish this assignment. We still have a few minutes left to see if this works."

I scoffed. "With you? Oh, fun. Considering you have no faith in me at all."

Kellan leaned in and whispered, "So prove me wrong."

"Excuse me?" I asked.

He shrugged. "Prove me wrong. Show me you have what it takes to heal."

Oh, it was on! Kellan was wrong about me. I belonged here at the academy, and I was going to graduate top of my class. Kellan—or anyone else for that matter—couldn't stop me.

"Fine," I said confidently, but my heart was racing. "Let's go again."

Kellan placed his hand back on my shoulder. This time, the essence current wasn't as overwhelming, but it was still strong. I could feel the channel opening wider and wider with each passing second. My fingers began to glow, but when I let out a cheerful gasp, they dimmed again.

Kellan leaned into me, until his chest was pressed against the side of my arm. The contact helped open the channel even more. "Relax, Cora," he reminded me softly.

I took a deep breath and forced the tension out of my shoulders. Essence traveled down my arms and to my hand. I held back on it since the rat was so small, and directed it only through the tips of my fingers. I tried to employ the techniques Professor Kovski had taught us in class, about how to visualize the healing process before it ever happened.

Right before my eyes, the incision began to glow. The skin began to knit itself together, and then...

Then the incision was gone. The skin was completely healed.

Kellan dropped his hand, and I felt my essence pull back. It was still there and a lot stronger than before, but not like it was when he was touching me.

I couldn't believe it. I stared down at the rat and ran my fingers over the stitches, but that was all that was left. The incision hadn't even scarred.

"Oh my God," I whispered.

When I finally lifted my gaze to Kellan, he looked impressed. He was speechless.

"I-I did it," I said breathlessly.

Kellan's surprise melted from his face, and it turned into a frown. "*We* did it," he clarified.

"Right," I agreed quickly. "We—"

"Very good job!" Professor Sanders said, clapping me on the back. "This looks excellent. Professor Kovski, if you would."

Kovski stepped up to our table and did the same thing she had with Celina's rat. A smile spread across her face, and pride filled my chest.

"Excellent work," she said as she pulled her hand back. "There are no internal injuries. It's rare for us to see such a great team on the first day. You two should be proud of yourselves. We only have a few minutes left, so you're free to leave for the day."

Kellan and I exchanged a glance as our professors moved on

to the next table. Kellan looked a little shocked, then smiled at me.

"How's that for proving you wrong?" I asked with a proud smirk.

"I'm impressed," he admitted, "but I don't take back what I said."

My jaw dropped. "You heard what Professor Kovski said. I healed this rat without any complications."

Kellan winced, like I'd said something wrong. "There's a lot more to healing than this."

I crossed my arms and glared at him. "Yeah, and that's what I'm here at the academy to learn. Clearly, I'm capable of something, or that rat wouldn't be healed right now."

Kellan reached down and grabbed his bag, which he slung over his shoulder. "I'm sure you'll do fine, Cora. Forget I said anything."

Kellan started for the door, and I quickly grabbed my bag and followed behind him. I'd meet up with Laura later.

"Forget it?" I asked when we were out in the hall.

He didn't even turn to look back at me. I quickened my step to walk beside him.

"But what if we're paired up?" I demanded.

"You heard Kovski," he said coolly. "Just because we did well today doesn't mean we're going to be paired up."

"It kind of increases our chances, though," I pointed out.

Kellan glanced down at me, then turned his gaze forward again. "Trust me, they're not going to pair us up if we don't want to be."

"Well, good," I snapped. "Because you're kind of a jackass."

"And you're a little irritating," he deadpanned. "We all have our flaws. See you later."

Kellan and I reached the front doors of the Elemental Building, and he pushed through them to outside. I'd had enough of him. I stopped inside the doors, fuming as I watched him go.

"Screw you, Kellan Green," I called before the door swung shut.

He gave a salute, like he didn't even care.

"Whatever," I mumbled under my breath. "I hope you and your partner are freaking happy."

As long as that partner wasn't me, everything would be a-okay.

6

"I got my assignment!" Laura said excitedly.

I was sitting in a study area in the Academy Center three weeks later when she rushed up to me. My laptop was set on the table in front of me, and I was studying for my Elemental Magic exam the following week. I tossed a flaming ball of fire from one palm to the other, following the instructions in our study guide.

I killed the flames when Laura sat across from me. "You did? Congratulations!"

"His name is Travis Marcos," she said.

"I don't think I've met him," I told her.

"I don't think so, either," she replied. "He's in the other time block for lecture, but we met during that testing I had scheduled last Thursday. We hit it off, and I guess we're almost a perfect match. He even has earth element like me, so I've decided to major in natural disasters with him."

I frowned. "I'm never going to get an assignment."

Laura sighed. "Don't say that, Cora. Kovski said it can take weeks."

"But almost everyone is already paired up," I pointed out. "I

46

barely showed promise with anyone, and the ones I did are already assigned. Shaylene and I would've been great together. She's even in the firefighting program. But she's with a guy from the other lecture block."

"What about Kellan?" Laura asked.

"Kellan's impossible," I said. "He has some serious issues. I'm not going to be paired with him."

"You should give him a shot," she encouraged. "He doesn't seem all bad."

"Just *some* bad?" I joked. I quickly changed the subject. "So, this Travis guy, is he Aedes or Davina?"

"Davina," Laura said. "I'll be doing the Aedes part with him."

"Good. It's just too bad we didn't get paired up," I complained. "We weren't half bad together after that first day."

"Yeah, but they look at more than just that," Laura pointed out. "Those personality tests weren't for nothing. And they look at your major—"

She was cut off by the sound of a notification on my computer. We both froze and exchanged a glance, like we could sense exactly what email had just come through.

I quickly looked to see that Professor Kovski had just emailed me. *Congratulations! You've Been Assigned*, the subject line read. My heart started to beat so fast that my fingers trembled.

"Is it—?" Laura started.

"Yes, oh my God. It is." I quickly opened the email and scanned it, until I found the name of my partner in the middle of the email. My stomach bottomed out.

"Holy shit," I muttered.

"What?" Laura asked eagerly. "Who'd you get?"

I didn't answer right away. I was still trying to convince myself it wasn't real.

"Come on, Cora," Laura pressed. "Who is it? Someone you know?"

"Yeah." My mouth felt dry and scratchy when I answered. "It's Kellan."

"Congratulations!" she cried.

"No," I said dryly. I crossed my arms and leaned back in my chair. "Not congratulations. This is a disaster. Kellan hates me. I can't work with him."

"Is it really that bad?" she asked.

I shrugged. "I don't know. Ask him what his problem is."

"So, contest it," Laura suggested, like people did that all the time.

"Contest it? Can I do that?"

"I don't know," she admitted. "Might as well try."

"You're right." I shut my laptop and shoved it in my bag, then stood. "I'm going to talk to Kovski now. I'll see you later."

"Good luck," Laura called as I started down the hall.

Professor Kovski's office was on the second floor of the Academy Center. I skipped the elevator and marched straight up the stairs to her office.

When I arrived, her door was open, and I could hear voices flooding out into the hall.

"It's very rare to refuse your assignment," Professor Kovski was saying, "but it can be done. We'll just need reasonable cause to know why you two can't work together."

Oh, good, I thought. *Kellan and I won't be the only ones contesting our assignment. Kovski will have to accommodate us.*

"She's unbearable," I heard a male voice say, and my jaw dropped. *Kellan?*

"I'm sorry, Mister Greene, but that's not—" Professor Kovski started to say, but she cut off when she saw me in the doorway.

Kellan glanced to me, and he looked like a deer in the headlights.

That's right. I've caught you talking shit a second time. What do you have to say for yourself?

I didn't say any of that. Instead, I said, "Kellan's right. We can't work together."

"Come in, Miss Marek," Professor Kovski said as she stood. She headed for the door and closed it behind me. "Why don't you both have a seat and tell me what's going on?"

I sat, but I crossed my arms to make it clear how much I objected to this assignment. "I don't know, Kellan. Why don't you tell her how much you hate me?"

Kellan sat, but he didn't look happy about it. "I don't *hate* you. I just… don't want to work with you."

"Why not?" I demanded, straightening in my seat. "What is it that you have against me? Is it something I said during that icebreaker? Because frankly, you've been an ass ever since, and I don't know why."

"Because it's obvious you're only here for one thing, and that's yourself," he snapped.

"How's that a bad thing?" I growled. "At least I *want* to be here. I *want* to help people. You act like you'd rather be doing anything else—"

"Well, maybe I do," he snarled back.

"Okay, okay," Professor Kovski said calmly. "One at a time. Cora, how about you go first?"

I felt like I could explode, but I kept my cool. "I think this must be some sort of mistake. Kellan has made it very clear that he has a stick up his ass, and I can't—"

"Whoa," Kellan cut in. "I do *not* have a stick up my—"

"Please, both of you calm down," Kovski demanded. She looked to me to continue.

I huffed. The truth was, I didn't know what it was about Kellan. He was just an ass.

"He's arrogant," I said, but that was all I could come up with.

"And Kellan?" Kovski asked. "What's your problem with Miss Marek?"

He answered without even having to think about it. "She's stuck up."

"I am not!" I defended. "Do you not like me because I'm a legacy? Well, news, *son of Ronan Greene*, so are you."

"That's not it," he shot back. "You don't work well with others, and that's been apparent since day one."

"That's not true," I insisted. "It's just *you* I can't work with."

Professor Kovski pressed her fingers to her temples. "Can't you two at least *try* to get along?"

"Why can't we just be reassigned?" I asked.

She dropped her hands and folded them on her desk. "Because you two showed the most promise than any other pairing we could come up with."

"I performed well with Celina," Kellan pointed out.

"Yes, but she performed better with Rhys, and they've already been paired up," Kovski said. "You two didn't just perform very well in class. You're also a match on the personality tests, and you're majoring in the same field. On paper, you're the perfect match."

"I'm still undecided," Kellan said.

Kovski frowned. "That's not what your file says."

"Yeah, well, I'm changing my mind," Kellan claimed.

My jaw dropped. This was bullshit.

Professor Kovski sighed and stood. "Look, you haven't given me a real reason to reconsider this pairing, so I'm afraid we're going to have to escalate this matter. Follow me."

She opened the door and breezed out of the room. Kellan and I exchanged a quick confused glance before both rushing to follow behind her.

"Where are we going?" I asked.

Her heels clicked against the tile. "It doesn't appear that I can help. I'm taking you to someone who can."

We ascended the stairs and came to a pair of double doors at the end of the hallway. A reception desk sat in front of them.

Kovski stopped and told us to stay where we were, then stepped forward to talk to the secretary.

"Is Chancellor Harris available?" she asked in a low voice, so low that I could hardly make out their conversation.

My gaze shot up to Kellan's. "Did she just say Chancellor Harris?"

He kept his arms crossed and didn't look down at me. "Sounded like it to me."

The secretary pulled the phone to her ear. She said a few things into it that I couldn't hear, then stood and said, "Follow me."

She guided us through the double doors. We entered a large office with tall bookcases, wooden accents, and a huge mahogany desk in front of a wide window that overlooked the courtyard.

Chancellor Harris stood from her desk, and Kellan and I both froze in the doorway. "Come in," she said kindly, gesturing us to step forward after Professor Kovski. "Please, have a seat."

I nervously took the chair across from her, and Kellan sat in the one beside me. Professor Kovski remained on her feet.

"Chancellor Harris," Professor Kovski greeted as the secretary closed the doors behind us. "These are my students, Kellan Greene and Cora Marek."

Chancellor Harris stretched her hand out over the desk to shake my hand, then Kellan's. "It's so great to meet you. I knew both of your parents very well."

"It's great to meet you, too," I said kindly.

"What seems to be the problem?" Chancellor Harris asked.

Professor Kovski explained how we both refused to go through with the pairing. "Unfortunately," she concluded with, "most other students have been paired up, and I just don't see the alternative."

Chancellor Harris frowned. "You both realize what will happen if you don't accept this pairing?"

"What will happen?" I asked curiously.

She sighed. "You will have to go through with the semester alone."

"Great. Let's do it," I said quickly.

Chancellor Harris continued. "Our classes are not designed for individuals. They are designed for teams. You might pass your written exams, but without a partner, you have no hope of passing the practicals or your final."

"Fail the final?" I balked.

"You're both in the firefighting program," Chancellor Harris pointed out. "As I'm sure you're well aware, your final will consist of grueling obstacles inside a burning building. I'm afraid it would be too dangerous without a partner."

"So that's my only choice?" I asked. "I work with Kellan, or I flunk out of the academy?"

Chancellor Harris seemed sympathetic. "It's possible that we can find another partner for the two of you, but we'll have to see how the other teams perform first. If another team is not working well, we can reconsider swapping the pairings. But I'm confident in Professor Kovski's assignments. She is very good at what she does. I suggest the two of you spend some time together, get to know each other. If it doesn't work out by the end of the semester, we'll reconsider things."

"The end of the semester?" Kellan sounded just as hopeless as I felt. "What if we can't get along enough to pass by then?"

Chancellor Harris looked disappointed in us. "If your preliminary tests showed that the two of you can heal, I'm not sure what you have to worry about. I suggest you find some way to get along."

Kellan dropped his shoulders. He looked to me, like he was finally giving in. It wasn't like we had any other choice. Chancellor Harris was the ultimate voice at the academy. If she said we were locked into this assignment, we were locked in—unless one of us wanted to drop out.

No way in hell.

"We'll try," Kellan said, like he actually meant it.

He turned to me, expecting my answer. I had to agree with him—because there wasn't any other choice. Kellan and I were hopeless. It was go through with this, or fail, and I wasn't going to do that.

So I was just going to have to suffer through this semester, pass, and then wait for a reassignment when our final was over with. My dream of graduating top of the class had effectively been crushed, but without a partner, I wouldn't graduate at all.

"I guess we have no other choice," I said to Kellan, then I turned back to Chancellor Harris. "We'll try our best."

And I meant it. The only problem was, I wasn't sure that Kellan did.

"I don't get this guy," I complained to Laura later that evening. I lay on my bed in our dorm, picking at a thread on my blanket.

"I'm sure it'll be fine," she said, turning to check out her shoes in the mirror. She wore a short, sleek black dress and four-inch heels. "They wouldn't have paired you up if they didn't think you'd work well together."

I frowned. "They paired us up because we were the last two without partners."

Laura turned from the mirror to look at me. "Chancellor Harris said you could switch partners next semester, right?"

I pushed myself to a sitting position. "Yes. I'm going to do my best to work with him. I think I'm just... nervous. I don't really know the guy."

Laura came to sit beside me on the bed. "There's your solution. You have to get to know him."

I reached for my phone. "Okay, let's stalk his social media."

Laura chuckled. "Not like that. Talk to him. Figure out why he's such an ass."

I laughed. "I think I can do that."

"Perfect," she said with a smile. "Now, are you going to get dressed and come to the party with me?"

"You sure you wouldn't rather study?" I asked, only half-serious.

Laura nudged me. "It's Friday. You need to get out and forget about Kellan for the night."

I fake groaned and got to my feet. "Okay, you've twisted my arm. I'll go."

I stripped off my boots and placed the Davina Blade I kept there on my desk beside my antiques collection. There were things like buttons, pocket watches, jewelry, and an old silver bowl that belonged to my great-great grandmother. Laura's eyes widened when she saw the blade.

"Is that a Davina Blade?" she asked breathlessly.

I nodded shyly.

"As in, one of the ancient blades that came from Vehena?" she asked. "That the Davina once used as weapons against the Aedes?"

"Yeah," I admitted. "My uncle Kyle gave it to me. It kind of started my antiques collection."

She reached her hand out. "May I?"

I handed her the blade, and she looked it over in wonder.

"You're not really supposed to have weapons on campus," she said with a chuckle, "but this is really cool."

I shrugged. "Who's going to notice? I'm not going to hurt anyone with it. It's just sentimental to me."

She set the blade back on my desk. "Your collection is really cool."

"Thanks," I said. "I'll collect anything with a story behind it."

"Well, let's go make our own story," she said, beaming.

I dressed in a summery navy-blue dress with tiny pink flowers all over it. Laura let me borrow a pair of fancy sandals to go along with it. I wore my brown hair down in waves and added a light layer of makeup.

We took the city bus several blocks away until we came to a residential area. We followed the sound of music as a pumping bass pounded through the street. Hoards of people stood in front of a big white house with a towering turret on one corner. Lights flashed inside, and I could hear the sound of cheers above the music. Next to the house, the garage door was open, and a group of guys were playing beer pong on a fold-out table.

"I'm the king of the world!" a guy shouted as he burst out of the front door in nothing but his underwear and a red cape. He jumped over the porch banister and raced down the street. A group of guys hurried outside behind him, cheering and hollering as he streaked down the sidewalk. Most of them held up their phones to film.

Laura and I stopped in our tracks. I turned to her in uncontrollable laughter. "Oh my God."

"*Somebody's* a little drunk," Laura said with raised eyebrows.

I grabbed her hand. "Come on."

Laura and I stepped inside, where the music was deafening. The living room was crowded, though people more or less milled around chatting instead of dancing to the music. When we got to the kitchen to find drinks, a Davina guy was standing on the counter shirtless and with his wings out.

Another guy reached up and tugged on his arm. "Put your wings away, Jett!" he demanded. "Do you *want* the neighbors to see? The Alliance will be all over your ass, and my parents will kill me."

"Save it for campus!" a girl shouted up at him.

Jett sighed and relaxed his shoulders, and his wings disappeared. "Screw you," he said lightheartedly. "You're no fun."

Laura and I maneuvered past a group chatting—I thought I heard the word *infantry*—and grabbed some wine coolers from the fridge, before she led me down a hall that opened to the garage. It was quieter out here, and I preferred that.

We arrived just as two guys were finishing up their game of

beer pong. One had a single cup left, and the other guy sank the ball in. He shot his hands into the air in victory, while the other guy groaned and chugged his beer.

"Travis!" Laura hurried over to the guy who'd won. He was tall, with dark hair and kind eyes.

"Laura, you made it!" he said in excitement, though he seemed like he'd already had a few.

"Travis, this is my roommate, Cora," Laura introduced. "Cora, this is my partner, Travis."

"Hey," he greeted with a smile. "It's nice to meet you."

"You, too," I said.

"Looks like you're having fun," Laura told Travis. It almost sounded like she was flirting.

Girl, don't get involved with your partner. What if you break up?

"Reigning champion of the night," Travis said cheerfully. "Have you come to challenge me?"

Laura laughed. "Uh, no. I can't play to save my life. We're just here to watch."

He shrugged. "Suit yourself. Who's up next?"

"I'll go." Kellan's voice came from out on the lawn. I hadn't even noticed him until now, and I didn't think he'd seen me. I took a step back into the shadows.

"But Kellan," Celina complained from beside him. "I thought we were going to get drinks."

"I'll take you," the guy beside her said. He was all muscle and a head taller than Kellan. He was kind of scary-looking.

"Aw, thanks Rhys." Celina's eyes sparkling up at him.

I leaned over to Laura and whispered, "That's her partner?"

She nodded. "They seem like total opposites, right?"

I just shrugged. I didn't know enough about Celina to say one way or the other.

Travis clapped his hands and rubbed them together. "Okay, Kellan Greene. Prepare to have your ass handed to you."

Kellan smirked as he arranged his cups on the table. "Don't get too cocky, Travis. You haven't seen me play yet."

"Oh no," Travis feigned dryly. "I'm so scared."

"You should be," Kellan challenged with a smile.

Kellan blew on his ping pong ball for good luck, then tossed it across the table. It landed square in one of Travis's cups before he even finished arranging them. Travis's eyes widened, then his lips formed into a playful smirk.

"That's it." Travis held his hand out to the guy beside him but didn't take his eyes off Kellan. "Caleb, it's time for the lucky underwear."

"Are you sure?" Caleb asked. He was shorter than Travis, with dark skin, tight black curls, and an attractive smile. I was pretty sure he was the guy Shaylene had been partnered with. "It's still early in the night."

"Do it! Do it! Do it!" The garage broke out into a chorus of chants.

"I want to see this," I whispered to Laura, before joining in on the cheers. "Do it! Do it!"

"Should I?" Caleb asked for show. "Should I do it?"

He held up a backpack and slowly reached inside. "Here it comes. Are you ready?"

"Do it! Do it!" The chanting continued.

Caleb whipped a pair of golden spandex underwear out of the bag and held them up like a victory flag. The crowd broke out into cheers and applause.

"The lucky underwear!" Caleb shouted, waving them around.

He handed them to Travis, who pulled them on over his jeans. Several people cat-called, and Travis turned around to show them off. He held his hands in the air and gestured for more applause. Laura stuck her fingers in her mouth and whistled loudly.

"Oh my God!" I grabbed on to Laura's shoulder as I doubled over in laughter. "He's hilarious."

"I know." She beamed. "Isn't he great?"

Laura's eyes sparkled when she looked at him, and I could already tell she was crushing on him. Travis caught her eye and winked at her. Their connection was undeniable.

The crowd quieted as Travis stepped up to the table. "Think you can one-up this, Greene?"

Kellan shrugged. "I've got all the guns I need, Captain Underpants."

Kellan flexed his biceps, and the garage broke out into cheers again. I even found myself cheering for him.

"I don't know why you don't like Kellan," Laura said to me. "He seems fine."

I shrugged, unable to take my eyes off him. He seemed so confident, which I found both attractive and repulsive at the same time.

Kellan's eyes met mine, but he looked away quickly, like he hadn't noticed me. I finally turned my gaze away as the game started, so he wouldn't think I was staring. But when I looked out the door and over the lawn, I saw something that made my gut sink. I threw myself behind Laura.

"What?" she asked curiously. She stepped aside, and I quickly followed to stay hidden.

"Um... I just saw someone I know," I admitted.

"Well, why are you hiding? Go say hello."

I bit my lower lip. "I-I can't."

She tilted her head in question. My eyes stayed fixed to the guy with curly black hair as he strutted up the lawn. His arm was around a girl that kind of looked like me, and I felt a pang of envy stab my gut.

Laura followed my gaze, but he was out of sight the next second. "Who is he, Cora?"

I relaxed and stepped out from behind her. "It's Drew, my boyfriend from high school."

I'd told her about him weeks ago. I knew Drew was attending the academy, but I'd done all I could to avoid him so far. Things hadn't ended well between us. The only solace I found was knowing we wouldn't be paired up since we were both Davina.

Laura's eyes widened. *"He's* the guy who—?"

"Used me for sex then stomped on my heart?" I finished for her. "Yep."

Her shoulders fell. "Cora, I'm so sorry."

I shook it off. "No, it's fine. It happened over a year ago."

"That doesn't make what he did okay," she said. "If you want, I can go spill my drink on him."

I laughed. "No, it's cool. Besides, you'd ruin your shoes."

She glanced to her feet. "Good point."

Laura and I stayed to watch the rest of the beer pong match. It was really close, with each of them getting down to only one cup, but eventually, Travis won. He shot his hands into the air, then did a victory dance, before pulling on the golden spandex waistband and letting it snap back against his jeans.

Kellan chuckled. "I guess those really do hold some power."

Travis took a swig of beer. "These panties are undefeated, sweetheart."

"Good game, bro," Kellan said, shaking Travis's hand.

Travis patted Kellan on the back, though he swayed a little on his feet. "Okay, losers. Who's up next?"

Laura quickly rushed over to him. "Travis, I think you've had enough. Let's take a break."

He waved his hand. "Nah, I can keep going."

"Travis," she persisted.

Travis burped, then clutched his stomach. The color drained from his face. "Okay, partner. You might be right."

He turned and hightailed it inside, making a mad dash to the bathroom.

The garage went silent for a second before Caleb said, "Okay, who's up next?"

I followed Laura and Travis inside. Laura sat on the edge of the tub, rubbing Travis's back while he puked into the toilet.

"Is he going to be okay?" I asked from the doorway.

"Totally fine," she assured me.

Travis gave a thumbs-up, then started retching again.

I couldn't watch, so I turned from the door and started for the kitchen to wait for Laura. I tossed my empty bottle into the recycling, then grabbed another drink from the fridge. I noticed the music had changed, and it sounded like someone was singing karaoke—and really well, too. I decided to check it out and stopped in the doorway to the living room.

It was Celina. She was standing on the coffee table with a microphone in her hand while words played across the TV. People were cheering for her. She swayed her hips while she sang and held one hand into the air, creating a swirling display of fire above her head. She was in the firefighting program like me, but I only had her in a few classes.

"She's good, isn't she?" a male voice asked.

I turned to see that Kellan had come up beside me. "I-I guess so," I stammered. What was I saying? She was amazing. "Do you know her well?"

"We went to high school together," Kellan told me over the loud music.

I quickly realized this was my opportunity to get to know him better, but I didn't know what to say. The guy was intimidating as hell.

"So, you two are dating?" I asked. I wanted to shove the words back in my mouth.

Kellan took a swig of beer, then chuckled. "Uh, no."

I couldn't read his tone. It was almost like if it were up to him, they would be dating. He certainly couldn't take his eyes off of her.

"So, um, where'd you go to high school?" I asked, but it came off nervous-sounding.

"Jackson High," Kellan said, then quickly added, "in Iowa."

"Oh, right," I said. "I've heard of it. I went to Galen High in Eagle Valley."

Kellan nodded, like he already knew. "Sounds cool. I've always wanted to visit the site of the Malum portal. Haven't had the chance yet."

I shrugged. "It's just a bunch of rocks. Nothing special."

He didn't respond. Silence settled between us, but I couldn't take it.

"Hey, since we're partners and all, maybe we should think about scheduling some study sessions," I suggested. "You know, to get to know each other."

"Sure," he agreed, but he was still looking up at Celina while she performed. "Just name the time and place."

"We could meet Monday after class, like three o'clock in the Activities Center," I said.

He shrugged again. "Sure, sounds good."

Celina finished, and the living room broke out into cheers. She handed off the microphone to Shaylene, who was wearing skin-tight jeans and looked ready to put on a show. Rhys reached up to help Celina down from the coffee table, then handed her a drink. She fell into his arms, laughing.

"How was it, Rhys?" she asked him. "Was it good?"

"It was great," he said. "You're really talented."

She smacked him playfully. "Oh, stop."

Kellan's eyes darkened from beside me. He was obviously jealous. "Hey, Celina!"

She looked over to us and waved. She quickly pushed through the crowd and stopped in front of us. "Kellan! Where have you been?"

"Playing beer pong," he said, like it was obvious.

"It took you that long?" she said with a fake pout.

Kellan shot a glance at Rhys, then took Celina's hand. "Maybe we can go get that drink now."

"No worries!" she said chipperly, holding up a plastic cup. "Rhys already got me one. Who's this?"

She looked over to me, eyeing me up and down. I suddenly felt like I should be pulling her hair out or something. I didn't like the way she looked at me.

"Nobody," Kellan said casually, and my stomach sank. "Just my partner."

Celina's face lit up. "Oh, *you're* Cora Marek. Of course. I should've known. I'm Celina Dyer. Perhaps you've heard of me?"

She stuck her hand out, and I had no choice but to shake it.

"Yeah, Kellan's mentioned you," I said. She was so fake I could hardly stand it.

Celina giggled, then swatted Kellan in the shoulder. "Kellan, you talk about me?"

"Only good things," he teased.

Ugh. Gag. This flirting was more uncomfortable than Travis's barfing.

"I'll see you on Monday," I said to Kellan before turning toward the hall to get away from them.

"Wait, Cora!" Celina called, following me.

I stopped in the doorway to the kitchen. Though we weren't far from Kellan and Rhys, they couldn't hear us over Shaylene's singing.

"Yeah?" I asked as politely as I could manage.

"Look…" I could hear the fake kindness in her voice. "Kellan and I kind of have a thing going."

I laughed out loud. "Oh, God. You don't have to worry about us. We're changing partners by the end of the semester."

"See, that's the thing," she said carefully, like she was

speaking to a child. "I want Kellan to stay in school with me, so let's make one thing clear. You *better* work your ass off for him. He *needs* to pass that final."

Oh, this bitch was *not* threatening me.

I took a step closer to her, finally feeling the alcohol kicking in and lowering my inhibitions. Yeah, I was a lightweight—so sue me. "And what are you going to do about it if he fails?"

Celina's gaze roamed over me, but that threat never left her eyes. "I'll make sure you never return to the academy."

I scoffed. Was she serious?

"Relax," I said, rolling my eyes. "I want to pass as much as he does. By the end of the semester, Kellan and I are going to be the best team Harris Academy has ever seen."

Celina smirked. "Oh, that I would very much like to see, considering Rhys and I are already working on that title. But have fun trying."

I didn't back down. I raised my eyebrows and stepped toward her, until we were almost touching. "Bitch, it is on."

Celina's lips twitched. "I always did like a little competition."

Before I could say anything more, she whirled around and started back toward Kellan and Rhys. Kellan's eyes darted between the two of us, like he couldn't figure out what that was all about. I shot him a half-hearted smile, but inside, I was reeling.

Celina thought she could threaten me? Well, fine. I was up to the challenge. My team was going to blow all others out of the water.

I just needed to get Kellan on board.

8

I paced nervously in the entrance to the Activities Center the following Monday after class. Kellan was fifteen minutes late, and I was starting to get a little peeved. We'd talked earlier that day in our Introduction to Firefighting class, so I knew he wasn't out sick. I glanced down at my phone. I would've messaged him, but he still hadn't accepted my friend request online, and I didn't have his phone number.

I was starting to hope he was waiting for me at a different entrance and hadn't completely blown me off, but as the minutes ticked by, the more I realized that was unlikely. This was the obvious place to meet. A half an hour passed, and then forty-five minutes. I huffed and finally gave up.

I stomped out of the Activities Center and across the lawn toward the dining hall, where I knew I'd find Laura. The cafeteria was huge, with a maze of tables and a long buffet line. Huge floor-to-ceiling windows lined the outer wall, letting in the sunshine. It was the end of September, so it was one of the last nice days we might have.

I piled my plate with food from the salad bar, then found

Laura sitting at a table in the corner beside Travis, Caleb, and Shaylene. They were discussing anatomy homework and arguing over which bone was the radius and which was the ulna.

"Your radius is this bone," Laura insisted. She ran her fingers over her forearm, drawing an invisible line down to her thumb.

"Are you sure?" Caleb asked, giving her a quizzical look.

"Positive," Laura replied.

He glanced to Shaylene beside him for confirmation.

"She's right," Shaylene said. "Didn't we go over this last night?"

Caleb held back a smile. "I was, uh, a little distracted."

Shaylene blushed and wiggled her eyebrows. "*Yeah* you were."

It was no secret that those two had hit it off the moment they'd been paired up.

Travis took immediate interest. "Ooh, give us the details."

"Get lost." Shaylene shoved Travis playfully.

Laura's gaze darted up to mine as I sat across from her. "Oh, hey Cora."

I smiled. "Hi."

Shaylene had made it clear to Travis he wasn't getting any details of last night. He gave up and turned to Laura. "Okay, smarty pants. You seem pretty confident you're going to ace this test. What's this called?"

Travis pointed to his elbow. Without hesitation, Laura answered, "Olecranon process."

Travis frowned. "I was hoping you'd forget that one."

She shrugged. "I study."

"So, can you take this test for us?" Caleb joked.

"Sure," Laura said casually. "If you want to be kicked out of the academy for cheating."

Caleb's face fell. "Flash cards, it is."

Laura giggled, then turned to me. "What's up? I thought you were meeting with Kellan tonight."

I pursued my lips. "I was *supposed* to, but he never showed."

"What a jerk," Laura said lightheartedly.

"He is," I laughed. "At least I'm trying to make an effort. I can't do all the work for him."

"I hope nothing happened to him," she said in concern. "I hope he's okay."

"It's Kellan Greene," I pointed out. "I'm sure he's fine."

Travis's voice cut through our conversation. "Hey, Laura. What's the kneecap called again?"

"Patella," she answered. "We've gone over this at least fifteen times."

"Right," Travis replied. "We might need an extra study session before Thursday's test. My dorm room?"

Laura shrugged. "Sure."

Travis turned back to Caleb and Shaylene, and I gave Laura a wide-eyed look.

"What?" she asked innocently.

I whispered quietly, though Travis was ignoring us. "He did *not* forget what the kneecap is called. He just wants to get you alone."

Laura turned bright pink, then her lips formed into a smile. "I don't have a problem with that at all."

I nudged her with my foot playfully under the table. "Don't have too much fun."

Laura smirked at me. "Please. We're partners. We're not dating."

"Yet," I added for her.

"Shh…" she hissed, glancing to Travis, but he was still talking to Caleb and didn't hear us. She straightened in her seat. "What will you be doing tonight?"

I poked at my food. "Probably studying. And hoping I don't fail the semester."

I gave a nervous chuckle, but the sad part was that it was true.

~

My stomach sank when Kellan entered our anatomy classroom the following morning. Laura, Shaylene, and I were seated beside each other toward the front. My eyes followed Kellan all the way to the back, until he slid into the empty seat beside Celina. He had a cocky smirk on his face and didn't even bother a glance my way.

I started to stand, but Laura tugged on my wing.

"Where are you going?" she asked.

"To confront Kellan," I said. "He stood me up."

Before I could start down the row of chairs, Professor Braff entered the room. I sighed and returned to my seat. Short of pulling Kellan out of the room and chewing him out in the hall, I wouldn't get a word in with him before class started.

"Okay, everyone," Professor Braff said as he stopped at the front of the room. The class quieted. "Get out a pencil. Pop quiz."

The entire class let out a collective groan, and Professor Braff laughed. "Kidding, but it sounds like most of you aren't ready for the test later this week. And I'll tell you why that's a big mistake."

Professor Braff was younger than most of our professors and had a great sense of humor. He was my favorite professor.

He continued. "As you may have noticed by now, attendance makes up ten percent of your grade. And still, many of you see it fit to skip my class."

He shoved his hands into his pockets and stared out at our faces with a pointed expression. He'd dropped his sense of humor and was getting serious now. It was strange, to say the least.

"We've spent the last two weeks studying the bones of the body. But why does it matter?" He paused for dramatic effect, though it was clear the question was rhetorical. "Every semester, I have at least one student come up to me and say, 'Professor, all these bones and muscles are too hard to remember. What do I have to know them for anyway?' And you know what I say? I say, 'You're right. I can't remember them either.'"

The class broke out into laughter.

Professor Braff's smile returned. "No, but seriously, you need to all understand why this class is important."

He continued to speak while he pulled up his slideshow presentation on the computer. "We all know that widespread chronic conditions are the most difficult to heal. Why do you think that is?"

Laura raised her hand.

"Yes, Miss Blake?" Professor Braff called on her.

"Healing requires the healer to target the area of treatment," Laura answered. "Without guidance and care, the essence that enters the body is useless, sometimes even damaging. The Davina administering the essence must be able to feel and target what they're healing."

"Precisely," Professor Braff said. "It's why lacerations are easy for us, because we can see the area that needs healing and focus on it. Once we get into internal injuries, such as broken bones or torn ligaments, things get trickier. You have to be able to identify which bone is broken, or which ligament needs healing. You target the wrong metatarsal, and you could injure your patient further."

Professor Braff changed the slide, and the entire room broke out into murmurs of disgust. The photograph he showed us displayed disfigured toes that were purple with bruises and twisted in unnatural directions. I remained calm. I was sure I'd see much worse than this in the field.

"As you can see, healing magic is as dangerous as it is helpful," Professor Braff pointed out. "So if you want to become a healer, don't blow off my class."

The whole room went silent for several seconds. I could feel the tension in the air as he narrowed his eyes into the crowd.

Finally, Professor Braff turned on his heel and started for the whiteboard. "Moving on."

I swore I heard the class take a collective breath. I leaned over to Laura and whispered, "That was a little intense. Usually he's so laid back."

"Agreed," she whispered back. "But he's right. If we don't get this down, we'll never learn to heal."

She stared down at her open textbook with a terrified look on her face. I suddenly felt bad for her.

Shaylene seemed to notice and quickly said, "It's fine. We can all study together."

Laura would pass this class for sure, but what Professor Braff had said clearly made her nervous.

My hand shot into the air before I really thought about it. "Professor?"

He turned to me with a raised eyebrow. "Miss Marek?"

I dropped my hand to my desk. "Yeah, I was just wondering… If it's the Davina's task to find the site of the injury and do the actual healing, why is this topic important for Aedes?"

Professor Braff looked confused by my question, and I felt like I'd just asked the stupidest thing in the world. But it was a valid question, wasn't it?

"Because, Miss Marek," he said kindly, "the Aedes are there to help. You are partners, and though they don't do the actual healing part of things, they should be supporting their Davina partner in every way possible. At times, that may include confirming their diagnosis. Don't underestimate the power of your partner just because they have a different job than you."

With that, he began his lecture, and I was left considering his words. I'd been trying to ease some of Laura's nerves, but I didn't think it helped.

For the next hour, all I could hear was the sound of Professor Braff's voice echoing in my head. *Don't underestimate the power of your partner...*

It felt like a personal attack, like he knew Kellan and I weren't working well together. But was I *underestimating* him? I didn't know.

By the time class ended, I was ready to figure it out.

"Kellan!" I called down the hallway as the class dispersed. I told Laura to go on without me, then quickened my pace toward Kellan. He didn't hear me, so I called his name again.

He let out an exasperated sigh and stopped in the middle of the hallway. "What is it?"

He sounded like he was trying to be nice, but I could hear the irritation in his tone.

Celina looked me up and down, then said, "See you later, Kellan."

He shot her a quick wave and said, "Bye."

"What happened yesterday?" I asked him.

His eyebrows knitted together. "Yesterday?"

"Yeah, were you sick or something?" I was trying to be nice, but the way he looked at me—like just the sight of me made him want to vomit—suggested he blew me off on purpose. "We were supposed to meet up in the Activities Center to train."

"Shit, I totally forgot about that." His tone was totally unreadable.

I crossed my arms. I couldn't tell if he was being honest or not. "Really? Or are you trying to be difficult?"

"I'm not *trying* to be anything," he insisted, though it didn't sound like the accusation bothered him at all.

I raised an eyebrow. "You sure? Because you never wanted to be my partner in the first place. We're a terrible pair."

"On the contrary, we're the perfect pair," he argued.

I was speechless. All I could do was make a face at him.

"What do you mean?" I finally asked.

Kellan shrugged. "No big deal."

"It *is* a big deal," I snapped. By now, we were the only two left in the hall, so I didn't mind raising my voice. "This is our future we're talking about. Do you want to flunk out? Because I'm willing to put in the work so that doesn't happen, but I can't do it without your help. What's your deal, anyway?"

Kellan frowned. "I don't have a *deal*."

"Sure you do. Everyone does," I pointed out.

Kellan shifted his weight between his feet and looked away from me.

"Well...?" I pressed.

Kellan sighed, finally looking me in the eye. "Look, I'm sorry I ditched you. I really did forget."

He sounded like he was telling the truth.

"Fine," I said, accepting his excuse. "But from now on, we need to communicate better with each other. We're partners, and I know that doesn't mean much to you, but it means something to me."

"It *does* mean something to me," he argued, then held his hand out. "Give me your phone. I'll put my number in."

I unlocked my screen and handed him my phone. He entered his number, then handed it back.

"I really am sorry," he said softly. "Let me make it up to you. Can we meet later tonight?"

I pressed my lips together, trying to get a reading on him, but he was impossible. I couldn't tell if his offer was genuine or not. Finally, I said, "Yeah, I'm available after class."

"Okay," he said. "Let's meet up then."

He started walking away, but I quickly stopped him. "Hold on. Where should I meet you?"

He paused, then said, "My dorm? Clark Hall, room 313. Four o'clock?"

"Okay," I said reluctantly. I'll bring the ham."

He shot me a quizzical look. "Ham? For dinner?"

I rolled my eyes. "Lord, you've missed too many lectures. You'll see."

A smile passed his lips. "It should be interesting."

I wasn't amused, but I replied anyway. "Yeah, it should be."

9

I arrived at Kellan's dorm room at four o'clock on the dot. I knocked, and the door swung open.

"Come on in," Kellan said.

I followed him inside. It was quiet, since his roommate wasn't around.

Kellan's room was the same dimensions as mine, but apart from that, they looked nothing alike. All the furniture was set up in different spots, and he had a futon that faced a huge TV. For some reason, I expected his room to be a mess, but I was surprised to see that it was neat and tidy. On one side of the room, band posters were hung all over the wall, while the other side had a mural of a forest tacked from floor-to-ceiling.

Kellan sat on the side with the mural. I tried to take in everything I could about the room to see if I could figure out what his deal was, but it was all trivial. There was a pair of hiking boots at the foot of his bed, a basketball on the top of his dresser, and a fishing pole propped up in the corner.

"The suspense is killing me," Kellan said from the bed. "What's the ham for?"

I took a seat at his desk chair and pushed aside a thick law book and an empty takeout container of Pad Thai to make room. I placed the ham on the desk and began to peel back the plastic covering. "In one of Professor Kovski's lectures, she talked about using meat to practice on. It won't actually heal it, since it's not alive, but it gives something for us to channel our essence into. It'll help us practice while we get a feel for each other's power."

Kellan sat up a little straighter, looking intrigued. "So, what's the plan?"

"Suffer through this," I joked. I was relieved to hear him laugh a little in agreement. I quickly turned serious again. "I wanted to start with feeling our connection again, since we haven't had a chance to work together since that first lab. I was planning to do some elemental work in the Activities Center, but now that we're stuck here, it's probably best if we don't burn the dorm hall down."

Kellan smirked. "No, let's not do that."

"So instead, I thought we could try some healing techniques together," I said. "It's not going to do anything since we don't have a living being to practice on, but at least we can get the techniques down."

Kellan stood and came up beside me. "Okay. Let's see what we're capable of."

He placed a hand on my shoulder. My essence felt like a rocket whipping through my body and leaving behind a tingling trail of fire. For a second, it felt like Kellan had sucked all my essence energy out of me. Then it came flooding through me like the wall between the earth and my body had broken.

Essence flowed through me and into Kellan. He took a deep, calming breath, and I could tell it was energizing him.

Maybe he'll be more bearable once his essence energy is balanced, I thought.

"Our connection is really strong," I remarked. I was starting to see why Professor Kovski had partnered us up. Something about Kellan's power opened my channel wider than I'd ever felt it before. I could tell by the faraway look in his eyes that he felt it, too.

"Yeah," he said without looking at me. "I guess we do."

I was ready to get down to business. "Still, I need you to open my channel wider. I need to access more essence to heal."

I could feel the moment he began to siphon more, because the energy began to buzz throughout my body at a higher frequency. The feeling that came with it made me actually like Kellan a little more.

I waited until I felt the channel stop expanding, then closed my eyes and placed my hands over the ham. I guided my essence down my arms like I had during our class with the rats, then let it settle in the palms of my hands. I pushed just a little to test it out, but I could feel my hands heating from my fire.

"Do you want roasted ham for dinner?" I asked, only half-serious.

"It's free food, right?" Kellan chuckled.

"Yeah, but that's not the point," I said. "I need more essence for healing, or I'm going to fire-roast this ham. Can you pull any more?"

"I'll try," he said.

My essence intensified, and I felt the heat in my hands wane to nothing more than a warm, comforting sensation. I pushed more essence into my hands. When I opened my eyes, they were glowing.

"That's it!" I cried, but as soon as I said it, the glow shifted from white to a red burst of energy.

Kellan and I both jumped back. I nearly tipped the chair back, while he stumbled into the corner of the bed. My essence channel immediately waned, until all I could feel was a light buzz. It'd be enough to conjure fire for a few days, but definitely not enough to heal.

"I thought we weren't having fire-roasted ham for dinner," Kellan teased.

"Shut up," I shot back playfully. I looked down at my hands, wondering where I went wrong. "I know what I'm doing."

Kellan shifted uncomfortably between his feet. "If it's okay, can I give you some advice?"

I raised an eyebrow at him. "Says the guy who didn't know you could use a ham to practice your essence."

Kellan held his hands up in surrender. "Look, I know you have all the textbook stuff down. You know the technique. But putting it into practice is a lot different. There are things no professor can teach you; you have to figure them out on your own."

I sensed some sort of insult was coming on, but I had to remind myself that Kellan and I were in this together. I didn't have any intention of fighting with him.

Don't underestimate him, I reminded myself.

"So, what am I missing?" I asked, though my guts churned. I wasn't sure I was ready for the answer.

"Your emotions are getting in the way," Kellan said.

I crossed my arms. "Are you suggesting I don't know how to deal with my emotions?"

He shrugged. "I don't know. Do you? You're acting pretty defensive right now, and all I'm trying to do is help."

I quickly dropped my arms to my sides. "Okay, so what do I have to do?"

Kellan reached out for my shoulder again. "Try to forget that I'm here."

"Forget you exist," I said, making a check sign in the air. "Got it. I can do that."

"Ha ha," Kellan said dryly. "Don't let your feelings for me get in the way of your essence."

I took a deep breath. "Okay, let's try this again."

Kellan and I did as we'd done before. He drew my essence

into himself, which opened up my channel wider and allowed me to gather more into my palms, but they barely glowed.

"I can feel you resisting against me." Kellan had his eyes closed and was focusing intently on the flow of essence between us. "You need to let your essence flow to me *and* to your palms. Don't divert it all to healing."

"But I need all I can get to heal," I pointed out.

"Let me take what I can, and you'll have plenty more to work with," he said.

I relaxed and tried to follow his instruction, but I couldn't feel my channel opening wider. It was like it was all flowing straight to him, and I needed more if I wanted to conjure healing essence.

"Cora," he pressed. "You're pulling away from me again. Don't resist."

I gave in, and I suddenly felt my channel opening wider. I gathered what I could and directed it down my arms and to my palms. My hands began to glow, but when I tried to transfer the energy into the ham, I couldn't make the transfer.

"Something's wrong," I said in frustration.

Kellan dropped his hand, and my essence pulled back as my channel shrank.

"What?" I asked in surprise.

"You're not following my instructions," he accused.

I looked up at him. "Yes, I was."

"It's not enough to give me just a piece of your essence," he explained. "You can't hold back. I'm not going to drain it from you, Cora. It doesn't work that way."

"Kellan, I did exactly what you asked," I said as I wiped my hands on my jeans. I was getting ham grease all over them and felt gross.

He shook his head. "But you didn't. I can feel it. I can sense the flow of essence through you. You're still holding back."

"If I am, I don't mean to." Irritation entered my tone again.

Kellan noticed. "Getting frustrated isn't going to help either of us."

"You're getting frustrated, too," I pointed out.

"Christ," Kellan sighed. "We've barely started, and we're already arguing."

"I don't think we're arguing," I said. "We just have to talk this out."

Kellan plopped onto his bed. "So, what's the problem? Why are you trying to do all this work alone? Why won't you let me do my part?"

"Maybe the problem isn't me," I suggested. I really tried to keep a level head, but it felt like he was accusing me of being incapable before we'd even gotten to the root of the problem. "Maybe you're not taking as much essence from me as you could be."

Kellan frowned. "That's ridiculous. Why would I do that?"

I shrugged. "I don't know. Because you've been doing the bare minimum all semester just to get by."

Kellan raked his fingers through his blond hair. He looked like he'd just about had enough of me today. "I'm trying the best I can. You're the one with healing power, so I think it's logical to work on that first."

"Yeah, I *am* the one with healing power, so why am I taking lessons from you?" I raised a challenging eyebrow.

Kellan's lips tightened. "Just because I don't have healing power doesn't mean I don't understand the theory behind it. I'm taking the same classes you are—"

"And you've missed half of them!" I exclaimed. He couldn't even argue with that, because it was true. "Don't even pretend like Professor Braff wasn't talking about you today when he chewed us out about attendance."

"My attendance has nothing to do with what I know," he defended. His eyebrows just kept falling deeper and deeper over his eyes.

It was clear we were both fed up with each other already. I stood and swung my bag over my shoulder. I left the ham behind on his desk. He could eat it for all I cared.

"Wait!" he demanded, shooting to his feet. "Where are you going?"

I whirled around before I got to the door. "Clearly, this isn't happening tonight. Let's take a break and try again later."

Kellan's shoulders fell. "Wait, Cora. I really want to try to work with you."

"So take some time to figure out what the deal is," I suggested. "You said it yourself. I have more power than you, which means I should be able to do this."

Kellan pressed his fingers to his eyes, like he was dealing with a migraine. He dropped his hands and rolled his eyes at me. "You really think that you're better than me because you're a Davina, don't you?"

I scowled at him. "I never said that."

"But you meant it," he accused, his voice rising.

"Your part is easy!" I shot back at him. "All you have to do is stand there while you fuel up on my essence. I'm the one who has to conjure healing essence, diagnose the issue, and heal without fucking it up. So sorry if I think my part is a little more involved than yours."

Kellan burst. "See? This is why we can't work together. Your head is too big!"

"And you're not dedicated enough!" I accused.

Kellan gritted his teeth and stared me down. I held his gaze.

"Fine," he snapped. "Just go. I thought you cared about passing this semester. I wanted to help you with that, but I can't if you're going to act this way."

"Act what way?" I snapped. *He* was the one being a major douchebag.

Kellan reached around me and swung the door open, then

started pushing me out of the room. "Have fun trying to heal without me. Come back when you appreciate my role in this."

"Kellan," I protested as he shoved me out into the hallway. "Stop it. I never said I didn't appreciate you—"

He slammed the door in my face.

Fine. I wasn't going to stick around if he didn't want me here. I stormed down the hall, getting away from him as quickly as I could.

One training session down. Only three months of training with this asshole to go.

I couldn't stop replaying my encounter with Kellan the following day. I barely paid attention in my Art of Healing lecture, and Kellan didn't show up for our Introduction to Firefighting class. I had a feeling he was avoiding me.

"I know what your problem is," Travis claimed during lunch.

I swallowed my bite of chicken and lifted my gaze to meet his. "What's that?"

"You two don't know each other well enough," he said. "See, Laura and I were good together during testing, but the more we get to know each other, the better we work together."

"It's true," Laura said as she stabbed her salad with her fork. "It's the same with Caleb and Shaylene."

At the sound of their names, they both looked up. They'd been in their own little world, talking lowly to one another.

"We tried getting to know each other," I said. "Didn't work out so well."

"Have you tried hanging out with each other outside of class?" Travis asked.

"I mean, yeah… last night," I said, poking at my food.

"Yeah, but you were studying," he pointed out. "You need to get out of that environment."

"We were both at that party together." I was grasping at straws. That hadn't gone well, either.

"See?" Travis said. "That's good. You should get together like that more often."

Shaylene quickly piped up. "We're getting some people together in the Activities Center tonight. You should come. Bring Kellan."

I twisted up my nose. "Me? Play sports? With Kellan? That'll be fun."

"Yeah, it will," Laura said chipperly, ignoring my dry tone.

"Shit," Caleb said, checking his phone. "We're going to be late for class, babe."

Shaylene quickly stood beside Caleb. "I expect to see you there tonight, Cora. Gym C, six o'clock."

I faked a groan. "Do I have to?"

"You don't have a choice." Caleb winked at me, then grabbed his skateboard from under the table. The two hurried out of the dining hall side-by-side.

My eyes followed them as they passed the large windows, holding hands. I turned back to Laura and Travis once Caleb was out of sight. "What do I do if Kellan doesn't want to come?"

Laura shrugged. "Come anyway. It'll be fun."

I sighed and pulled out my phone to message Kellan. *You busy tonight?*

You ready to talk? His text came only a minute later.

Ugh. He was so passive aggressive.

My fingers punched the screen quickly. *Depends.*

On what?

Are you ready to be a decent human being?

I thought you knew. I'm not quite human.

I nearly snorted on my water I was drinking while I read the text. Laura and Travis gave me concerned looks, but I assured them I was fine and returned to my phone.

Fair enough, I texted. ***You up for a game?***

What kind of game?

Idk. Something in the Activities Center. My friends didn't say.

Do I have to be on your team? he asked.

I won't make you, I texted back.

Then I'm in.

"What are *you* smiling about?" Travis asked.

I slipped my phone in my pocket and returned my attention to my food. "Kellan agreed to join us."

"Ooh," Travis sang. "You *like* him."

My lips twisted in disgust. "Ew. Never say that again."

His features went blank. "What? What did I say?"

"Oh, Travis," Laura sighed. "You have so much to learn about women."

"Do I?" he teased. "I thought I was a pro."

Laura rolled her eyes. "Keep believing that."

By the time six o'clock rolled around, I was pumped. I spent most of my nights in my dorm room studying, so it was nice to get out for once. I dressed in a purple racerback tank top and a pair of black leggings, then followed Laura and Travis to the Activities Center.

The gymnasium was huge. A full track ran around the length of the room, and the ceiling was at least three stories tall. In the center of the track, endless foam pads had been set up. High above me, Davina and Aedes flew from one end of the gym to the other, performing aerial tricks and goofing off. It was mostly guys, and they were all shirtless. Large nets were attached to the walls on either end and secured high above my head to the level where people were flying.

Caleb swooped down from the air and tucked his white wings close to his back. He held a soccer ball and tossed it from one hand to the other. "You guys made it! Where's your partner, Cora?"

"I'm not sure," I admitted. "He said—"

"Right here!" Kellan jogged in through the doors and slowed beside us. He wore a tight blue t-shirt and didn't have his wings out.

"You're late," I joked.

Kellan looked out toward the middle of the gym, where Aedes and Davina were landing on mats and gathering together. He shrugged. "Looks like I'm right on time."

Kellan pulled his shirt over his head. Holy mother of God— those abs! He flexed his shoulders, and feathery midnight-black wings grew out of his back. I stared a little too long, then forced my gaze off of him.

Beside me, Travis had also stripped his shirt off and spread his white wings. He clapped his hands together and said, "Let's do this!"

"Okay, everyone gather round!" Caleb called.

There were around twenty people, and only two other girls besides Laura, Shaylene, and me. I knew about half of the guys from class, but the others I hadn't met before.

"Does everyone know how to play?" Caleb asked.

"I don't," a petite girl with jet-black hair said.

"This is what we call aerial soccer," Caleb explained. "It's a little soccer, a little football, but with a few modifications. For one, it takes place in the air." He gestured up to the nets on the wall that would serve as our goals. "Unlike regular soccer, you can touch the ball with your hands. The goal is to get the ball into the other team's net. Tackling is allowed, but the Activities Director has urged us to use caution, as we don't want to send anyone to the hospital with a broken wing."

"Eh, it'll be practice," Travis said with a shrug. "We'll get that patched up right here."

Caleb laughed. "If you screw up trying to heal me without a medical license, I'll sue you."

Travis's face paled, then he saluted Caleb. "No injuries tonight. Got it."

"We need team captains," Caleb said.

"I'll be one," Kellan offered, raising his hand.

"Cool. Anyone else?" Caleb asked.

"I will," I said quickly. Kellan didn't want me on his team anyway. Might as well get on the other team as fast as I could.

Caleb stepped aside for me. "Kellan, you get first pick."

"I'll take Travis," he said without hesitation.

Travis beamed and moved to stand beside Kellan.

"Laura," I said.

"Sweet! I'm not last for once." She fist-bumped the air, then bounced over to stand beside me.

"Caleb," Kellan said.

"We'll take… Sorry, I forgot your name." I looked to a tall, athletic guy with black wings in my Introduction to Firefighting class.

"Miles," he said as he came to join Laura and me. He leaned over to her and whispered, "Your wings are sweet, by the way."

"Oh, these old things?" Laura joked.

We continued on choosing our teammates until we each had a team of ten. Shaylene looked pleased to be on Kellan's team with Caleb. Miles claimed the role of goalie, and the rest of us positioned ourselves in the air. Kellan and I faced each other as we hovered at the center of the gym. He shot me a challenging smirk.

"Ready?" Caleb asked from where he flew beside us.

"Ready as I'll ever be," I said.

"And… Go!" Caleb called. He tossed the ball between me and Kellan.

Kellan shot forward and reached out for the ball, but I kicked my foot at it instead. My toes connected with the ball, and it flew out of his grasp and toward Laura. She caught it and flew toward the goal, dodging out of the way of other players as she went. Kellan and I both shot toward her to stay on top of the ball.

"Over here!" a guy on my team named Everett called to Laura. Just before a girl on the other team swooped down to tackle Laura from above, she tossed the ball to Everett. He whacked it with his wing. It made a painful-sounding *smack*, but bounced into the net.

My team cheered. I stole a glance at Kellan, but he didn't seem bothered that we were already in the lead. He just looked like he was having fun.

The ball soared out into the middle of the gym after the other team's goalie kicked it. Kellan shot past me and caught it mid-air. He flew beneath one of my teammates, then shot back into the air once he passed them. I sped up to catch him, but before I could get there, he'd already handed off the ball to one of his teammates.

"Over here!" Kellan called just before his teammate was about to get tackled. He threw the ball back at Kellan.

I reached my hand out to stop it. It just barely grazed the ends of my fingers. Kellan caught it, then tossed it to another teammate, who took it all the way to the goal and shot it in before Miles could stop it.

"Tied game!" Caleb shouted.

Miles kicked the ball, and I quickly shifted course to follow it. I caught it, and Kellan's team started closing in on me at all angles. I twisted my body to dodge around one guy, then flapped my wings hard to shoot up and over Shaylene. I tucked my wings close to me and dropped several feet, then shot them out again to catch myself in the air as I dodged around another guy.

Then suddenly, something wrapped around my ankle, and I was falling. I let out a shriek and clutched on to the ball, flapping my wings harder to rip free. But it was evident my attacker wasn't going to let me go.

"Here!" a guy on my team named Tucker called.

I hurled the ball at him, but one of Kellan's teammates swooped in and caught it. My attacker let me free, and I finally saw that it was Kellan.

"Not fair," I said playfully.

"Hey, I don't make the rules," he replied innocently.

"Oh, so we're playing dirty now?" I laughed.

He shrugged, then continued on his way.

"Two can play at that game!" I called after him. I smiled as an evil plan began to form in my mind.

When the ball came toward him, I shot a white ball of essence in front of his face. It was the least powerful kind—the kind that would only stun him and wouldn't burn him—but it was enough to get him to twist out of the way. I swooped down and caught the ball he'd missed, then flew as fast as I could toward the goal. I threw it as hard as I could, and it soared past the goalie and into the net.

"Hey!" Kellan called. "Is that legal?"

I shrugged and hovered near the goal. "I don't make the rules."

"No stunning!" Caleb shouted. "It's a good way to break a wing."

"What if we're on the ground?" Kellan asked.

"Sure. Whatever," Caleb said. "Just don't stun anyone out of the air."

The game continued, and we were neck-and-neck the entire way. I'd scored two more goals, but so had Kellan. I got ahold of the ball again, and almost instantly, someone's arms wrapped around my legs. I tossed the ball to my nearest teammate as fast as I could.

I took my eyes off the game as I tumbled toward the mats. I drew my wings into me until they disappeared, then rolled across the mats to catch my fall. I turned to see that Kellan had landed gracefully on the mats and was smiling in my direction.

I struck before he could. I shot a white glowing ball of essence out of my palm. He ducked, just barely missing it. It landed several yards beyond him and exploded like a fire-cracker. Kellan quickly shot his own essence back at me, though his was a dark color with a red center. I threw my body to the mat to avoid it.

"I don't think this is how the game's played," I told him.

"You keep scoring goals," he chuckled. "I gotta give my team a fighting chance to get ahead."

I threw another ball of essence at him, but he pulled his wings into himself and dodged out of the way. He quickly threw another ball at me, but I rolled out of the way to avoid it. It wasn't long before we were running around the mats and firing essence at each other in quick succession. Kellan kept coming closer and closer to me, and I was already out of breath.

"Can't we work out some sort of peace treaty?" I asked, just as I shot more essence at his head.

It whizzed just inches from his face, and his eyes went wide. "Try asking when you're not trying to knock me out."

I held my hands up in surrender, but he didn't give in. He shot another ball of essence at me, and I jumped to avoid it. While my attention was on the essence, he sprinted forward and caught me by surprise. He grabbed me around the waist and tossed me over his shoulder.

"Hey!" I pounded my fists into his back, but he barely seemed to feel it. Instead, he spun us around on the mats until I got dizzy. I couldn't control my laughter. "This... is not... how the game... works."

He dropped me to the mat, then fell beside me, so close that we were almost touching. We were both out of breath and laughing. I turned my head in his direction and caught sight of his dimples. My laughter quickly died as I was reminded who I was goofing off with. Was this seriously the same Kellan I'd been having issues with all semester? It was so strange to see him in this new light—like we could actually get along.

Kellan caught my eye, but didn't lift his head off the mat. "What?" he asked innocently.

"I just… didn't know you were any fun." My cheeks flamed as I said it. I nudged him in the side, hoping he didn't notice my flushed face.

"Me?" he laughed. "I could say the same thing about you. Perhaps there's hope for you after all."

"Hope?" My eyebrows shot up. "You should be hoping I don't kick your ass in this game."

He looked up to the Aedes and Davina flying above us. "Eh, your team is doing fine without you."

Neither of us moved. It was silent on the ground for several seconds before I said, "I'm sorry about yesterday."

He waved it off. "Don't worry about it. We'll figure it out."

"You think?" I asked. "Because it feels like we do better when we're on opposite sides."

Kellan sighed, then pushed himself to his elbows. Hot damn. Those abs were still on full display. It'd be a sin not to admire them. He didn't seem to notice my eyes darting downward every now and then.

"Whether we like it or not, we're stuck with each other for now," he said. "So we're going to have to work as a team either way."

"Agreed," I said, sticking my hand out toward him. "Partners? Like, for real this time?"

He nodded, then shook my hand. A tingle of essence shot through me, and I knew he'd siphoned some just for fun. "Partners."

"Incoming!" someone shouted.

Kellan and I looked up to see essence raining down on us from all directions. He kept holding my hand and pulled me to my feet as we dodged out of the way. My heart lurched up into my throat, but the essence aimed at us had missed us. It all exploded into the mats, then disappeared.

"Attack!" someone shouted.

The players all landed on the ground, and our game of aerial soccer quickly turned into a game of essence dodgeball. Somehow, the teams shifted—like we could all just sense where our loyalties lied. Kellan and I ended up defending each other. We ran over to Laura and Travis and formed a group as we dodged essence whizzing in all directions.

It was the most fun I'd had all semester. By the end of the night, I'd nearly forgotten how much I despised Kellan as my partner.

"Thanks for suggesting this," I told Shaylene as we left the Activities Center. "It was a lot of fun."

"And Kellan?" she asked. "Did it help?"

I contemplated it for a minute, but the answer was obvious. "Yeah. I think things might actually work out between us."

11

When I entered my Introduction to Firefighting class on Friday, something seemed different. I didn't realize what it was until I saw Kellan waving me over. He wasn't sitting in his usual spot. Instead, he was sitting next to the chair I normally sat in. We didn't have assigned seats, and most of the class so far had been lecture instead of practical application. When we worked with fire before, Kellan had avoided me, since I could work with any Aedes on my element and we only needed each other for our healing classes. But today, he seemed to think it was a good idea for us to pair up.

"Hey," I said as I sat. "What's up?"

"We're killing flames today," Kellan reminded me. "I thought it'd be good if we worked together, since we'll be up against this during our final."

"Good idea," I said.

Kellan eyed me. "You look kind of… unenthused."

I shrugged. "I'm just waiting for this class to get exciting, you know. I can't wait to dress up in firefighting gear and walk into a burning building."

Kellan chuckled. "We have a long semester left. But you have to learn how to kill flames first."

"I know how," I said confidently.

Kellan rubbed his hands together like an evil mastermind. "Well, I can't wait to see it."

I shook my head and rolled my eyes.

"Okay, everyone. Settle down," Professor Arnold said as he strolled into the room with Professor Taylor on his heels. The two were both middle-aged men and best friends, which made them perfect teaching partners. "Today, we'll be focusing on our Davina students and practicing killing flames. However, that doesn't mean that your Aedes partner doesn't have a very key purpose in this. Allow us to demonstrate."

Professor Arnold gestured for the class to come forward. We gathered around a large glass window that took up the entire wall. On the other side was an empty room made entirely out of fireproof materials. The only thing inside was a pile of firewood for fuel. We'd watched several demonstrations here before, but I could tell today was going to be good.

Professor Arnold turned to his teaching partner. "Professor Taylor, if you will."

"Yes, sir." Professor Taylor stood at a control panel and let out a maniacal laugh that made the class burst into laughter. The two played off each other and always made sure we were having fun in this class.

"Bombs away," Professor Taylor joked.

He pressed a button on the panel, and flames immediately ignited. They quickly engulfed the wood while Professor Arnold continued to speak.

"Over the past several weeks, we've covered the basics about firefighting," he said. "You know your equipment. You know your safety procedures. Now it's time to learn how to put your essence to good use in the field."

Professor Arnold turned back to the fire and aimed his

palms to the glass. The flames instantly shrank, but they didn't completely disappear. "As you can see, I'm only capable of so much on my own. Professor Taylor?"

Professor Taylor came to stand beside him. He placed his hand on Professor Arnold's shoulder, drawing essence into him. I could tell the moment it happened, because the flames died quicker as Professor Arnold accessed more essence so he could perform more advanced magic. It seemed like only seconds before the flames died to embers, then the embers fizzled out to nothing.

"You see?" Professor Taylor said, turning back to the class. "This is why we continue to stress how important it is you get powered up before you go into a burning building, and why it's important you stick together. Your element will be stronger."

"Now, for the Davina in the class," Professor Arnold continued. "Don't get too hung up on extinguishing the flames completely today. All we want to see is that you're using the techniques from your Elemental Magic class and applying them to this setting. If you can't extinguish them fully today, you'll be able to by the end of the semester. I guarantee it."

"And if you can't," Professor Taylor cut in. "Good luck on the final."

The class shared a laugh, because we all knew what the final entailed. No way were any of us jumping into that without mastering this first.

"Are there any questions before we begin?" Professor Arnold asked.

Caleb raised his hand from the other side of the group, and our professor called on him. "So when we're actually extinguishing flames, are there any techniques to keep humans from noticing what we're doing?"

"Excellent question," Professor Arnold said. "We will be addressing those concerns another day. Right now, we want to master the art of our element before diving into that."

Shaylene's hand shot into the air next.

"Yes, Miss Hargrove?" Professor Arnold said.

"I'm just curious, why is it so important we keep our essence hidden from them?" she asked.

The question was innocent, but the entire room quieted. Professor Arnold shifted his weight between his feet.

"Coming out to the public has never ended well for us," he explained in a soft tone. "Humans greatly outnumber us. People are afraid of the unknown, and they react quickly and violently against the things they can't understand. We've kept our races secret for our own protection. At times when word has gotten out, we've been hurt for what we are."

"Hurt how?" Shaylene asked curiously.

Professor Arnold pressed his lips together, like the thought was uncomfortable for him. "A recent example involved a group of Aedes. It was around the time when their curse was broken and the Alliance was still working on assimilating the Aedes into our society. A group of humans caught some Aedes in their supernatural form. They called them spawns of Satan, captured them, and tortured them."

He didn't go into detail, but I'd heard the story before. They'd had their wings torn off and were beat to unconsciousness before the Alliance got word and made it there to save them. It wasn't the only time it'd happened, either. Of course, the Alliance kept it out of the media as much as they could.

"These past few years…" Professor Arnold trailed off, like there was something he wanted to say but couldn't. He had this faraway look in his eyes that made me shiver.

"Anyway…" Professor Arnold cleared his throat, cutting the tension in the room. "Back to our lesson. Who'd like to go first?"

A girl at the front shot her hand into the air. I would've half expected it to be Celina, had she been in this class. She was in the other time block, though, which I considered a blessing. I knew she'd show off if she had the chance—and she'd probably steal Kellan as her partner to do it.

Professor Arnold gestured her forward. "Pick a partner and step right up!"

The first team managed to reduce their flames by about half, but they couldn't get them down to embers.

"That's a great start!" Professor Taylor encouraged. "We'll make experts out of you by next week."

The next group was able to kill their flames to embers, but the wood still burned a hot red. When they pulled back their essence, the fire grew again.

"It's okay," Professor Arnold said. "You did great. Who's next?"

"We'll go," Kellan offered.

I froze. I'd wanted to watch a few more people before we went, but Kellan didn't seem to care.

"Come on up!" Professor Taylor said, like we were on a game show. "Show us what you've got."

Kellan and I made our way through the small group of students and stopped in front of the glass. He leaned over to quickly whisper to me. "We've got this."

"Thanks," I whispered back.

Professor Taylor pressed the control panel again, and the wood beyond the glass lit up in flames. We waited for Professor Arnold's signal, then Kellan placed his hand on my shoulder.

Essence flooded through me. I seemed to forget what it was like each time. That, or each time was more powerful than the last. I took a breath to steady my shaking hands, then held them up toward the glass.

"Remember that killing flames is different from creating them," Professor Arnold said to the class, though it felt as if he was reminding me. "You don't push your essence outward. You feel the essence all around you. You connect with your element and make it your own."

I concentrated on the flames in front of me. I tried to picture them as my own, as those that would come shooting out of my palms if I commanded them to. I ordered the flames to die, but nothing happened. I didn't feel anything.

"Take your time," Professor Arnold said softly.

"Relax, Cora." Kellan squeezed my shoulder, as if letting me know he could feel the tension in it. I hadn't even realized it was there until he pointed it out.

I took a deep breath and did as he instructed. Then I felt it. A warmth spread across my hands, but it came inward instead of going outward. I pulled back on my essence, as if tugging on that might bring the flames into me and tone them down, but all that happened was that the warmth in my hands disappeared.

I suddenly felt very self-conscious. All eyes were on me, and I was taking longer than the other teams had. I glanced to Professor Arnold, and he looked to be analyzing me, like he could see my struggle.

"What are you feeling right now, Cora?" Professor Arnold asked.

"I felt my hands get warm for a second," I told him.

Professor Arnold nodded thoughtfully. "Good. That means you connected with the flames. But you must go beyond a simple connection and make them your own. Feel them as if they're your own essence, and then control it as you would the element that pours out of you."

I nodded and tried again. Kellan dropped his hand from my shoulder, since I didn't need the constant power-up for elemental magic as I did with healing magic. He stepped close to me and whispered under his breath. "You've got this, Cora."

I knew I could do it, but his encouragement meant a lot. I took another deep breath and let my essence flow around and around in my body, swirling instead of going out through my palms to make flames. I focused on the fire beyond the glass—and felt that heat again. I didn't pull back this time. I just let the heat come. Slowly, it crept over my skin, washing over me until it overtook my whole body and became one with the essence inside of me. When I could no longer tell the difference between the fire in front of me and what it felt like to conjure my own flames, I did as I would my own magic. I commanded it to die down. And like my own magic, it did. The flames went from licking three feet high in the air to nothing more than an inch.

"That's it," Professor Arnold encouraged. "Keep it going. You can do it, Cora!"

I commanded it further, and the small flames died out, becoming nothing more than lingering embers.

"You've got this, Cora!" Kellan sounded excited. "We're almost there."

I held my breath and pushed harder as the last few embers held on. I couldn't leave a single one behind. It wasn't acceptable in the field, which meant it wasn't acceptable in class.

Come on. Come on. Come on.

The last embers glowed a bright red, then instantly died. I breathed a sigh of relief as the class clapped for me.

"We did it!" Kellan cried.

"Excellent job!" Professor Arnold applauded. "You've done great. You two make a really great pair."

He clapped us on the back as another team stepped forward to give it a shot. Kellan and I stepped aside. I was still trying to wrap my head around what I'd done.

"Wow," I said. "I don't think I expected to get that on my first try. I mean, I've extinguished flames plenty of times, but they were my own, you know? Taking an existing element and *making* it mine was cool."

"Yeah," Kellan said. "I guess we really do work well together."

I held in a laugh and teased, "If you say so."

"Would you have done better with someone else?" He raised a challenging eyebrow.

I shrugged. "I don't know. But we still have a long way to go. Especially with healing."

"True," he agreed. "But this is a good start."

12

"I need an update," Laura said.

It was mid-October, and the trees around campus were beautiful shades of reds, oranges, and yellows. The sun was shining, but the air was chilly enough that I wore a thick sweater and a knit beanie. It was Saturday, and Laura and I decided to take the bus downtown to do some shopping. She wanted to buy a new pair of winter boots, and I wanted to go to an antique store that had just opened up. We'd asked Shaylene to come along, but she was busy with Caleb.

I shoved my hands into my pockets as we walked toward the front gates. "Update on what?"

She nudged me with her elbow. "Duh. You and Kellan. You've barely talked about him over the past few weeks."

I shrugged, but a slight smile touched my lips. "Things are better. Introduction to Firefighting is going great. Our connection makes my element stronger, which means I'm getting really good with my fire. But we could still use the extra practice with healing. He always claims he's busy when I suggest we study."

"What about in class?" she asked.

"I don't know," I admitted. "I thought we were doing better, but Professor Kovski seems disappointed in us. Which I don't get, because we healed those frogs last week just fine. We still barely passed the assignment, though."

"Mm…" Laura pressed her lips together in thought. "I don't know… Hey, how's your anatomy homework going?"

"Fine. Why?" I asked.

Laura shrugged. "I did great with the bones unit, but now that we're working on muscles, I'm having a hard time."

"We'll study together later," I promised.

We reached the front gates. The security officers gave a polite nod, then let us pass.

We walked the long stretch of sidewalk to the corner. When we reached the intersection, we both slowed. Down the wide sidewalk along the busy road, a group of at least twenty people were pacing the wall with picket signs that read things like *What are they hiding?* and *The truth will set you free!*

"Let us in! Let us in!" they chanted.

Next to them, two guys were fiddling with a remote control and bitching about how it wasn't working. When their eyes turned skyward, I noticed a drone buzzing high above our heads. The losers were trying to get footage of campus—and I was pretty sure the Alliance had some sort of device to jam their feed.

My eyes caught sight of another guy, and a chill traveled down my spine. He had blond hair and wore a blue blazer. It was the same guy I'd seen on my first day here, the pompous ass who tried to sneak onto campus.

I grabbed Laura's arm. "Let's cross the street."

She eyed the protesters, then said, "Good idea."

Before the light changed to let us cross, the group spotted us.

"Colt," a girl said to get their leader's attention. "There's some!"

Colt and three girls hurried over to us. I wanted to just ignore them, but they swarmed us on all sides.

"What are you hiding behind these walls?" Colt demanded. He was so close that he was practically touching me.

"Nothing," I insisted, stepping away from him.

"You're hiding something, or you'd let other people in!" His nostrils flared.

"Yeah," one of the girls sneered, getting up close to Laura. "Tell us what it is."

I saw the fear in Laura's eyes and threw myself between the two of them. "Seriously, lady. Back. Off."

"Not until you tell us—"

"Nothing," Laura snapped. "We're not hiding anything. It's just a private and sacred campus."

"If that's true, why can no one join your religion?" Colt snarled.

He was getting way too close for comfort. I was very conscious of the Davina Blade tucked into my boot and was seriously considering using it if it came to that.

"You're a cult," he accused. "You're hiding something!"

"Dude, take it up with the administration," I growled. "Leave us alone."

"Leave you alone!?" he roared. His face was starting to turn red, and spittle flew from his mouth. "You're one of them!"

I'd had enough. I was seriously starting to feel like they'd jump us at any moment, so I struck first.

"I said, leave us alone!" I shoved Colt, and he stumbled backward into a few other protestors who had made their way over to us.

His eyes widened in surprise, like he couldn't believe someone had the audacity to put their hands on him. He straightened up and pointed a finger at me. "She assaulted me! You all saw it."

"You came at me first!" I defended.

"What's your name?" he demanded. "I'll be filing a police report for this."

Good Lord. Was he serious?

I couldn't stand around and watch any more of this bullshit. The light changed, giving Laura and me the signal to cross. I took her hand, but we didn't make it a step off the sidewalk before one of the girls stepped in front of me to block my path. She was young like the rest of them, maybe only a few years older than me.

"You're not going anywhere until you answer the question," she demanded.

"Um, yeah, I am," I stated, stepping around her and pulling Laura after me.

Seeing she couldn't mess with me, she went for Laura instead. She grabbed Laura's wrist and yanked her back onto the sidewalk.

"What the hell?" Laura shouted.

I shoved the other girl off her in an instant, and that's when it turned into a full-on brawl. Someone—I didn't see who— threw a fist at my face. My cheek throbbed in pain. Before I really knew what was going on, Colt had grabbed ahold of me and shoved me up against the wall surrounding campus. He leaned in to say something, but I didn't give him the chance. I shoved my knee up into his royal jewels, and he fell to the ground, clutching his groin.

I started to run over to Laura, but Colt reached out and grabbed my ankle. My body went tumbling, and my face smashed into a sharp rock on the sidewalk. Pain shot across my cheek, and I felt the warmth of my own blood running down my face.

"Let go of me, you freak!" I used my free leg to kick Colt's arm.

Just then, the sound of a horn honking cut through the screams. I looked up to see a black sedan rolling its passenger-side window down. I was surprised to see Kellan's face staring back at me from the driver's seat.

"Get in!" he shouted.

I scrambled to my feet and shoved two girls off Laura, who was fighting back fiercely. We jumped in the back seat of the car before anyone else could get their hands on us.

Kellan punched the gas, and we left the protestors in our wake. I finally breathed a sigh of relief. Laura lightly touched a tender bruise above her eye, and I clutched my cheek, which coated my hand in warm, sticky blood.

"Holy crap!" Kellan cried from up front. "What's wrong with you?"

"Wrong with me?" I asked in disbelief. "We're not the ones who started it."

His voice softened as he slowed the car at the next stoplight. "I'm sorry. I didn't mean that. It's just… you should know better than to get involved with people like that."

"Get involved?" I gaped at him. "We didn't mean to get involved in anything. We didn't know they'd be there or try to attack us!"

Kellan grabbed a handful of napkins from the front seat and shoved them at me. He looked concerned as his eyes traveled from my cheek to the blood on my hands. "Here. To stop the bleeding."

Kellan gently pressed on the gas when the light turned green. He turned down a quiet street. "All I meant is this group is kind of… crazy."

"Those are the protestors Kane Harris talked about during orientation, aren't they?" Laura asked.

"Yeah," Kellan said, holding tight to the wheel. "They call themselves the Infantry. And there are more of them."

I felt like I'd heard of them before but couldn't remember where. Then I remembered I'd briefly heard a group talking about them at the party we went to a few weeks ago.

"What's their deal?" I asked.

Kellan shrugged. "Don't know. They're just desperate to

know what goes on inside the academy, I guess. Usually, they're harmless."

"Well, they're stepping up their game," I said. "I mean, they attacked us."

Kellan gritted his teeth. "I should turn around and—"

"No," I said quickly. "We don't need more trouble."

Kellan let out a heavy breath. "Fine. But we should tell Chancellor Harris."

"Do you think she can do anything about it?" I asked. "Like stop the protests or something?"

"Technically, the school can't do anything since they're protesting outside campus boundaries," Kellan said. "But she can report the incident. Maybe local law enforcement will actually do something about it."

"So it was a *good* thing they jumped us?" Laura asked.

"Depends on how you look at it," Kellan said, glancing back at us. "I'm sorry they hurt you. I really am."

"How'd you know they'd attack us?" I asked.

"I didn't," he said. "I went to pick up some pizzas for my study group since I'm the only one with a car, and I saw you on my way back."

"Study group?" I asked with a raised eyebrow.

He caught my expression in the mirror. "For... one of my other classes."

We made it back to campus, and the three of us showed our student IDs to the security guards before they let us through. Kellan parked the car, and we got out. Before I could start for the Academy Center, Kellan stopped me. He grabbed the napkins from me and took my face in his hand.

"Let me see," he said.

I held still, completely in shock at his touch. He stared down at me and dabbed at the blood, but I barely felt the sting. All I could focus on was his warm fingers against the side of my face. I was acutely aware of his breath brushing across my skin as he inspected my wound, which wouldn't stop bleeding.

"Should we heal it?" I asked, mostly to break the silence. I couldn't tear my gaze from Kellan's face.

He shook his head. "Not yet. You'll want to show Chancellor Harris."

Kellan finally dropped his fingers, and I felt like I could breathe again.

"Are you okay, Laura?" I asked, turning to her.

She touched her bruise again. It was darkening by the minute. "Just a little shook up."

I had a feeling she was downplaying the pain. It looked bad.

We stopped outside Chancellor Harris's office, and Kellan explained to the receptionist what had happened.

"I'll let Chancellor Harris know right away," she said as she picked up her phone. "Please, take a seat."

We only waited a minute before the doors opened and Chancellor Harris invited us inside.

"I'll see you later," Kellan said with a wave.

"Wait," I blurted. He turned toward me expectantly, but I'd already forgotten what I was going to say. Instead, I said, "Thank you for your help."

He shot me a smile. "No problem."

I turned and followed behind Laura into Chancellor Harris's office.

"Please, girls," Chancellor Harris said. "Take a seat."

Laura and I sat in the two chairs in front of her desk. She took the seat behind it and folded her hands on the desktop in front of her. "I hear you had a run-in with the protestors outside campus."

"Yes." I quickly dove into the story of what happened.

Chancellor Harris looked more and more upset as the story went on.

"I can't believe anyone would protest the academy," I concluded with. "I mean, who could ever see us as a threat?"

Laura shrugged. "I mean, they don't know we're *not* a threat."

"I guess I get why we keep things a secret," I admitted.

"It's not really up for debate," Chancellor Harris pointed out. "It's our duty as supernaturals to keep our true nature secret."

"True," I agreed. "What can we do about this?"

"I think it's best if we report the incident to the police," Chancellor Harris said. "Perhaps then we can get these protestors off campus."

"Will it help, though?" Laura asked. "I mean, they could've done worse."

"Don't underplay it, Miss Blake," Chancellor Harris stated sympathetically. "What they did to you wasn't okay. You two were right to fight back. Will you be okay with filing written statements with the police?"

"Yes," the two of us answered simultaneously. We weren't going to let these assholes beat up any other students.

Chancellor Harris nodded. "I'll help you every step of the way to get this reported. In the meantime, be careful when you leave campus. I would hate to see this group targeting the two of you."

"We'll be careful," I assured her.

Chancellor Harris picked up her phone and began dialing a number.

While she was preoccupied, I turned to Laura and whispered, "I'm glad Kellan showed up and got us out of there when he did."

"Agreed," she said. "I guess he's not such a bad partner after all, is he?"

My lips twitched at the corners. "No, I guess he's not."

13

J tossed and turned all night. I couldn't stop thinking about how Kellan had shown up out of the blue to help save us from those protestors. It was like he was a guardian angel himself—though I knew what he'd say to that if I ever accused him of it. I could hear his voice in my head. *I'm no angel, sweetheart.*

Don't ask me why dream-version of Kellan called me sweetheart. It was just his thing, okay?

When I woke the next morning, all I wanted to do was show Kellan how much I appreciated his small act of kindness. I brought it up to Laura and Shaylene while we were at the gym.

"Kellan doesn't seem like the kind of guy who takes thank yous well," Laura said as she bent into a squat. Her face looked better since we'd visited the health services center and gotten healed.

"No," I agreed. I picked up a fifteen-pound weight to test it, then opted for the twenty-pounder. "I don't think he is. But I can't just do nothing, you know?"

"What should we do?" Laura asked. "Get him a gift basket or something?"

Shaylene snickered from beside her. With weights in her hands, she bent into a lunge and kept her eyes on the floor-to-ceiling mirror ahead. "Oh, Lord. Can you imagine that? What would Kellan do with a *gift basket?*"

"Good point," Laura said. "That idea is out."

Shaylene straightened, then switched legs. "If you really want him to know how much he matters to you, you have to make it personal."

"What?" I forced a laugh as I began curling the dumbbells. "Kellan does not *matter* to me."

Shaylene turned from the mirror and raised a skeptical eyebrow. "Let me rephrase. If you want him to know how much *what he did* matters to you... Do something that matters to him."

"Like what?" I asked.

Shaylene shrugged. "What does he like to do?"

I thought about it for a moment. "I don't know."

Laura sat on the bench press and took a swig of water. "Seriously, what do you two do when you're hanging out? Travis and I know practically everything about each other."

"Shaylene and Caleb don't talk either!" I defended. "They're too busy sucking face."

Shaylene threw her head back in laughter, then quickly said, "It's funny because it's true."

"At least Shaylene and Caleb interact like real people," Laura joked. "You can learn a lot about someone by the way they are in bed."

"Oh, God," I groaned, dropping my weights at my side. "Kellan and I are *not* getting into bed together. Besides, you're one to speak. You and Travis haven't even kissed yet."

"He hasn't made the move," she shot back playfully.

"Back to the topic at hand." Shaylene set her weights on the ground and came to stand by us. She stuck her hip out and said, "Doesn't Kellan have any hobbies or something?"

I shrugged. "I guess. He likes sports and fishing and stuff."

Laura wrinkled her nose. "I don't know if you can thank a guy with a fishing trip."

"I'll buy him a tackle box or something," I joked, but the sad part was it was the best idea we'd had yet.

Shaylene quickly shot the idea down. "Don't buy him a tackle box. In fact, don't buy him anything. If you really want to say thank you, give him an experience you want him to remember."

Laura wiggled her eyebrows suggestively.

"Ugh. Ew," I groaned. "Don't even joke about that."

I turned back to Shaylene. "You make a good point. I'll have to think about it."

It took me the rest of the morning and into the afternoon, but something Kellan had said weeks ago finally jumped out at me. I had an idea.

That afternoon, I knocked on his door, hoping he wasn't out. It swung open, and my jaw dropped. Kellan stood in nothing but a towel wrapped around his waist. His wet hair dripped water onto his muscled chest.

"You gonna stand there and gape at me all day?" he deadpanned.

I quickly shut my mouth and forced my gaze up to his face. "I, um, no…"

He stepped away from the door and gestured for me to come inside. "What's up?"

I hesitated a moment. I mean, the guy was naked and inviting me into his room. And it didn't sound like his roommate was around, either. My pulse quickened as I stepped inside. The door swung shut behind me, but I just stood there in the tight space between the closet and the bathroom, not stepping into the room fully. What was the protocol for being alone in a naked guy's room? I clutched the straps of my backpack tight in my hands.

Kellan reached into his dresser for a pair of jeans, then turned back to look at me. He raised a curious eyebrow. "Well…?"

"I was wondering if you wanted to go for a drive," I blurted.

"Am I the only guy you know with a car, or what?"

"Kind of," I admitted.

He pressed his lips together, like he was thinking hard. "Where are you planning to go?"

"It's a surprise," I told him.

Kellan stepped past me, and I had to push myself up against the closet door to let him through. His towel brushed against me, sending tingles up my body. He stepped into the bathroom and closed the door behind him.

"What kind of surprise?" he called through the door.

I smirked. He wasn't going to let this be easy. "The kind where you don't ask questions."

"Oh, that's how you're going to play it," he teased back. "So, this surprise… is it for me? Or are you just using me for my car?"

"I don't know," I said. "I guess you'll have to find out."

The door swung open, and Kellan stood there in all his gorgeousness. His jeans hung from his hips at just the right angle, and he didn't have a shirt on yet. His blond hair stuck up in every direction, which I thought actually made him hotter.

What the hell? I didn't find Kellan attractive!

"Well, are you intrigued or not?" I asked.

"A little," he admitted. He stepped back into the room and pulled a T-shirt out of his dresser. "But…"

"But what?" I asked. "Are you busy tonight?"

He hesitated. "No, not really."

"Then come with me," I begged. "I'll even pay for gas."

Kellan sighed. "Well, how can I argue with that?"

I bounced on my toes, beaming. "So, you'll come?"

"Will it help us as a team?" he asked, sitting down on the bed to pull on his socks.

"I hope so," I said truthfully.

"Then I guess I'm coming," he replied.

I smiled. "Awesome. I'm driving."

Kellan groaned. "Seriously?"

I shrugged. "It wouldn't exactly be a surprise if I told you where we were going, would it?"

Kellan frowned, but it was all in good fun. "Fair enough. Lead the way."

An hour later, I pulled down a long, secluded road with a line of trees on one side and a grassy field on the other. It was just outside of Eagle Valley, where I'd grown up. Almost no one came down here, except Aedes and Davina. No one else understood the significance of the landmark.

Kellan looked confused as we pulled into a small parking lot in the middle of nowhere. The sun was just setting, casting evening rays over the mounds of rocks in front of us. The rocks were out of place in the flat field, calling attention to the historic event that took place here twenty-five years ago. It was like a scar in the earth, marking the moment the realms nearly collapsed in on one another.

Kellan gaped, unable to take his eyes off the earth. "This is... this is the Malum portal site, isn't it?"

I nodded. "You said you hadn't had a chance to see it yet. I thought you'd like to."

Kellan's hand rested on his door handle, but he didn't open his door right away. "I didn't think you remembered."

"Hey," I joked. "I'm not totally heartless. I remember what my friends say to me."

Kellan finally tore his gaze from the mound of earth to look at me. "Are we friends?"

His question caught me off guard. I shrugged. "I don't know. Are we?"

He pressed his lips together in thought, but didn't answer.

I opened my door. "Let's go check it out."

I swung my backpack over my shoulder as we stepped out of the car and started for the portal site. Grass had overtaken the rocks over the years. Mom and Dad said that when the Malum portal collided with earth, a cavern had opened. When they'd destroyed the portal, the cavern came together to heal. It left behind this huge strip of heaved-up earth that overlooked the beautiful fields beyond.

Kellan and I climbed side-by-side to the top, using our hands to get over large boulders. By the time we reached the top, we were maybe only twenty feet up from the parking lot, but the site felt so significant that it seemed like we were on the top of the world.

Kellan took a seat on one of the boulders and looked out over the colorful landscape. The autumn leaves seemed to be every color of the rainbow. It was gorgeous.

I sat beside him. The boulder was big enough for two people, but small enough that we nearly touched.

"The actual portal opened up right there," I told Kellan, pointing to the end of the mound. "My parents said that you could see straight through it to the Aedes' realm."

Kellan shook his head lightly. "It's not our realm anymore. It hasn't been for a long time."

"I know," I said quickly.

Kellan turned to me. "Earth's our home, you know. We've been here as long as the rest of you. It's just that now…"

He reached for a small rock beside himself and tossed it in his hands. "Now it's *really* our home, you know."

I nodded, but inside, my chest was twisting into knots. I

didn't know what it was like for the Aedes. Before my parents destroyed the portal, the Aedes had been cursed, invisible to everyone but the Davina. Back then, the Davina hunted them. I wondered how much it still affected them—even Kellan, who never had to live through any of that.

His voice cut through the silence. "I know what you're thinking."

"Oh?" I asked, a little intrigued. "What's that?"

"You're wondering why I care, since I wasn't alive when any of it happened," he said.

I frowned. "Yeah, kind of."

He took a long breath, staring down at the rock in his hand. "It's not over, you know."

My brow furrowed. "What do you mean?"

He paused for a few moments, then said, "Your parents did a lot of good for our races in unifying them, but it's still a rocky ride for some of us."

"I get what you mean," I said softly. "We still have to hide ourselves from everyone else."

"I don't know that you *do* get it," Kellan said lightly. He wasn't accusing me of anything. It was more like he was stating fact.

I suddenly felt a sting in my chest. He looked kind of sad—vulnerable. It was strange, to say the least.

"Explain it to me, then," I offered.

He shook his head. "Nah, it's fine."

"I'm sorry that your parents had a tough time when their curse was broken," I said honestly. "Just because mine didn't doesn't mean I don't care. Help me understand. What was it like for your parents to go through that?"

Kellan hesitated, looking back over the landscape. "It wasn't my parents," he admitted. "Just my dad. My mom's human."

"Oh," I said flatly. "That's really uncommon."

I wanted to smack myself. That was all I had to offer? Seriously?

Fuck me. I was totally not offering any comfort. All I was doing was sticking my foot in my mouth. I did the only thing I could think to turn the moment around and changed the subject.

"I brought you something." I swung my backpack off my shoulder and set it on the rocks at my feet. I unzipped the zipper and pulled out a can of beer.

Kellan took it, and I noticed a slight hint of a smile cross his face.

"That's the kind you like, right?" I asked. It was the same kind he'd been drinking at the party.

"It's fine," he said, straightening up. He set the rock in his hand beside himself and popped open the top. He took a sip and smacked his lips. "Thanks. Where'd you get it?"

I smiled as he relaxed. "Bought it off Kumar. But wait; there's more."

His smile grew. "Is there?"

I reached back into the bag and pulled out two takeout containers of Pad Thai. I called upon my fire to warm it a little before I handed him one, along with a plastic fork. "You're okay with Thai food, right?"

"Yeah…" He sounded confused as he took the container from me. "I love it. How'd you know?"

I shrugged. "I saw an empty container in your room."

I reached back into my bag for one more item. "And if you're still hungry, I brought this."

I held up a bag of fresh-sliced deli ham. Kellan nearly choked on his beer.

"Oh my God," he chuckled once he finally swallowed. "Ham? Seriously?"

I smiled proudly, then placed it back in my bag.

Kellan rolled his eyes at me as he opened his take-out container. "I ate the ham, you know. The whole thing."

"Oh, I believe you," I said as I started digging into my own food. "Who can argue with free food?"

Kellan smiled. Silence settled over the portal site after that. All I heard was the gentle breeze brushing past us. It was kind of nice—serene. It wasn't until we finished eating and the last few rays of sunshine were fading that Kellan finally spoke.

"So, why'd you bring me here?" he asked. He'd set his beer and takeout container aside on the rocks and leaned back onto his hands. One arm kind of rested behind me, and I quickly became acutely aware of his proximity.

I blushed and turned away from him so he wouldn't see. "I wanted to thank you. For yesterday."

Kellan shook his head. "You don't have to thank me. I did what anyone would do when they see a girl getting beat up."

I finally turned to him with a raised eyebrow. "What *anyone* would do? Apparently that Colt asshole didn't get the memo—seeing as he was the one doing the beating."

Kellan pushed off the rock and sat up straight. His arm brushed against mine, sending tingles up and down the surface of my skin. "Yeah, well, guys like that are scum. He doesn't count."

I chuckled. "I don't know. I kind of think it's guys like you who are in the minority."

"Guys like me?" he asked.

I blushed even harder. What the heck was wrong with me today?

"You know," I said. "Nice guys?"

"Nice guys?" he repeated. "Is that a question?"

I shrugged. "I don't know. I guess the jury's still out on you. Sometimes you're nice, and sometimes you're a jerk. I haven't made up my mind which one you are yet."

A smile crept across Kellan's face. In the dying light, heavy shadows crossed his face, accenting his sharpest features. For some reason, I couldn't take my eyes off him.

"Maybe I'm both," he offered.

"Yeah, maybe," I agreed. "Or maybe you're one of the jerks and just saved me because you need me to pass the semester."

"That must be it." He bumped his shoulder into mine, and my whole body came alive with butterflies. He didn't seem to notice.

I laughed, mostly because I was starting to get uncomfortable with how my body was betraying me. I mean, I shouldn't be feeling this way. Especially not around Kellan. I had to be sick or something.

Kellan joined in on the laughter, but it was quiet, nothing more than a chuckle shared between the two of us. Then our eyes met, and we both went utterly silent. Our eyes locked, and we froze, like we were both waiting for the other person to say something. Without realizing it, my body inched closer and closer to his, as if magnetized. With each inch, my pulse increased, until my knees were shaking. I tilted my head up—

"Eh-hem." Kellan cleared his throat, breaking the spell between us.

We both jumped back from each other, like nothing had happened. My heart pounded violently against my rib cage, so hard that I wouldn't be surprised if Kellan could hear it. Had he felt the pull I'd felt? Did he even realize what was going on, that I would've kissed him if he let me?

The air suddenly felt heavier. Everything had quickly turned very awkward.

"It's, uh, getting dark," Kellan said. "We should probably get back to school. Early class in the morning."

"Yeah," I quickly agreed. I stood and reached for his trash. "I'll take that."

Kellan rose to his feet. He was so close to me that all I'd have to do is lean forward and we'd be pressed chest-to-chest. He looked down at me, but I couldn't read his expression.

"Thanks for bringing me here," he finally said.

I shrugged like it wasn't a big deal as we gathered our things. "Well, thanks for saving me yesterday. It was the least I could do."

But as we started on the drive back home, I couldn't help but think that maybe the night would've ended differently if I'd done more for him.

14

Several weeks passed, and Kellan hadn't mentioned the night in Eagle Valley to me again. I didn't know if it was because he didn't care or because he'd said all he could on the topic. I hadn't seen him since our Introduction to Firefighting class on Friday, since he wasn't in my Elemental Magic class that afternoon.

Laura and I were walking back to our dorms after lunch one Saturday when I caught sight of him in the distance. My pace slowed as my eyes followed him past the Winged Fountain. He was walking in a large group toward the Activities Center, with Celina at his side. My stomach felt hollow as he threw his head back in laughter at something Celina had said.

A sudden thought invaded my mind. He should be laughing at *me* like that.

Before I knew what was happening, my feet were carrying me in his direction.

Laura quickened her pace to follow me. "Where are you going?"

I pulled my jacket collar tighter around my neck to ward off the early November chill. There were flurries on the ground, though the snow wasn't sticking yet. "Um… I thought maybe we could go rock climbing?"

I couldn't tell her the truth—that some invisible force was pulling me toward Kellan. Half of me wanted to be with him at all times, and the other half of me was repulsed that the thought ever crossed my mind.

"Sounds like fun," Laura said. "Beats studying."

I kept my eyes on Kellan, and I was kicking myself the whole time. What was up with me? I was being a crazy, weird stalker. But turning back now would only make me look weirder.

When we got to the Activities Center, the entrance hallway was more crowded than usual. We noticed Travis and Caleb filling their water bottles at the drinking fountain. I finally tore my gaze off of Kellan as we made our way over to them. Kellan's group started in the opposite direction.

"What's going on?" Laura asked Travis.

He took a swig of water, then screwed the cap on his water bottle. "It's Grand Opening, babe."

Laura blushed a little when he called her *babe*. Those two needed to admit their feelings for each other already and make it official.

"Right," I said in realization. "The renovations on Gym B. We totally forgot."

Caleb turned away from the drinking fountain. "Exactly. Everyone wants a shot at it."

Laura bounced on her toes. "The obstacle course is finally open?"

Travis nodded and draped an arm around Laura's shoulder. "And it looks like we're partners."

Caleb groaned. "Come on, man. I thought we were going to dominate this thing together."

Laura giggled. "We can trade off."

Caleb scrunched his nose playfully, then his eyes caught

someone else's in the distance. "I guess I'll partner up with Shaylene."

I faked a jaw-drop as he hurried off the meet up with her. "What about me?"

I heard someone sigh behind me, then a deep male voice said, "I need a partner."

I whirled around to see Kellan standing there. "How did you—?"

He was just ahead of me! Sneaky little bastard.

I eyed him skeptically. "I thought you'd team up with Celina."

"She's with Rhys," he said with a shrug. "Besides, the point of the course is to build up teamwork skills, and well… we're a team."

For some reason, my heart lifted in my chest when he said that. "O-okay. Teammates it is."

Kellan shot me a quick smile that sent my stomach somersaulting in my abdomen.

The four of us headed down the hall toward Gym B. We came to a pair of double doors and entered a huge room bigger than a basketball court. Almost the entire thing was taken up by a horseshoe-shaped obstacle course, apart from the bleachers that were full of people. I kept my eyes on the course as we joined the line behind the sign-up table.

There were eight obstacles in total, all with tons of foam padding all around them. It seemed like half the school was here, with professors and teams roaming the gym. Over the loudspeaker, an announcer called teams up to the main platform. It looked like we'd already missed the opening ceremonies. Normally, the course wouldn't be so crowded, but the grand opening was kind of a big deal. They'd been building this course for months.

One team I didn't know was already working their way through the obstacles. They made it across a balance beam set over a large foam pit easily, thought it looked as if the beam was made to wobble beneath their feet.

The crowd cheered as we watched the team move on to the second obstacle. It was a set of monkey bars and looked easy to pass. The first team member jumped off a small trampoline at the platform below the bars. She got her hands around the first bar, but it spun on an axel, and she lost her grip. She tumbled downward with a scream and landed in the foam pit below her. A horn sounded, signaling the team's failure.

Ahead of us, Travis and Laura were discussing strategies. Kellan didn't say a word to me, so I scanned the gym, just for something to do. I spotted Celina and Rhys ahead of us, then glanced behind myself to see Caleb and Shaylene a few people back.

"Any ideas?" Kellan asked as the next team stepped to the first platform.

"Huh?" I asked, looking back to him. It felt strange to be standing here beside Kellan. Sure, we worked together in class all the time, but it was different being with him outside of class —since we weren't obligated. I wasn't sure why he'd even asked me to be on his team.

"Ideas," he repeated, gesturing toward the course. "Strategies?"

"Oh." I shrugged. "I was just going to wing it."

Kellan smirked, like he was amused. Was there ever a time this guy wasn't smirking? For whatever reason, I found it deadly attractive.

I quickly shot the thought down. What was wrong with me? Kellan wasn't attractive. He was still an asshole. Not as big of one as he was at the beginning of the semester, but an asshole nonetheless.

"Wing it?" he asked.

He eyed me skeptically, and I suddenly felt like I was being put under a microscope. I blushed and turned away to watch the team on the course. They wiped out on the third obstacle, one where there were three robes suspended in a row and you had to jump from one to the other to make it across.

"Hey…" Kellan nudged me with his elbow.

Heat pooled low in my belly. What was with my body today? It was like my element was going haywire or something. Plus, every time I looked at Kellan, all I saw was his face through the car window, offering safe haven from those crazy protestors.

"What's up?" he asked. "You're acting weird."

I shrugged and crossed my arms. "I don't know. I just… didn't expect you to ask me to be on your team."

Kellan stole a glance to Celina and Rhys ahead of us, who were laughing with one another. "Rules are rules. The obstacle course is for teams. I couldn't sign up alone."

"I thought you and Celina had a thing going on," I blurted. I wanted to quickly shove the words back in my mouth.

Kellan shifted his weight between his feet. "It's complicated."

Good. The thought came out of nowhere.

I breathed a sigh of relief when we reached the sign-up table and added our names to the sheet. We followed behind Travis and Laura to sit beside them on the bleachers, leaving some room beside us for Caleb and Shaylene.

I kept my eyes forward, studying the teams as they made their way through the course. For some reason, I couldn't look at Kellan. I felt like I had to keep my emotions under control around him, like if I looked him in the eyes, he'd read my mind or something. I watched the course as a Davina used his air magic to blow the ropes his way toward the platform he stood on so he could reach the first one.

Caleb and Shaylene joined us shortly after. None of us spoke until Celina and Rhys started the course.

"Bets?" Travis asked our group. "How far do you think they're going to make it?"

"I hope they fall off the balance beam," I mumbled. I thought it was quiet enough that no one heard me, but Kellan started laughing.

"What?" I asked innocently. Meanwhile, Shaylene was betting they'd wipe out on obstacle number three, and Laura bet they'd make it to the end.

"Do you have something against Celina or something?" Kellan asked, like it was a shocker.

"No, of course not," I lied.

"Then maybe you should hang out with us sometime," Kellan offered. "You two would like each other."

I nearly choked on my own saliva. Was he serious? This girl had threatened me at the beginning of the semester. I didn't want to be *friends* with her.

But for whatever stupid reason, I found myself saying, "Yeah, sure. Sounds fun."

The team began the course. I held my breath as Celina ran across the balance beam. She was so quick that it seemed like her feet barely touched the beam. Rhys stood on the other side with one foot on the first platform and the other firmly on the beam, holding it steady for Celina. She made it safely to the other side, but I was still hoping to see her wipe out later. Rhys followed quickly behind her.

The two worked in sync to make it past the next five obstacles with incredible speed. They barely looked tuckered out. What the hell? The whole crowd was on their feet cheering for them as they neared the end, as they were the first team to get this far all day.

The seventh obstacle was a set of transparent walls with a foam pit between them. To get through, you had to tension your arms and legs between the walls to make it across. But when Rhys came up to the obstacle, it was clear that the walls were set too far apart for even him—and he was a huge guy. The two paused as their timer kept ticking away. We could see them talking from here, though we couldn't hear what they were saying. Finally, they parted and stepped up the wall.

The crowd went silent as we watched curiously. Celina and Rhys turned back-to-back and hooked their arms together. Each put one foot on either wall, then they pressed their backs together and put their next foot up.

"Holy crap," I said under my breath. "That's genius."

"It must be designed like that, so you can only get across as a team," Kellan replied.

Celina and Rhys inched across the length of the obstacle, using the tension of their teammate to keep themselves suspended above the pit. The further they made it, the more the crowd cheered.

Finally, they reached the other side, and the crowd erupted. People were on their feet, clapping and hollering as Celina and Rhys raced toward the last obstacle. The final obstacle was a rope net they had to climb to get to the buttons they pressed at the finish line. They seemed to scale the net at an inhuman pace.

They reached the top, and the crowd couldn't contain themselves. Together, Celina and Rhys pressed the buttons, and a loud buzzer sounded throughout the gym. Their timer stopped, and the announcer came over the speaker to recap their amazing run.

I clapped, because even though I didn't like Celina, what they'd done was an incredible feat. I leaned over to Kellan and said, "If they can complete the course, we can, too."

He was also clapping, looking out toward the course at Celina while she waved to the crowd. "If we finish, that's good enough for me."

It wasn't long until Travis and Laura were up. Since Kellan and I were on deck, we stepped up to the starting platform behind them. We cheered as they began the course.

Travis and Laura held on to each other as they passed the balance beam, using each other as an anchor until they made it to the other side. Travis let Laura go first on the monkey bars. It looked like she was about to slip off, but she grabbed the next bar quickly and caught herself. It seemed like some of the bars rotated while others were stationary, and you had to figure out which ones to grab.

The two made it through the ropes next, then came up on the fourth task. Only a couple of teams had made it this far today. A timer high up on the ceiling counted the seconds they'd been on the course. So far, they had the best time, even better than Celina and Rhys.

The fourth task was a series of swinging steps. They were like the swings we'd played on as kids, only with hard bases for your feet. Laura nearly fell into the foam pit as the swing behind her slipped beneath her feet, but she caught herself on the ropes that held the swings up. Travis was behind her in an instant, helping her back up onto the swing.

I breathed a sigh of relief. "Only four more to go. I think they could make it!"

The fifth obstacle was a tall wall set at a steep incline that you had to run up to get onto the platform at the top. It was practically a ninety-degree angle and over a dozen feet tall, with a curve at the bottom that reminded me of the ramps at a skate park. The rules said you couldn't use your wings and that you only got three tries. Laura gave it a shot twice, but she couldn't get herself high enough to reach the platform. Travis said something to her, though we couldn't hear it. She backed away, and he took a running start at it. His fingers reached the platform, but they slipped before he could pull himself up. His second attempt yielded the same result, as did his third.

The buzzer rang, signaling that the team had failed. They didn't look disappointed, though. If anything, they looked like they'd had a lot of fun. The two stepped off the course smiling and laughing with one another. Then, in front of everyone, Travis leaned down and planted a kiss right on Laura's lips. She seemed shocked at first, until she brought her hands up behind his neck and kissed him back.

My jaw dropped, but I was beaming. I was happy for them.

"We're up next," Kellan said, pulling my attention away from the couple. "Mind if I power up?"

I shook my head, and Kellan placed his hand on my shoulder, drawing my essence into himself. Color filled his cheeks, and he looked energized.

He gestured to the balance beam in front of me. "Ladies first."

I took a deep breath and fixed my eye on the course. I knew this was all just fun and games—a training exercise—but I didn't want to be the girl who wiped out on the first obstacle. I glanced back to Kellan for a moment, but my gaze traveled beyond him. I caught Celina's eyes in the crowd. She stared me down, wearing a challenging smirk on her face. It was in that moment that a stone-cold resolve came over me. I was going to beat Celina's time and shove it in her face.

I slammed my hand down on the button at the beginning of the course, which started our time on the clock. I began across the beam quickly, but it wobbled so much that I had to slow down. I held my wings out at the sides to help me balance as I inched across to the other side.

You're going too slow, one voice in my head chastised.

Slow and steady wins the race, I shot back at myself. It was better to get across slowly than not at all.

I reached the other side, and Kellan started across the beam himself. At some point when I'd been walking across, Kellan had ditched his shirt. His black wings were at his sides, steadying himself. I hesitated a moment. He was moving much faster than I was, so I turned to the next obstacle to get ahead of him so I wouldn't slow him down.

I pulled my wings into me, then bounced off the trampoline to the monkey bars. Instead of going for the rotating spokes, I held on to the thick support bars on the sides. My body swung side to side as I moved my hands forward, until I was over the next foam platform. I gave my body one final forward swing, then jumped down onto the safety of the platform. I turned to see Kellan was using my same strategy and was close behind.

The next obstacle was the ropes. The first was close enough to reach, so I grabbed as high as I could and kicked off. I reached for the second rope and caught it, but I didn't let go of the first soon enough. I swung backward with both ropes in my hands, until I was at a standstill between the two of them. I didn't give myself too much time to hesitate. I dropped my feet from the first rope and twisted them around the second. I went swinging toward rope number three and caught it without a problem. At the peak of my swing, I let go and went flying toward the next platform. I landed with a hard thud and rolled across the foam to catch my fall.

By now, my arms were aching, and I was breathing heavily. But I was no stranger to heavy physical activity, since I had to train for firefighting. I knew I could do this.

I shook my shoulders out and eyed the sharp incline in front of me. I took a running start and jumped up the wall. My fingers just barely touched the platform, but they slipped. I went tumbling down the wall and rolled to keep from twisting an ankle. I heard the crowd react, but I tried to block it out. It'd only distract me.

Kellan had caught up to me. While he took a momentary break, I turned back to the wall and prepared to tackle it again.

"Wait," Kellan said quickly, stopping me. "We each only get three tries. Let me give it a go."

Was that a challenge?

"As you wish." I stepped aside.

He ran up the wall, giving one last thrust upward at the peak of the incline. His fingers curled around the platform, and his muscles rippled as he pulled himself upward. The crowd cheered, and I went breathless as he stared down at me with a proud smile on his face. He bent to one knee and held an inviting hand out.

I grumbled. If he helped me, it'd make me look weak. I wanted to do this on my own.

I backed up and ran up the wall again. Instead of reaching for his outstretched hand, I went for the bottom of the platform as he had, but my fingers slipped again, and I tumbled back toward the ground.

"Come on, Cora," Kellan's smooth voice said from above me. He kept his hand out toward me as I righted myself again. "Let me help you."

"It makes me look weak," I said up to him.

He frowned. "This is a team course, Cora. The only weakness you can show is not letting me help you."

I stood at the base of the wall for several seconds, trying to catch my breath. Above us, the clock continued to tick, counting our time. We were quickly reaching Celina's time.

"Do you want to get up this wall or not?" Kellan asked. I could see the challenge in his eyes.

Shit. He was right. I only had one shot left, and I didn't have the strength or the height to do it on my own.

Sighing, I backed up and ran toward Kellan. My left hand curled around the platform, while my right caught his hand. Electricity shot between us when we touched, but he didn't seem to notice. He pulled me upward, until I hooked my foot on the platform and pulled myself the rest of the way. I stood beside him, catching my breath.

"See?" he said. "A little teamwork goes a long way."

I rolled my eyes and punched him playfully in the shoulder. "Yeah, yeah. You were right. Next obstacle?"

To get to the next platform, we had to use our wings to glide down. Kellan and I flexed our shoulders at the same time, and our wings shot out on either side of us. Mine smacked into his, and he went stumbling forward. Before I knew what was happening, Kellan's foot slipped off the edge of the platform. My heart sprang into my throat as he went tumbling down to the mats below us. He landed with a loud *thud*, and a *crack* sounded across the gymnasium.

The crowd gasped and rose to their feet as Kellan rolled on the ground, spewing a sling of curse words.

"Oh my God!" I cried.

I flung myself off the platform and spread my wings out wide, soaring down to him. A knot formed in my chest as I knelt to his side.

"Kellan…" I reached out to touch him, but he curled in on himself, shying away. His wing was twisted in the wrong direction, sending my stomach plummeting to my toes. My own wings ached at the sight. "Oh, God. I'm so sorry. Can I heal you?"

Kellan cradled his wing into himself but didn't say anything. I felt completely hopeless. Travis and Laura rushed over to us and knelt beside Kellan.

"Dude, are you okay?" Travis asked, inspecting the broken wing.

"Do I look fucking okay?" Kellan growled through gritted teeth.

"It's fine," Laura said softly, trying to be the comforting friend she was. "We'll heal you—"

She was cut off as Professor Kovski and Professor Sanders arrived. "Move aside," Professor Kovski commanded.

Travis and Laura stepped back just as Caleb and Shaylene arrived. Celina abandoned Rhys and shoved her way over to us. She practically knocked me over as she dropped to her knees beside Kellan. She took his hand in hers, and he squeezed it back.

"I'm here, babe," she said in a voice that made me want to hurl. It sounded so fake.

"Everyone back!" Professor Kovski barked.

It was like I was watching myself from above as I rose to my feet and took a step back. I was still in an utter state of shock. Broken limbs and bloody wounds I could handle. I was going into the medical field, after all. But watching Kellan squirm in pain was entirely different. It made my stomach twist into knots and sent a lump forming in my throat. My eyes welled up for him.

"Kellan, I'm sorry," I said, but he didn't seem to hear me as Professor Kovski inspected his twisted wing.

"It's definitely broken," she announced. "You'll need to keep your wings out while we heal it, Mister Greene. If you shift, you could do more damage the next time you bring them out."

Kellan squeezed his eyes shut and gritted his teeth. He still hung on to Celina's hand, like he needed her to get through this. I suddenly had the thought that *I* should be the one holding his hand.

"I'll do whatever you say," Kellan said. "Just heal me."

Professor Kovski frowned. "I'm afraid it's not that simple, Mister Greene. We have to set the bone before we can transfer our essence, or it will heal wrong."

He knew that. It'd been discussed in class plenty of times. But he didn't look like he was thinking straight. His face had paled, and sweat had broken out on his forehead. He'd gone into shock.

Two professors I didn't know ran over with a stretcher and a first-aid kit. Everything happened so fast. They hoisted Kellan onto the stretcher, with his wings hanging limply at his sides.

"Miss," one of them said to Celina, who was still holding Kellan's hand. "I'm going to have to ask you to step back."

"No," Kellan said weakly. "She's good."

My chest twisted into a tight knot.

They let Celina walk with him as they rushed him out of the room and toward the health services center on campus. I found my feet moving under myself before I made the conscious decision to follow. I rushed up alongside Kellan.

"Kellan," I said breathlessly. "I'm so sorry. It was an accident."

"Miss, please," one of the professors begged. They paused at the gym doors as several onlookers rushed to hold them open for the stretcher.

Kellan took the moment to open his eyes and look up at me. For a moment, the deep blue of his eyes melted my heart, and then he opened his mouth—and shot a dagger straight through me. "Every time I think you've made progress, you turn around and show me just how wrong I am."

That was all he said before he was rushed out of the room. I remained firmly planted in place, staring after him as his words sunk in. The knot in my chest tightened, until it felt as if I was suffocating.

Laura came up beside me and touched my wing to get my attention. "He'll be okay, Cora."

I swallowed hard and turned to her, blinking away the tears. "I know, but…"

She caught the horrified look on my face. "But what? What'd he say to you?"

I shook my head, trying to get the words out of my mind. "Nothing," I lied. "I just… I think I broke more than his wing… I think I broke our trust."

15

I wanted to see how Kellan was doing, so I texted him and asked him to tell me when he was healed. Hours passed, and his reply never came. I was starting to get worried, so I visited his dorm room to make sure he was okay. His roommate, Warner, answered and told me Kellan wasn't around. Worry tightened in my stomach. I texted Kellan again.

Did everything heal okay?

No response.

I knew it was only a broken wing, but my anxiety kept telling me there were complications that killed him or something. Yeah, it was over the top, but what else was I supposed to think?

I went to the health services center, and the receptionist there told me he'd been released over an hour ago. That jerk! I was seriously worried about him. Without any other options, I returned to our dorm hall and sat outside his room, waiting for him to return.

While I waited, I played with my element. Fire danced around in my palm, warming up my skin. I played with controlling the angles of the flames, trying to get an image to form like

133

I'd seen Celina do on move-in day. I'd been working on it all semester. The best I could do was sustain the figure of a kitten in my palm, but as soon as I tried to add motion, my flames became unstable.

It was an hour before Kellan showed up. He noticed me as soon as he entered the hallway. His step slowed, but he approached me anyway.

"What do you want, Cora?" He barely looked at me as he made a beeline for his door.

I quickly stood. "I wanted to apologize. I feel awful."

Kellan paused with his hand on the door handle. "Good. You should."

My jaw dropped at his tone. "What the hell?" I snapped.

Kellan opened the door, barely acknowledging me. He left it open behind him, but didn't invite me in.

I crossed my arms in the doorway. "Are you really going to act like this?"

He turned to me. "Act like what?"

"Like… like…" I couldn't find the words. "Like *you*."

Kellan scoffed, but it was more like my choice of words amused him than upset him. "Sorry, sweetheart. It's who I am. Take it or leave it."

Holy crap! He actually called me *sweetheart*. What the heck was up with that?

Warner looked uncomfortable and started toward the door. "I'm just gonna…"

He didn't finish his sentence as he stepped past me, gesturing for me to step inside.

I took the invitation and let the door swing shut behind me, leaving Kellan and me in privacy.

"I just mean…" I started. "I came to apologize, and you're kind of being a jerk about it."

He plopped down on the bed, not even looking at me. It was like he *wanted* to prove my accusation.

I moved to the foot of his bed, where he couldn't ignore me. "It was an accident, Kellan. Why are you so mad at me?"

He crossed his arms and looked to the mural on his wall.

"Besides that, why didn't you answer my texts?" I demanded. "I was worried. You let me think something bad had happened to you. And when I went to the health services center, you weren't there."

His gaze darted to mine. "Oh, so you're stalking me now?"

"No!" I pressed my fingers to my eyes. "God, what is going on, Kellan?"

He sat up in bed and looked straight at me. "I get that it was an accident, Cora, but it was more than that. We were supposed to be working as a team. You hurt me because you'd rather do things on your own than work with me to get ahead."

My stomach sank. There was something in his tone that suggested I'd hurt him in more ways than one. My knees suddenly felt weak, so I sank into the chair beside his desk. "I'm sorry, Kellan," I whispered. "I didn't think—"

"Exactly," he cut in. "You didn't think."

"Seriously?" I snapped. "You're going to call me stupid now? I won't put up with that shit from my partner."

"So request another one," he insisted. "I've been putting up with your shit all semester."

"What shit?" I demanded. It was like he was grasping at anything he could to get angrier at me.

"You're not a team player," Kellan accused. "And you keep proving to me that that'll never change."

A lump formed in my throat. "How am I supposed to be a team player with someone who doesn't want to be on my team in the first place?"

"I *do*!" Kellan practically shouted. "I'm the one who asked you to team up with me on that obstacle course. Yet you still think I'm the same guy you started the semester with. A lot has changed since then."

It was hard to see it when he was acting like the first week I'd met him.

"So, what?" I asked softly. "Do you want to quit being my partner? We've worked so hard."

Kellan clenched his jaw, considering the question. Instead of answering, he said, "Can I ask you something?"

I hesitated, not sure where he was going with this. "Sure."

Kellan's tone softened. "What do you think of me?"

The question caught me off guard. What *did* I think of Kellan? It sounded like a trick question. I went with the easy answer.

"I think you're kind of a jerk." It wasn't anything he didn't already know.

Kellan looked like he wanted to smile but was holding back. "Guilty. But no, I mean…"

He paused. "What do you want? From me, as your partner?"

"I don't know," I admitted. "I just want to finish what we started and get through the semester."

Kellan's shoulders fell, like it wasn't the answer he was looking for. He lay back down in bed and turned on his side toward his wall. "Apology accepted. You can go now."

Except it didn't sound like he accepted it at all. He seemed very hurt.

"Kellan," I said softly, feeling the weight of his rejection in my guts. "I really, *really* am sorry. What can I do to make this up to you?"

He shook his head, like there was nothing I could do. It wasn't even about the broken wing—that could be healed. It was about something bigger, something I didn't really understand and couldn't wrap my head around.

"Please talk to me," I begged. "I want to understand."

"I think we're both on the same page," he grumbled. "By the end of the semester, we'll change partners, like we agreed."

My jaw dropped. It felt as if he'd shoved a dagger into my stomach and twisted it around.

He didn't seem to notice. "I'll see you Monday in class."

It was clear there was no wiggle room with him. He wasn't going to give me any more than he already had. Though I didn't want to leave him, I stood and made my way toward the door. It seemed like that was what he wanted right now.

And that was all I could give him.

16

Over the next few weeks, Kellan and I didn't talk much. We just kind of went back to being lab partners—nothing more. When I tried to talk to him and get him to open up, he barely humored me with a response.

At least I didn't have to work with him in my Elemental Magic class. It was the one class we didn't have together.

"Today, we'll be shaping our elements," Professor Swan announced one day in class. She was an older woman, who had been studying elemental magic since the Davina discovered it. "The more you learn to control your element in the classroom, the more control you will have over it in the field. Celina, would you help me a moment?"

Celina stood proudly and walked to the front of the room. Our class was small, only about thirty people, and entirely Davina—all except Laura, who was half Aedes, half Davina.

"Celina, can you demonstrate creating and sustaining a fire tornado?" Professor Swan asked.

"Can I get a power-up?" Celina asked.

Professor Swan stepped aside. Her teaching partner,

Professor Roberts, who was a younger Aedes woman, pulled Celina's essence into herself to open up her magical channel.

Celina took a refreshing breath. She didn't say anything before she started swirling her hands in front of her. Fire seemed to grow out of her palms like vines, each stream wrapping around one another until they formed a large funnel that hovered only an inch above the tile.

"Excellent!" Professor Swan praised.

I sat back in my chair, observing closely. I could create and sustain fire tornados, too. What was the big deal?

"Now, create a scene for us," Professor Swan instructed.

Celina smirked proudly as her fire tornado split into two, then settled down until the tornados transformed into two human figures. They looked like flaming marionettes as she twisted her hands to control them. One figure was clearly a woman, and the other a man. The woman twirled and danced around the man while he watched in admiration. As the woman slowed, the man got to one knee and held up a flower. A fricken flower! How'd she get that kind of detail? It was insane.

The fire girl shied away, then continued dancing, while the man continued to hold the flower up to her. When she didn't respond, he put the flower in his pocket and got to his feet. The woman stopped dancing and came running toward him, pressing a kiss to his lips as he pulled her into an embrace.

The story looked like it was going to continue, but Professor Swan cut Celina off. "Very well done!"

"Thank you." Celina smiled proudly.

The class applauded as Celina returned to her seat. I joined in, but I was still dumbstruck as to how she'd worked in so much detail to her flames.

"That was amazing," Laura leaned over to me and whispered.

"Yeah," I said flatly. "I don't know how she did it."

Laura shrugged. "I guess she's just really good."

"Each of you will be shaping your element like this today,"

Professor Swan said. "We'll be going around to your tables to observe. You're free to take any props you'd like from the table up front."

She gestured behind her, where rocks sat for earth Davina, along with vials of colored smoke for air and water bottles for water.

"If you need a power-up, please raise your hand," Professor Roberts offered.

Almost half the class raised their hands, and she started her way around to open their essence channels.

Laura turned to me. "Do you need a power-up? I can help."

"Yeah, that'd be great."

When Laura channeled my essence, it wasn't nearly as strong as when Kellan did it. It wasn't enough to heal, but it'd let me conjure fire for a day or two.

"Thanks," I told her as I held my hands up and summoned flames.

"I'll be right back," she said. She bounced up to the front table and came back with a bowl full of pebbles.

"That's pretty cool," Laura said, eyeing the bird I'd made in my palm. It hovered there like a mere silhouette. I couldn't get the details in the feathers.

"Thanks," I said. "What can you do?"

Laura held her hands over the bowl. "I could use a power-up, but we'll see what kind of juice I have left over from our last class."

Laura twisted her fingers, and pebbles rose out of the bowl, creating a corkscrew spiral. When she tried to expand them into another shape, they shuddered in the air, then rained down onto the table.

"Crap," she mumbled, diving for the few that had bounced off the table.

"No, it was good," I assured her.

She gathered her pebbles back into the bowl. "Can you make the eagle fly?"

"Oh, um…" I looked back to the flaming eagle I'd made. "I don't know. I'm still trying to work out the details in it."

Laura looked thoughtful. "Maybe try animating it first, then adding the details later. It might be easier."

I wasn't sure, but I decided to give it a shot. "Okay."

I commanded my essence to move to the rhythm of flapping wings. But instead of making just the wings move, the entire figure bobbed up and down above my palm.

"Good start, Cora," Professor Swan said.

I hadn't noticed her approach. I got a little startled, and my fire fizzled out. "Um, thanks."

"Your control is very good," Professor Swan told me. "I really enjoyed the figure you created. But when you animate your essence, you must focus on each moving part as a separate piece to a larger puzzle—just as if you were controlling a large fire, you would begin by extinguishing it in sections rather than trying to do it all at once."

"That makes sense," I said. "Thanks for the tip."

Professor Swan nodded, then moved on to the next table. I glanced around to see that several of the other fire Davina were having trouble shaping their essence into anything but a sphere. One water Davina had created a mass of water that defied gravity. It hovered above his table and fell like raindrops onto the surface. Beside him, an air Davina creating a purple smoke swirl, then directed his air through the raindrops, dodging them as they fell.

Professor Roberts came to our table a moment later. "Do either of you need a power up?"

"Yes," Laura said. "I do."

Once her essence channel was open, Laura was able to control the pebbles with such finesse that she created a sculpture of a cat and made it walk across the desk. It sat in front of me and started licking its butt.

I broke out into laughter and couldn't focus on my element. "Oh my God, Laura. Seriously?"

She couldn't contain her laughter. "You think *that's* funny?"

Laura twisted her fingers, and the rocks moved to her command. They rearranged themselves into a very crude sculpture that made even cruder movements.

"Laura!" I cried.

She died of laughter, and her rocks went scattering across the table. "Your reaction makes it worth it."

I caught Celina glancing our way. She looked at us like we were a bunch of freaks.

Laura finally composed herself. "Okay, I'll behave myself. Let's see you try again."

I took a deep breath. "I'll *try*."

Celina had finally looked away, thank God.

I formed the eagle in my palm again. This time, I focused on keeping the body in place and only giving motion to the wings. To my surprise, Professor Swan's advice worked immediately. The eagle animated and began flying around the table.

Laura clapped and cried, "Awesome job, Cora!"

Celina shot another glance our way. I held my head up proudly as my tiny fire eagle soared above my head. She looked less than pleased.

I ignored her and turned back to Laura. "Look at us. We work well together. I don't know why *you* can't be my Art of Healing partner."

Laura sighed. "Because our essence isn't compatible for it. Plus, I like being Travis's partner."

I wiggled my eyebrows suggestively. "In more ways than one."

She giggled, but didn't deny it. "I don't get how you and

Kellan can be so compatible with healing magic but like, not in actual life."

I shrugged. I didn't get it either. "Maybe we're too similar and that's why we butt heads. I seriously just want to get through this semester and change partners."

Laura frowned. "Are you sure? I mean, will being with someone else make things easier, or do you think you and Kellan can work things out?"

"I don't know," I admitted. "Even if I stick with him through school, it doesn't mean we'll be together in the field forever. It might be good to give it a shot with someone else."

"Don't make any fast decisions," she warned.

I chuckled. "Fast decisions? This thing with Kellan has been going on for months."

"Exactly," Laura said. "And you've worked so hard. And I can tell—"

She cut off.

"You can tell…?" I pressed.

She sighed. "I can tell you guys enjoy working together when you try."

I raised my eyebrows. "I doubt it. Besides, he already made his decision. He's going to request a reassignment before next semester."

She frowned. "Maybe you can change his mind."

If only.

"Take the Thanksgiving break this weekend to think it over," she suggested.

I wasn't feeling confident about that, but I answered anyway. "Yeah, okay. I will."

I only said it to end the conversation. For some reason, I was starting to get uncomfortable with it. But as I considered what she said, I realized I really didn't know what I wanted. Did I want to fight to stay Kellan's partner or opt for a new one?

I guess I had a long holiday break to decide.

17

Dad picked me up from school Wednesday night, and we drove home in silence. He tried to get me to talk, but I didn't know what to say. That I'm having guy troubles? I could see that going down so well. Dad would drive straight to the academy with his police cruiser and gun on his hip to give Kellan a piece of his mind. So I just gave him the standard answers and told him things were going great.

When we arrived home, Mom had just returned from the restaurant. She was still climbing out of her car, and her face lit up when she saw our headlights pull into the driveway. We lived on a two-acre wooded lot just outside of Eagle Valley. Our house was two stories, with brown siding and stone accents.

"Cora!" Mom squealed, rushing over to the passenger side as Dad parked the car.

I flung open my door and rushed into her arms. She squeezed me tightly, and I inhaled the fresh scent of her lavender shampoo. "Mom! I missed you."

She gave me one last squeeze, then drew away. "We missed you, too."

"Well, if you bought me a car, I could come home more often," I teased.

"In your dreams," she joked back. "Here. Let me help you with your bags."

"I don't need any help," I told her as I reached into the back to grab my backpack. It was all I had, since I was only staying for the four-day break.

"Oh, okay..." Mom looked a little flustered, like she was disappointed I wouldn't be staying longer. "In that case, I brought some leftovers home from the restaurant. Can you help me with them?"

"I've got it," Dad said quickly. He hurried over to her car to grab a stack of pies out of the back. There must've been at least five of them.

"Holy crap!" I said. "Are we hosting the whole town for Thanksgiving?"

Mom laughed as we started for the door. "Not unless you invited them. It's just going to be us three."

"What about Grandma Gloria?" I asked.

"She and Calvin are spending Thanksgiving on a cruise," Mom explained.

"What?" I squeaked. I paused to hold the front door open for Dad. "She didn't tell me."

"She's too busy having fun," Dad joked.

We stepped inside, and the smell of home hit my nose. I didn't even know our house had a smell until I'd spent time away. The scent of cinnamon candles and fresh linen was an instant comfort. Kellan quickly fell to the back of my mind as I stepped back into my old life. A huge TV sat across from the brown leather couches, with a stone fireplace set into the wall between them.

"Do you want these in the kitchen?" Dad asked Mom, gesturing to the pies he was carrying.

Mom rolled her eyes. "No, I want them in the garage. Yes, I want them in the kitchen."

Dad disappeared down the hallway, and Mom turned to me. "Sit down, Cora. Tell me all about how school's going."

"I'm actually really tired," I admitted. "Can we talk tomorrow?"

She frowned. "Okay. Are you going to help me cook? I'm making your favorite: honey glazed ham."

I laughed, but Mom just looked confused. "It's nothing," I told her. "My partner and I just kind of have an inside joke about ham."

Her brow furrowed even further, like she couldn't understand how that was even a thing. "Well, you can tell me all about it tomorrow. Your room is all ready for you upstairs."

"Thanks, Mom." I hugged her again. She seemed surprised at first, then relaxed into it. "I love you."

"I love you too, sweetheart," she said. "Goodnight."

"Night."

I hurried upstairs, where my room was exactly as I'd left it. The only thing different was that Mom had washed my sheets and made the bed. The walls were a light pink, leftover from when we'd painted when I was six. A blue bedspread accented the room. There was a white tree decal decorating one wall, along with a large wooden "C" above my bed. An entire bookcase was filled with my antiques collection, including everything from old thimbles to a music box I picked up at a yard sale a few years back. Pictures of my family were plastered all over the room, along with several of me and my best friend Kaylee. I wouldn't see her this weekend, since she was still traveling Europe. God, I missed her. We talked online occasionally, but she didn't get a lot of time to talk, so we barely knew what was going on in each other's lives anymore. It made me kind of sad.

I closed the door behind myself and dropped my bag onto my bed. I changed into my pajamas—the fluffy ones with cartoon sheep on them—then sat at my vanity to brush my hair into a high ponytail. As I moved through the quiet space, I couldn't get Kellan off my mind. I thought it'd be easy, until Mom mentioned the ham. Now that he'd invaded my mind, I was hopeless.

Sighing, I stood and walked over to my window. I sat on the cushioned bench beneath it and stared outside at the starry sky. Kaylee and I used to sit here and talk for hours. Sometimes, I'd lie down here and read. When Drew broke up with me, I spent hours crying into the pillows stacked against the window. Whatever it was, this bench was my place of solace, where I could relax and work through my issues.

But now, I felt stuck.

I woke early the next morning. When I glanced outside, frost had coated the ground, and little snow flurries were floating through the air. The sun was just barely coming up. I wasn't ready for the day—to cook Thanksgiving dinner with Mom and play board games with Dad, all while they grilled me on my classes. This semester was supposed to be the best four months of my life. Instead, it'd turned out to be the most frustrating I'd experienced yet. I didn't know if Kellan and I were supposed to stick this out or go our separate ways, and that frustrated me more than anything else.

I showered and dressed, then headed downstairs. I found Dad in the kitchen sneaking a piece of pumpkin pie. He jumped when he heard me and whirled around, shoving the plate behind himself on the counter. His mouth was full, and he had an innocent look on his face, like he was a kid who'd been caught with their hand in the cookie jar.

"Cora." He relaxed. "It's just you."

"Is Mom on your case about saving it for dinner?" I asked.

"What can I say?" he said. "Your Mom's a great cook."

I crossed the room to the fridge and opened it, then pulled out the pie tin on top. "I won't tell if you won't tell."

A smile crept across Dad's face, then he hurried to get me a plate and a fork. We sat at the kitchen table and ate our pumpkin pie together.

"Hey, Dad," I said when I was halfway through. "Do you mind if I borrow the car?"

"For what?" he asked.

"Nothing really," I said honestly. "I just want to drive around town. I miss it."

"You know your Mom wants your help cooking this morning, right?"

I nodded. "I won't be long."

Dad sighed, then reached into his pocket for his keys. "Fine, but be back in an hour."

"Thanks, Dad." I took the keys and headed to the front door to grab my shoes and jacket.

Eagle Valley wasn't very big, so it didn't take a long time to drive around. Still, I was surprised at how much had changed since I'd been gone. There was a new bookstore next to the restaurant on Main Street, and the bank had moved to a new location. The antique store I loved so much had expanded, but they were closed this weekend, so I didn't get a chance to go in. I drove by Kaylee's house, as if hoping to spot her car—like she might've come home from Europe to surprise me or something. But she wasn't there.

Eventually, I found myself at the edge of town, parked across the street from the Galen High Mansion. It was all red brick and endless corridors, with trees surrounding the property. The street was completely deserted, and everything was so silent it almost seemed unreal. The snow had picked up from earlier, dusting the high peaks of the mansion with little flurries. It seemed picturesque. I just sat there in the car, looking up at the mansion. I wanted to go inside and visit Grace's tomb. She was one of the Originals, a child of the higher gods. It seemed like finding direction when nothing else made sense started with turning to your ancestors for answers.

But I knew she wouldn't have them. She was gone—her essence returned to the earth and now a part of the rest of us.

I didn't know what I was doing when I stepped out of the car. I put my hood up and walked across the vast lawn to the front doors of the school. I tried to open them, but they were locked. No surprise there.

Still, I felt a pull to the school I couldn't explain. It was like it held the answers—as it did throughout my entire high school experience. Maybe I was just being nostalgic. Or maybe I was a little insane. Either way, I didn't want to leave.

I started walking around the side of the school, like I might find a window cracked open or something in this chilly weather. But all the windows were locked tight, as were the back doors. My feet continued to carry me into the woods behind the school, down a long, narrow path I'd become accustomed to over the years. After several minutes of walking, the trees opened up to a wide, grassy clearing that sloped downward at a steep angle. It was our training site for flying and elemental essence when I went to school here.

I stepped out of the trees and took in a deep breath as my eyes scanned the deep valley. It was cold out, but not so cold that it was unpleasant. The light snow muffled any other sounds, and a single ray of sunshine shone down into the valley. It was beautiful and so, so peaceful. I felt the urge to fly around like I had so many times here.

Why the hell not?

I stripped off my jacket and set it on the ground, then pulled my t-shirt over my head until I was standing in only my tank top. The cool air brushed across my skin, sending goosebumps all over my arms. But I didn't care. I just wanted to fly.

I flexed my shoulders, and my wings grew out of my back. I spread them out wide, then took a running start and leapt off the ground and into the sky. My stomach somersaulted in my abdomen, and my heart beat in exhilaration. I spread my arms out to the side and closed my eyes, letting my wings carry me slowly to the ground. I felt so free as I soared around the secluded valley.

I got close enough to the bottom of the valley that I could land, but I decided not to. Braving the cold winds, I flapped my wings and shot upward into the sky. I raced to one end of the valley, and then to the other, performing flips and aerial tricks as I went. After several rounds, I began feeling the strain, so I started my descent to the ground again. When I reached the snow-coated grass below, I fell onto my back with my wings stretched out at my sides. I expected the air to be cold down here, but it wasn't. It was actually kind of pleasant.

I looked up to the clouded sky to watch the snowflakes gently fall toward me. I was surprised at how good it felt to just sit here out in the winter weather, as if I didn't have a care in the world. I didn't know how long I lay there, just thinking things over.

Maybe I'd just stay here and not go back to school. It was easier. If I went back to school, I'd have to deal with Kellan again, and he was impossible. He couldn't seem to make up his mind. One second he was joking with me and we were laughing, and the next he was making some backhanded comment or *blaming* me for an accident. What did he even mean that I constantly proved him wrong? That was some next-level emotional manipulation or something. Did he not realize how hard I'd worked these past few years to get into Harris Academy? Did he not see how much I'd been studying this semester to make it through our finals? Did he not notice the effort I put in to make our team better? Did he not realize that I actually *cared*?

No, probably not. Because he didn't care. I didn't know why, but it just didn't seem like any of this mattered to him as much as it did to me. He was probably only there to get with Celina anyway. Freaking perfect, show-off Celina.

Oh my God. What was wrong with me? I was being obsessive. I was—

"Cora."

A male voice sounded from directly above me. My eyes shot open, and I was surprised to see my dad staring down at me. He nudged my leg with his foot. He breathed a sigh of relief when I moved.

"Are you alive?" he joked.

I groaned and pushed myself to a sitting position. I suddenly realized how cold it was and wrapped my wings around myself. "Yeah, I'm alive. What are you doing here?"

Dad held my coat out to me. He must've retrieved it from the top of the valley before he ventured down here. I pulled my wings in and slipped my arms into the warm jacket.

"It's been over an hour," he said. "I called your phone, but you didn't answer. Your mother and I were worried."

"Oh, sorry." I reached into my jacket pocket and pulled out my phone. The screen read three missed calls. "I lost track of time."

Dad must've caught my low tone, because he suddenly looked concerned. "Are you okay?"

I didn't look up at him. I just shrugged and said, "I'm fine. It's just…"

Dad didn't care that the ground was wet and cold. He saw that his little girl needed him, and he plopped down on the ground next to me and wrapped a warm arm around my shoulder. A lump rose to my throat as I leaned against him.

"What's wrong?" Dad asked in concern. "You can tell me anything. You know that, right?"

I nodded, but I didn't answer right away. Finally, I found my voice. "I've just been dreaming about the academy my entire life. I've never wanted anything more than to become a firefighter and a healer. And I wanted to be great, but…"

Dad didn't prod. He was nice like that. He let me come to him at my own pace. Tension wrapped around my head, and a burning sensation stung my eyes.

"It's not what I dreamed it would be," I admitted.

It pained me to say. How could the academy be anything less than I dreamed? I didn't think I wanted to admit it to myself until now. I wanted everything to work out with Kellan and me because if it didn't, it meant that on some level I had failed. It meant that the academy wasn't the dream I'd always pictured it to be. Even now, the words didn't feel right on my tongue.

Dad squeezed me tight to his chest as I blinked the tears away. "I understand, Cora. Sometimes reality isn't as great as our dreams."

"It isn't," I agreed. "Not even close."

"Do you want to tell me about it?" he asked.

I pulled away from him and ran my hands over my face. "My partner and I don't get along well. We haven't all semester. It feels like we've just been going through the motions so we can pass, but that we aren't making any real strides. And when I thought we were starting to get along, he decided that he doesn't want to keep working with me."

Dad frowned, looking concerned. "I'm so sorry, Cora. I know this is what you've always wanted."

That was an understatement. It was more than just *want*. It was a passion, a desire that had consumed me to my very core since I was a kid.

"Tell me about your partner," Dad encouraged. "Why is it that you don't think you two get along?"

I shrugged. I wasn't sure how much I could tell Dad. He'd think I was making a big deal over nothing. But it *was* a big deal.

Not just because the academy mattered to me, but because *Kellan* mattered to me.

Oh, shit!

It hit me like a ton of bricks. Why hadn't that occurred to me before? How could I be sitting here thinking Kellan's comments hurt because all I wanted was the best shot at my academic career? Chancellor Harris had already promised a reassignment if we wanted it.

But that was just the thing. I *didn't* want it. I wanted Kellan on my team, because even though we had our differences, and even though we didn't always get along, we had some damn good successes. We had the potential for so much more—and in more ways than one. So, where was the problem?

"Do you want to know why your mother and I get along so well?" Dad asked.

I knew Dad was only trying to make sense of the things I didn't want to say aloud, but I decided to humor him anyway. "Because you were made for each other?"

Dad chuckled, then said, "No. It's because we put the work into our relationship. There are two things that are the key to holding our relationship together. The first is communication."

"Yeah, because you two disagree all the time," I said sarcastically.

"It's true," he argued. "We do. But we also *listen*. We hear each other out, until we understand where the other person is coming from. And when we do that, we almost always find that we're on the same page and just translating our feelings into different terms."

I carefully considered his words. Lack of communication was definitely one of mine and Kellan's downfalls. He barely talked about himself, and when I tried to get him to, he shut down.

"What's the second key?" I asked.

Dad looked me straight in the eye and gave me a single-word answer. "Trust."

I waited for him to say more, but that was it. "Trust? Isn't that kind of a given?"

"Is it?" Dad asked challengingly.

Silence settled between us for a few moments. Snowflakes continued to fall, lightly dusting our clothing. "So, you think that's my problem? Communication and trust?"

Dad shrugged. "I don't know what your problem is. I was just talking about me and your mother."

I knew Dad sensed what was going on more than he let on, but I didn't push it. He'd given me something to think about.

"Any other words of wisdom?" I asked. I was half joking, but I kind of wanted more anyway—anything to help.

Dad thought about it for a moment, then said, "You need to treat each other as equals. That said, before you can work together, you have to learn to work with yourself."

I scoffed. "That makes no sense, Dad. They're two completely different things. Besides, I could never heal on my own."

"I didn't say you had to heal alone." Dad pressed a finger to my chest. "Good teamwork comes from the heart—when you're confident in yourself and no longer in competition with your teammates."

I am not in competition with Kellan, I wanted to say, but I bit my tongue. It would only result in some sort of lecture from Dad that I wasn't actually listening to what he was saying.

"Here, Cora." Dad leaned over and picked up a couple of sticks that had blown from the trees in the last storm. They were thicker than my thumb and longer than my forearm. He handed one to me. "Break this."

I eyed him curiously, but I took the stick anyway. "Why?"

"Just do it," he encouraged.

"Okay…" I took the stick in both hands and easily snapped it in half.

From beside me, Dad snapped the other. He looked back to me proudly. "See? We're each strong enough to break these sticks on our own. Now break them together."

He took one half of my stick and one half of his and handed the two of them to me in one hand. I didn't know where he was going with this, but I was intrigued, so I followed his instruction. I tried to snap the sticks together, but it wasn't as easy as snapping the first. I even pressed them against my leg to get them to give way, but no matter what I tried, I couldn't get them to break.

"I can't," I told him, handing them back.

He shook his head and pushed them back into my hands. But instead of making me try again, he placed his hands beside mine, his fingers curled around the sticks. "Do you trust me?"

"Yes, of course." What kind of a question was that?

"We'll do this together, then," he stated. "On three? One… Two… Three."

Dad and I tightened our hold on the sticks and twisted. A satisfying *snap* sounded, and the sticks broke in two. I smiled proudly.

"Some challenges are too big for a single person," Dad said. "But before we can break the sticks together, we must know how to break them on our own. Get it?"

I nodded as I let his words sink in.

Communication. Trust. Find myself.

It couldn't be that easy, not after Kellan and I spent an entire semester back and forth trying to make this thing go.

But maybe it *was* that easy…

I looked up into my father's blue eyes. "Thank you, Dad. You've been a big help."

"Have I?" he sounded shocked, but I could sense it was for show.

My lips twitched at the corners. "Yeah. We should probably get home and help Mom with the cooking."

"Good idea," he said. "She's probably worried sick."

Dad and I stood and headed back to the parking lot. I followed behind him as we drove home in separate vehicles. When we arrived home, Dad stopped me on the porch steps.

"Cora, there's one more thing I think you need to hear." Dad sounded serious.

"What?" I asked, trying to keep an open mind.

He took a deep breath. "Essence isn't the only thing we leave behind when we go. We also leave our legacy, our mark on the world. And no matter how big or how small that mark is, it's still there. The gods who created us are long gone, and we have no one to answer to. All we have left are basic human values, and we must adhere to them—not because there's something for us after this life, but because there isn't. This is your one and only shot, Cora. What will you leave behind?"

My mouth hung agape. It wasn't a question I thought I could answer. Months ago, I would've said my purpose was to heal, but after talking to Dad today, that seemed so superficial.

Dad turned to the door and stepped inside, leaving the question hanging. And it was in that moment that I finally realized what I had to do.

$\mathcal{I}$ took a deep breath as I entered the Activities Center Sunday night. I hoped Kellan would make it. I'd sent him a text hours ago, and he still hadn't responded. Typical.

It was dark out, and the campus was quiet, since most people didn't want to venture out in the snow. But I'd brave any weather to see Kellan again. Things were about to change, and I had to prove to him the academy didn't make a mistake putting us together.

The Activities Center hallways were eerily silent. The only sound I heard was the beat of my own footsteps against the tile. When I got to Gym B, I was pleased to see that the lights were on, inviting me inside. No one was around.

I dropped my gym bag at the foot of the bleachers and stripped my coat off, shoving it inside the bag. I sat down and opened my phone—waiting...

I expected to see a response from Kellan by now, but I didn't. While I waited, I scrolled through my phone, but that didn't help calm me. I tapped my foot and watched the door as the minutes ticked by. It seemed like an hour, but I'd only been there ten minutes.

I was so full of energy that I couldn't stand to just sit. So I stood and let my feet carry me to the starting platform. Dad's words echoed in my mind, his lesson resonating louder than a bass drum pounding against the side of my skull. Kellan and I had to work together—truly *together*, as pieces of a whole. But to do that, I had to know where I stood first—where my strengths and weaknesses lied, so that he could fill in the missing parts.

I placed my foot on the balance beam and spread my wings out to the side to keep myself steady. I began inching my way across the beam, wobbling as I went. I was almost to the other side when I lost my footing and nearly fell into the foam pit, but I spun my arms and flapped my wings to regain my balance. My heart was pounding at the near-failure, but I straightened up and crossed to the other side. I breathed a sigh of relief when I was once again standing on a solid platform.

The monkey bars were next. I used the same strategy I had the last time by grabbing on to the outside support bar instead of the rotating spokes in the middle. I made it to the other side with ease, then started on the ropes. The swinging steps were just as easy.

When I reached the incline wall, I paused at the bottom. This was the task I couldn't complete on my own last time—the first in the course that required teamwork... But Kellan had reached the top of the wall himself.

Because Kellan is taller and stronger than you, I thought to myself. I didn't feel bad about it. It just was what it was. Kellan had used his strengths to get us up that wall, and this was one area where he was stronger than me.

I already knew we could conquer this obstacle together, so I skipped over it and walked around to the next platform. We hadn't gotten this far before, so I had to study these tasks to come up with solutions to get the two of us through them.

The sixth obstacle had a small trampoline at the base of the platform, with a large, rotating spoke hanging above the pit. It looked like a steering wheel on a car, only parallel to the ground and much bigger. A platform had been placed in the middle of the pit. When I'd watched the other teams, I saw that the platform was on some sort of track that made it move when you landed on it. If you didn't push the platform back once you made it to the other side, your partner had no hope of completing the task.

I eyed the moving platform, calculating my aim. After taking a deep breath, I leapt onto the trampoline, then sprang upward. My hands curled around the metal spoke, and my body's momentum sent me swirling in an arc. I let go before I made a complete rotation and landed firmly on the platform beyond. It moved easily beneath my weight, shooting down its track and slamming against the side of the stationary platform at the end. I bent my knees to stay steady. Finally, everything became still, and I stepped off onto solid ground.

Looking back toward the rotating spoke, I tried to calculate how hard I'd have to push the platform to get it in the right position for my teammate to land on it. I thought I had it down, but the platform moved easier than I anticipated. It bounced off the stoppers at the end of the track, then started back in my direction. When it stopped, it was several feet away from me, but too far away from the spoke. I couldn't reach it to try again. Had we been competing against other teams, we'd have failed.

But we weren't, so it didn't really matter. I just had to try again until I got it down.

Walking around the side of the course, I came up beside the platform and pushed it to the end, where I tried again to get it back to where my teammate would need it. I tried four more times. Each time, I pushed either too hard or too soft, and it never ended up in the right location.

Finally, I got it to stop right where I aimed. I tested it twice more until I was sure I had it down, then moved on to the next obstacle.

This one was the one that was made of two panes of glass set parallel to each other. Celina and Rhys had climbed across going back-to-back. As I paced around to look at it from every angle, I realized that strategy was probably the smartest idea, but I still wanted to figure out if there was a better solution.

I stood on the platform between the two walls and placed my hands on one side and legs on the other, wedging my body between the two large panes of glass with my belly pointed at the ground. I was thrilled to see it was working, but it was hella hard to keep myself upright. I was a little shocked at the core strength it took to accomplish.

Though my limbs shook, I began to inch myself across the pit. Every movement I made was calculated so I wouldn't slip. But I was taking too long, and my body was getting tired. I moved my foot to the right—and that was it.

My whole body went tumbling down into the foam pit. I landed on my front and rolled over, but that only sent me sinking further into the pile of foam cubes. I tried to find my footing, but it was like the pit was endless. I only sank in further.

A male voice chuckled from above me, and my gaze darted in the direction of the sound. My heart flipped wildly in my chest when I saw Kellan's blue eyes staring down at me from the platform above. He looked thoroughly entertained.

My whole body went still as I drank him in. He looked even better than the last time I'd seen him. He wore a white t-shirt that stretched tight across his muscled chest, with a blue zip-up hoodie over the top. His legs were exposed beneath black athletic shorts. Could a guy's calves be considered sexy? Because Kellan's definitely were. And then there was the blond hair falling into his eyes, the dimples, and the slight smirk I no longer wanted to slap off his face. In fact, there were other things—much better things—I'd like to do to his lips.

"How long have you been watching?" I asked, though I didn't take the harsh tone with him I normally used.

"Long enough." He leaned down and held out a hand. "Need help?"

I felt like I should reply with a snide comment or something —since that was the usual dynamic between the two of us, but I hesitated.

"Yeah, thanks," I said instead.

I took Kellan's hand, and my whole body came alive. Butterflies danced around in my stomach, and my mind raced with what I would say to him. Luckily, he spoke before I did.

"So, what are we doing here?" Kellan asked once I'd crawled out of the pit and was standing beside him. He crossed his arms, like he was still in defense mode. I didn't blame him. I'd be mad too if someone broke my wing—no matter the circumstances.

I gestured around at the gym. "To finish the course!"

Kellan looked confused at my chipper mood.

I sighed, then plopped down on the foam platform, with my feet hanging off the edge into the pit. I patted the spot beside myself and said, "Sit."

Kellan pressed his lips together, looking skeptical.

I raised an eyebrow at him. "I don't bite."

He hesitated, then sat beside me. We were so close that we'd be touching if I leaned over only an inch.

"I'm not sure I believe that," he said.

"Okay," I caved. "I don't bite *hard*."

I playfully snapped my teeth at him. He rolled his eyes.

Silence settled a moment later, and I knew we could both sense things were about to get serious. Kellan turned his gaze down into the pit and swung his legs, lightly kicking at the end of a foam cube. He took his sweatshirt off and set it beside himself, perhaps just for something to do with his hands.

I took a deep breath before I dove in. "Look, Kellan. I know you want to quit working with me when the semester's over, but whether you like it or not, we're a team until our final. Please give me another chance. I know we can do amazing things—together."

Kellan raised his gaze to mine, giving me a shell-shocked expression. I suddenly felt self-conscious. I could feel myself turning red.

"What?" I asked, pushing my hair out of my face.

"You said *we*," he pointed out.

"Well, yeah," I said. "Because we're a team."

"But you never call us *we*."

I furrowed my brow. "What do you mean?"

"It's always *me*. *I* healed. *I* put out that fire. It's like, one of your Cora-isms."

My eyebrows shot up. Did I actually talk that way?

Instead, I said, "Cora-isms? Is that a thing?"

"It is now," he said. "This is the reason we're no good together. You're always trying to do things on your own, like with the obstacle course. But I'm not here as your sidekick, Cora. I'm here as your equal, your partner."

I opened my mouth to say something, but he continued before I could get a word in.

"The only reason you work with me is because you're forced to."

"I could say the same thing about you," I reminded him.

He shrugged, like he couldn't argue. "The thing is, if you didn't need an Aedes to heal, you'd be on your own. That's no way to live, Cora."

Every time he said my name, it was like warm, smooth honey washing over my skin. I loved hearing the sound of my name on his lips.

"I know all that now, Kellan," I said. "But please don't pretend like you were perfect."

"I know I'm not," he said quickly. "Far from it. But I already knew it wouldn't work from the start."

"So you didn't even try?" I asked.

Kellan frowned, and I could see the guilt on his face. "You're right. I didn't try."

"I want to try," I said. "We still have two weeks until the final. I can't make up for breaking your wing—which I'm so, *so* sorry about. But maybe I can make up for the rest of it. I'm sorry about everything. I want to work together now."

Kellan stared down at me, like he was trying to figure me out. I just sat there staring back to let him know I wasn't messing around. The whole time, my heart beat wildly. I feared he was going to shut me down.

"Okay," he finally said.

I breathed a sigh of relief.

Kellan rose to his feet. "Show me what you've got, Cora. Let's beat this course."

I beamed as I followed Kellan to the starting point. He stripped his white t-shirt off, and I had to tear my gaze away so I wouldn't stare.

"Okay, Team Captain," I said. "You take the lead."

"Me?" He sounded shocked.

"Yeah," I said with a shrug. "I trust you."

Kellan cracked a smile. "In that case, ladies first."

"Ooh," I joked. "Such a gentleman."

He pressed the button to start the timer, then gestured me forward. I stepped onto the balance beam, and he placed one foot on the other end to steady it. I barely had to use my wings to balance. When I reached the other side, I did as he had and placed my foot on the beam so he could cross.

I stood in front of the next obstacle, ready to jump and grasp the bars, but instead Kellan said, "Up you go."

Before I knew what was happening, his hands were grasping my hips. I was too stunned to question it, so I just went along with it. I jumped, and Kellan hoisted me upward effortlessly, like a cheerleader. I climbed on top of the bars, feeling steady even over top of the rotating spokes. I turned back and held my hand out for Kellan, then helped him up with me.

"This was smart," I said as we crawled across.

"It's best to conserve our energy for the end," he said.

"See?" I replied. "Look what happens when we work together."

I jumped down on the other side, and Kellan quickly followed.

"Go ahead," he said when we reached the ropes.

I grabbed for the first one then swung across to the next. I didn't hesitate, or the rope might not have had enough swing left in it to get back to him. I finished the ropes, then glanced back to see he was close behind.

The swing steps were easy. I couldn't recall a time when Kellan and I moved together in such synchrony. It felt different... and intense.

Next came the wall Kellan had fallen off last time. He ran ahead of me and got to the platform on the first try, then held his hand down to help me up. He shot me a glance when I got to my feet at the top.

"Don't worry," I assured him. "I have no plans to throw you off this time."

"Throw me off?" He raised a teasing eyebrow. "Is that what you did the first time?"

"Do you really think I'd do that?"

Kellan shrugged, but I could see the hint of a smile tugging at the corner of his lips. "Dunno."

"Well, you better get going before I do it again," I teased.

Kellan nudged me. "Stand back."

I did, and beautiful black wings sprouted from his back. He leapt from the platform and soared down to the next one. I stared after him, practically drooling at the sight of his wings spread out in all their glory. It was even hotter than his exposed chest.

Kellan landed, and his wings disappeared. "Well, are you coming?"

Oh, shit. He'd caught me staring.

I quickly flexed my shoulders and spread my wings, joining him on the ground.

"I saw you practicing this one, so I think you should go first," Kellan said.

"Okay." I retracted my wings and stepped up to the trampoline, then did as I practiced before. I went swinging around the spoke, then flung myself to the moving platform. When I reached the other side, I pushed the platform back to Kellan. I held my breath, hoping I'd given it just the right amount of force. It bounced off the other end of the track a little, but only came back a few inches. Kellan could still make it.

"Come on!" I cheered for him, clapping my hands together. "You can do this!"

He glanced up to the rotating spoke and looked as if he was calculating his jump. He gave the trampoline a few test jumps to see what kind of force it had. Then he backed up and took a running start. His hands curled around the spoke, and his legs flew in an arch, before he let go and swung onto the platform. It shifted under his weight and sent him gliding over to me.

"Woohoo!" I cried. "We did it."

Kellan looked like he was getting tired, but so was I. "We're not done yet, sweetheart."

My heart lurched at the term of endearment. He didn't mean it in *that* way, did he?

"Come on," Kellan said, like he hadn't just called me sweetheart. He kicked his sweatshirt aside that was still sitting there from when he took it off before. We stood back-to-back and hooked our arms together like Celina and Rhys had done during Grand Opening. I was acutely aware of Kellan's bare skin pressing against my shoulders.

"Press against me as hard as you can," he said. "Don't hold back, okay? We need to create as much tension as we can."

"Okay. I can do that," I agreed.

We each placed one foot on the walls in front of us, then I felt him press his back tightly against mine. I pushed my leg hard against the wall, until we were locked tight enough that we could both get our other foot up without falling over.

"This is a good start," I said.

"Yep," Kellan agreed. "We have to keep this kind of tension the whole time. Understand?"

"Yes," I answered.

"Okay. One foot at a time."

"Got it."

Kellan and I started inching across the obstacle. It took a lot of strength to stay pressed up against him, but I pushed through it.

"Almost there," Kellan said.

My knees were wobbling, but I forced them to steady and continued moving along with his rhythm. I stared forward, trying not to focus on the pit beneath me. Before I knew it, I caught sight of the end of the wall in my peripheral vision. I glanced down to see we were already over the finishing platform.

"Down on three?" Kellan asked.

"One, two, three," I counted.

We stepped down at the same time, but I lost my balance and stumbled into him. Kellan caught me before I face-planted into the pit. His hands were warm on mine—comforting. What I wouldn't give to have him touch me in other ways…

Kellan straightened and cleared his throat. "One more obstacle to go."

"Right." I nodded, then turned to the final obstacle.

It was a giant rope net that climbed to a high platform above us. After all the energy we'd put into the last few obstacles, it looked like an impossible feat. My legs groaned beneath me, and my arms felt like noodles. But I wasn't about to give up now, not when we were so close.

I looked up to Kellan. "Together?"

He gave a firm nod. "Together."

We raced to the net and began climbing, keeping pace with each other as we went. The net was incredibly wobbly, which made it even harder to climb than it looked. But I kept moving forward, pushing as hard as I could without worrying about how far away the finish line was.

Kellan and I reached the top at the same time. We climbed onto the platform, both breathing heavily. He reached out and helped me to my feet. Together, we stumbled toward the buzzers at the end.

My hand hovered above mine as I glanced to him. He did the same.

"Ready?" he asked.

"Ready," I confirmed.

We pressed the buttons at the same time, and the scoreboard let out a loud *buzz*. I sighed in relief and plopped onto my butt, trying to catch my breath. I expected Kellan to be out of energy, too, but he wasn't. He walked to the end of the platform and shot his fists into the air.

"Woohoo!" he cried toward the direction of the bleachers. "That's right, bitches! We did it!"

I chuckled. "There's no one out there, you weirdo."

"Well, there should be," he replied. He hammered his fists against his chest like a gorilla, then let out another loud *whoop!* Wings shot out of his back, and he jumped off the platform, gliding down into the foam pit between the glass walls.

"Oh my God, Kellan," I said between laughs. "Calm down. It's only an obstacle course."

Kellan pulled his wings in and twisted in the air. He landed on his back in the pit, sinking deep into it. He looked up at me and said, "Get down here, Cora."

I rolled my eyes, but I couldn't resist. I spread my wings wide and soared down to him. I did as he had done and pulled my wings into me, then twisted in the air and landed in the foam pit beside him. I giggled as the rush overcame me.

The two of us were still trying to catch our breath as we stared up at the gymnasium ceiling.

Kellan was the first to break the silence. "You look freezing."

I glanced over to him to see he was eyeing my arms, which had broken out in goosebumps. "No, just cooling off."

He wouldn't take that for an answer. He rolled onto his stomach and crawled through the foam pit to the edge, where his sweatshirt was lying. He grabbed it and tossed it over to me. "Here, take this."

I was about to protest, but then his scent hit me. I couldn't even describe what it was like. It smelled like a warm embrace—if that made any sense. All I wanted to do was wrap the sweatshirt around me and never take it off.

"Thanks," I said sheepishly as I slipped my arms into it.

It was soft and smelled like Kellan. This guy didn't know what he'd just done.

He plopped onto his back again beside me. I lowered myself to my back until our heads were almost touching. I could feel the heat coming off of him, and it made my whole body quiver. I wanted to move closer—to touch him—but I didn't.

"Kellan," I finally said when my breathing slowed.

"Yeah?" he asked.

"I think I know why we've had such a hard time this semester."

"Oh?

"I don't think we understand each other," I admitted.

He chuckled. "That's the understatement of the year."

"No, I'm serious." I kept my eyes on the ceiling while I spoke. It seemed easier to talk without looking him in the eyes. "I hardly know anything about you."

"What do you mean?" He nudged me with his elbow, and my breath caught in my chest. "You call me an asshole all the time."

I smirked. "That's because you are."

"See? That's all you need to know."

"I don't know what you think about me." I held my breath, awaiting his response. The truth was, Kellan had told me more than once what he thought about me, but I couldn't help but wonder if things had changed. They had for me. "Why'd you hate me so much when we were paired up?"

He took a long breath, like he was contemplating the question. "It was that whole icebreaker thing," he admitted. "You kept blaming everyone else and wouldn't take responsibility. You didn't trust anyone."

I blinked a few times, absorbing his words. Had I really been that much of a bitch?

"And then there was the whole *Davina power* comment," he said.

"Oh, come on," I defended. "I was just… you know."

"No, I don't know," he replied. "The Aedes and Davina are equals, and you kept acting like the Davina were better."

I frowned. "I never meant to. I'm sorry."

Kellan sighed. "The truth is, I never wanted to come to the academy anyway."

"Wait. What?" I finally lifted my head to look at him. I knew I'd said before he acted like he didn't want to be here, but it was different hearing him admit it.

Kellan didn't even look at me. "I'm only here because my dad wanted me here. He wanted me to become a healer like him, but I've always wanted to be a lawyer."

I suddenly remembered the law book I'd seen in his dorm room. I should've realized.

"Why do you want to be a lawyer?" I asked.

He finally tore his gaze from the ceiling and turned to look at me. "Remember how I told you my mom is human?"

I nodded. "Yeah, how does that even work when we can't tell humans what we are?"

"The Alliance put laws in place to keep us from revealing ourselves to humans," Kellan explained. "In special circumstances, however, they make exceptions. My parents fell in love, but before my dad could tell her the truth, he had to undergo an application process, interviews, and get a license so they could make sure she wouldn't tell anyone. Then once he told her, *she* was rigorously interviewed, and honestly, the secret itself was a lot to swallow. She almost left my dad for keeping it from her."

I gasped. I couldn't imagine.

Kellan took a deep breath. "Anyway, Mom says it would've been a lot easier if there was a bigger support network in place for mixed families and that the laws were a little more lenient so you didn't have to go through such a long process just to share your secret with someone you love. Mom never felt like part of our world, even though she married into it."

With every word Kellan spoke, my heart sank for his family. His mom obviously really mattered to him. I could tell there was more to the story than he was saying, but I didn't prod.

"You want to change all that," I guessed.

He nodded. "I want to create a program for mixed families, a way to educate and support the spouses and children. My ultimate goal is to get voted into the Alliance and work with them to make better laws."

"I think that sounds great, Kellan," I said honestly.

"Anyway," he continued. "My dad and I agreed that I'd spend one semester at the academy, and if I didn't like it, he'd pay for the rest of my schooling. Do you know how expensive law school is? I couldn't exactly say no."

"So… what'd you decide?" I was scared to ask. "Do you like the academy, or are you giving it up for law school?"

Every muscle in my body froze as I awaited his response. My chest twisted into knots. I wanted him to stay with me, but I feared he wouldn't.

"Wait, Kellan." I stopped him before he could open his mouth.

I shocked the both of us when I rolled over and threw my arms over his chest, pulling him into an embrace. It should've been awkward, since we were sinking further and further into the foam pit and it wasn't much of an embrace anyway. But we were touching, and it felt right.

"Before you say anything, let me say something first," I said into his shoulder.

Kellan relaxed and rested a hand on my back. Oh, God. Something about that gesture was everything I needed. It was like he was accepting me.

I drew away and stared into his eyes. They would've made my knees go weak if I were standing up. I spit the words out before I could stop myself. "Kellan, at the beginning of the semester, I hated you as much as you hated me. But… something changed. I don't know what it was. Maybe it was when you saved me from those protestors. But whatever it was, you showed me that you weren't the guy I thought you were. I know I tell you you're a jerk all the time, but it's not true. You're actually kind of nice, and you can be sweet sometimes."

His expression remained blank the entire time. I had no clue what he was thinking, but I pushed on. If I hesitated, I'd never finish what I had to say.

"I stuck with you, but it turned out to be better than I imagined. I don't want to lose you. I want to stay on your team. If that means working harder, then I'll take it. But…"

Kellan's expression finally shifted to curiosity. "But…?"

I swallowed down the lump in my throat. I couldn't sit here

and guilt him into staying on my team just because I felt something for him. It wouldn't be fair. I knew what Dad had been trying to tell me now with his last bit of advice. My parents' legacy wasn't the sealing of the realms and the breaking of the Aedes' curse. Their legacy was in the kindness they showed and the differences they embraced—and they'd shown me that through every step of my life. They supported me in everything I did. And I wanted to pass on the same legacy, which meant I had to do the same for Kellan now—no matter what he decided.

"But," I said, "I'll support you in whatever you want to do."

Kellan took a deep breath, then started to get up. I drew away from him and sat up in the pit, until we were facing each other. My hands quivered. I couldn't believe I'd just said all that to him. I was dying to hear his response.

"I'm glad you feel that way, Cora," he finally said. "Because there's something I need to tell you."

My blood ran cold. Yeah, I was wearing this wonderful warm sweater that smelled like Kellan, and my blood ran cold. Whatever he had to say didn't sound good.

He glanced down to his hands and started picking at his fingernails in his lap. Yep. Definitely not good.

"I'm not coming back next semester," he spat out.

My heart sped up a little, but I couldn't say it wasn't what I expected to hear. It wasn't what I *hoped*, but I wasn't surprised. "Then that's what you have to do," I told him, trying to be the supportive partner I said I'd be.

He shook his head, still refusing to meet my gaze. "There's more. Over break, a friend of my dad's called me up and said he'll be in town in two weeks. He's the president of Dunmar University."

"Oh my God," I said. "That school's super prestigious."

He nodded. "I know. And they have the best pre-law program in the country. He's invited me to dinner. If I go, it could secure my entire future—the university, the pre-law program, and everything after that."

"Then you have to go," I encouraged, even though my stomach felt empty and that knot in my chest kept tightening.

"The thing is, Cora…" Kellan hesitated, and I instantly knew there was more. "He's only in town on the night of our final."

I recoiled. It felt like he'd just slapped me across the face. "Wait. Hold on. Are you saying you're *ditching* our final?"

Tears began to well in my eyes. This was way worse than leaving at the end of the semester. This was a complete betrayal of our partnership! If I didn't pass this final, I could flunk out. He was gambling my dream away at a chance to get his!

"Cora…" He reached for me, but I instantly backed away.

I glared at him, unable to truly wrap my head around what he'd just told me. "I thought part of being partners was that we trusted each other," I snarled, blinking away the tears.

"Cora, I'm sorry," he insisted. "But this is my future."

"And this is mine!" I exploded.

I was so angry that when I opened my mouth, I couldn't get any words out. I thought I could support him, but this went beyond any decision I thought he'd ever make.

I couldn't even look at him right now. I started toward the edge of the pit, but it wasn't the dramatic exit I was hoping for. My arms and feet sank into the pieces of foam, and I moved at a snail's pace. I probably looked like an idiot, but I didn't care. I had to get out of here.

"Cora, wait," Kellan called.

I reached solid ground and whirled toward him. Unlike me, he moved through the foam with ease. He reached the platform and pulled himself up before I could get a word out.

And now I was a freaking mess, so I couldn't talk anyway. Tears streamed down my cheeks, and I wiped them away with the sleeve of Kellan's sweatshirt.

"I—I thought—" I sobbed.

"I'll talk to Chancellor Harris," he promised.

"What good is that going to do?" I snapped, still wiping at my eyes. "I can't go through the final without a partner. I'm going to flunk out."

My chest heaved, and uncontrollable sobs bubbled up in my throat. I was so embarrassed.

"Cora, they're not going to flunk you because I—" he started, but I quickly cut him off.

"This academy is all about teamwork, Kellan," I snapped. "They grade you based on how your team performs. So yeah, if you're not there, I can pretty much guarantee I'll fail."

"Cora—"

I didn't want to hear any more. If Kellan had stuck this out until the end of the semester and *then* decided to leave, I could've lived with that. I would've even thrown him a going away party or some shit like that. But this...

I whirled around and stomped toward the bleachers to grab my bag, then headed for the door, fuming. It was just my luck that Celina decided to step into the gym at that exact moment. Her eyes met Kellan's first from where he stood dumbstruck on the obstacle course.

"Hey, babe!" she called over to him. "I've been looking every-where for—"

She cut off when she noticed me approaching, a hard expression fixed to my face. I didn't mean to, but I was so mad I barely noticed where I was going. I slammed my shoulder into hers on the way out.

"Hey!" she cried. "What's your problem?"

I whirled toward her, my breath hot. "You wanted him to stay at the academy with you? Maybe *you* can convince him. Because I sure as hell can't."

Celina's gaze darted to Kellan. He was already making his way toward us from across the gym.

"Kellan, what's she talking about?" Celina asked.

Part of me was glad he hadn't told her. It was the one ray of sunshine on this whole matter. But I couldn't bring myself to rub it in. I turned and started down the halls toward the doors. He called for me, but I ignored it.

As the sound of my name echoed down the halls, one thing became very clear. Kellan Greene didn't want this life—the healing, the firefighting, any of it. But I had enough determination and resolve for the both of us.

With or without him, I was passing that exam.

19

 ven though it was late, I marched straight to the Academy Center and to Chancellor Harris's office. It was a long shot that she'd be here at the end of a holiday weekend, but I had to at least check. The reception desk was empty, but her office door was open a crack. I stepped toward it and knocked.

"Come in."

My heart skipped a beat when I heard Chancellor Harris's voice behind the door. I pushed it open, and she glanced up to me from where she sat at her desk. Her lights were off, but her computer glowed brightly.

"Cora," Chancellor Harris said lightly. "What can I do for you?"

I stepped further into the room. Anger continued to course through my body, but it was more than that—it was disappointment. I tried not to let any of that show.

Instead, I found myself saying, "You're still here."

She gave a slight smile and said, "Yes, I'm known to overwork myself a little. Please, have a seat."

I sat in the chair across from her. My lips tightened, and my jaw tensed. "Chancellor Harris, I'm here to petition to complete my final exam on my own—without a partner."

Her brow furrowed, and she tilted her head to the side a little. "Why would you want to do that?"

An image of Kellan's face flashed through my mind, and my hands tightened in my lap. "My partner's bailed on me."

Chancellor Harris frowned. "Your final exam requires a group effort, Miss Marek."

"I know," I said. "But what happens if I don't go through with it?"

She took a deep breath. "You'd fail out of the academy."

"I can't let that happen," I stated. "This has been my dream since I was a kid."

"Perhaps I can talk to Mister Greene," she offered.

"It doesn't matter," I replied. "He doesn't care if he flunks out, and he's already made plans for the night of the exam."

Chancellor Harris looked speechless, like she wanted to help but didn't know what options to give me. "I'm sorry that you were put into this situation, Miss Marek. I know it isn't fair. The risks are simply too high to send an individual into the exam without support."

"The risks are high regardless," I argued.

"There's a healing portion to the exam that can't be performed alone," she pressed.

I was starting to get more upset by the minute. It was like I was being punished for Kellan's choice—and I hadn't done anything wrong. "Kellan can't be the only person on campus that I can heal with. Let one of my professors help."

"The exam doesn't just test practical skill, Miss Marek," Chancellor Harris said. "It also tests the team skills you've developed over the course of the semester."

"I was going to be reassigned anyway," I said. "Besides, it's unrealistic to expect any of us to work with the same partners the rest of our lives. People are reassigned to new locations all the time. Others die on the job and their partners have to work with someone else."

I rose to my feet, my face heating. "You and I both know I have what it takes to pass this thing. Please just give me a chance to prove myself."

I was fuming, but Chancellor Harris's expression was unreadable. I expected her to shoot back how this was the academy's policy and how they'd never had issues before. Instead, she took a deep breath and folded her hands in front of herself on the desk.

"I understand your frustrations, Cora," she said. "But no one has ever gone through this exam on their own."

I crossed my arms. "So I'll be the first."

She hesitated, then said, "Okay."

I blinked a few times. Had I heard her right? Was she really going to let me do this on my own?

"I'd like to see you pass your exam as well," she told me. "I'm willing to let you go through with it."

Excitement filled my chest. I could hardly believe she was agreeing to this.

"*But,*" she quickly added. "Should you fail the test, I can't allow you to retake it."

I swallowed the lump rising in my throat. "So I can take the test on my own, but I can't ever reapply for the program if I fail?"

She nodded. It was better than skipping out on the test altogether and flunking out. At least this gave me a chance.

"And I'll still be reassigned next semester?" I asked. "No repeating my classes?"

Chancellor Harris nodded. "Provided you pass."

"I will," I stated confidently. Inside, I was giddy with excitement. "Thank you so much for this opportunity."

"You're welcome, Miss Marek," Chancellor Harris said as I started for the door. "Good luck on your exam."

I only hoped that the second chance she'd given me was enough to get me to pass.

20

Two weeks later, I stood in front of the burning building questioning everything I'd gone through this semester. The sky was dark, in stark contrast to the bright orange flames and white snow on the ground. The heat came in waves across my face like a warning, like I shouldn't be going into this test alone. But this was my future we were talking about. If I didn't do this, I'd never become the EMT I'd always dreamed of being.

"Are you okay?" Laura asked from beside me. She'd come for emotional support, since she wasn't in the firefighting program and already took her earth final yesterday.

I nodded, but inside, I was screaming.

We stood on the corner of an intersection across the street from a burning house. It was a controlled fire, one that the school had been hired to start as part of a demolition project. It doubled as the perfect location for our final exam. I knew I wasn't in any real danger, since my professors would be keeping close watch, and we each had an alarm attached to our uniform, but it was nerve-racking nonetheless.

All along the block, people had come to watch the fire.

Some were students and faculty here to support their students. Others were nearby residents who couldn't resist checking things out. Down the street, the protestors that called themselves the Infantry walked with picket signs. I hadn't seen them around campus since the incident, but this was new turf for them to play on. I could see that Colt douche from here. He was yelling obscene things into the crowd so fiercely that his face had turned beet red. Campus security was doing their best to keep the protestors far away from the fire.

Close by, Celina and Rhys were staring up at the fire, looking like they'd already won the challenge. Caleb and Shaylene were on the other side of the lawn, going through their dressing drill.

I'd already completed the drill and wore my heavy firefighting gear—helmet, jacket, gloves, and all. I even wore a pair of steel-toe boots that I'd secretly slipped my Davina Blade into for good luck. My breathing apparatus cylinder was attached to my back, and I held my mask in my hand. Even though I could control fire, my essence wasn't enough to protect me. There was still a chance of falling debris, unexpected flames, and poisonous gas. The gear provided an extra layer of protection should something get out of hand. Just thinking about it made my guts twist.

Laura stepped in front of me to look me in the eyes. She took me by the shoulders. "Before you go in there, Cora, I want you to know how incredibly proud I am of you. Kellan never deserved to be your partner. You have the determination and the skill to do whatever it takes to get through this. It's time to show Kellan how wrong he was about you. You can do this. Make me proud."

I forced a smile. "Thanks. I will."

Laura didn't take her hands off me. Instead, she drew my essence into herself, and I felt my channel opening, the essence buzzing through my body. It was enough to power me up for the night.

"I'll be here when you're finished," Laura said, dropping her hands. "Then afterward maybe we can get a bite to eat to celebrate."

"Celebrate what?" I asked.

"Your test, of course!" she said. "Because you're going to pass. I know it."

I felt her confidence wash over me. "Yeah, I am."

"You are what?" Travis asked as he came up to us. Caleb and Shaylene were at his side in their gear.

"She's going to pass," Laura said brightly.

Travis draped an arm over her shoulder and gave her a light kiss. "Good. We want you around next semester, don't we?"

"Absolutely," Shaylene agreed. "I still can't believe you're doing this on your own, though."

"What choice do I have?" I asked. "Chancellor Harris said I'd flunk out if I didn't go through with this."

"Don't worry," Caleb said. "I'd do the same thing. You'll do great."

Shaylene stepped toward me and slipped her arm into mine. "You should stick close with us. After all, in a real scenario, there'd be multiple teams going in at once."

"Are you saying this isn't a real scenario?" Travis balked, pointing to the burning building in front of us.

"Fair enough," Shaylene said.

Caleb looked deep in thought. "I don't know if it'll work for her to follow us. Each team gets a different route."

Shaylene's shoulders fell. "Right."

"Guys, I'll be fine," I assured them. "Laura powered me up for this part, and I've got Professor Sanders waiting on the other side to power me up for healing."

"That's the spirit!" Laura encouraged.

"Okay, everyone!" Professor Kovski called. She stepped up to the middle of the lawn with a clipboard in her hands. "All fire-fighting students, please gather around."

I waved to Travis and Laura, then followed Caleb and Shaylene to stand beside our classmates.

"This is a three-part test," Professor Kovski explained. "It simulates a real-life situation using the key lessons you've learned in your classes over the past four months. This test will prepare you for the next three semesters. If you cannot complete the tasks, you will not be deemed a fit for the remainder of the firefighting and EMT courses at Harris Academy."

She continued. "In this mock scenario, the house caught fire when a burning candle was knocked into the curtains. The parents escaped, but their six children are still trapped inside. Your first task is to follow your route—which I'll provide you with in a moment—and retrieve the dummy in the room marked on your map. You will rescue them following the safety procedures you've learned in your firefighting class."

She pointed to a group of ambulances parked at the curb. "Once you retrieve your dummy, your team will make its way to these ambulances, where we'll swap the dummy for lab rats and you will be tested on your healing abilities, as would be required of you in the field."

She continued. "Once you're finished there, you will join Professor Taylor and Professor Arnold at the back of the house and attempt to extinguish the flames coming from the bathroom. Any questions?"

Nobody raised their hands.

"Good," Kovski said, giving a firm nod. She reached for the papers on her clipboard and began handing them out. "Study your routes carefully. In a real-life setting, you will not be blessed with a map."

She handed me my paper, then lowered her voice just for me. "I'm sorry to hear about Kellan, Cora. Good luck in there."

I forced a smile. Just the mention of Kellan made me want to punch something. "Thanks."

She turned her attention back to the group. "Remember, should anything go wrong, we highly encourage you to use the alarms on your belt to call for help."

She held up a small red device, which we'd covered many times in class. It attached to our clothing and made a high-pitched squeal when you pressed the button.

"Your test starts now."

Kovski said it so casually that it took me a second to realize she meant *now* now. Groups started moving, and I quickly followed behind. I slipped my mask on, which covered my entire face, then attached my regulator to it—the device that connected to the tube for my air tank, which would allow me to breathe in the fire. Finally, I added my hat, then raced inside behind the other teams. My map showed that my target was located upstairs in the second bedroom, so I immediately started toward the stairs. The entire building was up in flames, and it was nearly blinding. I was hot everywhere beneath my uniform, but my air tank made it easy to breathe.

When I reached the stairs, I was ready to do a quick assessment of the structure to see if they were safe, but Celina and Rhys were already rushing up them. I deemed it safe and climbed the stairs. In front of me, Celina was using her essence to calm the flames along the walls. I decided to save mine for the final task, since I didn't have a partner to power me up.

Celina and Rhys went into the first bedroom, and I immediately went for the second. There, I found a nursery set up, with a crib, rocking chair, and chest of drawers. I ran to the crib and found a dummy the size of an infant lying there. I wrapped the doll in its blanket and turned back to the door.

I stopped in my tracks when I saw Celina standing there. Even though her mask covered her face, I could see the anger knitted in her eyes.

"You dumb bitch!" she shouted. Her voice was a little distorted behind her mask, but I could still hear her clearly.

I was so shocked that I stumbled back a step. Was she seriously going to do this in the middle of a burning building?

"Excuse me?" I snapped.

"You heard me," she snarled.

"Celina," Rhys called from behind her. He was carrying their dummy.

"Just hang on," she growled at him. She stepped into the bedroom, blocking my only exit.

I took a cautious step back. The murderous look in her eyes was freaking me out. "Aren't you wasting time?"

She didn't respond. Instead, she marched forward and slapped her hand as hard as she could across my face. You would've thought my mask would protect me, but it didn't. It only dug into my skin, then dislodged. I breathed a gulp of thick smoke, and my lungs burned. Primal anger pulsed through my veins.

I dropped my dummy and resituated my mask, then faced her. "What the hell is your problem?"

"You're my problem!" she shouted.

"Celina, stop," Rhys begged, tugging on her. He was so huge he could've just tossed her over his shoulder, but he didn't. "Save it for later."

She ignored him and took another step toward me until our masks were practically touching. "What did I tell you at the beginning of the semester? Kellan's quitting, and it's all your fault."

She was getting way too close for comfort, and the whole building was up in flames. The longer we stayed, the more dangerous the structure became.

"Back off!" I shoved her, and she went stumbling backward.

Her features hardened. "You don't deserve to pass this test."

"Fuck off!" I shouted. "Kellan made his choice on his own. I wanted him to stay."

"Bull shit!" she cried.

Then she lunged. Her hands went straight for my face, but I ducked, and she ended up landing on top of me. She grabbed me by the jacket and dragged me onto the ground. Suddenly, her hands were all over me. I fought back. *Hard.*

I thrust my hand outward, clipping her in the chin. Her head snapped back, and she screamed. A second later, her fist slammed down on the side of my face. Pressure shot out through my ear, and a ringing filled my head.

"Bitch!" I roared as I brought my knee up into her gut.

She grunted. A second later, Rhys was dragging her off of me.

"What the hell, Celina?" he yelled at her, trying to restrain her. "Leave it. Let's get this test over with!"

Celina elbowed Rhys in the stomach and broke free. She lunged at me again, clawing at anything she could. She ripped my hat off my head and flung it across the room, then grabbed my mask and tore that off, too. Heavy smoke assaulted my lungs and eyes. I was so pissed I could literally throw this bitch down the stairs right now.

I kicked her in the stomach as hard as I could. She went stumbling back but grabbed on to my uniform so she wouldn't fall. Even though I punched her again, she still hung on.

Rhys grabbed her around the middle and tried to drag her away from me, but she wouldn't let go. She tugged and tugged on my uniform while I tried to go the other way, but even Rhys couldn't pull her off of me.

"It's all your fault!" she shouted.

Suddenly, something on my uniform gave way. I thought I saw a chunk of something fly off, but I didn't see what it was. Celina and Rhys stumbled one way, while I went the other. I slammed into the burning wall and quickly jumped away before the flames could hurt me.

When I righted myself and turned back to Celina, she'd grabbed whatever had come off my uniform and was reaching for my dummy. "Have fun passing without this," she growled, before turning and rushing out of the room behind Rhys.

"Celina!" I shrieked, heading after her. My insides were blazing red-hot, and it had nothing to do with the fire all around me.

All I heard was her evil laughter over the sound of roaring flames. I reached the doorway and saw her stop at the top of the stairs, one arm raised. In the blink of an eye, flames burst around me with such force that I was blasted back into the room. I went reeling onto my back, but an ungodly pain shot through my skull on the way down. My head had slammed into the side of the rocking chair.

The world blurred around me as I lay there, unable to find my balance. As the burning building spun around me, I continued to inhale poisonous gas that made my airways feel as if they were on fire. I grabbed for my mask, but I could barely feel my fingers. Something warm and sticky touched the back of my head as darkness swirled around me.

Blood.

I was a fool to think I could do this alone. I reached for the alarm on my belt, but my hands couldn't find it. Was I *that* disoriented?

I was a moment from slipping into unconsciousness when I saw a figure making their way through the flames and over to me. They wore a firefighting uniform, so I couldn't make out who it was. My best guess was Celina. Had she come back to make sure I was dead or something?

Except the figure was too tall and their shoulders too broad to be Celina. The fire blazed behind him in a way that outlined his form, like he himself was glowing. He bent down to me and reached for the back of my neck to cradle my head in his arms.

"Cora," he said breathlessly.

Shock riveted through me, and I actually felt the heat melt away for a second. I turned my gaze up to his eyes through his mask, and there was no denying those beautiful blue eyes. The fall must've been worse than I thought, because there was no way this was real.

"Kellan?"

21

"Cora, you have to get up!" Kellan commanded.

"Kellan, I'm—" I started to say, but he already noticed. He pulled his gloved hand away from the back of my head to see it was coated in blood. He cursed under his breath.

"Kellan, what are you doing here...?" I paused to go into a coughing fit. Kellan's eyes widened, and he quickly grabbed for my mask hanging off my air tank and slipped it back over my bloody head. I breathed a greedy breath of fresh air.

"Cora, you're badly hurt," he said, ignoring my question.

I blinked a few times. My mind began to clear as the fresh air filled my lungs. "I—I can heal myself."

"Do it quickly then," he instructed.

Essence poured through me as Kellan channeled my power into him. My hand shook as I brought it to the back of my head, but I didn't give it too much thought. The more I contemplated it, the harder it would be. I felt my essence leave my hand, and a warm tingle spread across my skull, numbing the pain. My head began to clear.

"Good enough," I said quickly, pushing myself to my feet.

Kellan grabbed my arms to steady me. He glanced around

189

the room. "Where's our dummy? We'll fail this portion if we leave without it."

"Celina took it," I told him. "What are you doing here anyway? I thought you had a dinner with some big law professor."

Kellan shook his head. "I did, but I got there and I realized—"

He was cut off by the sound of collapsing debris in the next room. His hands tightened on my arms, and we both startled.

"We can talk about it later," he said quickly. "Let's get out of here."

Kellan pushed at me, and I started for the door. By now, the stairs were completely covered in flames. I aimed my palms at them to calm the fire and get a look at their structural integrity.

"They're too far gone!" I shouted at Kellan over the groaning of the building. "The map showed a second staircase that way!"

I pointed. Kellan took my hand, and we started down the hall together. When we reached the second staircase, we saw that it was engulfed in even more flames than the last.

"I think we're going to have to take a window," Kellan said.

My heart hammered. Fire, I could deal with. Jumping out a second-story window? Not so much.

"There has to be another way," I said.

"I don't think—Look out!"

Before I knew what was happening, Kellan lunged forward and shoved me out of the way. I slammed into a door, and the wind left my chest. Debris went everywhere, kicking up smoke all around us so that I couldn't see. Then suddenly, the flames were back, burning a pile of boards and drywall that had caved in from the ceiling. Above us, a gaping hole had opened in the roof. Dark smoke billowed out of it.

All I heard were the sounds of Kellan's screams. My stomach plummeted to the floor when the smoke cleared and I saw him lying beneath the debris pile.

"Kellan!" I shrieked.

I immediately aimed my hands at the pile and killed the flames faster than I thought possible. The instant they were gone, I rushed forward and started pulling pieces off Kellan. At the same time, I used my other hand to search for the alarm on my belt, but my hand met nothing. I glanced down to see my alarm was missing.

Fuck! That must've been the thing that tore off when Celina and I were fighting.

"Relax, Kellan," I said with all the gentleness I could muster. Inside, I was a wreck. Nerves were racing through my veins, and every inch of my body was shaking. "We're going to get a rescue crew in here."

"Shit, Cora," he cried. "There's something in my leg."

I pushed enough debris out of the way to get to his alarm, only to see that it'd been crushed under the weight of the debris.

Shit. Shit. Shit!

There was no way to alert our professors. No one was going to save us.

I quickly turned my attention to his leg. A sharp piece of metal from the roofing material had sliced through his uniform and stuck into his flesh. It was attached to a bigger piece of wood that looked almost as heavy as Kellan. Blood oozed out of the wound and dripped onto the floor.

"It's okay, Kellan," I assured him in a shaky tone. "I'm going to get you out of here."

He sucked in a sharp breath and tried to say something, but he didn't get it out.

"This is going to hurt, but if you work with me, we can get it healed and get out of here," I said.

He shook his head, but his eyes looked anything but on board with this. He looked terrified and in unimaginable pain. His face had paled, and I worried he was about to pass out.

"On three?" I said, but he just gritted his teeth and didn't respond. "One… two…"

I pushed on his leg and tore the piece of metal out before I reached three. He screamed so loud that it shook me to my very core. But we weren't out of the woods just yet. The piece of metal had caught on his uniform. I tugged on his pant leg, but it wouldn't break free.

"I can't move!" he cried, trying to roll away from the debris, but it held on to him firmly.

I pulled a second and third time, but it was determined to hold Kellan down. The debris itself was too heavy for me to move. The best I could do was rip his pants off.

Rip his pants.

I remembered the blade in my boot and reached for it. The fire was hot on my exposed skin as I pulled my pant leg up to get to the boot. I pulled my dagger out and pressed it into the fabric. Kellan's uniform finally tore away from the debris.

"Okay, let's get you healed up so you can walk," I said as I slipped the knife back into my boot.

But when I looked back to Kellan, he wasn't moving at all. Shock had set in, and his eyes had rolled back into his skull.

"No!" I cried.

I slapped him in the chest, trying to get him to wake up, but nothing happened. A heavy weight settled on my chest, and my throat burned at the threat of tears. What was I going to do? I couldn't get to the stairs, and both our alarms were out. If we waited for our professors to come searching for us, we could be burnt to a crisp by then. The only other thing I could do was throw Kellan out the window—but who knew how much that could seriously hurt him?

Shit!

My eyes turned upward, and an idea suddenly struck me.

No... It was stupid. Beyond stupid.

I knew the consequences if I did this. I knew what people would see—and what they would say. I knew everyone in the supernatural community would judge me. They'd all say how they'd have done it differently. But if I didn't do it, Kellan could die, and I wasn't willing to let that happen.

I stood and took a deep breath. "I'm sorry, Kellan. But it's the only way to save you."

Then I did the only thing I could. I stripped off my mask, air tank, and jacket, then flexed my shoulders. White wings grew from my back.

They say adrenaline can do crazy things to you. It's true. Kellan was heavy as hell, but somehow, I found the strength to cradle his body in my arms. I shouldn't have been able to fly with all the extra weight, but I jumped and shot out of that hole in the roof like I was a freaking superhero.

All those people on the ground—the Davina, the Aedes, and the humans—their eyes gravitated toward me like I was a divine angel sent from the heavens.

Cell phone cameras pointed my way. People screamed. I don't remember much, but I remember thinking one thing: *I don't care.*

Yeah, we had our secrets, and yeah, I got that exposing ourselves could lead to serious consequences. But Kellan was alive and free from that fire because of me. And nobody— *nobody*—could convince me that wasn't the right thing to do.

I soared over the crowd, searching for a place to land. My feet made heavy impact with the pavement next to the ambulances, and I pulled my wings into my back. The air was ice cold on my skin. Professors Kovski and Sanders raced over to me with a gurney.

"Do you have any idea what you've just done!?" Sanders yelled at me.

"Yeah," I snapped back, helping Kellan onto the gurney. "I saved my partner's life. Want to grill me about it?"

"We'll deal with that later," Professor Kovski said quickly. "Mister Greene needs immediate medical attention."

"Kellan! Kellan!" I shouted.

I quickly followed them. At the back of the ambulance, they removed his mask. He blinked a few times, and relief flooded through me. I was so happy I could cry.

Before I knew what I was doing, I flung myself over him and planted a kiss firmly on his lips. It wasn't how I planned for our first kiss to go. I didn't even realize it was going to happen until it did. My heart lifted in my chest. It felt like my first flight, my stomach somersaulting in my abdomen and my pulse tapping to the beat of a quick drum. For one split-second, the entire world stood still.

The next, it was over. Everything happened so fast that I barely felt the rush of the kiss before his hands were on my shoulders, pushing me away.

"No, Cora," he groaned.

His pained eyes met mine, and I read something in them—something that buried deep down into my heart and tore it just a little. It wasn't that he was in too much pain. He really didn't want me in that way.

I knew it shouldn't matter. There were more important things happening right now. You know, like saving his life. But the mix of sorrow and regret that entered his eyes was enough to get me to stop and slow down. And when I did that, the weight of everything that had happened tonight came crashing down on me.

I stepped away before I really decided to. It was like my feet had a mind of their own. It felt like I was floating as all sounds around me faded. Celina ran over to Kellan. I was mostly grateful, because he needed someone right now, and I couldn't handle another fight with her.

My knees were shaking so badly, and my heart pounding so fiercely, that I couldn't stay on my feet. I ended up in a secluded corner of the street and turned to the curb behind me. I sank to the ground, burying my face in my hands. Cold air brushed across my exposed skin.

Please be okay. Please be okay, I begged as they worked on Kellan.

I couldn't stop the flood of tears that rained down my cheeks as I rocked back and forth. Davina couldn't fix everything. They'd heal the wound for sure, but if something else went undiagnosed, he might experience permanent damage. I felt like a total failure—and the test wasn't even on my mind anymore. Who cared if I passed now? All I cared about was making sure Kellan was okay. And he didn't even want my help…

"Well, well, well…"

I whirled around as the sound of a sinister male voice met my ears. Colt Walter approached me through the darkness. He was alone, but there was a look in his eyes that said I should be very afraid. I shot to my feet and backed away.

"I have to say, I didn't expect that." He spoke coolly, like he was hiding some sort of secret.

"Leave me alone," I said, sounding more confident than I felt. I quickly glanced toward the ambulance, but no one was looking my way.

"There's no reason to be afraid," he sang, like he was toying with me.

"Don't you dare come any closer," I snarled in the most threatening tone I could.

To my surprise, he stopped in his tracks. "I don't want to hurt you."

"Then what do you want?" I snapped.

Colt straightened his blazer. "I want answers. I knew something was going on at this school, and this just proves it. What are you? What do your people want?"

"We just want to help," I insisted.

"Help what? Yourselves?" he accused.

"What are you talking about? No!" I cried. "Why do you hate us so much?"

"I'm not here to answer your questions," he growled, his lips curled back over his teeth like an animal.

I crossed my arms. "Then I'm not here to answer yours. Leave us alone. We aren't hurting anybody."

His nostrils flared, but he spoke in a cold tone. "Oh, but you are. And that little stunt you just pulled? It didn't go unnoticed. Soon enough, everyone will know that the people at Harris Academy aren't really people at all."

I curled my hands into fists. What was he implying? That we were aliens or something?

"We're not dangerous," I told him, but he didn't look like he wanted to hear it.

"You're not what you seem," he said, "and that means you should be feared. And believe me, everyone will fear you. Watch out, because that can of worms you just opened can never be closed again."

"What are you suggesting?" I bit at him.

"The academy's going down," he threatened. "A war's been brewing for a long time, and now there's nothing you can do to stop it."

My blood ran cold as Colt turned on his heel and walked away from me.

A war? He couldn't be serious.

Except he didn't sound at all like he was joking.

Everyone had been right. The Aedes and Davina had kept their identity secret for a reason. Because there were people out there like Colt Walter who would stop at nothing to kill the thing they feared.

And something told me he had the means to actually do something about it.

22

I sat in Kellan's hospital room the next morning, waiting for him to wake. The minutes turned into an hour, but they felt like an eternity. I didn't quite feel whole, and it had nothing to do with failing my exam. It wasn't about Kellan, either. At least, I didn't think it was. I couldn't really explain it. All I knew was that my insides felt raw—empty. I'd come to the academy to make an impact on the world... and now I wasn't sure that was going to ever happen.

Celina had been here earlier, probably to gloat about winning the Chancellor's Award. I'd hid out in a corner of the waiting room until she left, then snuck inside while Kellan was sleeping. What I could gather from listening to the nurses was that the cut had been deeper than we thought and he'd lost a lot of blood. He'd recover, but he was very fatigued from it all.

I thought coming here would allow me to apologize to Kellan about everything that had happened. I knew it wasn't my fault that the roof had collapsed on him, but I still felt like I should be sorry about something. Maybe it had to do with everyone yelling at me afterward about it. My professors, my parents when they heard... Laura seemed sympathetic—she said

I'd done the right thing—but I hadn't had a chance to talk to any of my other friends yet.

Maybe that's what I was hoping for from Kellan, that he'd confirm what Laura said and tell me I did the right thing. I mean, would he rather I left him? Tossed him out the window? I did what I had to do… right?

Kellan shifted a little, and I straightened in my seat. His eyelids fluttered open, and he glanced around in confusion, like he couldn't figure out where he was. Then his eyes caught my face, and he relaxed.

"Kellan…" I said softly, not sure where to start. My body involuntarily moved toward his, but I jerked back before I could touch him. "I'm sorry."

"Sorry for what?" he asked in a strained voice. "You saved me, didn't you?"

I shook my head, though I didn't know why. I *had* saved him.

I knotted my hands in my lap. "I—I guess so, but I don't know if I did it in the right way."

"Is there a right way to save someone?" he asked. He started to sit up, but he groaned and fell back down onto the bed.

I was on my feet in an instant. "Does it hurt? What's wrong?"

"No." He waved me off. "Just stiff is all. And hella thirsty."

I grabbed the water bottle beside his bed and handed it to him. He slowly pushed himself to a sitting position.

He took a swig, then spoke in a clearer voice. "Did they freak out?"

"Did who freak out?" I asked.

"Everyone?" he asked with a raised eyebrow. "You exposed yourself last night. It's kind of a big deal."

"Oh, so you remember," I said flatly. Somehow, I had hoped he'd forgotten most of the night.

"Yeah, I remember."

"All of it?"

He didn't take his gaze off me when he spoke. "All of it."

I sat back in my chair and buried my face in my hands. "Oh, God, Kellan. I'm sorry about kissing you. It was just the heat of the moment kind of thing and…"

I wished he would've kissed me back. I wished he hadn't pushed me away. But he was right to. It wasn't fair of me to do that to him when he'd been lying on a gurney.

"Celina and I are together," he blurted, like he couldn't hold it in any longer.

My heart stalled, and I gaped at him. "*Together* together?"

He nodded, his cheeks reddening a little. "When she visited me this morning, I told her that I couldn't go through with the law school thing, that I'd stay here. And so we made it official."

"But she's been stringing you along all this time!" I practically shouted. How could he have feelings for this girl? She was insane! They had no chemistry. "She tried to kill me during that test, you know."

Kellan gave me this look like he thought I was overreacting. "I talked to her. What happened was an accident."

I crossed my arms and looked away from him. How could he be on her side? "You weren't there."

"I came, though," he said softly. "That has to count for something, doesn't it?"

I turned my gaze back to him, my hands shaking. He was right. It did count.

I softened my tone. "About that… what changed your mind? Why'd you come?"

Kellan shrugged. "I got to the dinner, and everything was great, but I couldn't get you off my mind."

My heart fluttered when he said that.

"We got our food, and I couldn't eat it," he said, staring at the floor and looking deep in thought. "That's when I realized that if I truly had any integrity, I wouldn't be sitting there. I'd be at the test. With you."

He lifted his gaze to mine, and I saw a sparkle in his eyes I hadn't seen before.

"I'm glad you came," I whispered. "I couldn't have finished the test without you."

Kellan scoffed. "Well, you didn't finish it with me, either."

I cracked a smile.

"Thanks for everything you did," he said. "It's more than I could've asked of my partner."

The tension in my body melted. "Thanks, Kellan. I really needed to hear that."

A knock came at the door. We turned to see Travis's face through the glass. He was beaming and waving his hand comically at us.

"Hey, guys!" he said as he pushed the door open. Laura, Caleb, and Shaylene piled in behind him.

Laura was carrying a pile of balloons. She stepped further into the room and set them—along with a card—beside Kellan's bed. "We came to see how you were doing."

Kellan sat up straighter and set his water bottle aside. "Fine, thanks. But you guys really didn't have to come."

"Of course we did," Caleb said. "Our fellow classmate gets impaled by a piece of building. We're all here for you, bro."

Kellan offered a small smile. "Thanks."

"Have you guys been online?" Shaylene asked.

Kellan looked between the four of them. "No. I've kind of been sleeping off the whole *being impaled* thing."

"What's going on?" I asked. Concern washed over me. I didn't like the look on Shaylene's face.

"Here, I'll show you," she said.

Shaylene turned on the smart TV in Kellan's room and hooked her phone up to it. She mirrored the screen for all of us to see. As she started to scroll through social media, my stomach sank deeper and deeper in my abdomen. There were pictures and videos from all angles of me flying through the air carrying Kellan.

"You've gone viral," Travis said, like it was some sort of badge of honor.

"Viral?" I squeaked. "Guys, this isn't good. I mean, I knew people would see, but I didn't think the whole freaking *world* would see! The Alliance has strict laws about this."

Laura's face paled. "Do you think you'll get arrested?"

"Arrested?" Disbelief fell across my face. "I didn't exactly think of it as a possibility until now."

"You should see what they're saying about you," Travis said, like it was cool. "An angel sent from the heavens. Archangel Michael himself."

"Archangels are only stories based off the Originals," I said. "They were never real."

Travis shrugged. "Yeah, but *they* don't know that."

"Besides, do I really look like a *man*?" I rolled my eyes, but it was only to lighten the mood. Inside, my mind was running zigzags. I knew what I was getting into when I flew Kellan through that roof, but I thought I'd get a slap on the wrist for showing myself to a few people. The videos Shaylene was casting on the screen showed millions of views.

"Calm down, Cora," Kellan said, keeping the level head he always did. "The Alliance will understand you were trying to save me. They've dealt with this stuff before. It'll be old news by this afternoon."

His reassuring tone helped calm me.

"I hope so," I said.

A second knock came at the door, and we all turned to see Chancellor Harris stepping into the room. We all exchanged a quick glance, but no one seemed to be able to explain what she was doing here.

"Hello," she said, nodding toward each of us. Her tone wasn't as bright as usual, which made my mouth go dry. She'd probably come to drag me away to the Alliance or something.

Caleb cleared his throat. "Um, you're probably here to talk to Kellan. We'll give you some space."

I stood to follow my friends out the door, but Chancellor Harris stopped me. "Sit, Cora. I'm here to speak with you, too."

I ducked my head and returned to my seat, waving to my friends as they left the room. When the door shut, silence fell between the three of us. Uneasiness twisted in my gut. Chancellor Harris stood at the end of Kellan's bed in a black pantsuit looking super prim and proper. Her expression was hard to read, but I sensed it couldn't be anything good.

"You're coming back to the academy," she stated, like it was mere fact.

"Wait… what?" I couldn't be sure I heard her right.

"What do you mean?" Kellan asked at the same time. He shot me a quick, confused glance. "But we failed. If you fail your exam, you're dropped from the program."

Chancellor Harris took a deep breath. "I need you two close… So I can protect you."

Kellan and I shared another glance.

"Protect us from what?" I asked.

She frowned. "The Alliance isn't pleased with what happened last night. They'll find a way to cover this up, but I'm sensing that won't be enough. Things have been changing these last few years, and it's only a matter of time before all hell breaks loose."

"All hell breaks…" I could hardly process what she was saying. So Colt had been right. A war was coming. "But we help people!"

She shook her head. "Sometimes, that is not enough."

"Why do you want to help us?" I asked.

"The academy will be under close watch given the location of the incident," she said. "If anyone comes after you two, they come after the academy. And I can't let that happen. This world needs us."

Kellan's confusion dropped from his face. He held his head a little higher and said, "You're damn right they do. We'll help any way we can."

It hit me instantly that Kellan had said *we*—as in, we were a team. Like he took responsibility for what happened as much as I did. And when he turned his gaze to mine, I saw it in the way he looked at me.

In that moment, one thing became very clear. Kellan maybe didn't like me in *that* way, the way he liked Celina, but I was important to him in another. We were partners—for good.

I was touched. I couldn't explain it, but that emptiness inside of me seemed to fill when I saw that look in his eyes.

I turned to Chancellor Harris. "So what are we going to do?"

Chancellor Harris took a long breath. "The only thing we can do, Cora. Prepare for what's coming."

END OF BOOK ONE

EXPOSING MAGIC

DIVINE DESCENDANTS BOOK TWO

1

"What are we going to do?"

"The only thing we can do, Cora. Prepare for what's coming."

Chancellor Harris's words echoed in my mind even after she left the hospital room. I lifted my head from my hands, and my gaze turned to Kellan's. He sat in the hospital bed looking as worried about Chancellor Harris's words as I was.

I'd screwed up. I screwed up big time. Our semester final had gone down in flames—literally. The only way to save Kellan from the burning building was to fly through the collapsed roof. The decision led to me exposing myself as supernatural, and the whole thing had gone viral. A stupid, stupid mistake—one I wouldn't take back for anything, because my partner was lying here beside me alive because of it.

"At least we get to go back to the academy," Kellan said.

I nodded, but my hands tightened around the armrests of the leather chair I sat in. Attending Harris Academy was all I ever wanted. I should have been relieved. And I was—on some level. But I couldn't get the rest of what Chancellor Harris had said out of my head. She seemed to think a war was coming, and she wanted Kellan and me safely within the walls of Harris Academy when that happened.

This world needs us, she'd said.

Hell yeah, they did. The Aedes and Davina had revolutionized the medical field. We *helped* people more than they could possibly imagine. Hell, it was because of us people healed so quickly and there were virtually no risks to surgery. And yet… people feared us.

People like Colt Walter, who'd threatened me the moment I exposed myself. For whatever reason, he hated us. I wouldn't let the rest of my people go down with me. I had to do whatever I could to fix this.

The sound of the door swinging open came from behind me. I turned to see a man in a black suit step into the room. He was tall, with short gray hair and age lines around his eyes. He looked like he could be a stock broker. I couldn't place my finger on it, but something about him chilled me to the bone.

Kellan sat up straight in the bed, fully alert. "Can we help you?"

The man cleared his throat and kept his eyes on Kellan. "I'm John Maddox, a Davina and Chief of the Public Relations department of the Alliance." Even his voice sounded terrifying. "I'm here to speak with Cora Marek."

My blood ran cold. Oh, shit. Was he here to arrest me or something?

I stood on shaky knees. "I'm Cora Marek."

Mister Maddox looked at me, but there wasn't an ounce of respect in his eyes. He folded his hands in front of him. "Miss Marek, I'm afraid you're going to have to come with me."

I froze. Kellan must've noticed my unease, because he reached out and took my hand. We both jumped at the contact. Kellan didn't like me like that. He was with Celina now. Still, his touch brought the nerves in my stomach to life. He squeezed my hand tightly, then pulled back, as if afraid to show any more affection toward me. We were, after all, only partners.

When my eyes met his, he gave me a firm look, as if to tell me I wasn't going anywhere with this guy.

I crossed my arms and turned back to Mister Maddox. "We can talk here. Whatever you have to say can be said in front of Kellan. He's my partner."

Maddox's lips tightened, like he was shocked a young girl like me had the balls to stand up to him. The truth was, I was quaking in my shoes, but I wasn't going to let it show.

"Very well," Maddox said stoically. He gestured for me to return to my seat, then moved across the room to stand at the foot of Kellan's bed.

I was relieved to sit back down again. I feared he was about to deliver some very bad news.

"As I'm sure you're well aware, Miss Marek, the events of last night are not to be taken lightly." Maddox spoke in a slightly threatening tone. "What happened was… unfortunate."

The way he spoke didn't reflect his words. It was like he was choosing his words carefully as to not insult me to my face—like there were deliberate insults running behind his seemingly innocent words.

He continued. "The supernaturals have hidden their existence for ages. We must be diligent to keep it that way."

"Why?" I asked. The question slipped out before I could stop myself.

Maddox frowned, and his tone hardened. "To keep ourselves safe, of course."

I suddenly felt like I'd asked the stupidest question on the planet. I swallowed, but held my head high. "So, what's going to happen now?"

"Damage control," he answered bluntly.

"Wait, so she's not being prosecuted?" Kellan asked, looking relieved.

"The Alliance, of course, considered the possibility." The way Maddox spoke made it sound like he was on the side who wanted me prosecuted. I had the strangest urge to throw a ball of essence at his head. "But the board understands that this was an act of desperation. We don't believe Miss Marek poses a threat to exposing us in the future." He sounded doubtful, like if it were up to him, I'd be rotting in a supernatural prison by now. "Even if she did, prosecuting Miss Marek would look bad…"

Maddox trailed off. He'd said too much. It was obvious what he was about to say. My parents were so high-profile that this sort of thing would make national news within the supernatural community. Too many Aedes and Davina would take my side, and it would damage the Alliance's image. Thank God for famous parents, right?

Maddox cleared his throat. "The Alliance is willing to offer you a deal, Miss Marek."

My mouth went dry. "What kind of deal?"

Maddox paused a moment, as if deliberately dragging out the suspense. "We want you to go public and tell the world the entire thing was a hoax."

"What?" I balked. "How am I supposed to convince them of that?"

Maddox eyed me up and down with a look of disgust. "That's for you to figure out."

What the hell was this guy's problem? I'd never met him before, and already he hated me.

I lifted my chin. "And what happens if I don't take the deal?"

Maddox smirked, like he'd like to see me try. "Exposing the Aedes and Davina in a criminal offense, Miss Marek. You're lucky the Alliance is forgiving this incident as an accident and giving you a chance to fix it."

Kellan's eyes darkened, and his tone became harsh as he

repeated my question. "What happens if she doesn't take the deal?"

"What happens to all criminals, Mister Greene?" Maddox practically sang, as if calling me a criminal pleased him. "She'll be imprisoned for her crimes."

My stomach plummeted to my toes. No way in hell. I wasn't some sort of traitor. I did what I had to do to save Kellan's life.

And now I had to do everything to save mine.

I crossed my arms and got to my feet. "Fine. I'll do it. I'll convince them."

"No, Miss Marek." Maddox chuckled, and it sent a shiver down my spine. "Convince *me*."

2

My heart pummeled against my rib cage as Maddox left the room. The white walls spun around me as I lowered myself back into the chair. Convince John Maddox? How was I supposed to do that?

"Cora. Cora." Kellan's voice sounded like it was coming through a thick vat of jelly. I barely heard him.

Once the initial shock waned, I lifted my head to meet Kellan's gaze. "What am I supposed to do? If I can't convince him, I could end up—"

"Relax, Cora," Kellan said in a soothing tone. It was weird to hear him reassure me like that. Normally, we were yelling insults at each other. "We'll figure something out."

I furrowed my brow. "Like what?"

Kellan smirked. "I have an idea."

~

"Are you sure this is going to work?" I asked.

Our friends had already come and gone, and Kellan and I were alone. We'd been rehearsing for an hour already. He had a great idea. The only problem was I didn't know how well I could pull it off.

"For sure," he said confidently.

Kellan pushed the bed sheets off his legs and stood on shaky knees. The wound on his leg had been healed, but he'd lost a lot of blood and hadn't eaten much since last night. Until this morning, he'd been hooked up to tubes to help with the dehydration.

My gaze roamed up and down his body. I didn't mean to check him out; I was just concerned about him. But looking at him made my cheeks flame nonetheless. "Are you sure you're up for this right now?"

Kellan placed a hand on my shoulder. "Absolutely. We've got this, partner."

Butterflies danced in my stomach when he called me his partner. It was stupid, because we'd been paired up all semester, but something about hearing that word come from his mouth made it seem... sexy.

I raised an eyebrow as I looked over his hospital gown. "Are you wearing that?"

Kellan chuckled. "No. Celina brought me clothes this morning. I'm going to change."

The mention of Celina made my guts sink. What did he see in her anyway?

Kellan reached for the curtain beside his bed but paused before tugging on it. He winked at me. "No peeking."

"Please," I scoffed. "Like I want to see *that*."

I did. I *so* did. But no way in hell was I going to tell him that.

Kellan rolled his eyes, then pulled the curtain between us and began getting dressed. "All you have to do is be confident," Kellan said from behind the curtain. "Believe it yourself."

"How can I believe in something I know is a lie?" I asked.

"You just... pretend, I guess," he said.

"Pretending is the exact opposite of believing," I pointed out.

Kellan whipped the curtain back, and I jumped a little. I went still the moment my eyes fell upon his torso. He wore jeans that hung off his hips in a way that made me want to drool, and his black shirt lay tight across his muscled chest. The color reminded me of his wings, which made me hot just thinking about. He was hella sexy when he went shirtless and took his feathery black wings out.

Crap. How was I going to focus at all this semester now that I knew I had feelings for my partner?

I shook the thought off. I didn't need to be thinking about any of that right now.

"Let's practice," Kellan said. He sat on the bed again and looked me in the eyes.

Damn it. Taking him off my mind was *not* going to work when he looked at me with that smoldering gaze.

"I'm going to ask you a series of questions," he said. "And I want you to make me believe the lie."

I shifted in my chair. "Okay…"

"What's your name?"

I hesitated. Nothing but my real name came to mind.

"Err." Kellan mimicked the sound of a buzzer. "You hesitated too long. Now I'm not going to believe anything you say. Let's go again. What's your name?"

"Shay—Laura," I answered, stumbling over my words. My two friends' names got mixed up in my mind.

Kellan raised an eyebrow. "Shaylaura?"

I bit my lower lip. "No?"

I mentally kicked myself. Why was I being all shy and weird around him? I wasn't normally like this. Damn hormones.

Kellan sighed. "Rule number one about lying, go with your first instinct. Rule number two, never change your mind. Rule number three, always answer with yes."

"Oh, so you're an expert at lying now?" I teased.

He chuckled lightly. "You'd be surprised."

"Hang on." I crossed my arms. "What exactly have you been lying about?"

"Nothing," he assured me.

"See, now how do I know *that's* not a lie?" I pointed out.

His tone softened. "Because I don't lie to you, Cora."

My heart lifted in my chest. I didn't care how good of a liar Kellan was. When he said those words, I believed him whole-heartedly.

Kellan clapped his hands. "Again. What's your name?"

The first name that popped into my head was my mother's, so I went with it. "Kathryn Marek."

"Where did you grow up?" he asked.

Eagle Valley came to mind, but I was supposed to lie, so I went with the next thing I could come up with. "Right here in Celia, Minnesota."

He started throwing questions at me faster and faster. "What's your favorite pizza topping?"

"Mushrooms," I lied. Pepperoni all the way.

"Favorite hobby?"

"Ice skating." If I sounded convincing, it was a miracle. I'd actually never been ice skating before. My favorite hobby was collecting antiques.

"What's your element?"

"Fi—water."

Kellan frowned, but he continued anyway. "What's your major?"

"Surgical studies," I spat out before I could question it.

"Which are you: A morning person or a night owl?"

"Night owl."

"Do you love me?"

"Yes." The word slipped out before I could stop myself. My entire body went rigid, and I held my breath as I awaited his reaction. I hadn't even known until that moment that I felt that deeply about him. Of course I knew I was crushing on him, but *love?* Deep down in my soul, I felt the truth to my answer. I loved Kellan Greene.

A smile spread across Kellan's face. Time seemed to stand still, and my mind raced with theories to what it meant. Was he going to say it back?

"See?" Kellan said. "You're already a pro at this."

I released the breath I was holding, but with it came the sinking of my stomach. Of course Kellan thought I was lying. It was part of the game.

"Are you ready?" he asked.

"As I'll ever be," I answered, trying to keep my tone steady. "Let's get this over with."

"Let's do it over here." Kellan pointed to an empty corner of the room. "It's not quite as convincing when people can tell we're in a hospital room, is it?"

"No, it's not."

Kellan and I pulled two chairs together, and I took out my phone. My hands shook a little. If I didn't get this right, that jerk from the Alliance was going to make sure I was put on trial for exposing us. It was a lot of pressure to put on a girl.

Kellan nudged me in the side, making me nervous for entirely different reasons. "Nervous?"

"Of course not," I lied. "I don't get nervous."

"Good job," he praised. "Even *I* believed that one."

I rolled my eyes at him.

"Okay, let's go," he said.

I pulled up my camera app and paused. I shoved my phone in his direction. "You do it."

He pushed the phone back. "That Public Relations guy wanted you to do it."

"Ugh," I groaned. "At least help me out, okay?"

Kellan nodded. "Of course, partner."

I mentally swatted away the butterflies in my stomach and swallowed my nerves, then pressed *record.*

"Hello, Internet!" I practically sang. Oh, God. I didn't sound *anything* like myself. It was sickening. "I'm Cora Marek."

"And I'm Kellan Greene," he cut in like we'd practiced.

"And we have a confession to make," I said.

I didn't like using my real name, but Kellan thought it was best to put some truth into the lie. It would make the rest of it more believable when people started digging for confirmation.

"You don't know who we are, but by now you've *seen* us," I continued. "Last night, we performed an experiment for our social media class. There are no words for how incredible this experience has been."

"We're definitely getting an A," Kellan joked.

"For sure," I played along. "By now, you've all seen the video of what *looks* like an angel flying out of a burning building to save an injured man. Well, we hate to burst your bubble, but it was all fake." I put on my best expression of disappointment.

Kellan subbed in for me. "See, while our classmates were testing for their final in firefighting, Cora and I were preparing *our* final for our social media class. The assignment was to create something that would get the highest number of likes, shares, clicks, you name it. Of course, we thought the best way to do that was to put on a show."

Kellan was such a natural at this. If I didn't know what had really happened, I'd have believed every word he said.

"With the help of our professors, we got in costume, hooked up to some wires, and made it look like an angel was flying out of the flames," Kellan said.

"Well, I mean, it was a little more complicated than that," I joked. "But we won't go into all the specifics. We just wanted to let everyone know that the videos aren't real. We really would've loved to see how much farther this could go, but we already have plenty of data for our class, so we thought it was best to tell everyone the truth."

Crap. I was rambling now. Time to wrap it up.

"If you guys see a real angel, let us know," Kellan laughed. "But for now, it's just the brainchild of two college kids who wanted to see how far they could go on social media. Again, thank you guys for all the likes and shares. If you want to stay updated, we've got links in the description, and don't forget to hit that follow button before you leave. *Chao!*"

I held my smile until I hit the button to stop recording. I turned to Kellan with both my eyebrows raised.

"What?" he asked innocently.

"You're a natural," I complimented.

He scoffed and rolled his eyes.

"No, I really mean it," I said.

Kellan shrugged. "It's nothing. I used to run my own channel."

My jaw dropped. "I didn't know that. What was your username?"

I turned to my phone and scrolled through the apps.

Kellan groaned. "Oh, come on. Don't go looking for it. It's so cringe-worthy. There's a reason I stopped."

"I want to check it out," I insisted.

Kellan leaned over to grab my phone out of my hand, but I held it out of reach. Good God. He was almost on top of me now. "Cora," he complained.

I laughed. "It can't be that bad."

"Oh yeah?" he challenged. "Maybe we should go look at your photos and videos from five years ago?"

My laughter instantly died, and the blood drained from my face. "How about no?"

"See?" he said.

I let it drop, while secretly making a mental note to search his channel later. "How was our first take?" I asked. "Do you think it was good enough?"

"I think it was perfect," he told me. "The first one is always the most natural."

I snorted. "Says you."

"I did say so," he teased. "Are you ready to tell the world the truth?"

I rolled my eyes. "You mean the lie?"

He narrowed his eyes. "But is it?"

"Yes," I deadpanned.

Kellan frowned. "Cora, if you're going to stick to this lie, you've got to believe in it yourself. So let me ask you again. Are you ready to tell the world the truth?"

I straightened my spine and saluted him. "Yes, sir."

Kellan chuckled and shook his head. "You're such a nerd."

"Hey! I wear the title of *nerd* proudly, thank you very much."

Kellan got serious. "Cora, you're stalling."

My shoulders fell. "Okay, maybe I am."

"Send me the video, and we'll do this together," Kellan offered.

"Okay," I agreed. "Together."

3

I held my breath as Kellan and I blasted the video across social media. I couldn't take my eyes off my phone, waiting for the numbers to start climbing. My stomach sank as it became more and more apparent that this video wasn't going to go viral as quickly as the last.

And then something miraculous happened. All at once, it seemed like comments started flooding in to Kellan's account. He already had a huge following, so when his followers started sharing it, it was like we couldn't turn off the flood of comments.

Of course Kellan would do something like this. It's so like him.

Congrats on pulling it off, buddy!

I knew it! I kept telling people the video was faked.

I looked back at the original, and you can totally see the wires holding them up.

I breathed a sigh of relief.

"See?" Kellan asked brightly. "I told you everything would all work out."

I frowned as my eyes scanned a new comment. "Apparently, not everyone believes us."

Angels are real! This video is the real hoax!

And then came a long rant from another commenter who called us sick for using someone's religion in our social experiment. *I hope you eat a ghost pepper and choke on it!*

"Forget about them," Kellan said. "They're just trolls."

"What about the people who don't believe us?" I asked.

"We don't need everyone to believe us," Kellan reminded me. "Just enough to mark those videos as unreliable."

"True," I sighed, standing from my chair. "I think I need a break from all these comments. I'm going to head to the cafeteria and bring you back something to eat."

"You don't have to do that, Cora," he assured me. He didn't sound like he was just being kind, either. He sounded like he meant it.

"You don't really have a choice," I told him. "You're still recovering from the blood loss, and you need something to keep your strength up. Until they discharge you, I'm here to take care of you."

Kellan leaned back in his bed and made a show of snuggling in. "In that case, bring me back chocolate."

"Okay, your Highness."

Kellan grinned as I headed out the door.

The hospital was quiet as I started down the hall. I finally had a chance to breathe, and everything that had happened over the last twenty-four hours began racing through my mind—the test, how Celina had sabotaged it, and Kellan showed up to help, how the roof had caved in and I had to fly Kellan out... Colt's threat to me, Chancellor Harris's visit, everything John Maddox had said. It was all so much to absorb. I didn't even know where to start with it all.

My mind wandered so far that I didn't realize where I was going. I missed the turn to the cafeteria and started weaving through the maze of hallways. I didn't realize where I'd ended up until I heard the sound of a voice coming from one of the open doorways.

"Hey! It's her! Hey, lady!"

I backpedaled a few steps and looked into the room to see two girls lying on identical beds. The older of the two must've been at least ten years old, but she was barely alert. She was attached to a bunch of tubes, and her lips were pale. Whatever happened to her must've been really serious if the Davina hadn't healed her yet.

The other girl looked around six, and she was very cheerful as she poked at a tablet in her lap. My gaze darted up and down the hall, and I wondered if they were alone. I didn't see anyone nearby who could be their parents.

"It's you!" The younger child smiled brightly at me and held up her tablet. The video from last night played on the screen. "You're the angel. Are you here for Rebecca?"

My face paled, and I stepped closer to the room. Kellan's words echoed in my mind. I had to stick to this lie and believe it myself.

I shook my head. "I'm sorry, but I'm not an angel."

"You look like one," she told me.

My heart melted on the spot. The way she looked up at me with those big brown eyes made me want to cry.

"Thank you," I said. "You and your sister look like angels, too. You are sisters, right?"

They shared the same curls and chocolate eyes.

The young girl nodded. "I'm Saddie, and that's my sister Rebecca."

"It's Becca, Little Mouse," her sister corrected her. She spoke in a strained voice, which only tugged on my heartstrings further. I still couldn't figure out why she'd been hooked up to all those tubes, not when there were Davina healers on staff.

"What are you two doing here?" I asked curiously. "Where are your parents?"

Saddie frowned and spoke in a serious tone. "Grandpa doesn't like it when we talk about them."

My stomach sank. "I'm sorry. Is your grandpa around?"

"No," Saddie said. "He had to leave to get cigarettes."

"Saddie," Becca hissed, but she didn't stop talking.

"We were in a car accident," Saddie announced. "But I'm all healed up. See?"

Saddie held out her arm and pointed to nothing. She must've had a nasty gash or broken bone the way she looked at it so proudly, but the Davina had already healed her.

"Not me, though." Becca's gaze fell.

"What's wrong?" My voice filled with concern.

"It's normal for her," Saddie told me matter-of-factly. "She's *always* in the hospital."

"Not *always*," Becca shot back, before looking to me. "My immune system doesn't work right. I don't heal as fast as Saddie."

My heart fell. On the outside, Becca looked okay. There were no lacerations or bruises that I could see. But I'd learned in my classes that chronic, wide-spread conditions were difficult to heal with essence. We had to be able to pinpoint the site of the injury and direct our magic into it with care, or we risked hurting our patients even more. It was why we could heal cancerous tumors easily but not wide-spread cancers like those in the blood. It was the same with chronic conditions like immune deficiencies. We could help speed the healing process along, but if the body wasn't working right to begin with, our essence could only help so much. The body had to do the rest of the work itself.

Saddie studied her tablet closer. "Do *you* have a sister?"

"No, I—"

I cut off as she turned the tablet screen back toward me. It was the same video from last night, when I flew out of the burning building, but this time it was zoomed in on my face so I was easily recognizable.

"She looks just like you," Saddie accused.

Rebecca's gaze darted to the screen, then she narrowed her eyes at me. "Why are you lying to us?"

"Lying?" I balked.

"You said you're not an angel, but that's you." Rebecca pointed to the tablet.

"It is," I admitted, "but—"

Tears welled in Rebecca's eyes. She bit her lower lip, and it nearly tore my heart to shreds. I couldn't stand to see *children* like this. I was a Davina. I should be able to heal them.

"Have you come to take me to heaven?" Rebecca asked as a single tear fell down her cheek.

"No, of course not." Instinct took over, and I rushed to her bedside. I knelt beside her and ran my thumb along her cheek to wipe away the tear.

I opened my mouth and waited for the lie to come, to tell the girls the video was nothing more than a trick. But a hollowness opened in my stomach, swallowing the words.

Rebecca spoke before I could. "Tell me the truth. What's going to happen when I die?"

Rebecca's eyes gleamed as she looked up to me, and my guts sank. In that moment, something inside of me changed.

I was suddenly taken back to the time when my best friend Kaylee fell out of our treehouse and broke her arm when we were nine. Kaylee was tough and refused to let anyone see her cry—until we were alone in the hospital. She turned to me and said, "*Promise me I'm not going to die, Cora.*"

Rebecca gave me that same pleading expression. I knew in that moment I couldn't lie to her. Rebecca was just ten years old, and already she'd been worn down by her pain. The least I could do was offer her comfort—to serve and heal. That was what it meant to be a Davina.

I took a deep breath and reached out for her hand. "When you die, your essence will be restored to the earth."

Rebecca blinked away the tears. "Essence?"

"Your soul energy," I clarified. "You'll be reunited with all the people who died before you. And you'll become a part of everyone who comes after you. You'll feel nothing but peace. It's a wonderful, beautiful process."

Crap. Now *my* eyes were watering.

Rebecca's eyes cleared, and a smile tugged at the corners of her lips. "So I'm going to be okay?"

I nodded. "Of course you are. But it's not your time yet, Becca."

I couldn't know that for sure, but it felt like the right thing to say.

"What do I do?" she asked. "What do I do before my time is up?"

I squeezed her hand. I didn't know what to say, but the words started tumbling out of me before I knew what I was saying. "You find your purpose, Becca."

"What's my purpose?" she questioned.

"It's whatever you want it to be," I told her. "You get to decide what you want your legacy to be, Becca. The world is a scary place, but each and every one of us get to add our own beauty to it."

Becca closed her eyes, and her lips stretched into a wide smile as she relaxed into the pillow. "I like pretty things."

"Like unicorns," Saddie cut in.

Becca chuckled. "Yeah, Little Mouse. And wings." Becca opened her eyes again and looked at me. "Can you show me yours?"

Every muscle in my body tensed. I glanced toward the door, but Saddie had already jumped out of bed and was closing the curtain on the other side of the bed.

"Yes, show us!" Saddie sang as she jumped back onto her bed.

I hesitated. "I- I can't. Not here."

Becca's bottom lip poked into a pout, and Saddie frowned.

"Please?" Saddie begged.

"We won't tell anyone," Becca promised. "We swear it."

I couldn't. Exposing myself was a huge offense. I already had one strike against me. The Alliance would never forgive me if they found out about this.

If...

I stopped and seriously contemplated what to do. These girls looked at me like they needed hope in their lives. If I wanted to leave anything behind when *I* died, it was inspiring others to do good. For as long as I could remember, all I wanted was to make the world a better place—to make a difference. In that moment, a sense of peace washed over me when I realized I had the opportunity to do just that in these two little girls' lives.

"Okay," I agreed.

The girls' eyes lit up in unison.

My heart pounded. I couldn't believe what I'd just said. I'd just agreed to break the law, to go against the Alliance *again*. And the weird thing was, *I didn't care.*

I took a deep breath and stood, then flexed my shoulders. Glorious white feathered wings grew from my back as I shifted into my Davina form. They fit perfectly past the straps of my tank top. The two girls drew a breath in unison, and their eyes widened.

"So beautiful…" Saddie whispered.

Her sister had gone speechless. She threw her hand over her mouth, and the tears returned to her eyes. But they were no longer tears of sadness. They were tears of joy, and that filled my heart to the very brim, until it felt as if my emotions were overflowing.

"You've made me so happy," Becca whispered.

In that moment, I knew I made the right choice by showing them my wings.

4

I couldn't stop thinking about Saddie and Becca, even after I left the hospital. I didn't tell Kellan about what I'd done. I knew he would only chastise me for it.

Luckily, we didn't talk much over the next week, so even if I wanted to break down and confess, I couldn't. It was winter break, and I was staying at my parents' while Kellan went back to Iowa to visit his family for Christmas. I should've been spending time with my parents, but I spent most of my time in my room, going over everything that had happened.

I wished I could see those girls again. I had to know—did exposing myself leave a lasting impact on them?

Of course it did. They were ten and six. That was the kind of thing you remembered your whole life.

Oh, crap. Did I make a mistake? They were just children now, but of *course* they would grow up someday. Would exposing myself come back to hurt my people in the future?

I jumped out of bed when the thought hit, and I scrambled over to my laptop across the room. I pulled it onto my lap as I snuggled back under the covers. I furiously typed into the search bar and brought up endless stories of people who

227

claimed to have near-death experiences and interactions with angels. I sat there for hours listening to video interviews and reading first-hand accounts. I didn't know what I was looking for, but I couldn't keep from diving deeper into the stories.

Hours later, the doorbell rang. I didn't think anything of it until I heard my mom's voice calling me from downstairs.

"Cora!"

I paused the video I was watching and set my laptop aside. I was still in my pajamas, and I wore Kellan's sweatshirt I still hadn't returned to him. My hair was tied into a high ponytail, and I wasn't wearing any makeup. I furrowed my brow as I got out of bed, wondering who could possibly be here. I headed over to the window, and my heart stalled in my chest when I saw the vehicle parked in the driveway.

"Oh my God!" I cried. I raced across the room and flung the door open, then tore down the hall and pounded down the stairs.

"Kaylee!" I screamed as I ran into the living room.

My best friend from high school stood just inside the door. She wore a huge smile and spread her arms out wide. I slammed into her, pulling her into a tight hug. She squeezed me back and lifted me off the ground.

"Cora! I missed you so much!" she cried.

She set me down, and I stepped back to look her up and down. Kaylee looked the same as always. She was several inches taller than me, with long flowing brown hair and beautiful eyes. But there was something different about her, too. There was a glow to her that I'd never noticed before. Her brunette hair seemed more vibrant, and a touch of a smile lit up her face.

"I can't believe you're back from Europe," I said. "I thought you had at least six months left."

"Oh, I do," she replied in an excited tone. "I came back for Christmas. After New Year's, I'm headed on a plane to Italy!"

"Oh my gosh, that's great!" I told her. "You have to tell me all about your trip."

"Absolutely," she gushed.

I led Kaylee up to my room, and she immediately pulled out her phone and started showing me pictures of her travels.

"Okay, so Paris… You *have* to come with me sometime, Cora. It's to die for," Kaylee said. "The Eiffel tower was amazing, and I met this *crazy* hot French guy who showed me around the city and took me to all these wonderful places to eat."

Kaylee continued on, telling me about all the cities she'd visited during her time abroad and the sites she'd seen. Mostly, though, she talked about the hot foreign guys.

"I got you something," she announced after finishing her stories. Kaylee reached into her purse and pulled out a little pink gift bag. I smiled at the gesture and took it from her hands.

"What is it?" I asked.

She giggled. "You'll have to open it and look inside."

I pulled open the bag, and my heart warmed. Inside was a collection of trinkets from all the countries she'd been to. I pulled each one out one by one. The first was an old statuette of the Eiffel tower. It wasn't the kind you picked up at a gift shop, either. It looked hand-crafted and had a genuine weathered look to it. I pulled out a wad of tissue paper and unrolled it to find a teacup that had the English flag on it. At the bottom of the bag was a miniature Christmas ornament of a beer stein from Germany. I drew a breath as I emptied all the contents from the bag.

Kaylee smiled proudly. "I went to every flea market I could find to get you antique souvenirs."

"Kaylee, that's so thoughtful," I said. "You didn't have to."

"Of course I did," she said simply. "You're my best friend."

I set the gifts aside on the bed, then pulled her into a hug. "Thank you. I wish I could go with you."

She tilted her head to the side. "But what about Harris Academy? It's all you've ever wanted."

I didn't really want to admit to Kaylee that it wasn't everything I dreamed. She spent years listening to me talk about how amazing life would be once I got to the academy. She'd be disappointed to hear how everything turned out.

"Yeah, it is," I said. "But it sounds like you had so much fun."

"I'm *having* a lot of fun," she reminded me. She nudged me in the side. "What's up with you? You sound... not quite like yourself."

I dropped my gaze and picked at my fingernail. "I just have a lot on my mind."

Kaylee frowned. "Is this about your semester final?"

I groaned. "You heard about that?"

Kaylee chuckled. "A Davina exposes themselves and it goes viral? Of course I'm going to hear about it."

"Oh, God." I covered my face. "Please don't tell me that's why you came home. I don't want you to stop your trip for me—"

"No," Kaylee said quickly. "Absolutely not, Cora. I've been planning this trip home for months. I just didn't tell you because I wanted to surprise you."

Kaylee crossed her legs on the bed and turned to face me. "I want to know all about your first semester."

"There's not much to tell," I admitted, though I wasn't sure that was true.

"What about your partner?" she asked. "Last time we talked, you sounded unsure of him. Did you get reassigned?"

"No," I said. "We actually worked things out. Problem is, I like him now, but he's dating this horrible girl."

With that confession, everything else just started pouring out of me. I told Kaylee all about Kellan and myself—how we couldn't get along, how I took him to the Malum portal site, how I broke his wing, and how he decided to ditch me for our final last minute. I couldn't stop talking as I recounted everything that happened during the semester final—how Celina had tried to make me fail and Kellan showed up anyway to help. It felt good to finally be saying everything out loud—and to someone I trusted.

"The Alliance threatened me, Kaylee," I said as I reached the end of my explanation. "I guess the video Kellan and I put out explaining the whole thing as a hoax satisfied them, because I haven't heard from them since. But Kaylee, I'm not sure I did the right thing."

I didn't realize I felt that way until I said it out loud.

She eyed me sideways. "What do you mean? You did what they wanted."

I bit my lower lip. "Yeah, but what if…?"

I trailed off.

"What if, what?" Kaylee asked.

"What if the Alliance is wrong?" The words felt dirty coming from my own mouth. I'd never questioned the Alliance before. They were here to protect us, to keep the Aedes and Davina a secret. People had retaliated against us before—tortured us, even. We were powerful, but not powerful enough to survive the kinds of weapons that could be used against us. That's why we had to hide in the shadows. But maybe coming out wouldn't be all bad…

Kaylee furrowed her brow. "What are you trying to say, Cora?"

I swallowed. "I've been listening to all these stories about people who have had these amazing spiritual experiences. Maybe the people who fear us are in the minority. Maybe we can bring hope and beauty to people if they just knew the truth."

Kaylee's features hardened. "Do you really want to take that chance, Cora? People motivated by fear are… deadly."

My mouth went dry at the word *deadly*.

"Not if we fight back," I argued. "Look at the world. We're in constant war about one thing or another. It's human nature to fight. But do you know how many people have died in the name of their gods for centuries? If people knew the truth, maybe we could get along."

Kaylee eyed me cautiously, as if I'd gone insane. "Even if they knew the truth, people would deny it. You saw what everyone said about that video. The evidence was right there, and people didn't want to believe it."

"That's one video," I said. "One that was easy to explain away as false. The Aedes and Davina have years of proof that we can heal and so much evidence that we *help*."

"Yes, but you have to get people to *believe* you," Kaylee pointed out. "Cora, I'm not saying you're wrong. I'd love if we didn't have to hide who we truly are. But this isn't that simple."

My throat closed up. "The Aedes and Davina used to fight, too, Kaylee. My parents changed that. Maybe it's time we figure out a way to work alongside humans, too."

"We do work with them through the Alliance," she reminded me.

"Yeah, a *select* group of government officials," I said.

"Cora..." Kaylee trailed off, like she didn't know what else to say.

"You'd get it if you saw the kind of peace people get when they know the truth." The words slipped out before I could stop myself.

Kaylee stilled. "What are you talking about?"

My whole body tensed, and I hesitated.

"Cora." Kaylee's voice became very stern. "What do you mean?"

I couldn't hide it from Kaylee. She was my best friend, and I knew she'd pry it out of me one way or another. I lowered my voice anyway, though my parents were downstairs. "When I was in the hospital with Kellan, I showed my wings to these two little girls—"

"Oh my God, Cora!" Kaylee threw her hand over her mouth.

"Shh…" I hissed.

She dropped her voice. "You know exposing yourself is strictly forbidden!"

"I know," I said. "But these girls… one of them was sick, and—"

"So what?" Kaylee asked. "Let the other Aedes and Davina help her."

"It wasn't about healing her," I replied. "Not physically, at least. Kaylee, you should've seen her face. She was… completely at peace."

"Okay, but that's a child," Kaylee pointed out. "What about adults who are so stuck in their ways that they'll *kill* you just to maintain their own worldview?"

"I don't think that would happen—"

"Think harder!" Kaylee snapped.

I recoiled. Kaylee pressed her fingers to her eyes. After a few moments, she dropped them and looked up at me. "I'm just worried for you, Cora. I don't want you getting hurt."

"Relax, Kaylee." I reached out and placed my hand on top of hers. "I'm going to be fine."

I wasn't sure how well I could keep that promise.

"Are you ready for your second semester?" Dad asked brightly as the tall white boundary walls of the Harris Academy campus came into view.

Winter break had passed far too quickly, and Dad had offered to drive me back to the city. He was trying to make me feel better, but I could sense the unease in his tone. Mom hadn't come with, as she had to stay back at the restaurant.

"Ugh," I groaned, leaning against the passenger side window. "Don't ask."

He nudged me. "Everything's going to be fine, Cora. It's a new semester—a fresh start. You can put your semester final behind you."

My guts sank. Putting the past behind me was all I wanted to do, but somehow, I didn't think that was going to happen—not the way Chancellor Harris had talked about things. No matter what I did to convince the Alliance and the rest of the world of my lie, there was no coming back from this.

Dad slowed the car to follow traffic. It was like move-in day all over again, except it felt melancholy. I wasn't excited like I used to be. The car remained quiet, as if Dad could feel my low mood in the air.

"What's going on up there?" Dad mumbled. He craned his neck to look ahead of us.

I hadn't been paying attention to the streets outside until he said something. When I looked ahead of us, I saw what was holding up traffic. My jaw tensed. People walked up and down the sidewalk holding picket signs. It wasn't like the last time I ran into the Infantry, the group that frequently protested outside campus. They'd grown in numbers, so much that there were at least a hundred people yelling obscenities as cars passed.

Barricades had been set up along the street to the academy entrance, and campus security was trying to keep all cars out who weren't faculty or students. Aedes and Davina students stood behind the barricades, as if standing guard in case a brawl broke out. My stomach dropped when I saw a face I recognized and despised.

Colt Walter stood atop a parked car and yelled into a megaphone. "They're not what they seem!" he screamed, pointing to all the cars. "They're not even human! They're demons come to steal our souls straight from our bodies."

"*We want the truth. We want the truth,*" the group chanted.

I pressed my hand to my face. "Dear God. Are they serious?"

Dad shifted his hands on the steering wheel. "If you don't want to go, you don't have to, Cora."

I hesitated as an internal battle raged inside of me. Of course I wanted to go. I still wanted to become an EMT, and nothing—not even Colt Walter and his Infantry—could stop me. I'd just like to go back knowing campus was safe.

"I'll be fine, Dad," I told him.

"Okay," he replied with a frown.

Another fifteen minutes of silence passed as we crept along the street. I sank lower and lower in my chair as we neared the line of protestors. But it didn't matter how deep I sank or how much I tried to conceal myself. As we neared the barricades, Colt Walter's eyes turned inside my vehicle, and his gaze locked on mine. His lips twisted into a sneer, and a shiver traveled down my spine.

Colt pointed straight at me. "It's her!"

My heart leapt into my throat as dozens of Infantry members started running toward our vehicle.

"Lock the car!" I shouted to my dad.

He jumped in his seat and clicked the button next to him with not a moment to spare. My pulse quickened as people surrounded our vehicle and started pounding on the windows. Dad laid on the horn, but it didn't do any good.

"Go away!" I shouted. Another useless attempt.

Colt shoved his way through the Infantry members around the car and walked straight up to my dad's window. He held his megaphone up and held it so close to the car that it almost touched the glass. "She's the demon who exposed herself!" he spat. "She's living evidence of the truth! Get out of the car and show us what you truly are!"

"I'll get out of the car and kick your fucking ass!" I screamed back at him. I could light the jackass up in flames, too—if I had an Aedes to power up my essence. Problem was, I hadn't been powered up all break, so the best I could do was knock him out. It was good enough for me, at least.

"Is that a threat?" Colt growled through the megaphone.

My hands quivered. If it were just Colt and me, I could totally take him on, but my dad and I were surrounded by so many angry people that they were starting to shake the car. Even if I wanted to fight this self-righteous asshole, I'd never get a shot at him before the rest of them took me down.

"Relax, Cora," Dad said in a calm, collected tone. "I've got this."

Dad shifted the car into park and reached for the police-issued gun on his hip. But before he could grab it, the crowd began to disperse. I didn't realize why until I saw a muscular figure step in front of Colt. He stood with his back to me and his arms crossed over his chest, looking out at the Infantry members.

"Step away from the car," he said firmly.

Kellan?

My heart lifted as more and more people like him began to surround the car, all sharing the same protective stance.

"Dad, roll your window down," I begged.

Dad frowned, but he rolled it down a crack. The cold January breeze entered the car.

"Kellan?" I called. "What are you doing?"

Kellan turned around, and my heart melted when his eyes met mine. "I've got this, partner."

Kellan turned back toward Colt. "If you want her, you're going to have to go through us to get her."

Colt's face paled momentarily, but a second later, it turned into a sneer. He glared at Kellan with pure hatred in his eyes and chuckled. "Oh, I'll get her. You just wait and see."

My mouth went dry. Colt cocked his head to the group, and the people surrounding the car dispersed. Kellan and the other supernaturals didn't move, though. They followed us along the road until we made it through the barricades. I was acutely aware of Dad's hands tightening on the steering wheel and his eyes continuously flickering down the gun on his belt.

The whole time, I couldn't stop thinking about what Colt had said.

I'll get her. You just wait and see.

He wasn't the kind of guy to just walk away. I wasn't looking forward to whatever it was he had in store for me.

"Cora, we need to talk."

I'd barely had a moment in my dorm before Chancellor Harris summoned me to her office. I hadn't even seen my roommate, Laura, or got the chance to unpack my suitcase.

"What's wrong?" My knees shook as I stepped into her office. It was a relief to sit in the chair across from her. Normally, I wasn't so nervous and timid, but I usually knew what to expect. Lately, surprises were being thrown at me from all directions. I had a feeling Chancellor Harris was about to throw me another one.

Chancellor Harris ignored my question and instead said, "Are you okay?"

I tucked a strand of brown hair behind my ear. "Yeah, of course. Why do you ask?"

She took a deep breath. "After everything that happened, I just wanted to make sure you're getting along well. The group outside campus hasn't hurt anyone yet, but I fear..."

She trailed off, and my stomach sank.

"You're afraid I'll be the first one?" I guessed.

She pressed her lips together and nodded. "I've seen all this happen before, Cora, and I would hate to see any one of my students get in the middle of it."

I furrowed my brow. "You've seen what happen before?"

"The fear." She swiveled her chair to look out the big window behind her desk. She stared out into the distance to the walls surrounding campus. We couldn't see the Infantry from here, but the deep, contemplating look in her eyes told me she was thinking about them.

"Years ago, the Aedes and Davina didn't get along," she said without looking at me. "We fought for millennia—all because we didn't understand each other. All because we *feared* each other. It was only when we learned that our powers worked better together that we finally declared an end to the war."

I didn't know why Chancellor Harris was telling me all this. I knew the stories well and had heard about the war first-hand from my parents, who'd been there with Chancellor Harris when it all happened. It was almost like… like she was trying to tell me something she couldn't say out loud.

I spoke slowly and deliberately, trying to decode her message. "So, if we want to prevent something like that from happening with the humans, we have to find a way to benefit everyone… But we already help them."

Chancellor Harris's eyes met mine. "They don't know that, though. And they mustn't."

I couldn't explain it, but there was something behind her eyes that conflicted with her words. Of course I knew we had to keep our existence a secret. We were outnumbered, and it was the only way to protect ourselves. Helping the humans by using our healing abilities had been a compromise with the government when they discovered what we were. They wanted to use us in war, but we wouldn't do it, and they were too afraid of us to force us. And yet, we were too afraid to expose ourselves.

Is that what our existence had come down to—fear? Were we perhaps hiding ourselves from the world because we feared what the humans would do to us? It was just a vicious cycle. One set of fear right after the other.

I hated fear. Fear was the worst of all emotions. It stopped you in your tracks. It put you at a standstill. Every other emotion drove you in one way or another, but fear halted progress all together. But right now—the way Chancellor Harris was looking at me like there was something I needed to know—fear chilled me to the bone.

I swallowed. "So, what can we do before things get out of hand?"

Chancellor Harris cleared her throat. "Well, anything we *could* do is banned by the Alliance." Chancellor Harris crossed her hands over her desk and looked to me without blinking. "Short of starting a revolution, there's nothing we can do, Cora. Understand?"

My breath stalled in my chest. Chancellor Harris was saying all the right words to keep her place as head of the academy, but there was an underlying message in her tone I couldn't deny. Chancellor Harris knew she couldn't get involved in whatever happened next, so she was asking me to do it for her.

Holy crap! Did Chancellor Harris seriously want me to start a revolution?

"I'm only a freshman, Chancellor Harris," I reminded her aloud. "Even if I wanted to do anything, I'm not cut out for it."

Her lips curled into a smirk. "Of course you wouldn't do anything, Cora. It's against Alliance laws. But don't ever underestimate yourself because of your age or experience. Need I remind you that your parents and I were younger than you are now when we closed the portal to Malum and facilitated peace among the supernatural community?"

I'd never thought of how young my parents were when

they'd done all the wonderful things I'd heard about. It was crazy to think about.

Chancellor Harris looked at me in warning. "Whatever you do, Cora, I hope you will make the right choice."

I swallowed. Yeah, I hoped I did, too.

7

I hadn't stopped thinking about my conversation with Chancellor Harris by the time classes started on Monday.

"Are you okay?" Laura asked as we headed to the Science Building together.

I kept my face buried in my scarf. "I'm fine. Why do you ask?"

"Because you've been really quiet since we got back from break," she said.

"I'm just tired." The lie slipped out. I should've told her the truth—that I just had a lot on my mind—but I didn't know how to say it without worrying about her. I was still trying to figure out how to tell her about everything, so I decided to change the subject. "Hey, you finally got those new winter boots."

Laura opened the door to the Science Building and stomped her boots off inside the entrance. "Yeah, I got them for Christmas. Do you like them?"

She stuck her foot out to show me the black boots with fur on the top.

"I love them," I said.

"My class is this way." Laura pointed down the hall. "I'll see you at lunch. We're going to talk about this then, okay?"

I nodded. I knew I couldn't keep all this from Laura much longer. "See you."

Laura and I waved goodbye to each other. I headed in the opposite direction of her toward my Intermediate Firefighting class. My gut sank when I stepped into the room and saw Kellan and Celina sitting up front. He had an arm draped over the back of her chair and was leaned in close to her. He brushed her short hair away from her ear and whispered something into it. She giggled in a way that made me want to hurl.

Kellan caught my eye as I passed by their table. He hesitated, like he wasn't sure whether to sit next to me—his partner—or Celina—his girlfriend. Celina's laughter instantly died, and she shot me daggers. I breezed past their table and took a seat in the back. Kellan shot me a look of apology, and I forced a smile back. I'd be lying if I said I wasn't disappointed that he didn't want to work with me in this class.

Professor Taylor and Professor Arnold entered the room a few moments later. They were the same teaching pair who taught our Intro to Firefighting class last semester.

"Welcome back, students!" Professor Arnold said at the front of the room. He was in a good mood like always. "Before we begin, I'd like to congratulate you all on passing your first semester final."

At the front of the room, Celina scoffed. She glanced in my direction and mumbled something under her breath. I couldn't hear her from here, but I was pretty sure it was along the lines of, "*Some* of us passed."

My lips tightened. Did she not realize she was insulting her boyfriend right in front of him? I wasn't the only one who'd failed.

"You've all come a long way and have proven you have what it takes to continue in the program," Professor Arnold continued. "This semester, we'll be diving into more advanced tactics for controlling fires and new scenarios with your essence. Let's get started."

I still had my eyes on Celina and Kellan. Kellan said something I didn't hear. Celina placed a gentle hand on his shoulder and replied, "Oh, no. Not you. I know what happened wasn't your fault."

Her comment was laughable. When you really thought about it, it was all Celina's fault.

~

Kellan approached me in the hall after class. "Hey, Cora."

I stopped in my tracks and glanced around, expecting Celina to be attached to his side, but she was headed off toward another class in the opposite direction.

"What is it, Kellan?" I snapped without meaning to. "Come to insult me some more?"

His brow furrowed deeply. "Insult you?"

"Isn't that what you and Celina were doing the whole lecture?" I accused.

I pressed my lips together. I didn't want to fight with Kellan. It would only make the whole situation worse. Besides, he wasn't the problem. His girlfriend was.

Kellan sighed. "Come on, Cora. She didn't mean it. She's just upset because I got hurt."

"Why are you making excuses for her?" I asked.

Kellan frowned. "Look, I'll talk to her, okay?"

I relaxed a little. "So, what do you need?"

"I was wondering if you wanted to get lunch together," he said.

My whole body tensed. "You—you want to get lunch with me?"

"Well, yeah," he replied simply. "We're partners." He paused a moment before adding, "Wait. We're not still fighting, are we?"

I let out a light chuckle. "After everything that happened? No."

"Oh, good." He pressed his hand to his heart for show.

Damn it. It was hard not to like him when he wasn't acting like a jerk all the time.

I didn't say anything while we walked, and the silence was awkward. Kellan must've noticed, because he stopped just inside the front doors.

"Cora?" he asked. "Are you okay?"

I was still getting used to him showing concern for me, and it made my head spin every time.

I pushed a strand of dark hair behind my ear. "Okay? Of course I'm okay."

"You don't seem like yourself," he observed. "It's like you have something on your mind."

Only everything.

"Is this about that Colt guy?" Kellan asked.

I shook my head. "No, but thanks again for stepping in."

Kellan smirked. "Hey, I'm your partner. It's what I'm here for."

I raised a playful eyebrow. "Protecting me from weirdos? Because you've done that more than once."

I still hadn't forgotten how Kellan had shown up last semester when the Infantry attacked Laura and me outside the academy.

Kellan shrugged. "I've gotta protect my own. Who would I heal with if I didn't have you?"

My heart lifted in my chest while he spoke, then quickly plummeted at the last comment. I knew he didn't mean it like that, but it sounded like he was only keeping me around so he could pass his classes.

"Aw, you're such a sweetheart," I teased as I punched him lightly on the shoulder. Inside, a rock had settled in my gut. "The truth is, Kellan, I have something I need to talk to you about."

Kellan glanced around at the people coming in and out of the building. He cocked his head, and I followed him into an empty classroom. He closed the door behind us and turned to me. I was surprised by the deep look of concern in his features.

"What's wrong, Cora?" he asked, like he genuinely cared.

I took a deep breath and clutched the strap of my bag tighter. "Chancellor Harris and I spoke."

Kellan furrowed his brow, as if wondering where this was going. "About what?"

"Well, about..." I pressed my lips together. "It's hard to explain, because she didn't really *say* anything to me."

"What do you mean?" he questioned.

"It was like... like she was trying to send me a silent message," I admitted. "She said she worried that the Infantry was going to hurt me, but that there was nothing we could do about it. But then she started talking about how she and my parents closed the portal to Malum and how they were younger than me. It was like she wanted me to take action somehow."

Kellan considered my words. "Take action?"

"Yeah, like try to make peace with the Infantry or something," I said. "Kellan, I think she wants us to reveal ourselves."

Kellan's features fell, and the muscles in his jaw tightened. "No, Cora. You must've misread her."

I crossed my arms. "I don't think I did."

"You've heard Chancellor Harris say it a million times—keeping our secret is vital," Kellan pointed out. "Besides, the Alliance would have you arrested. Why would you want to reveal yourself after you just covered up the last incident?"

I thought back to the girls in the hospital room, but I didn't mention them to Kellan. "I think the truth will bring people peace, Kellan."

"You can't make that decision for everyone," he shot back.

I ran my fingers through my hair, trying to find the words that could explain how I felt. "Look, I… I…" I didn't even know where to start.

Kellan raised an eyebrow, waiting for my explanation.

I sighed. "I used to think all that mattered was getting through school and shit like that, but life is so much more complicated."

"You're right," he said bluntly. "It is."

A silent beat passed where we just stared at each other. I didn't expect him to agree with me.

Kellan breathed a deep sigh. "But exposing ourselves, Cora… That only makes things *more* complicated."

"For a while, maybe," I agreed. "But once things settle down—"

"How do you know they'll settle down?" he interrupted, taking on a harsher tone.

I gaped at him. "I just have to trust that they will."

Kellan started pacing through the classroom. "You have to remember history, Cora."

"I know my history," I shot back.

He raked his fingers through his hair and turned back to me. "Then you'll remember when we were kids and that story about the people who captured those Aedes and ripped their wings off."

I swallowed. "I remember the story."

"Right, but do you *feel* it?" he asked harshly.

My voice became small. "What do you mean?"

"Have you ever felt the persecution for what you are?" Kellan repeated. "Do you have even the slightest idea what it'd be like if you exposed yourself?"

I wanted to tell him about how I showed myself to the girls in the hospital, but he was so worked up that I couldn't do it. My heart sank.

"You have no idea, Cora," he said through clenched teeth, like he was trying not to freak out on me. The truth was, he was scaring me. There was a look in his eyes I'd never seen before, one that chilled me to the bone. I didn't know what it meant. "Before you go exposing yourself, think of how it would affect everyone else."

I opened myself to reply, but my phone began ringing in my pocket, cutting me off. I grabbed it and saw my dad was calling. I turned my gaze to Kellan before I answered. "I'm not trying to be selfish, Kellan. I'm trying to do what's best for everyone."

I punched the screen on my phone and turned away from him. "Hey, Dad. What's up?"

"Cora?" he asked breathlessly.

My stomach plummeted to my toes. I could instantly tell by the sound of his voice something was wrong.

"I'm here. What is it?" I demanded.

"Where are you, Cora?" Dad asked. "Are you safe?"

Kellan heard my father through the phone, and his features instantly softened. He stared at me wide-eyed.

"Yeah, Dad. I'm fine," I answered. "I'm with Kellan at school."

Dad breathed a sigh of relief. "I'm so glad to hear that."

"Why, Dad?" I pressed. He was really starting to freak me out. "What's wrong?"

The line went silent for a moment, until Dad took a big breath. "It's the restaurant, Cora. There's been an explosion."

8

The room spun around me. I was sure my father was saying something more, but I couldn't process it. Mom's restaurant was gone? The business she built from the ground up? Our family's prime source of income? Her very passion?

I could hardly wrap my head around it. I'd spent so many summers there, coloring in the booth in the corner or helping fold napkins in the back. How could something like this happen?

Minutes must've passed, but it felt like a lifetime. I sank into one of the seats at the front of the empty classroom. Kellan grabbed my phone from my hand and started talking to my dad.

"Mister Marek," he said.

Dad replied to him, but I didn't hear what he said. I was still trying to make sense of what my father had said. How could my mother's beautiful restaurant be reduced to nothing by my very own element? I wished I'd been there to put out the flames. Hell, why didn't my dad do it? He had fire essence the same as me.

They exchanged a few more words I couldn't process.

"Are you sure it can't be salvaged?" Kellan asked my father.

I snapped back to attention, curious to hear his answer.

"The building's too far gone," Dad said. "They suspect some sort of accelerant was used, but they're also considering the possibility of a gas leak. We won't know more until the investigation concludes."

"Was anyone hurt?" I blurted. "Where's Mom?"

"Shh…" Kellan said, listening closely to my dad. "Okay. We'll be there as soon as we can."

Kellan hung up, and I gaped at him.

"Why did you do that!?" I yelled as I shot up out of my chair. "I had more questions."

"I'll tell you in the car." Kellan grabbed my elbow and dragged me out of the room.

I pulled against him. "No, Kellan! Stop!"

He dropped my arm, but his lips tightened in anger when he looked at me. "Look, do you want to go home and see your parents or not?"

I planted my feet firmly in place. I didn't care that there were a group of people passing by. I wasn't moving until Kellan gave me answers. "Tell me what my dad said."

Kellan pushed his hand through his hair. "Your mom's going to make it, but—"

"Oh God!" My hand shot over my mouth. I didn't like the way he said that. It wasn't good at all.

Kellan placed his hands on my shoulders to get me to calm down. "*But…* she was badly burned."

Tears pricked at my eyes. "How bad? Will they be able to heal her?"

"They're working on it as we speak," Kellan told me.

I dropped my shaking hand. "What else did my dad say?"

"He wanted you to stay here at the academy."

"No. No way," I replied. I started walking briskly toward the door. "I'm going to see my mom."

"I knew you'd say that," Kellan said as he fell into step beside me. "Which is why I told your dad we're going to Eagle Valley. I'm taking you. I'm not letting you do this alone."

My chest twisted into knots as I thought of what my mother must be going through right now. But when Kellan said that, the knot eased ever so slightly.

We hurried out of the Science Building and to the parking lot. The cold wind bit at my nose, and my hands shook as I reached for the passenger-side door of Kellan's black sedan.

Kellan drove out of the academy gates. The street was empty, save for a few cars passing along.

It was an hour drive back to Eagle Valley, and it must've been the longest hour of my life. I had no idea what sort of condition my mother was in, and I was imagining the worst. Even with essence to heal and powers of her own, burns were dangerous. If they burnt through layers of skin, it took great care to heal each layer.

Kellan glanced to me from the driver's seat the closer we got to Eagle Valley. "Cora, please say something. You haven't talked the whole ride."

I kept my eyes on the landscape out of the window. This area was home, but it didn't feel right. I swallowed the lump in my throat. "I'm scared, Kellan."

"Your mom will be fine," he assured me. "Your dad said—"

"That's not the only thing I'm scared of," I admitted.

"Then what, Cora?" he begged. "Whatever it is, you can tell me."

"I know," I said in a small voice. He was my partner. We were supposed to trust each other, but I just couldn't bear to say what I was thinking out loud. I took a deep breath and forced the words out. "I'm scared because I'm afraid someone did this on purpose."

Kellan pressed his lips together. He didn't answer right away, like he was wondering the same thing.

"My dad basically admitted it," I pointed out. "He said an accelerant might've been used. Kellan, what if this was my fault?"

"No!" He slammed his hand against the steering wheel, which made me jump. "Don't say that."

"But it's a real possibility," I argued. "Nothing like this has ever happened to my family. Now my mom's restaurant burns down days after Colt Walter threatened me."

A shadow fell over Kellan's face. "Even if he did this, you can't blame yourself. You're not the one who started the fire."

Kellan's words should've reassured me, but they didn't. My pulse quickened the closer we got to my hometown. By the time we entered the outskirts of town near Galen High School, my heart was hammering against my chest.

"Are you sure you want to see this?" Kellan asked me softly.

I closed my eyes and nodded. "This is what I'm going to school for."

"Cora, this isn't some class assignment," he reminded me. "This is personal."

My hands knotted in my lap. "I know. I can handle it."

I wasn't lying, but I also wasn't prepared for what I was about to see. Ahead, Main Street was blocked off by a *Road Closed* sign. All I saw were the barricades and a huge crowd of onlookers. Kellan parked along the street as close as we could get. I jumped out of the car before he even shut the car off.

I sprinted toward the intersection—and my feet halted beneath me when I rounded the corner. Time seemed to stand still as an invisible knife pierced my stomach and gutted me.

Behind all the emergency response vehicles and flashing lights of police cars, Mom's restaurant was nothing more than a charred memory of what it once was. The fire had already been put out, but it was like I was still watching it burn. I didn't even recognize the restaurant, and I'd never know what the building was if it hadn't been there my whole life. The roof had completely caved in, and the sign that read *Cozy Cafe* was nowhere to be seen. Anywhere that wasn't charred to bits had soot all over it. The businesses that sandwiched my mom's restaurant had experienced minimal damage. It was clear that whoever had done this had intentionally targeted my mom.

My gaze darted around the area, searching for any signs of my parents. My eyes fell on my dad next to the other police officers. He was in his usual police gear and was talking to his deputy.

"Dad!" I cried as I raced over to him.

The officer who was trying to keep people away from the area let me pass.

Dad turned in my direction. He looked relieved to see me. "Cora."

I slammed into him, throwing my arms around his neck. Dad hugged me back tightly. He ran his fingers through my hair as I buried my face into his shoulder. The smell of smoke filled my nostrils, and tears began to stream down my face.

I heard Kellan come up beside us, but I didn't want him to see me cry, so I wiped the tears into my dad's shoulder and put on a mask as I drew away from him. The longer I held it, the tighter the knot in my chest became.

"Dad, where's Mom?" I demanded. "How bad is it?"

"Cora, calm down," Dad insisted, placing a hand on my shoulder. He held on tight, like he couldn't contain his anger. "Your mother is in good hands."

"Why aren't you with her?" I cried.

Dad's lips tightened. He was always trying to play the hero. I knew why he wasn't with Mom, though he wouldn't say it. He wanted to catch the bastard who did this to her.

"How did this happen?" I demanded. "How many people were hurt?"

Dad shot a glance to the other officers, then guided me away. Kellan was polite and didn't follow.

Dad took a deep breath. "Everyone else got out when the fire started. Your mom…"

My hands shot over my mouth. "What'd she do?"

Both of my parents sort of had a hero complex. Mom was almost too kind-hearted for her own good.

A muscle in dad's jaw popped. "Your mom went back inside to save her recipes moments before the explosion."

"Oh my God!" I cried. "Why doesn't she keep those on a damn computer like a normal person?"

"Well, they came from Grandma Gloria, and—"

"I don't care!" I shouted. "She could've been killed."

Dad's tone softened. "Do you want to go see her?"

"No, Dad," I said sarcastically while wiping tears from my eyes. "That's not why I came all the way home."

Dad frowned, but he didn't reprimand me for my sarcasm. "Okay, let's go."

Dad started leading me toward his police cruiser. Kellan stopped me before I could get in the car.

"Hey, Cora," he said softly. "You take all the time you need. I'll be here for you when you get back."

"Wait," I replied. "You're not coming?"

"This stuff with your mom is private," he told me. "Go visit her."

My stomach sank. "You don't have to wait around."

Kellan frowned. "How are you going to get back to the academy."

Right. I glanced to my dad, who was climbing into the driver's seat. "I'll get my dad to drive me back. Thanks for driving me, Kellan. And just… being here for me."

"Of course." Kellan reached out and wiped a tear from my eye before I even realized it had formed. We both stilled at the contact.

Kellan cleared his throat and broke the silence. "You should go."

I didn't feel like I could leave him like that. Before I knew what I was doing, I threw my arms around his neck and squeezed him into a tight hug. He tensed for a moment, then relaxed as he hugged me back. It was weird for us, but somehow, it also felt natural.

I drew away from Kellan, though I didn't want to. "Really, Kellan. Thank you."

At that, I turned around and climbed into my dad's cruiser. "Let's go see Mom."

I stepped into the hospital with a heavy sense of dread in my stomach. The nurse pointed us in the direction of Mom's room. I pushed the door open, and my heart stalled in my chest.

Mom lay on the bed with bandages covering her arms and legs. Burn marks marred her face, and patches of hair were missing. It was obvious they'd already tried healing some of it, but I couldn't imagine it looking any worse.

Mom's eyes darted to Dad and me when we entered, but she didn't move. It was so bad she could hardly show emotion on her face.

"Cora," she breathed, like she was relieved, though her voice came out strained.

"Oh my God, Mom," I whispered as I stepped into the room. I stopped at her bedside and ran my hands lightly over the bandages. "It's bad…"

"I'll be okay," Mom said, but I didn't know how she did it when she looked like this.

I sniffled. "I know you can heal, but to be in that kind of pain in the first place…"

I looked down to her arms, though I tried not to picture

what was beneath the bandages. Mom must've noticed my expression because she rushed to explain. "I'm not going to lie to you, Cora. There are some deep burns. The healers have already taken care of the minor ones, but the others they'll have to do in stages. I'm less worried about the injuries and more worried about the restaurant."

I scoffed. That was such a Mom thing to say.

"Ryn," Dad said to her sternly. "You need to worry about healing. Forget about the restaurant."

Mom pressed her lips together. "That restaurant is my life, Marek."

"And the insurance will pay for it." Dad took her face gently in his hands and tried to reassure her. "We'll get through this, Ryn."

Dad pressed a kiss to Mom's forehead. She swallowed as he drew away.

"At least I still have you two," she whispered, looking at us both longingly.

The lump in my throat grew bigger. "Mom, I'm so sorry."

"Don't be," she said gently. "It's not your fault."

I shook my head. "You don't know that."

"What do you mean, Cora?" Dad demanded. "You don't think those people from the academy had anything to do with this?"

I turned my gaze up to Dad. "I don't know. It's too big of a coincidence. If someone wanted to hurt me and couldn't get inside the academy, what do you think their next move would be?"

Mom's lips turned down at the corners, but it looked like it pained her. "Going after our family restaurant. Cora..."

"I know I don't have any evidence," I said. "And you may never catch the guy who did this. But something deep in my gut says this is about me."

Dad pressed his lips together. "They're afraid of you," he said thoughtfully.

"No." I shook my head. "This isn't the kind of thing someone does out of fear. Whoever did this—and I think I know who—they did it out of anger."

And that was the most dangerous motive of all.

After the fire, I didn't feel like myself. Every now and then, I'd forget that anything had happened, and then it came rushing back like a tidal wave. Colt Walter had hurt my family. That wasn't something I could easily forgive.

I hoped that the justice system would run its course, but according to Dad, Colt Walter had a rock solid alibi backed up by his Infantry group. I was shocked at first, but then I started to wonder if Colt had somehow fabricated the alibi. As for suspects, they had none, which seemed awfully fishy to me considering Dad basically admitted it was arson.

At this point, I didn't know what to do. Chancellor Harris wanted me to fight back, but Kellan wasn't on board, and neither was Laura.

"Kellan's right," she told me. "Exposing ourselves will only get you arrested by the Alliance."

"They didn't arrest me last time," I reminded her.

She frowned. "What will happen on your second offence? They won't forgive you again, Cora. You won't get a second chance to explain it away. I'm not sure I get what you hope to accomplish."

Laura's words felt harsh at the time, but the more I thought on it, the more I wondered if she was right. Even when I exposed myself at my semester final, people wrote it off as unbelievable. Perhaps they'd never believe what was right in front of them, no matter how many times I showed them.

But Laura hadn't seen those young girls' faces at the hospital. She didn't know what it felt like to be someone else's source of hope. All I wanted was for everyone else to feel that sense of peace.

I tried to put it out of my mind, but it kept creeping back in even weeks later. I was sitting alone in the Clark Hall rec room, going over my human physiology homework, when the sound of a child's voice came over the TV. I looked up to see a young girl with pretty curls and chocolate eyes staring back at me. She was standing outside in the snow with a thick coat wrapped around her, and she was talking to someone beyond the camera. She held something in her hand, though I couldn't see what it was.

Saddie?

"It was my sister's idea," she told the interviewer. "She wanted everyone at school to know that even if they're bullied or they feel bad sometimes, they're not alone. All the kids will see the tree when they're walking into school, so they remember all day that everything's going to be okay."

The camera angle shifted, and it showed this large, beautiful evergreen growing at the front of one of the local schools. Hundreds of angel-wing ornaments hung from the branches. Names had been scribbled across each one in permanent marker—one for each student at Becca and Saddie's school.

My heart warmed.

The camera shifted back to Saddie. "I think if my sister were here right now, she'd be really proud. She never got to see the tree, but she would've loved it."

My stomach dropped. Becca was gone?

The news hit me like a bulldozer. If I hadn't been sitting, I'd have been knocked off my feet.

Gone...

No, she wasn't gone forever. Her essence was out there. That peace she'd found had inspired her to create this angel tree for her classmates. Her legacy lived on.

Something sparked in my heart at the realization. I barely knew what I was doing when I jumped up from the couch and shoved my textbook in my bag. All I knew was that I had to see Becca one last time. I had to witness the legacy she left behind.

I ran back to my room to drop off my homework and pick up my jacket. Laura wasn't around, since she was in her elementals class. I threw on my jacket and tightened my scarf around my neck as I left the dorm hall. I left out the back gate to the academy and walked the next block to the bus stop.

What am I doing?

The thought crossed my mind while I was waiting, then I wondered why I even questioned it in the first place. I shouldn't be ashamed of this. I couldn't turn back.

I rode the bus all the way across town, until it came close enough to the school that I could walk the rest of the way. I shivered at the cold winter air on my skin, but I didn't slow down. My heart pounded the closer I got...

And then I saw it, and everything stilled.

My heart slowed, and even the wind seemed to die down. A beautiful warmth surrounded me as I stopped across the street from the school and looked up at Becca's angel tree. The clouds parted, and sunlight shone down on the tree. The white angel wing ornaments twisted and turned in a beautiful, sparkling display. It was as if I could feel Becca's essence around the tree, sharing her message of peace and beauty.

The street was eerily quiet. It was so unusual that it snapped me back to attention. I looked both ways, then crossed the street to the angel tree. I stopped when I got close enough to touch it. I pulled my glove off and reached out to run my fingers over the nearest ornament. It was strangely warm, considering the chilly weather. As the ornament twisted around, the name written on it came into view.

Becca.

I inhaled a sharp breath. It was like a message from Becca herself, though I didn't know what it meant.

Moments later, the sound of a diesel engine met my ears, pulling me out of my trance. I glanced down the street to see a line of school busses driving toward the school. They turned into the parking lot and stopped next to the front doors. I didn't realize how late it was already, but it must've been time for school to let out.

I didn't pay much attention to the kids flooding out of the school and onto the busses. I kept my gaze on the angel ornaments, reading each name. I didn't know exactly what I was looking for. I hoped to see Saddie's name, but each name I read filled me with a warm, fuzzy sensation. It was like the entire tree was a list of the people Becca had inspired.

"It's you again!"

A familiar voice caught my attention. I turned to see Saddie letting go of an older man's hand and running in my direction.

A smile broke across my face when I saw her. "Hey, how are you?" I asked.

Saddie spread her arms and threw them around me, squeezing me tight.

"Whoa," I chuckled, totally caught off guard.

"I'm so glad you made it," she said as she pulled away from me.

"What do you mean?" I asked.

Saddie looked up to me with bright eyes. "Becca wanted you to see it," she stated simply.

"Me?" I balked.

Saddie nodded. "She made it because of you."

10

I couldn't get what Saddie had said out of my mind.

She made it because of you.

Becca had died, and her last wish was to inspire others—because of me. The idea had totally floored me. I'd never been an inspiration to anyone.

And maybe it was because I'd always had to hide who I was.

I still hadn't mentioned it to Laura or Kellan. I didn't know how to tell them that I'd shown my wings to those two girls. But the guilt at keeping my secret was eating away at me. A heavy rock seemed to settle in my gut over the next few weeks, and every time I opened my mouth, it was as if my throat was closing up. I feared that the secret might slip out before I could stop it, and I knew nothing good could come of it.

"Cora?" Kellan nudged me in the side.

I snapped back to attention. We were sitting in our Art of Healing II lab, and Professor Kovski had just finished giving instructions on how to use our essence to diagnose internal issues. Each of the rats placed in front of us had some sort of internal anomaly, and we were supposed to spend the lab diagnosing them.

I swallowed the lump in my throat. "Sorry. I just spaced out a second. Let's get started."

Kellan looked down to the paper that'd been handed to us with our rat. "Symptoms include limping and low appetite."

"That's it?" I asked.

Kellan nodded. "Do you want to try looking inside?"

"Sure." I took a deep breath as Kellan placed his hand on my shoulder. He held my shoulder so many times throughout the past few months, and it was still like an electric shock every time he made contact—and it wasn't from his power, either.

Kellan drew my essence into himself, and power rushed through me as my essence channel opened wider. I let it flow into him for several moments before turning my attention to the sedated rat. I placed my hands over the creature and closed my eyes. I pushed a small amount of essence into his body. My magic explored the rat's body effortlessly. As I turned my focus to its legs, I felt my magic pushing back and resisting me.

"I can feel an injury in the left leg," I told Kellan.

"Perfect," he said. "Any idea what it is?"

I honed my attention on the leg, but no matter how hard I pushed, I couldn't pinpoint which tissue had been affected or how severe the injury was.

"Whoa!" Kellan grabbed my hands and yanked them away from the rat.

My eyes shot open. "What's wrong?"

Kellan stared back at me with knitted eyebrows, like he was trying hard to read my expression. "We're not supposed to heal them, Cora. The assignment is just to diagnose them."

"I wasn't trying to heal it," I told him.

He raised his eyebrows. "Your hands started to glow."

I glanced down to them. I'd never healed without purposely trying to. "I didn't mean to."

Kellan pressed his fingers to his eyes. "Cora, what's going on?"

I recoiled a bit. "What do you mean?"

He sighed and dropped his hands. Next to us, Caleb and Shaylene cried out in victory as they diagnosed their rat with a digestive disorder. No one was paying attention to Kellan and me, but he lowered his voice anyway.

"Your head's been all over the place lately," Kellan said gently.

A few months ago, I'd have been offended by his statement, but I knew now Kellan was only saying it to help me. He wasn't exactly wrong, either.

"We need to talk about what's going on," he stated. "If this is about your mom, you know you can borrow my car to go see her. Or better yet, I'll drive you."

That weight in my gut seemed to lift slightly at the generous offer, but it quickly settled back in when I reminded myself I was hiding things from him.

"No, Kellan," I said. "It's not about my mom. I've talked to her. She's doing better, and she says not to worry. It's about…"

I glanced around the room. Though no one was listening to us, I didn't feel comfortable talking about this out in the open.

"It's about something else," I settled on.

Kellan eyed me curiously. "Something you're going to talk to me about? Because as your partner—"

"I know," I said, cutting him off. "I know. Partners need to work together. And be honest with each other. And I want to. I just…"

I took a deep breath. "I'll tell you after class."

"Okay," Kellan agreed.

We turned back to our rat, but now my mind was so consumed with how to tell Kellan that I couldn't concentrate on the assignment. I expected Kellan to push me, but he kept quiet and waited patiently.

By the time class ended, I could tell he was about to burst

with impatience. He grabbed his bag and practically pushed me out of the classroom.

"So, what is it you want to tell me?" he asked once we were out in the hall.

I bit my lower lip. "It's not really something I can tell you. I have to show you."

Kellan didn't seem too keen on the idea of being kept in the dark, but he seemed really curious. We got in his car, and I pointed him in the direction of the elementary school.

When we reached the angel tree, I pointed to the curb. "Right here's fine."

Kellan pulled over and parked the car. He glanced up and down the street, until his eyes finally fell on the sparkling ornaments in the front of the school lawn.

"This is what you wanted to show me?" he asked. "What is it?"

I steadied my hands in my lap. "There's something I need to tell you, but you have to promise me you won't freak out."

He eyed me up and down, and his lips pressed into a thin line. "I'm not making any promises."

There was the Kellan I knew.

"Let's just say I don't need a lecture on this, okay?" I said. "It'll only make it worse."

The curiosity in Kellan's features deepened. "Cora, what's going on?"

I didn't know why I was so scared to tell anyone—but Kellan especially.

All my life, it'd been ingrained in me that exposing myself was among one of the worst things a supernatural could do—that if you exposed yourself, you exposed everyone. Though a part of me questioned it, another part of me still believed it was true. I felt like I'd failed everyone—Kellan, Kaylee, Laura, my parents... I felt like a sinner.

And yet, I felt like I'd done the right thing. It didn't make any sense.

I took a deep breath. "A few weeks ago when you were in the hospital, something happened."

Kellan's hands tightened on the steering wheel. "With that Alliance guy? John Maddox?"

"No," I said quickly, though Kellan didn't relax. If anything, the shadow over his face darkened.

"Then what?" he asked firmly.

"I met these girls," I said. "They were young, and they'd just been in a car accident. One of them had an immune disease—the kind of thing we can't heal."

Kellan didn't say anything. He just sat there and listened, which almost felt worse than if he'd said something by now.

"Anyway, the girls... they recognized me, and it was like... like they wanted me to be real. Like they needed a real angel in their lives," I admitted.

Kellan's eyes widened as he realized where I was going with this. "Cora, you didn't—"

"I showed them my wings," I spat out.

Kellan's eyes widened, and his knuckles turned white on the steering wheel. His lips pressed so thin I could barely see them.

"Are you serious, Cora?" Kellan demanded.

His tone was harsh, but he didn't move.

"I am," I stated firmly.

Kellan raked his fingers through his hair, though he didn't look at me. He kept his gaze out the front window. "Cora, you *know* what exposing ourselves could do!"

"I know, but Kellan—"

He finally turned to me, his eyes dark. "People get hurt when this kind of stuff happens," he growled.

My heart rate spiked. Kellan and I had fought before, but I'd never seen him look so angry.

"God, Cora," Kellan huffed. "You were *just* let off for

exposing yourself once. You got lucky. If the Alliance finds out about this, they'll arrest you."

"I know," I said. "You don't think I've already considered that?"

Kaylee had made sure I knew it when I talked to her about this.

"But so what?" I continued. "Let them arrest me. I wouldn't take back what I did."

"That's because you didn't get hurt!" Kellan roared.

I drew away from him, pressing myself up against the passenger-side door. His tone was so harsh, it was like he was taking this too personally.

Kellan shook his head and looked out his window, then mumbled under his breath. "It's no wonder the Infantry is after you."

My jaw dropped. *"Excuse* me?"

Kellan's nostrils flared as he turned back to me. "You heard me. What you did was reckless, Cora. If the Infantry wants to make an example out of the supernaturals, they were smart to choose you."

I crossed my arms. "That's low, Kellan."

He shrugged. "It's true."

I narrowed my eyes at him. I was about ready to step out of the car and walk back to campus myself. I thought Kellan and I had gotten over all this fighting. I thought I could confide in him. "You haven't even heard everything I want to say."

"Do I want to?" he asked. "You can't just go around exposing yourself, Cora."

"I exposed myself to save you!" I yelled.

"Yeah, the first time," he shot back. "What's your reasoning for the second? And how are you going to justify the one after that? And after that? When people get hurt, how are you going to justify that, Cora? What about your mom? Tell me how you justify that."

A lump rose to my throat. I could hardly get the words out. "I'm not the one who started that fire."

"You started it the moment you flew out of that burning building," he accused.

A piercing stab like a knife to the gut tore through me. I couldn't stop the next words from flying out of my mouth. "Would you rather I'd have left you there to die!?"

The car went dead silent, but it was the loudest silence I'd ever heard. My ears rang, and the words I'd just spoken echoed in my mind. *I'd have left you there to die...*

Kellan glared at me, but his tone finally softened. "I don't know, Cora. To protect the supernatural community, maybe you should've."

Tears welled in my eyes. Kellan would prefer to die than expose himself?

Kellan's hands shook in his lap, but he wouldn't look at me. "You don't get it, Cora. You've never felt what it's like to be persecuted for what you are."

He was *not* using the Aedes card on me.

"You mean because you're Aedes and I'm Davina?" I accused.

"No," he said simply. "You grew up surrounded by people who were just like you. You didn't have to worry about exposing yourself, because you got to do it wherever you went without repercussions."

"You did, too," I reminded him. "You went to a supernatural high school, too."

Kellan nodded. When he looked at me, his expression had softened. It was so full of sorrow that my heart became filled with compassion for him—and I didn't even know why.

"It wasn't always like that, though," Kellan said. "I'm only half Aedes. Remember?"

After a beat of silence, he continued. "I grew up between two worlds—the human world, where anyone could be what they wanted and the only secrets were where you hid your candy after Halloween, and the supernatural world, where I was forbidden from speaking to anyone about what I was. I didn't really know which world I belonged in. I didn't know how to tell a human from a supernatural. Hell, I still barely know the difference."

"Kellan," I said softly, but he cut me off.

"When I was eight, I went to a sleepover at this kid's house. There were four of us upstairs playing video games. One of my friends asked the other when his dad was coming home, and he said he wasn't. When we asked him why, he said, *'Because he's an angel.'*"

My breath stalled. I didn't know where Kellan's story was going, but the way he spoke, it didn't sound like it was going anywhere good.

Kellan continued. "To eight-year-old ears that had really only heard the term used for Davina, I was obviously concerned. I thought he meant his dad worked an important Davina job and was gone from home a lot. So when the other two boys left the room, I confronted my friend. I told him it was against the rules to tell people his dad was an angel. He didn't have any clue what I was talking about. I thought he was just playing along, you know. So I said the Aedes and Davina had to be kept a secret. He still said he didn't know what I meant, so I told him we didn't have to lie to each other anymore because I was Aedes. He *still* didn't know what I meant."

Kellan pressed his hand to his temple, like looking back on the memory was particularly stressful for him. "I should've just stopped there, but in my little kid mind, I was convinced my friend was a Davina. When he asked what an Aedes was, I remember saying, *'I'm Aedes. If your dad's an angel, you must've heard of us.'* He asked if an Aedes was some sort of guardian angel. I told him I was just like his dad with black wings, so he asked me to show him."

Oh, shit. I knew now where Kellan's story was going.

"I should've realized at that point that he only meant his father was dead, but I couldn't see past my excitement for meeting another boy my age who knew about our supernatural gifts," Kellan said. "And so I showed him my wings. It was the biggest mistake of my life. The other two boys walked in just then. The three of them took one look at my wings and began chanting *demon*. The first insisted that I was nothing like his father, that my wings must be black because I was evil. They dragged me outside in the rain where his mom couldn't hear and beat me to a pulp. I remember crying and shivering beneath a cold downpour, wondering where I went wrong and how my friends could turn on me so quickly. I realize now that they were frightened of me and took to hurting me before I could hurt them, but at the time, I just thought they were cruel. I stumbled several blocks home in the rain. I could barely see past my swollen eyes. Each raindrop was a needle of pain on my tender cheeks."

I pressed my hand to my mouth, and my eyes burned at the threat of tears. I had no idea Kellan had gone through something so horrible.

"When I got home, I told my mom the fight had been over a video game, but sometimes I wonder if she sensed the truth," Kellan admitted. "She transferred me to a new school that fall, and I never saw those boys again. I've never told anyone this story until now."

A single tear streaked my face. "Kellan," I whispered. "I'm so sorry you went through that."

He stared out the front window. "I don't want that to happen to any other kid like me. I want them to know what to say in those kinds of situations, be taught how to handle it. That's why I wanted to be part of the Alliance."

"You're right, Kellan," I said. "That should never happen to any other kid. And that's why I think it's worth telling people, so we can educate them, so they don't have to be afraid."

Kellan shook his head. "You don't want to take that risk, Cora."

"Kellan, I already showed two girls what I am, and it inspired them," I told him. "That tree right there was made by these girls for the other kids, so they could walk into school every day with a guardian watching over them."

Kellan shot me a skeptical look. "Guardian angels aren't real, Cora."

"So what?" I challenged. "All that matters is if the kids believe it."

"And would they if you told them the truth?" Kellan asked. "Cora, I'm sorry, but a few ornaments that will be taken down in a month are nothing compared to what happened to me."

My jaw dropped. "I'm not saying it is. But if we can inspire people—"

"We can scare people, too," he reminded me. "The world isn't ready for this."

"The world will never be ready!" I argued. "And yet accidents keep happening. We continue to reveal ourselves despite the laws. The Alliance can't keep covering it up and locking people away forever."

"But they can," he insisted. "The Davina have been doing it for millennia."

"Kellan, you don't understand—"

"No, Cora," he said firmly. "*You* don't understand. If you think I'm going to support you in this, the answer is no."

It was clear Kellan wasn't budging on this issue. Which meant that somehow, someway, I was going to have to find another way to solve this.

11

My talk with Kellan didn't exactly go as I expected, but the outcome was essentially the same—he freaked out and still thought it was a bad idea to expose ourselves. Telling Laura the truth, at least, was a little easier to handle.

"I have a confession to make," I told her that night in our dorm room.

Laura turned from the homework she was working on at her desk. "Spill."

It was easier to tell Laura about what happened in the hospital after I'd already confessed to Kellan. Laura didn't interrupt, either. She just sat quietly and listened while I told her about the girls in the hospital and the angel tree they'd made.

"I took Kellan to see the tree, but he flipped," I said. I didn't tell Laura about the story Kellan told me—how he'd been beat up when he was a kid because of his wings—since I felt like that was his story to share. It wouldn't be fair of me to tell her.

Laura sighed. "Kellan has a point, Cora."

My stomach sank. I knew she didn't agree with me, but I was

hoping now that I told her about the girls she might take my side.

I dropped my head in disappointment. "Yeah, everyone seems to be making the same point."

"Then why do you keep pushing it?" she asked. She wasn't being mean. She was honestly curious.

"I don't know," I admitted. "Maybe I'm sick of hiding."

"Me too, Cora, but that doesn't give us the right to expose ourselves," she said gently.

"I know, but it's more than that," I said. "When I flew out of that burning building and showed the world my wings, it was… freeing. We talk about fear all the time. People think if humans knew about us, they'd be afraid. But maybe *we're* the ones who are afraid, Laura."

"We are," she stated. "Everyone's afraid of the unknown, Cora. And we don't know what might happen if everyone knew we existed."

"Exactly," I said. "All I'm saying is it might end up being good."

"Things are fine now, though," Laura insisted. "Why would we want to change things?"

"Because they're *not* fine," I pressed. "Look at what those assholes did to my mom."

Laura's face fell, but she didn't rush to agree with me. Instead, she said, "I think you need to get your mind off this for a while. What do you say we go down to the rec room and play a round of pool?"

I groaned. "I suck at pool. We could go to the Activities Center and fly around."

"Sure," Laura said. "*After* you beat me at pool."

She hopped up from her desk and started pulling on a pair of bright blue heels.

"Fine," I reluctantly agreed.

I pulled on my tennis shoes, and Laura and I headed downstairs to the rec room. When we got there, though, the doors were packed. Inside, we could hear the sound of screaming voices.

"I'm sorry!" a girl squeaked. I recognized the voice as Celina's.

"Sorry!?" Kellan snapped. "Sorry doesn't begin to cover this, Celina."

The sound of Celina's sobs traveled through the open doorway, but I couldn't see inside. Laura and I stepped closer to try to get a good look, but there was a guy blocking our way.

"What's going on?" I asked without really looking at him.

"Sounds like Celina—"

The voice stopped dead when he turned to look at me. My heart stalled in my chest as I looked into dark brown eyes.

Drew.

My high-school boyfriend. The guy I lost my virginity to—who'd dumped me the second we screwed. So far I'd done a pretty good job of avoiding him on campus.

Drew shifted his weight between his feet, like he was uncomfortable around me. Good. He should be after what he did.

He cleared his throat. "Celina cheated on Kellan with Rhys. He just found out."

My stomach dropped to the floor.

"What!?" I shouted so loud that a couple people turned to look at me. Inside, the fight was still going on.

Laura and I exchanged a wide-eyed look.

"Stay away from her!" a deep voice boomed across the rec room.

Rhys. Oh, shit. This couldn't end well.

"I didn't—" Kellan started, but Rhys cut him off.

"You want to go, man? Let's take this outside."

I elbowed my way through the crowd to get to Kellan.

People must've recognized me as his partner, because they made way for me. When I finally broke through the crowd of onlookers, Kellan was backing away from Rhys and Celina. Travis and Caleb stood behind Kellan with their palms held up, like they were ready to conjure essence at a moment's notice. Celina cowered behind Rhys, crying like *she* was the victim. My hands curled into fists, and I wanted nothing more than to throw a fireball at her head.

Kellan shot a scathing look at Celina and scoffed. "Forget it. She's not worth the fight."

Celina's mouth dropped open, but Kellan didn't see it. He whirled around—and slammed straight into me. He stumbled back a step and stared down at me. His eyebrows knitted tightly, and a muscle in his jaw popped. He looked so hurt.

"Kellan," I whispered.

He shook his head at me, like he couldn't bear to talk about it. Then he stepped around me and pushed through the crowd.

"That's right!" Rhys shouted after him. "You better run!"

Behind him, Celina's eyes were filled with tears. She shot daggers my way, then turned to the rest of the crowd. "What are you all still doing here?" she shouted. "The show's over."

Nobody moved, but a few people in the back began whispering.

Rhys took a step forward, his muscled hands flexing at his side. He used his most intimidating voice. "She said the show's over."

The crowd started to disperse. I had a clear shot at the door again, so I started for it.

Laura caught me at the entrance and pointed down the hall. "Kellan went that way."

"Thanks." I hurried off in the direction she pointed.

"So, you caught the end of it?" Travis asked Laura as I was leaving.

"Yeah," she said. "Crazy, right?"

The rest of their conversation faded as I turned the corner. I caught sight of Kellan's blond hair disappear through a door at the end of the hall, and I quickened my pace. I pushed through the door and entered the stairwell. There, I found Kellan sitting on the steps with his head in his hands.

He sighed as he stared down at my shoes, but he didn't move. "What do you want, Cora?"

I lowered myself onto the step beside him. "I'm sorry about what happened."

Kellan gritted his teeth. "What happened with Celina is none of your business."

"But we're partners," I stated. "I'm not going to let you deal with this on your own."

Kellan scoffed and finally lifted his head. I expected his expression to be knitted in anger, but instead, it was full of defeat. Celina had played with his emotions for so long. Last semester, she did all she could to play hard to get. Now she was cheating on him with her partner. It was clear Kellan was exhausted playing this game with her.

"I'm a man," Kellan pointed out. "We're supposed to deal with stuff on our own."

"Well, I'm a girl," I replied. "And we never let our friends deal with a breakup alone."

Kellan let out a puff of air. "Is that what I am? Your friend?"

"Yes," I said. "Haven't we already established that?"

He shrugged. "I just thought after the fight we had earlier, we were back to hating each other."

I shook my head as I stared into his ocean-blue eyes. God, I could get lost in them. My pulse spiked, but the breath in my chest settled as we stared at each other. All I wanted to do was reach over and touch him, to let him know everything was going to be okay. But I resisted.

"I can't stay mad at my partner when we have work to do," I told him. "We'll make up, but we have to get through this thing with Celina first."

Kellan turned his gaze away from me and stared out the door that went outside. "I don't want to talk about it, Cora."

"Okay," I said gently, but I didn't move. I just sat there in silence.

After a few beats, he added, "To be honest, I kind of want to be alone right now."

His tone was gentle, but my heart broke a little when he said he didn't want me there. And yet I knew that little pang I felt in my chest was nothing compared to what Kellan was feeling now. Screw Celina for doing this to him!

"Okay," I agreed, standing. "But I won't stand around and do nothing about this."

I started for the door that led back into the hall.

"Cora," Kellan groaned.

I didn't stick around to listen to what he had to say. I was still fuming over what Celina had done to him. I flung the door open and stomped down the hall in the direction of the rec room. A few people were standing in the hall, including my group of friends. Travis, Caleb, and Laura were explaining in hushed whispers to Shaylene about what had happened. Travis's eyes flickered upward, and he noticed the determined look on my face.

"Oh, shit," he mumbled. "Cora!"

Travis rushed away from the group and toward me, but I ignored him.

The rec room had completely cleared out, except for Rhys and Celina. They were having a heated conversation but stopped dead in their tracks when I stomped into the room.

Celina's gaze met mine, and she eyed me up and down with disgust. "Look, whatever Kellan told you, I'm sure—"

I walked right past Rhys and shoved Celina in the chest, cutting her off. "You bitch!" I screamed.

A heavy hand landed on my shoulder, but I spun around and slapped Rhys's arm away. A fireball formed in my palm, and I aimed it at the Aedes asshole. "Touch me again, and I'll burn your cheating dick off."

"Not if I burn yours first!" Celina growled from behind me.

I turned to her to see she had a fireball of her own in her hand. She held it up threateningly at me. "Don't fucking mess with Rhys."

"Me?" I balked. "*You're* the one who messed with Kellan."

I noticed my friends in the doorway, but I shot them a look to tell them I had it handled. Laura held Travis back.

"This is none of your business, Cora," Celina spat.

"When it involves my partner, it is!" I shouted.

"Lay off her!" Rhys growled.

He reached for my arm, but I pulled my fire power to the surface, and he jumped back as my skin burned him. He screamed and looked down to his red palm, then turned his angry gaze on me. Rhys lifted his good hand, and black Aedes essence formed inside it. He was a second away from slamming the sphere down on my face to knock me out when four figures jumped in front of him—Travis, Laura, Caleb, and Shaylene. Two of them raised white Davina essence, while another aimed dark Aedes essence at him. Laura held up Aedes essence in one hand and Davina essence in the other.

She glared at Rhys. "You want to hurt her? You'll have to go through us to do it."

"You think I won't do that?" Rhys threatened her.

Travis stepped forward. He matched Rhys's height, but Rhys had at least twice the muscle mass. And still, Travis didn't show one ounce of fear. "Try it," he sneered. "I dare you."

Rhys curled his upper lip back and stared at Travis several moments longer before backing down.

I turned toward Celina again. She had a hard look on her face, but I could see her quaking in her shoes. "For someone who wanted Kellan to stay at the academy so badly, you really didn't do much yourself to keep him around. Kellan loved you, Celina. And you did nothing but hurt him. I hope you're proud of yourself."

Celina narrowed her eyes at me. "What do you know, Cora? Except how to be annoying."

"I know how to treat people right," I snapped back.

"Well, you clearly don't know how to shut up," she growled. "Kellan was always mine, Cora. Believe me, he'll come crawling back."

"After what you did to him?" I asked. "What makes you so sure?"

"Because Kellan *always* comes back to me," she stated confidently, crossing her arms. "Besides, if you think he's going to go crying to you just because you're his partner, you better think again. Kellan would rather cut his own wings off than date you."

I totally lost it. Joking about cutting your wings off was unacceptable. To even suggest Kellan would do that to himself was lower than low.

I couldn't listen to her talk anymore. I lifted my palm and formed a white ball of essence inside of it. I was about to throw it straight into her face, but I didn't get a chance before she thrust her hands out and essence shot straight at me.

I ducked, and the essence soared over my head. Travis leapt out of the way, and the essence slammed straight into Rhys's chest. His eyes rolled back in his skull as he was stunned, and his huge body crumbled to the ground.

Celina's eyes went big, and her lips curled into a sneer. She readied her hands to throw another ball of essence at me, but another hand shot out of nowhere and caught her wrist.

The essence in my hand fizzled out as Kellan stepped in

front of me. "Don't talk to Cora like that, Celina," he demanded as he dropped her wrists.

She stared at Kellan wide-eyed, like she couldn't believe he was standing up for me. "Why not? You hate her, too."

Kellan chuckled lightly, but it sounded stilted and forced. "Not as much as I hate you. Believe me, I won't be crawling back this time. I hope you and Rhys are fucking happy."

And then Kellan whirled around and strolled out of the room. My friends and I exchanged a quick glance of shock, but I was the fastest to recover. I hurried out into the hall after him.

"Kellan!" I called.

He was already standing next to the elevator and pushing the button. He pressed his hand to his temple when he saw me coming, like the stress was too much right now.

"Kellan, I'm sorry," I said as I came to a stop beside him. "I hope I didn't make it worse."

"No," he sighed. "It was already bad enough."

The elevator doors opened, and Kellan stepped inside. I hesitated for a moment, but he stepped to the side, like he was waiting for me to join him. I stepped inside the elevator, and Kellan pressed the button for his floor.

Once the elevator started moving, a silent beat passed before Kellan said, "Thanks for what you did, Cora."

"What do you mean?" I asked. "I didn't do anything."

"You did," he replied. "You stood up for me."

I shrugged. "Well, yeah. That's what partners do."

Or girls who are hopelessly in love with you. Whichever.

The elevator doors opened, and we both stepped off. This wasn't my floor, but I found myself following him back to his dorm room anyway.

Kellan shoved his hands into his pockets. "This was different, Cora. You didn't stand up for me because you're my partner. You stood up for me because…"

"Because we're friends?" I filled in for him when he trailed off.

"Yeah," he breathed. "Because we're friends."

Kellan stopped at his door, but he didn't go inside right away. He just stood there awkwardly, like there was more he wanted to say.

He cleared his throat. "Anyway… thanks, Cora."

And then the strangest thing happened. Kellan reached out and pulled me into a hug. My heart jumped as his warmth surrounded me. A fresh linen scent filled my nose. I was surprised at first, but I found myself relaxing into the hug. I hadn't felt this relaxed in… well, forever.

Being in Kellan's arms was indescribable. I'd dreamt about this moment for weeks—what it'd feel like to do this and more to him. But I didn't ever dream it would feel so… right. I thought I'd be scared. And part of me was. But a larger part of me didn't know why, because being in his arms felt perfect, like I was right where I was meant to be.

As I wrapped my arms around him to hug him back, Kellan's arms pulled even tighter around me. Then he ducked down, and I thought my heart was about to give out. His lips connected with my forehead. A warm sensation tingled down my body and back up again, making my heart rate spike.

Kellan instantly dropped me, like he was just as surprised as I was. I stepped away and cleared my throat, because even though I was sure the hug was meant to happen, I didn't think he'd intended to kiss me.

Sure, it wasn't a *real* kiss. It wasn't even on the lips. But it was a kiss nonetheless, and even as partners we weren't supposed to get *that* close.

"I should probably, um…" I started.

"Yeah, me too." Kellan reached for his door handle. "See you later, Cora."

"Bye."

Kellan rushed into his room so quickly, you'd think there was an ax murderer coming down the hall or something. I just stood there in shock for several moments longer, wondering where the affection had come from.

It was the heat of the moment, I told myself. But a part of me wasn't sure if that was true... or if there was something more to it.

12

I didn't see Kellan until our Art of Healing II lecture the next week. He glanced at me from across the room, but I couldn't read his expression. I, on the other hand, blushed red like a freaking tomato. The guy did things to me that no one else could. I didn't get it.

I sat in my usual spot in the lecture hall beside Laura and Shaylene. I sank in my seat a little, trying to hide behind the trio of girls who sat in front of me. Sarah was showing Avery and Lisa a video on her phone. They had their heads close together, so it was easy to hide behind them.

Laura eyed me, and her lips curled into a teasing smirk.

"*Someone's* embarrassed," she sang lowly so only Shaylene and I could hear.

Shaylene followed my gaze, and her eyes landed on Kellan. She sat up straighter in her chair, her black wings brushing up against the table behind us. "Wait. Did something happen?"

I sighed. "No, nothing happened."

Laura leaned over and lowered her voice. "He kissed her."

"What!?" Shaylene balked. "Cora, why didn't you tell me."

"It wasn't a *real* kiss," I insisted. "We just hugged, and he kind of… kissed me on the forehead."

"That means something," Shaylene said.

"That's what I told her," Laura agreed.

"No, you guys," I groaned. "It's nothing. It was just a friendly thing between two partners. It meant nothing."

Shaylene scoffed and turned to face the front of the room. "Okay. If you say so."

Professor Kovski entered the room, and the chatter slowly died. She pulled up her lecture notes on the projector and dove right in. "Welcome, class. Last week I hinted that we'd be studying a very important concept today that you wouldn't want to miss."

She pressed a button on her remote, and the word *Channeling* came up on the screen. My spine straightened as I opened my laptop to take notes. I'd heard so much about channeling but didn't really know how it worked. I was really excited to learn.

"Channeling is an advanced type of healing power," Professor Kovski continued. "It's not something we practice in this class, but it's an important topic to cover, especially for those students who are accepted into our upper-level programs. So, what exactly *is* channeling?"

Professor Kovski changed the slide again, and a drawing appeared. It showed a patient lying on a bed with a glowing ball of essence hovering above them. "Channeling is a technique where a Davina transfers—or *channels*—their essence into another being's body. It intertwines with their life force and places them in a suspended state. Think of it as a medically-induced coma. It buys time in serious cases to administer blood transfusions or diagnose more serious issues."

I was so entranced by the concept that I found myself leaning forward over my table.

Professor Kovski pressed another button on her remote, and the drawing began to animate. It showed the essence lowering into the patient's mouth and then spreading throughout their body. "Once the essence enters a patients' body, it can stay there for up to twenty-four hours without causing damage. Once it's job is complete, the essence must be removed."

The animation changed to show the essence drawing out of the patient's body and forming into the glowing white ball again.

"As you can imagine, this technique is much different than the healing we've been practicing over the last two semesters," Professor Kovski said. "It requires a great deal of care and intent. I expect a two-page paper on this concept from each of you by the end of the week."

"That was a cool lecture," Laura said as we left the lecture hall.

Shaylene brushed out her dark hair with her fingers. "Agreed. Anyone want to get some grub?"

I shrugged. "I could eat."

We left the Science Building—and stopped in our tracks. A shadow passed above us, and the three of us looked up to see someone with black wings flying overhead. They were flying high, way higher than the walls of campus, which was totally off-limits in case someone outside saw.

I shaded my eyes to get a better look. "What is he—oh my God!"

As I watched the Aedes fly above us, I realized his flight trajectory was off, and he was teetering in the sky. Whoever it was took a nose-dive, and my stomach dropped as he tumbled toward the ground.

Laura, Shaylene, and I raced in the direction of the Aedes, but before we could get there, another flash of black wings streaked past us. I gasped when I saw it was Kellan. The first Aedes was about to plummet into a pile of melting snow when

Kellan swooped in and caught him by the shoulders at the last second. He slowly lowered him to the ground as we raced over.

"Oh God!" Laura's hands slapped over her mouth. "What happened?"

We stopped beside the two of them, who were slumped on the slushy ground. My guts twisted when I saw the state the Aedes guy was in. He was shirtless and had bruises all over his torso. Huge chunks of feathers were missing from his wings, and his eyes rolled back into his skull. With his ruffled hair and a swollen black eye, it took me a second to realize that I recognized him.

It was Kumar, the fourth-year Aedes who'd led my orientation group my first day at the academy.

"Kumar!" Kellan slapped his face a little to get him to wake up.

Kumar's eyelids fluttered, but he didn't completely come to.

"What happened?" I heard Travis ask from behind me.

By now, a huge group had formed, mostly the people who had been leaving our Art of Healing II lecture when Kumar flew overhead.

I immediately jumped into emergency mode. I turned to see Travis and Caleb looking shell-shocked but eager to help. "Travis and Caleb, go get Chancellor Harris. Shaylene and Laura, we need Professor Kovski out here right away."

"Got it!" Travis gave me a salute, and the four of them ran off.

Sarah, one of the girls who sat in front of me in class, looked at me like she wanted to help.

"Sarah, go tell the nurses," I instructed.

"On it," she said, grabbing her two friends and whirling around. The three of them rushed toward the health services center.

I leaned down to Kumar's level and took his hand in mine.

He squeezed it ever so slightly, so I knew he was still conscious, but barely.

"Kumar, take my essence," I told him.

He groaned a little, but his head lolled to the side like he didn't hear me.

"Kumar," I stated firmly. "You're badly hurt. Essence will help you heal. Take mine."

A familiar electric sizzle passed over my hand as he started drawing my essence into himself. It wasn't a lot, but it lifted his energy enough that his eyes opened.

"Chancellor Harris," Kumar groaned. "I need to talk to Chancellor Harris."

"She's coming," Kellan stated. "You just lie back and relax, buddy."

Kellan stripped off his jacket and laid it over Kumar. I shifted to cradle Kumar's head in my lap. He shivered from the cold, but he relaxed his head.

"They've got Annie," Kumar groaned.

"Annie?" I asked.

Kumar inhaled a sharp breath and stilled. "My sister."

I gasped. *Annie.* We'd played aerial soccer with her last semester.

"Who has her?" Kellan demanded.

"I-I don't know," Kumar admitted. "The Infantry, I think."

My hands curled into fists. "Colt has your sister?"

"I don't know," Kumar said through clenched teeth. "I didn't see their faces. They jumped us downtown. They sent me back to give Chancellor Harris a message."

"What message?" a stern female voice demanded.

My gaze snapped upward, and I saw Chancellor Harris pushing through the crowd. She wore a light t-shirt, like she'd rushed out of her office without her coat. Travis and Caleb looked worried behind her.

"Everyone out of the way!" Professor Kovski shouted. She

ran in from the other side of the crowd, and people parted to let her through.

Professor Kovski knelt down at Kumar's side and placed her hands over his stomach. She closed her eyes. I could tell by the knitted concentration in her face that she was using her essence to diagnose his injuries.

A few moments later, Professor Kovski opened her eyes and announced, "He's suffering from intense internal bleeding. We need to get him to the health services center."

Chancellor Harris turned to the crowd. "Everyone return to your dorms or classes immediately."

The crowd began to disperse, all except me and Kellan, since Kumar was still holding on to us. Our friends shot us a look before they left, as if to say they'd be waiting for us whenever we were ready. I nodded back to let them know we'd see them soon.

Professor Kovski stood and pulled her phone to her ear, while Chancellor Harris knelt in the snow beside Kumar.

"Kumar," she said softly. "What's the message?"

Kumar swallowed and licked his lips. "They want to talk to you, Chancellor. If you don't, they're going to kill Annie."

13

I was reeling from what happened in the courtyard with Kumar as I walked beside Kellan back to our dorm. Professor Sanders had arrived shortly after with a stretcher, and they took him away to be healed, while Kellan and I were dismissed. Everything happened so fast, and we were still trying to process what Kumar had told us.

"This is bad, Kellan," I said. "Really bad."

He swallowed. "I know."

I had so many questions, I didn't even know where to start. How did they know Kumar and Annie were supernatural? Had they followed them from campus? Did they attack Kumar in the middle of downtown during daylight hours, or did they take him somewhere else? What had they done to Annie, and how badly was she hurt? Was it safe to leave campus?

And most importantly, was it safe to stay?

I wasn't sure how long it would take to get answers.

"I'm scared," I admitted.

Kellan stopped just before the front doors of our dorm. He grabbed me by the shoulders and turned me to face him. "Nothing's going to happen to you, Cora. I won't let it."

My heart fluttered in my chest. I spoke in a small voice. "I'm not scared for me, Kellan. I'm scared for everyone else. I don't want anyone else getting hurt."

Kellan stared deep into my eyes. When he spoke, it was like a binding promise he'd never dare to break. "We're not going to let that happen, Cora. Come on."

He cocked his head toward the door. When we stepped inside, we found our friends sitting in the main study area by the front desk. Caleb sat on the couch and had his arm around Shaylene. Laura fidgeted in her chair, and Travis paced back and forth.

Travis stopped in his tracks when he saw us. "Did you learn what happened?"

Kellan shook his head. "All we know is someone jumped them downtown and hurt them. They're threatening to kill Annie if Chancellor Harris doesn't talk to them."

Laura's hands shot over her mouth. "Oh, God. She's going to talk to them, right?"

"She has to," I stated firmly. There was no alternative.

Laura's shoulders shook. "I can't believe this is happening."

Caleb shook his head, but his eyes weren't really focused on anything. "It's crazy. Annie's one of our own. We're in classes together."

"Yeah, she sits by us in our earth element class," Travis said. "She wasn't there today, but I never imagined it was… this."

"No one could've known this was going to happen to her," I stated.

"No," Kellan agreed, "but we have to do something about it."

"Do *what*?" I asked. "Go after Colt? We don't even know if it was him."

Kellan crossed his arms. "You don't know he burnt down your mom's restaurant, either, but you seem pretty adamant it was him. Don't you want to get back at him?"

"Of course I do," I snapped. "But we're not the Alliance."

Kellan's features hardened. "No, but they haven't dealt with Colt yet. *Someone* has to do something."

Laura's eyes lit up in interest. "What are you suggesting?"

Kellan raked his hands through his blond hair. "I don't know yet. A sort of security team, maybe?"

"I'm in!" Travis raised his hand before hearing any more.

"Me, too," Caleb agreed.

I crossed my arms. "And me."

"Wait." Shaylene shot to her feet. "You guys aren't suggesting like a vigilante group, are you?"

Kellan raised an eyebrow at her. "And if we are?"

"Violence isn't going to solve violence," she pointed out.

The room went silent, and I held my breath. After what Colt did to my mom, I wanted nothing more than to stab my Davina Blade into his chest. But Shaylene's words made me pause. I could do anything I wanted to Colt, but who's to say someone bigger and badder wouldn't rise up to get revenge on *us*? She had a point.

Travis cracked his knuckles. "Violence will solve something, I'm sure."

"Maybe our group could be about facilitating peace," I suggested.

Kellan sighed, like he was sick of me suggesting this. "This again, Cora?"

I turned on him, my nostrils flaring. *I* was sick of him shooting me down every time the topic came up. "My parents did it," I snapped. "Or maybe you forgot that thirty years ago, you and I would be trying to kill each other."

Kellan pressed his lips together, like he was trying hard not to shoot back an insult. His ever-changing mood left me in a constant state of whiplash.

"Either way," Kellan said coolly, "I can't sit around doing nothing. Annie's out there, possibly being tortured."

"I agree," I said, "but do you have any ideas on what we can do?"

"We're sitting ducks until we know more," Kellan said. "I'll talk to Kumar as soon as he's stable."

"Okay," I agreed. "But Kellan..."

Kellan stared down at me. Though he had a look of determination painted on his face, I saw the ache beneath it. None of us knew Annie well, but she was one of us. I could tell Kellan was taking it particularly hard because of what happened to him when he was a kid.

I took a long breath. "Whatever we do, we do it together."

It was late by the time the health services center returned Kellan's call and said he could come and visit Kumar. While Kellan went to talk to him, I headed to Chancellor Harris's office.

I walked through the darkness with my hands shoved in my pockets for warmth. I glanced around campus. It was quiet and a little eerie. I knew the Infantry couldn't get inside the walls. After what happened today, I was sure the academy had increased security. But still, I had images of the Infantry crawling over the walls and swarming the school to torture us all.

But nothing happened. I reached the Academy Building in one piece and walked upstairs to Chancellor Harris's office. Her receptionist wasn't at her desk, so I walked past it and knocked on the double doors. I didn't know what I was expecting, but no answer came. Of course she wasn't here. She was obviously dealing with the shit the Infantry was stirring up.

And then came the sound of heels clicking against the tile. I turned around to see Chancellor Harris rushing down the hall. When her eyes caught mine, she looked surprised.

"Cora, can I help you?" She spoke quickly, like she was in a rush.

"We want to help, Chancellor," I said.

She paused for a moment, then reached for her door. "Inside, Cora."

She rushed me into her office. I didn't even sit before I started talking. "Chancellor Harris, what's going on?"

She paced across the room and stood at the window. "It's the Infantry, Cora."

Surprise, surprise.

"They're holding a student hostage," she told me solemnly.

"What do they want?" I asked.

She pressed her lips together firmly and gazed out over campus. "They're making demands we simply can't meet."

My stomach plummeted to my toes. "Wait, so you can't save Annie?"

Her gaze snapped to mine. "We will. I assure you of that. But... it's complicated."

"What sort of demands are they making?" I questioned.

Chancellor Harris hesitated, as if unsure whether or not to tell me the truth. Finally, she said, "They want to expose the school."

"I thought you wanted us to expose ourselves," I mentioned.

She shook her head. "Not like this, Cora. Not on their terms. They intent to incite a panic. It could put the entire student body in jeopardy—not just Annie."

"So, how can we help?" I asked desperately. I'd do anything to protect my fellow students.

Chancellor Harris sat in her chair, looking defeated. "We need to change their minds."

I gaped at her. "How do we do that?"

She shook her head. "I don't know yet, Cora. But I have a call I have to make. I appreciate your eagerness to help, but I'm afraid there's just not much you can do right now."

"Thank you," I said. I knew whatever call she had to make was important, so I left the room quickly.

I was walking back to my dorm when I caught sight of Laura and Shaylene walking near the Winged Fountain. They'd left to get takeout from the dining hall before I'd gone to meet Chancellor Harris, but they had no food in their hands.

They both walked at a quick pace and looked around frantically. I could hear their voices traveling over the courtyard, but I couldn't make out what they were saying. The street lamps above them illuminated their faces, and I instantly became worried when I saw the expression of distress they shared. Their eyes landed on me, and they rushed over.

"Thank God," Laura said breathlessly. "We thought you guys had left without us."

"Left where?" I asked.

Shaylene pulled her coat tighter around her. "We don't know. The guys sent us to grab food, but when we got back, everyone was gone."

My body tensed. "Everyone? I know Kellan went to talk to Kumar."

"Well, Travis and Caleb disappeared," Laura stated.

"You don't think they're in trouble, do you?" I asked.

Laura crossed her arms. "Travis? In trouble? He hears the word danger, and he goes running after it."

"You don't think—?" I started, but Laura nodded, cutting me off. "You think they went after Annie?"

Laura's lips tightened. "Well, if Kellan found out where she was, what's to stop them?"

My hands tightened into fists. "We have to go help them! They could get themselves killed."

"Exactly," Shaylene said. "Except we don't know where they went."

I pulled my phone out of my pocket and punched the screen. *Where are you!?* I texted Kellan.

No response.

I huffed. "I bet they did this on purpose."

"Left us girls behind?" Shaylene asked, sounding less than pleased.

"Yes," I said. "We talked about doing this peacefully. They don't want our help."

Shaylene's features darkened. "Caleb's going to get an earful from me tonight. Jerk."

A silent beat passed as we all considered what to do next.

"We have to go talk to Kumar," I finally said. "If he told Kellan where Annie is, he can tell us. We can go after them and help."

"Or get everyone in deeper trouble," Laura pointed out.

"Well, I can't just sit around," I said.

I wasn't taking no for an answer. Laura finally caved, and the three of us walked to the health services center. But when we got there, the receptionist told us that visiting hours were over. She wouldn't let us through to Kumar, no matter how much we argued.

There was nothing we could do but wait for them. We returned to the Winged Fountain, since it gave the widest view of campus. We sat on the edge and shivered in the cold, but the three of us were determined to remain put until the guys returned.

It must've been an hour before we spotted the shadows in the sky. They were hard to see in the darkness, but I caught sight of dark wings against the backdrop of the moon.

The three of us shot to our feet as a group of guys swooped down onto campus and landed near the health services center. It wasn't just Kellan, Caleb, and Travis, either. There were at least a dozen other guys behind them. Most of them rushed inside, but three others hung back.

My friends and I ran over to them. They were all talking over each other and sounded distressed. Travis was shirtless with his wings out, and he paced back and forth with his hands fisted at his sides. Caleb and a guy I'd only met once, Tucker, were trying to calm him down.

"We should've burned that place to the ground!" Travis growled.

"Oh my God, you guys!" I cried as I sprinted over. "What happened?"

"Travis!" Laura gasped. "Are you okay?"

She reached up to the side of his face, which was swollen and bruised. He wrapped her in a hug. "Don't worry, babe. I'm Davina. I'll heal fast."

I looked around for Kellan, but I didn't see him. My breath stalled in my chest.

Caleb must've noticed, because he grabbed my arm. "He's fine, Cora. He's inside."

My stomach twisted into knots when he said Kellan was in the health services center. Had something bad happened to him?

I didn't ask. I just ran into the building and down the hall. When I got inside the doors to the health center, my heart lurched. Voices filled the entrance as nurses yelled instructions back and forth. Kellan was standing in front of the reception desk and placing a petite, unconscious girl onto a gurney the nurses had pulled out for her.

Annie.

She looked really pale and had gashes running up and down her arms. Her black wings were out and were twisted at odd angles.

Two other guys were being guided onto gurneys. One was unconscious and being carried by two other guys, and another was clutching his stomach and groaning as he lay down. I recognized the guys. The one clutching his stomach was Jett, a guy I'd barely met before but saw at a party once. Then there was Miles, a tall guy from my firefighting classes, and Everett, a Water Davina, carrying the unconscious guy together.

I didn't see who it was at first, until his head lolled to the side. I gasped when I caught sight of his face. It was Drew, my ex-boyfriend. I barely had a second to process it before he and Annie were being wheeled down the hall.

Kellan himself was shirtless, with his black wings on display. He was bleeding from a large wound on his shoulder. It looked like a bullet wound. My throat closed up as I took in his injuries. Just the thought of him being hurt worried me to my very core.

"Kellan!" I cried as I rushed over to him.

He let out a breath. "Spare me the lecture, Cora. I did what I had to do."

"You're shot!" I yelled.

"Sir," a nurse said to Kellan. "Sir, you're going to have to come with me."

"No," he snapped at her, but he quickly softened his tone. "Take care of the others first."

Her lips tightened, but they were obviously short-staffed at this time of night, so she didn't argue. "I'll get you some gauze for that, and we'll patch you up shortly."

Kellan turned back to me.

I had half a mind not to punch him in his injured shoulder. "You jerk! I thought we agreed that whatever happened, we'd do it together."

He gazed down at me with a soft expression. I didn't know if it was because he was kind of out of it from blood loss or if he was happy to see me. "I never agreed to that, Cora. But I am truly sorry about lying to you. I just knew you'd never agree to it."

He shifted his weight between his feet and glanced around the room.

I took Kellan's face in my hands and forced him to look me in the eye. I was so pissed at him right now, but I couldn't bring myself to fight when he was hurt like this. "What matters is everyone made it out, right?"

Kellan nodded as the nurse handed him the gauze. "Yeah, we all made it out. But Miles and Annie are hurt real bad. I didn't know they'd have guns."

The nurse turned to me. "You keep an eye on him, and if anything happens, you come and get me."

"Got it," I said.

The nurse rushed off after the others whose injuries were more life-threatening.

Kellan pressed the gauze to his wound and winced. He looked at me, but he could hardly focus.

"You need to sit." I grabbed his good arm and guided him over to the waiting area.

Kellan breathed a sigh of relief once he sat down.

"I can heal this if you let me," I offered. "As long as the bullet's not still in there."

He shook his head. "I got it out."

"Okay," I said gently, "but I'm going to have to double check. Do you trust me to diagnose it?"

Kellan nodded.

"I'm going to need your help," I reminded him.

Kellan grabbed my arm with his good hand and squeezed so tightly that I squeaked a little. He closed his eyes and gritted his teeth.

"Kellan, stay with me," I demanded. "We've got this."

I pulled the gauze away to look at the injury, but it was still oozing blood. I placed my hand over the wound and pushed my essence into it to explored his injuries. I could feel the warmth of his pain. There was a lot of tissue damage and grime shoved into the wound, but his immune system would take care of the bacteria once I healed it.

"It feels like all the bullet fragments are out," I said. "You ready?"

Kellan nodded, then started opening my essence channel. I guided warm, fuzzy essence into his wound, and my hand began to glow. He sighed in relief, and I knew his pain was melting away. It was a deep wound, so it took a while to heal, but it was simple, so I was able to sterilize it and close it up easily with my magic.

When I drew away, his shoulder looked as if he'd never been shot in the first place. I wiped the blood away with the gauze. "How does that feel?"

Kellan took my wrist, stopping me from wiping his shoulder. I glanced up to him, and he was starting at me in this intense way—almost like he wanted to kiss me. My breath stalled in my chest, but my heart sped up. Even though I was mad at him for going after Annie without me, I couldn't help but feel like I was melting in his presence.

"A little sore yet," he admitted softly without taking his eyes off me. "But I'll be fine now… Thanks to you."

Our eyes locked for several more seconds. His gaze flickered to my lips, and I felt a surge of excitement rush through my belly. Then another tingling rushed through me. My essence channel shot open, and power whipped through me, making my whole body come alive with an electric charge.

Kellan jerked away and dropped my arm. "Sorry. I didn't mean to do that. I just… needed the power-up."

He didn't sound convincing, though I didn't know why else he would take my essence like that.

"It's okay," I assured him. "You can take as much as you need. You've been through a lot tonight."

Then, without giving myself a chance to second guess it, I took his arm and put it over my shoulder, and I laid my head on his shoulder. It wasn't meant as a romantic gesture, just a way for us to keep in contact so he could channel my essence and heal faster. But I'd never felt so comfortable and at ease in someone else's arms. He didn't pull away, either.

Kellan relaxed. "Thanks, Cora."

After a few moments of silence, I said, "So, are you going to tell me what happened?"

"Do you really want to know?" he asked.

"Yes, I really want to know," I stated. "Why'd you ditch me? We're partners. We're supposed to do this kind of thing together."

He shrugged. "Because you'd never have let me go through with it. When Kumar told me where they were keeping Annie, I just... I lost it. When I got back to the dorms to get Travis and Caleb, they already had a group of guys together who wanted to help. And so..."

"You went after her," I finished for him.

He sighed. "It was risky, I know. It goes against everything we've been taught at the academy. But we got her."

"So, where *were* they keeping her?" I asked.

"She was at this abandoned warehouse on the other side of the city," Kellan said.

"And it was the Infantry?" I questioned. "You saw them?"

Kellan hesitated a moment. "Well, sort of. As soon as we got in, they put on ski masks and started shooting at us. We didn't see their faces."

I bit my lower lip. We now had two major crimes that I was sure connected in some way—the arson at my mom's restaurant and Annie's kidnapping. But we still had no proof who'd done it.

"Cora, it's them," he stated confidently.

"It's Colt?" I asked. I already knew it was him, but having the confirmation would be freeing. The last thing I needed was to be focusing on Colt when there was some other asshole out there hurting my people.

Kellan nodded. "I didn't see him, but I heard their leader shouting orders. It sounded just like him."

"I believe you, Kellan," I said. "But we have to be very careful going forward. I want to get back at him as much as you do, but hurting him is only going to make us bigger targets. I can't risk them going after my family again."

"You're right."

I was shocked to hear him say it. "You agree with me?"

His shoulders fell. "After tonight, we've all become targets. I've dragged other people into this, and they got hurt."

I sniffled. "Kellan, what are we going to do?"

"Excuse me?" A nurse walked into the waiting room and looked to us. "Are you Cora?"

I sat up straight. The air felt cold between Kellan and me. "I am."

She cleared her throat. "Drew Randall is asking for you. Would you like to see him?"

Drew was asking for *me*? Shit. It must've been really bad if my ex wanted to talk to me.

"Yes," I answered as I shot to my feet. "Yes, I'd like to see him."

14

I walked into Drew's room on shaky knees. The nurse shut the door behind us to give us privacy. Drew sat on the bed and looked up at me. His face was pale, like he'd lost a lot of blood, but he was alert.

I stopped a few paces from his bed, feeling really awkward being there alone with him. We hadn't really talked in over a year. I had no idea what he could possibly want from me.

"Did the wound heal okay?" I squeaked out.

Drew cleared his throat and nodded. "They healed the wound. My body will take care of any internal injuries within a few days. Perks of being a Davina."

He gave a nervous chuckle, but it sounded stale. He must've felt just as awkward as I did.

I steeled my nerves and looked him straight in the eye. "Why'd you ask me to come in here, Drew?"

He took a deep breath and gestured to the chair beside his bed. "You should probably sit down for this."

My heart pounded as I sat. A long silence stretched between us, until I dared to break it. "What is this about?"

Drew couldn't meet my gaze. "I have a confession to make,

Cora. After I was shot tonight, I thought I might not make it. My buddies tried to heal me on location, but we were so rushed and everyone was hyped up on adrenaline… the only thing we could do was come back to school."

I swallowed the lump in my throat. I couldn't imagine what he'd gone through tonight—what any of them had gone through.

Drew continued. "While they were flying me back and I was bleeding out, all these things started to rush through my mind."

He paused for a moment, and I dared to ask, "What kind of things?"

He frowned. "Things I'd done wrong."

He paused for a moment before continuing. "I was really out of it when they brought me back, but I saw you out there by the waiting room. It just made me think of what a jerk I was to you."

My stomach sank at the memories. Drew was the one and only guy I'd gone all the way with—and he dumped me the second he had what he wanted. He didn't even have the decency to do it in person. I had to find out we were breaking up over text.

"I just wanted to apologize, Cora," Drew said softly.

The look in his eyes told me he was being honest. It was hard to wrap my head around after the way he treated me in high school. But it was like there was something different about him now. I didn't know if it was because he'd grown in the year we'd spent apart, or if tonight had changed him.

"Cora?" Drew pressed.

It took me a second to realize I'd been sitting there for several moments without responding. I never thought I'd hear him apologize.

"It's fine, Drew," I found myself saying, though it was hard to get the words out.

"No, it's not, Cora," he insisted. "You're doing that thing again."

"What thing?" I asked.

"That thing you did when we broke up," he said. "You act like everything's fine when it's not. I know you hold the breakup against me."

It was true. I hadn't really ever gotten over it.

I shrugged. "It was a long time ago."

"I know," he said gently. "And it still hurts."

My breath stopped in its tracks. "I guess so," I admitted.

After a beat, Drew spoke again. "I want to join your cause, Cora."

I furrowed my brow. "My cause?"

He nodded. "I know you and Kellan are leading the charge. Whatever we have to do to keep what happened to Annie from happening again, I'm in."

"Even though you were shot?" I balked.

"Yes," he said simply. "But I don't want to ruin anything by causing tension between us. I just hope we can put the past aside and work together."

My chest softened at his offer. "I'd like that, too, Drew."

His eyes brightened. "So, you forgive me?"

I bit my lower lip. Instinct told me to say yes, but I didn't know if that was just because I was feeling sympathetic since he'd been shot. I'd spent so long holding it all against him that it was hard to let that go.

But I knew the future wasn't about me. It was about all of us.

"I'm going to try," I told him.

He breathed a huge sigh of relief, like he'd been carrying around a huge weight. "Thank you, Cora."

15

A week passed, and news about Annie and the rescue mission had spread throughout the school. Everywhere we went, people approached Kellan to ask about it. He gave curt answers and seemed annoyed when people commended him for his bravery.

"I didn't do this to be recognized as some sort of hero," he told me in our firefighting class one day. "I did it to save Annie."

"And you *did* save her," I pointed out. "But isn't all this recognition good for you? It could help you get a position on the Alliance like you want."

Kellan thought about it for a moment. "Yeah, I guess you're right. But people seem to keep forgetting that I got people hurt."

"Everyone's healed," I reminded him. "Drew was the worst, and he's out of the hospital."

Kellan raked his fingers through his blond hair. "Yeah, but I just keep thinking of how I'd do it differently. He never would've gotten hurt in the first place."

"You don't know that," I said.

Kellan sighed. "That meeting with Chancellor Harris didn't help how I feel about this, either."

Kellan had already told me about what went down in that meeting. Chancellor Harris and a bunch of faculty came together to reprimand the guys about going off and saving Annie without consulting anyone. They made a big deal out of how even though they were glad Annie was safe, they could've royally screwed things up and gotten her—and themselves —killed.

"Anyway," Kellan said. "Are you coming tonight?"

I furrowed my brow. "Coming where?"

He looked shocked that I didn't know what he was talking about. "To Heaven's Lounge."

"The bar beneath the dining center?" I asked.

He nodded. "Kumar invited us all out as a sort of thank-you."

"I guess I wasn't invited," I said.

Kellan nudged me in the arm. "Well, you can come as my date."

My heart lifted in my chest when he said it, but the look in his eyes told me he didn't mean it in that way.

"Say you'll come," he begged.

A blush rose to my cheeks. "Okay, I'll come."

Kellan came to my dorm room that night, and we walked to Heaven's Lounge together. The place was so packed we could hardly see to the back wall. The lighting was dim to begin with, so that made it even harder to spot our friends. I scanned the room, but I didn't see our friends anywhere near the bar or at the dining tables up front. I spotted Celina, but I was staying the hell away from her. I noticed Kellan's eyes fall on her for a second, but they continued to sweep the room, like he didn't care.

"There they are," Kellan said, eyeing the back corner.

My heart leapt when he took my hand and led me through

the crowd. We found our friends seated at a long table that was really four tables pushed together. Travis and Laura sat side-by-side, with his arm draped around her. Caleb and Shaylene were trying to throw peanuts in each other's mouths from across the table. Kumar sat at the head of the table and was chatting with Drew and Miles while he sipped on a beer. Everyone else was here—all the guys Kellan had recruited to help the other night.

When Kumar's eyes landed on Kellan, he jumped to his feet. "Kellan, my man!"

He came over to us and shook Kellan's hand, then pulled him into a one-armed hug. "How've you been, our big hero?"

He clapped him on the shoulder, then turned to the rest of the group. "Everyone, Kellan's here!"

A chorus of *hellos* traveled around the table.

I could tell Kumar was already a little drunk. He turned to Kellan and lowered his voice. "Thanks for saving my sister, man. I owe you big time."

Kellan's eyes roamed the table. "Is she joining us?"

"Nah," Kumar said. "She's staying with our parents for a while. It's safer that way. But she's doing a lot better."

"That's good to hear," Kellan said.

"Hey, why don't you take a seat," Kumar suggested. "Can I get you anything to drink?"

Kellan waved his hand. "Nah, I'm good."

"Pft," Kumar said. "I'll grab you a beer."

"Cora!" Laura called over the loud chatter. "We saved you guys seats!"

Kellan and I sat next to each other in the empty chairs beside Laura and Travis. It was only after I sat that I realized Drew was on my other side.

Great. I was sandwiched between the only two guys I'd ever had feelings for.

Drew noticed me immediately and offered a friendly smile. "Hey, Cora. How are you?"

"Fine," I said.

Kellan heard us talking, and his curiosity piqued. "You two know each other?"

I nodded. "Yeah, we went to high school together. Drew's my..." I trailed off when I realized I was about to say *ex-boyfriend*. Was that the right way to introduce him?

Drew cleared his throat. "We used to go out."

Kellan's face fell. I'd never told him about Drew or anything that happened between us, but he seemed to sense it wasn't good. "Oh," he said flatly.

When Drew turned away to talk to the guy next to him, Kellan leaned into me and lowered his voice. "Do you need to switch seats with me?"

My pulse quickened as his warm breath rushed across the side of my face. "No, I'm fine."

"Here you go." Kumar reached between us and set a beer in front of Kellan. Kellan wasn't twenty-one yet, but I didn't think anyone would notice or check his I.D.

"Thanks," he said, before taking a swig of beer.

"No problem," Kumar replied. "If you need another, you know who to ask."

He winked, then went back to his seat at the head of the table. The guys around him were all laughing and goofing off.

"Hey, Cora," Caleb called. "Open wide."

Before I could respond, he tossed a peanut at my face. It bounced off, and I caught it in my hand.

I laughed and threw it back at him. "Hey! I wasn't ready."

"Try me," Kellan said.

Caleb picked a peanut up from the bowl in front of him and tossed it at Kellan. He caught it in his mouth and ate it.

"Dude, you're a pro," Caleb teased.

Kellan shrugged and reached for a menu. "Or lucky."

Caleb held up a second peanut. "Another?"

"Nah, man," Kellan said. "I'm going to quit while I'm ahead."

"Toss me one." I opened my mouth wide, and it took two more tries before Caleb got one in my mouth.

We hung out for another hour, laughing with our friends and listening to Travis and Caleb tell stories of their parkour adventures, some of which I wasn't sure I bought. Kellan and I split an order of fries.

"Do you need another drink?" he asked, gesturing to my empty soda.

"If you're getting up, sure," I said.

My eyes followed Kellan as he walked up to the bar. Laura noticed me checking out his backside and shot me a knowing smile. I blushed and ducked my head. When my gaze darted back toward Kellan, my stomach dropped.

Kellan walked by a beefy guy and accidentally bumped into him, causing him to spill his drink on himself. When he turned around, I saw that it was Rhys. His lips curled into a sneer, and he puffed out his chest like he was trying to assert his dominance. Kellan took a step back, and the two exchanged a few words I couldn't hear. I was already on my feet, rushing over to him as back-up. Not like Kellan needed it, though.

"No need to get all bent out of shape," Kellan was saying when I approached. "It was an accident."

"Oh, really?" Rhys taunted. "So you're not still mad about what went down with Celina?"

Kellan scoffed. "If I was, I'd do more than spill a drink on you."

Rhys's hands curled into fists. "That a threat, Greene?"

Rhys formed essence in his hand, and I threw myself between the two of them. "Whoa, guys! Let's calm down."

"Take it outside!" one of Rhys's friends shouted. "We want to see a fight."

Kellan frowned. "We're not going to fight."

Rhys smirked. "Why not? You scared?"

Kellan didn't take the trash talk lightly. He chuckled and

glared at Rhys like I wasn't standing right between them. "Scared for you, bro."

Rhys narrowed his eyes. "Ah, I see. You think you're some sort of hero after what you and your friends did. Why don't you prove it?"

"Screw you, Rhys," Kellan growled. "I don't have anything to prove to you."

Rhys's lips tightened, and I could tell he was getting more and more frustrated with Kellan by the minute. It was clear he was itching to start a fight.

"Enough," I stated firmly. "Kellan, we're leaving."

I grabbed Kellan by the arm and tried to drag him away, but we barely made it a step before Rhys said, "I see you need your girlfriend to keep you in check. Good luck with that mess."

Kellan wrenched his arm away from me and whirled on Rhys, getting so close their noses almost touched. "*Excuse* me?"

My jaw dropped. Did he just call me a *mess*? Who the hell was he to say that about me?

Rhys scoffed, and his eyes darted in my direction. "Come on, man. She's the one who exposed herself. She's the reason Annie got hurt and you had to launch your *rescue* mission. What's she going to do next? How many people are going to get hurt because of her?"

Kellan's hands balled into fists. "This isn't her fault. I'm alive because of her. No thanks to your skank girlfriend, who tried to kill Cora in that fire."

My eyes went wide. I didn't think until now that Kellan believed me about what had happened before he'd arrived that night.

Rhys glared down at Kellan. "My girlfriend's a skank? What about yours? How many professors did she have to sleep with to get back into the academy after that disaster of a final?"

Kellan totally lost it. Before I could even react to Rhys's accusation, Kellan slammed his fist into the side of Rhys's face. I gasped as a cracking sound filled the air. Rhys formed another ball of essence in his hand and shot it at Kellan's face.

I reacted quickly and shot my own essence between them. My white essence collided with Rhys's black magic, and a loud *boom* sounded through the bar. A blast of air rushed through my hair, bur Rhys caught the brunt of the blow. Essence exploded in front of him, and he was blasted back into the table behind him, making the feet screech across the floor. Complete silence fell over the room as the whole bar turned to look at us.

I didn't care that everyone was watching. I stepped right up to Rhys, who looked down at me with a wary expression. It was like he thought I was going to slam essence in his face, and he knew he couldn't retaliate against a girl when everyone else was watching.

But I didn't touch him. Instead, I got up close in his face and sneered, "Believe me, you don't want to mess with us. You already know I'm not opposed to breaking the rules, so I suggest you don't test just how far I'd go to protect the people I love."

I whirled around, and Kellan was right there to catch me. My heart was pounding fiercely as he took my hand in his and we made a dramatic exit together. Celina stood a few people back with drinks in her hands. She'd gone still in shock. Kellan and I rushed out of there so quickly that I accidentally shoved my shoulder into Celina's. She gave a yelp as her drinks splashed up on her shirt.

Kellan took long strides, so I had to practically run to keep up with him. But I didn't care. I wanted to get out of there as soon as possible.

Kellan didn't stop until we were outside and far away from the dining hall. A cold rain was sprinkling down on us, but Kellan didn't seem to care. He stood in front of the Winged Fountain, rainwater starting to drench his hair, and looked down at me. It was impossible to read his gaze. I didn't know if he was mad at me or proud. It might've been a little of both.

"Cora, I thought I told you last time not to get involved in stuff like this," he growled.

"I wasn't just going to stand there!" I shot back.

"You're making yourself a target," he insisted. "Rhys never would've said those things about you if you didn't confront Celina the last time."

"Those are just words," I argued, blinking away the rain from my eyes. Given the weather, I should've been shivering, but I was so worked up right now I barely noticed the chill.

"Words that *mean* something," Kellan said.

"He could've hurt you, too!" I shot back.

Kellan winced, like I'd hit a nerve. I glanced down to his hand—the one he'd used to punch Rhys—and my stomach bottomed out. Purple bruises had formed all over his knuckles.

My tone softened. "You did get hurt, didn't you? That crunch I heard…?"

Kellan cradled his broken hand to his chest. "I can deal with that. What I can't deal with is if you got hurt because of me."

I took a step forward. I longed to reach out for Kellan, but I hesitated. "Rhys wouldn't have hurt me."

"You don't know that," he said. "He thinks we're dating. If he wanted to hurt me, he'd go after you first."

"Why didn't you correct him then?" I asked.

Kellan opened his mouth to say something, but he shut it a second later. Finally, he said, "Would it matter? You're my partner. He'd hurt you either way."

"I can take care of myself," I said.

Kellan's eyes darkened. "So can I. I don't need you stepping in to deal with Celina and Rhys. In case you haven't noticed, I'm not completely helpless."

My heart sank. Is that what he thought it meant when I stood up for him? That I thought he was *weak*?

"I don't think you're helpless, Kellan," I stated. "That couldn't be further from the truth."

"Then what's your fascination with getting into trouble for me?" he snapped.

I gaped at him. "I don't have a fascination with it. Is this some male ego thing or something? Is this why you didn't tell me you were going after the Infantry and left me behind? Because you thought I might screw something up?"

"No!" he yelled. "I did that to protect you."

"You can't protect me from everything, Kellan. That's part of the job we're training for."

Kellan raked his fingers through his wet hair with his good hand. "Well, maybe this job is too dangerous."

The words felt like a slap in the face. It was like he was saying I wasn't cut out for this. I blinked away the water from my eyes as the rain picked up, but I couldn't help but glare at him. He didn't freaking own me. He couldn't tell me what to do. And so what if this job was too dangerous? I was doing it anyway.

Kellan must've noticed the hurt look on my face, because he stepped forward and softened his tone. "Cora, it's not like I don't think you can't do it. I just... I just couldn't stand to see you get hurt."

I swallowed, and my pulse quickened. He was so close now that I could feel the heat coming off his body. "Well, you're probably going to," I said. "Fighting fires is dangerous, Kellan, but it's what I signed up for."

Kellan's features softened. He reached up to brush a few strands of wet hair behind my ear, and I gasped at the contact. "You'd do it with or without me, wouldn't you?"

I nodded, because I couldn't find my voice to answer. The way he looked down at me was so hypnotic.

"Then promise me one thing, Cora," he whispered.

"Anything," I replied breathlessly.

He stared with such an intense gaze it made my knees go weak. "Don't ever walk into danger without me."

I was shocked by the way he said it—like he never wanted to leave my side. "I can't make any promises. Why do you care so much anyway?"

Kellan's lips tightened, like he didn't dare answer. "Did you mean what you said in Heaven's Lounge?"

"Did I mean what?" I asked.

"You told Rhys you'd do anything to protect the people you love," Kellan reminded me. "Did you mean it? Do you love me?"

I was blindsided by the question. So he'd caught that, had he? The words were heavy and light at the same time. I wanted so badly to tell him the truth—that yes, I loved him. But I didn't know if that was what he wanted to hear, and I couldn't risk screwing up our partnership.

"Cora, do you love me?" he asked more clearly, more firmly.

"I—I might. I mean, I think so," I stammered. "But you just broke up with Celina, and you got shot, and if you don't feel the same way, I understand—"

Kellan pressed his hand to the side of my face and stared deeply into my eyes. "You've got it wrong, Cora. The reason I can't stand to see you in danger is because… I feel the same way about you."

Without warning, Kellan's lips swooped down to connect with mine. The kiss was unlike anything I'd felt before. My body reacted before my head caught up with what was happening. My stomach flipped in my abdomen, and all the rain pounding down on us seemed to disappear. It felt as if the sidewalk had dropped away and we were floating in midair.

I realized what was happening and relaxed into the kiss. As I wrapped my arms around him, he placed his good hand at the back of my neck and cradled me in his arms. Kellan's tongue rolled over mine, and he kissed me with a passionate energy that sizzled between us. It was as clear as when he siphoned my essence, but it was different. This energy went back and forth, instead of going in just one direction. It was something I received as much as I gave. It sucked the very breath from my lungs.

I thought kissing Kellan again would feel awkward. The first time I kissed him—right after we escaped from the fire—was anything but the passionate kiss our first kiss should've been. But this... this was different. This felt perfectly natural, even with the rain pouring down on us.

All too soon, Kellan drew away from me. My head was still spinning, and he inhaled deep breaths. Rain dripped down his face, but he didn't rush to wipe it away. I was frozen in place, still trying to wrap my head around Kellan's confession and the kiss.

Kellan stared down at me a moment longer, then wrapped me into a hug. He kissed the top of my head, and I suddenly felt more alive as my stomach flipped in my abdomen. Being in his arms felt perfect. I couldn't believe just months ago we were fighting about being partners. It felt like a lifetime.

"I don't want to keep fighting, Cora," Kellan whispered.

"I don't, either," I admitted. "But that means from here on out, we do things together. No running off without telling me."

"Deal," he said. "But you need to leave Celina and Rhys alone. We have bigger things to worry about, and I don't need to worry about them fighting with you."

I drew away from him and nodded. "Agreed."

Kellan took my hand in his, and I squeezed his hands to let him know we were on the same page. Kellan winced, and my heart lurched. I jerked away from him immediately and threw my hands over my mouth.

"Oh my gosh! I'm sorry," I cried. "I forgot—"

"It's fine," Kellan said through gritted teeth.

I rolled my eyes at him. "No lying to me, either."

He smirked. "Well, I'm just going to omit how bad that hurt then."

"Come on, Kellan," I said. "Let's get you healed."

We started in the direction of the health services center. The rain had let up, and I wasn't sure if it was the weather or how I felt around Kellan, but I felt warmer now.

"Is this going to start becoming a habit?" I teased, glancing down to his hand.

Kellan followed my gaze and chuckled. "As long as we're partners? Probably."

My jaw dropped dramatically. "What does that mean?"

Kellan smiled and put his good arm around my shoulder. "It means we'll have lots of stories to tell."

16

Kellan wasn't lying when he said we had stories to tell. I wished they were the good kind—like sneaking into each other's dorms when our roommates were away. But between our classes and homework, we only had a few moments here and there to sneak kisses in the stairwell. Any time we had alone was spent on bigger problems—mainly, figuring out what to do about the threats mounting outside the academy.

"We have a plan," Kellan announced a few weeks later.

The two of us stood at the front of the study room we'd reserved in the library. The crew who'd helped break out Annie —along with Kumar, Laura, and Shaylene—sat crowded around the table.

"Perfect," Drew said, tapping his fingers on the tabletop. "What's the plan?"

Travis rubbed his hands together. "Yeah, are we going to burn their warehouse to the ground?"

"No," Kellan answered in a sharp tone, but he quickly clarified. "We don't want anyone else getting hurt."

"To be honest, I'm starting to wonder why no one else *has*

317

gotten hurt," Shaylene pointed out. All eyes turned to her. "I mean, you stole their one bargaining chip. Why haven't they retaliated yet?"

"That's a good point," Kellan said, "and something Cora and I have been considering. Our best guess is they're planning something—something big."

Warner frowned. He was Kellan's roommate and hadn't been there the night of the rescue mission, but Kellan had managed to recruit him since. "I don't like the sound of that."

Kellan shook his head. "No, you shouldn't. But we have to be prepared for anything."

Kellan started passing out sheets of paper, while I stepped to the front of the room to explain.

"You all know that campus security has increased this semester," I said. "However, there are parts of campus that security doesn't have access to—namely, the students. We need eyes and ears everywhere. If you hear the slightest whisperings of a threat against campus—or against any of us—you report back to Kellan or me, and we'll relay the message to Chancellor Harris."

Kellan finished passing out the papers and stood beside me. "We've already talked with Chancellor Harris, and she's given us the go-ahead to form a student security team."

Caleb looked down at his paper. "The Supernatural Cavalry?"

Kellan shrugged. "Colt Walter has the Infantry. We'll fight them with the Cavalry."

Laura smiled. "I like it."

"These are your schedules," Kellan said, gesturing to the papers. "We've also emailed each of you a copy. We'll be patrolling areas campus security deems less important, like the dorms, dining hall, and the Activities Center."

Shaylene's jaw dropped. "Those are *less* important? There are students in those buildings all the time."

Kellan held up a hand. "I'm not saying security won't be

there, but they've allocated their resources to the perimeter and classroom buildings—especially the Academy Building where all the administrative offices are."

Laura bit her lip while she looked over the schedule. "Do you really think the school is in this much danger?"

"We can't know for sure," Kellan said, "but we have to be prepared. The Infantry has shown they're capable of anything. In the meantime, I've spoken to my father about getting a meeting with the Alliance. We need to escalate this issue to the proper authorities."

Kellan's gaze flickered to mine. "My dad made it sound like what happened last semester is a hot topic within the council. Maybe we can leverage that somehow. What we need from you guys is help developing a presentation that will ensure the Alliance takes us seriously and we can implement the most effective solution."

"Hold up," Miles said, raising his hand. "Why wouldn't the Alliance take us seriously?"

Kellan frowned, and his eyes darted toward me. "Well, we're already in deep, with what happened during our final last semester. My dad says they've heard whisperings of our rescue mission, but luckily the Alliance doesn't know all the details."

"Luckily?" Tucker asked.

Kellan raised an eyebrow. "You think they wouldn't prosecute us for flying through the city that night? They have their suspicions from the rumors, but they can't confirm anything."

Kellan and I exchanged a glance, but it was me who spoke. "We think Chancellor Harris might be protecting you guys to keep from attracting any more attention to the academy."

"Okay," Travis said, clapping his hands together. "Let's get started."

～

After our meeting with the team, I was starting to feel more positive. There'd been no attack on the school, and I was starting to wonder if maybe Kellan's rescue mission had scared the Infantry off.

"You might be right," Kellan said to me before class one day. We were hiding in an alcove by the stairs, talking in hushed voices. "But I'm not ready to get my hopes up."

"You worry too much," I told him.

Kellan brushed my hair behind my ear, and tingles spread all the way down to my toes. He liked to siphon my essence every time he touched me just to make me jump a little. It got me every time.

"There's a reason for that," he whispered.

My heart pounded as Kellan leaned in. He brushed his lips across mine, and they tingled where he touched. I took his face in my hands and pulled him closer to me. His hands roamed over my back, and I arched my spine to press against him. Kellan's hand traveled down further and further, until he was cupping my ass.

I gasped, but I didn't pull away.

He chuckled and spoke between kisses. "You like that?"

"I like everywhere you touch me," I said breathlessly.

Kellan's gaze darted down to my breasts, then back up to my eyes. "I think we can steal a few hours after class. Warner's got security duty in the dining hall tonight."

Please, God. Yes! Kellan and I had hardly gotten to second base. I was dying for more, and I knew he was, too.

"We should probably get to class," I whispered.

Kellan faked a frown, then squeezed my butt again. "If I have to."

I snickered. "We don't really have a choice."

"We could skip," he suggested playfully.

"And fail the kidney section of the final?" I reminded him.

His shoulders fell. "Fine. Let's go."

We walked hand-in-hand to our human physiology class and sat beside each other. Celina and Rhys were at the front of the class. She kept shooting Kellan glances, but he was making it a point to ignore her. She was obviously bothered by it.

Whatever. Screw her. She didn't deserve a second of his attention.

None of our other friends had this class with us. They'd all been put in the other lecture block and were always a day ahead of us on material. Kellan and I silenced our phones, since Professor Braff has a strict no-phone-in-class policy.

Professor Braff strolled into the room a few minutes later. He was my anatomy professor last semester and still one of my favorite teachers. He gave a few students high-fives as he walked in, and Everett made a few jokes about Professor Braff's skeleton tie.

"Okay, okay, settle down," Professor Braff said, straightening his tie. "Last week, we left off with an overview of the kidneys. Today, we'll dig in deeper."

Professor Braff opened up his slideshow on the projector and showed us a diagram of the kidneys. He clicked a button on his computer, and the image zoomed in to a small structure inside the kidney labeled *nephron*. I started taking notes immediately.

"We all know that the kidneys filter the blood," Professor Braff started, "but they don't do it by magic. Each of our kidneys is made up of millions of small units called nephrons. These are the filtering units that take waste out of the bloodstream—"

The door burst open, cutting Professor Braff off. I jumped in my seat when I saw Shaylene grasping the door frame with tears streaming down her face. She gasped for breath, as if she'd been running. Her eyes scanned the room, until her gaze fell upon Kellan and me seated beside each other. My stomach plummeted to my toes.

Professor Braff's eyebrows knitted together. "Miss Hargrove?"

"Sorry, Professor," she said breathlessly. "I need to talk to—"

Kellan and I were already on our feet. We grabbed our coats and rushed out of the room. I grabbed Shaylene by the shoulder and dragged her down the hall, since she seemed too shocked to move herself.

"Shaylene!" I shook her, but her eyes glossed over. I was aware that the classroom door had been left open and students were talking indistinctly about the interruption. There were even a few people who stuck their heads out the door to see what was going on. But I didn't pay any attention to them.

Kellan stepped between Shaylene and the classroom door, so people wouldn't see her cry.

"Shaylene, what's wrong?" he demanded.

She blinked a few times, then wiped the tears away. "S-something's happened."

Shaylene held up her phone, and my guts twisted at what I saw. A video played across the screen. It shook a little, like someone recorded it on their phone. It showed six people on their knees in the middle of a tiled floor. The angle looked down on them, so we couldn't see behind them. Their hands were held up in surrender. Tears glistened in several of the girls' eyes, but the guys kept a stoic look on their face, like they weren't willing to show their emotions.

"Oh my God!" I cried. "Is that Laura and Travis?"

Shaylene sniffed. One of the guys lifted his head, and I realize Caleb was there, too. I recognized the three other girls from my Art of Healing II lecture—Sarah, Avery, and Lisa. Laura sat still like Travis and Caleb, not giving her thoughts away.

Various sets of feet passed in front and behind them, encircling them like they were prey. We couldn't see their faces, but we could hear the indistinct voices of men whispering in the background.

"What is this?" Kellan demanded.

"It was sent to my ph-phone," Shaylene sniffled. "The three of them left a half hour ago with a group of girls who had to stop at the bank downtown. They were escorting them as part of the Supernatural Cavalry."

"Who sent the video?" Kellan growled.

Shaylene's bottom lip quivered. "It came from Caleb, but I-I think the guys who have them sent it, like they wanted me to see it."

Kellan and I glanced at each other, before realizing a second later we were in all their phones as contacts. We both scrambled to grab our phones out of our pockets. My body froze when I saw that I had messages from both Laura and Travis with a link to the video.

I glanced up to Kellan. "Do you think it's live?"

Kellan stared down at the video, his lips tightening with each passing second. "We better hope so. If we could only figure out where they're at..."

"I think they're still at the bank," Shaylene said. "When I first opened the video, I could see the teller windows in the background. But I don't know which one."

Kellan eyed the video a second longer. One of the men stepped in front of the hostages. "Here's what's going to happen," he sneered.

The sinking feeling in my gut turned to stone cold rocks as I heard the sickening cold voice of Colt Walter play over the speakers.

"You're going to expose yourself for what you truly are," Colt said. I couldn't see his face, but I saw the gun in his hand. "Then the whole world will know the truth."

Travis's lips tightened. "You think we're going to give in that easily?"

Colt lifted his gun and pointed it at Travis's face. My whole body began to shake.

"You will… or the girl dies." Colt shifted his gun, and the barrel pointed directly between Laura's eyebrows.

The camera angle shifted to fit the gun into the frame, and we caught sight of the pillars and dark wood tones around the room.

Kellan inhaled a sharp breath. "I know this place. It's on Bleecker Street."

Shaylene's eyes lit up. "Then let's go!"

The three of us took off in the direction of the parking lot. Outside, the sky was dark with storm clouds. The video continued to play on our phones, and my lungs felt as if they were going to burst from holding my breath. Colt was still negotiating with Travis, but I worried he might pull the trigger at any second.

"Wait, wait!" I cried as soon as we stepped outside and I spotted the bell tower of the Academy Center in front of us. "We need to tell Chancellor Harris before we run off."

"You guys go!" Shaylene told us. "I'll talk to Chancellor Harris."

Shaylene ran off in the direction of the Academy Center, while Kellan started toward his car. I took quick steps beside him, but I didn't really watch where I was going. I couldn't tear my eyes from the video in front of me. Colt had Travis pinned to the floor now, the gun pressed against the back of his skull. Colt's face finally came into view, but it was covered by a ski mask.

"You know what you are!" Colt was yelling.

I tore my gaze away from the video. "Shit, Kellan. They're going to kill our friends."

"No, they're not." Kellan pulled his phone to his ear as he wrenched open the driver's side door.

"What are you doing?" I asked breathlessly.

Kellan's lips tightened. "Calling in the Cavalry."

As I slid into the passenger seat, he stuck his key into the ignition. He turned his attention from me to whoever was on the other line. "Warner? They've got six supernaturals at the bank on Bleeker. We're going to need all the help we can get."

"I'm on it," I heard Kellan's roommate say.

Kellan punched his screen to end the call. My heart slammed against my rib cage.

It'll all be fine, I told myself. *Colt can't get away with this...*

Unless he killed one of my friends first.

I couldn't bear to think of that.

Kellan drove so fast through the academy gates that security barely had a chance to buzz us out. Word of the video must've not reached the highest authorities at school yet, or the place would be on lockdown. Right now, that wouldn't stop Kellan or me, though. We had to get to our friends—immediately.

Kellan stepped on the gas and tore through a yellow light at the end of the street. He took sharp turns and weaved between traffic like he was on a freaking racecourse. But I didn't care. I held on to the oh-shit handle and tried to keep my body from shaking as the video continued to play.

Colt ripped off Travis's shirt. "Show us! Show us who you truly are!" he yelled.

My eyes widened in horror. "Where's the Alliance!? They should be responding to this shit."

Kellan's eyes darkened, but he kept them on the road.

Another male voice came through the video. "They want to talk to you."

I glanced down to the video to see one of the masked men handing Colt a wireless landline phone. It must've been one of the bank's phones. Colt took it and walked off camera, until we couldn't hear him. Our fellow classmates didn't move, and the video had gone quiet.

"Why are they showing us this?" I demanded, though I didn't

think Kellan knew the answer. "Do you think it's everywhere? If they want to turn people against us, why are they being total assholes?"

Kellan shook his head. "I think this is for us."

"To scare us?" I asked.

He took another corner and said, "Exactly."

We turned onto Bleecker street, and I was half terrified, half relieved by what I saw. Police cars were lined up in front of the bank a block away, and barricades had been set up to keep traffic from coming through. Their lights blinked on top of their vehicles, and police pointed their guns at the entrance of the bank. In front of the barricades, traffic cops were directing cars through a detour onto the next street.

I swallowed the lump in my throat. "They think it's a robbery."

There was nowhere for us to park, but traffic was backed up as it was, so Kellan just shoved the car into park, and the two of us jumped out of the car. We ran toward the barricades, but two cops jumped in front of us to stop us.

"I'm sorry," one of them said, "but we can't let you go any further."

"Our friends are in there!" I yelled at them.

The taller of the two puffed out his chest at me. "Miss, I'm going to have to ask that you stand back."

"We have information that could help," Kellan insisted.

"What kind of information?" the cop asked firmly.

"They want to negotiate," Colt's voice came through my phone.

I held up the video. "We know what's happening inside."

The cop's eyes narrowed on me, like he suspected I might have something to do with this. "We're going to have to show that to the chief."

He reached for my phone, but I jerked it away. "I want to talk to him."

When the officer hesitated, Kellan added, "We have more information."

We didn't. Not really. But the officer must've believed us, because he said, "Wait here just a moment."

The second officer kept watch on us while the first walked over to the police chief. The chief stood next to a team of high-ranking officers. One of them was on the phone, which I assumed was the negotiator who'd called the bank phone to talk to Colt. The chief looked surprised when the officer approached him, then glanced our way. His lips tightened, but he made his way over to us anyway.

"Hi, I'm Chief Brown," he said as he approached. He sounded distressed, but he tried to remain friendly. "I hear you have information that can help us."

I handed him my phone. "They're recording what's going on inside. Our friends are in there, and they sent links to our phones to make us watch."

The chief's eyes went wide as he stared at the video. It was hard to tell what was going on now, because whatever was happening was taking place off camera.

Kellan inhaled a sharp breath. It was so quiet that no one else noticed, but I did. When I glanced at him, I saw his eyes were locked on the police chief's vest. I followed his gaze and noticed a symbol on his clothing. It was an embroidered Alliance symbol—three hands linked together. I realized what it meant right away.

"Chief Brown," Kellan said quickly. "If it helps, our friends and us go to Harris Academy."

The chief's eyes snapped upward, and they flickered between the two of us. He didn't look at the other police officers when he addressed them. "Please give me a moment with these students, if you will."

"But sir—" one of them protested.

"I said I need a minute," he repeated.

The officers stepped away, and the chief leaned in and lowered his voice. "You're both one of them, aren't you?"

The way he said *them* suggested he wasn't supernatural at all. He was human, but the symbol on his shirt told us he knew our secret.

Kellan and I nodded in unison.

The chief's face paled, and he glanced back down to the video. In it, Colt was saying, "This isn't a negotiation. We're going with the plan and exposing them."

"This isn't a bank robbery, is it?" the chief asked.

"No," Kellan said. "These people followed our friends and cornered them here. They're trying to get our friends to expose themselves on camera."

The chief frowned. "This changes everything about our negotiation tactics. Is there anything else you can tell me?"

"The group calls themselves the Infantry," I said.

Chief Brown's eyes narrowed. "These people again?"

"You've heard of them?" Kellan sounded irritated.

"We're aware of the problems you've had at school," he said.

"Then why haven't you done anything?" Kellan demanded.

The chief ignored his question.

Colt's raging voice came through the video. "Tell us the truth!"

There was so much anger in his voice. I just didn't get what he was so mad about. I'd said it before, and this just confirmed it. Colt wasn't scared of us. Though he'd amassed a following of terrified people who wanted to know the truth, it was clear that wasn't Colt's motives. He already knew what we were. He wasn't using *his* fear against us. He was using everyone else's.

The only thing was, I couldn't figure out why. What did he have against us?

I heard the sound of Laura whimper, and that was my moment of clarity. I turned to Kellan. "Kellan, we have to talk to Colt."

"What? No," he insisted. Darkness crossed his features, like he thought this was one of those dangerous situations I promised I wouldn't get into anymore.

"Colt wants to know the truth, Kellan," I said. "We need to show him who we truly are."

Chief Brown cut in before Kellan could respond. "I'm sorry, but I can't let you speak to him while there are hostages in there."

"Cora, he already knows what we are," Kellan argued.

"He doesn't," I replied. "If he did, he wouldn't be doing any of this. He thinks we're something we're not. If we could just show him how good we truly are—"

"Cora, you promised." Kellan pressed his fingers to his eyes. "No more putting yourself in danger."

"I never promised that," I reminded him. "I only said I wouldn't do it without you."

Kellan's features softened.

"I'm sorry, but no," Chief Brown insisted.

"Please," I begged. "I can help."

Kellan grabbed my arm. "Cora, you can't."

I ignored Kellan. "Make him a deal," I said to Chief Brown. "Let him take me in exchange for the other hostages."

"No!" Kellan cried. "If we're making exchanges, I'm going in."

I turned to Kellan. "We both know he's not going to make that deal with you. He's wanted me since the beginning."

Kellan's features were hard, but his expression wavered. He knew I was right.

"No one's going in there," Chief Brown insisted.

I crossed my arms. "Do you want to lose six people today? Ask for the exchange, and I guarantee he'll agree."

"I can't," he insisted again. "Why do you think you can talk him down? Do you have a personal connection with these criminals?"

Kellan and I exchanged a glance.

"Not really," I said.

"I really am sorry, kids," Chief Brown said regrettably. "But we're doing our best. I'm going to have to ask you to return behind the barricades and allow our officers to do their jobs."

"Of course," Kellan said, grabbing my arm tighter. "Thank you for your time, chief."

Kellan started dragging me away.

I ripped my arm out of his grasp. "Kellan, wait. We have to help! Our friends are in there!"

Kellan and I stepped to the other side of the barricade, and he whirled toward me, his nostrils flaring. There was a dark look in his eyes I'd never seen before. He pushed his fingers through his hair, then balled his hands into fists at his side. "I know, Cora. Believe me, I'm as pissed as you are. But we can't just run in there guns blazing."

"I'm not suggesting that," I said, though my eyes flickered upward.

Kellan noticed. "You're thinking of flying to the roof and seeing if there's a way in, aren't you?"

I crossed my arms. "Well, there has to be a back entrance somewhere."

"Or it's a bank and it's secure?" he retorted. "You don't think the police already have this place surrounded?"

"If we could just talk to him…"

"Then what?" Kellan pressed. "Cora, we don't want anyone getting hurt."

"People *are* getting hurt," I reminded him. "Kumar, Annie, all those people you went to the warehouse with. Kellan, if we don't do something, I'm afraid—"

Bang!

The sound of a gunshot rang through the street. My heart jumped and began racing a hundred miles per hour. Several people along the street screamed, and the chief started barking orders. Kellan grabbed me, and we ducked into a nearby alleyway.

Tears pricked at my eyes. "Oh my God! Do you think—?"

Kellan ripped his phone from his pocket and pulled up the video. My phone was still with the chief. He didn't let me look right away, until he breathed a sigh of relief.

"That was a warning shot," Colt's voice growled through the speakers.

My heart settled a little, but it was still racing. "Shit, Kellan. He's not screwing around. The only reason he's holding out is because the police are outside. We have to do something!"

Kellan's hands shook, but he wouldn't show his emotions on his face. "I know, Cora. I just…"

"You just what?" I asked.

He took a breath. "I don't want you getting hurt, too."

I crossed my arms, but my heart was still racing. "You may have to accept that as a possibility. Unless…"

Something hit me.

"What?" Kellan asked.

"We don't have a way in there, but we *can* talk to Colt," I pointed out. "He has our friends' phones."

Kellan inhaled a sharp breath. "Good idea. But *I'm* doing the talking."

"Anything to get Colt to step down," I said.

Kellan brought up his contacts and punched a few buttons on the screen, then pulled the phone to his ear. Each passing second felt like an eternity.

Please don't kill my friends. Please don't kill my friends.

Kellan's teeth ground together. "The bastard's not picking up!"

"Try again," I insisted.

Kellan called Travis's phone again, and then a third time after that. Finally, someone picked up.

"What the hell do you want?" one of Colt's cronies barked into the phone.

"I want to speak to your boss," Kellan stated firmly.

"Why would he want to talk to you?" the voice demanded. "Who are you?"

"I'm the guy who's going to give him what he wants," Kellan said.

The phone went silent, and I held my breath. For a moment, I thought they'd hung up, and I dreaded what might come next.

Kellan mumbled under his breath. "This bastard better—"

I cut him off by placing my hand on his arm. We both knew that kind of language could get one of our friends killed. He unclenched his jaw, and a moment later, a voice came over the phone. I recognized it as Colt's.

"I hear you have a deal for me," he practically sang.

"I do," Kellan said. "This is Kellan Greene, and I'm an Aedes."

Colt's evil laughter ran through the phone. "Oh, I know who you are, Kellan. I've been following you and Cora since you exposed yourselves. That was clever, by the way, telling everyone it was a hoax. So, what's this deal you have for me?"

"My friends won't give you what you want," Kellan said. "Let them go, and you can have me. I'll do whatever you say."

"Kellan!" I cried, but he shot me a dark look. My guts twisted in my abdomen.

Colt chuckled. "Is that her?"

"You're not getting her," Kellan growled. "You can have me. Just don't hurt my friends."

"Put your girlfriend on the phone, and I'll consider the deal," Colt replied.

Kellan hesitated. We both knew if we refused, we risked our friends getting hurt.

Colt spoke in a harsher tone. "Put her on the phone."

"Kellan, I've got this," I told him, reaching for the phone in his hand.

Kellan's nostrils flared, but he let me take it.

"I'm here," I said to Colt. "Look, all we want is our friends to be let go."

Colt chuckled. "And you know what happens the second I do that? The police come swarming in on all sides. I don't think so."

"Then what do you want, Colt?" I asked gently, though my hands were shaking in rage.

"I want everyone to know what you truly are," Colt said. "I want your kind to pay for what you've done."

"What is it that we've done?" I asked him.

"Like you don't already know," Colt sneered.

"I don't," I swore. "I'm sorry if one of us hurt you, Colt, but you have to know—"

"Hurt me?" he snapped. "Hurting me would've been preferable, little demon."

My guts twisted into a knot. It was obvious by the way he spoke that my theory was correct. He was *angry*—but angry at what, I didn't know.

"What happened to you?" I asked.

Colt laughed again, a laugh that sent a chill down my spine. "All you demons are the same—playing stupid when you know damn well what you've done! You took her from me! You took her!"

The phone shook in my hands. I knew now more than ever, saying the wrong thing would have dire consequences. And so, I had to make the best assumption I could.

"You loved her a lot, didn't you?" I tried my best to keep the shakiness from my tone.

"Of course I loved her," Colt snapped. "We were engaged. Your kind changed all that."

My pulse quickened. I had to keep Colt talking, to get him to tell me the rest of the story, but I had no idea where he was going with this.

"She got involved with the supernaturals, didn't she?" I asked, making the vaguest assumption I could.

"*She* got involved?" he balked. "More like *they* got involved."

"Involved how?" I asked. I didn't know how else to phrase the question, considering how little he was telling me.

"She was supposed to live!" he yelled.

That's when it hit me. He blamed *us*, the people who were supposed to heal his fiancé, for her death.

"Healing is a difficult process, Colt," I found myself saying.

"Healing?" he scoffed. "That's what you think you do?"

I furrowed my brow. "What do *you* think we do?"

"I know the truth," Colt growled. "After the accident, she was brought to the hospital and promised she'd make it. But I saw what those assholes with the winged emblem on their coats did. They drew her soul straight out of her body. I saw it. Seconds later, she went into a seizure, and she was dead before I could get the *real* doctors there."

I covered the phone's mouthpiece with my hand and looked to Kellan. "He thinks they took her *soul*. It makes no sense..."

Kellan looked as confused as I did.

I brought the phone back to my face. "What did her soul look like?"

"I don't know," Colt snapped. "Like all souls. White and glowing. You should know!"

My eyes widened, and Kellan had the same expression on his face. *Essence!* Colt had seen essence. My mind flickered back to one of our lessons earlier this semester. Professor Kovski had taught us about channeling, a technique where you place essence into someone's body to stabilize them until you can administer a transfusion or other care. What he must've walked in on was them removing the essence—but she wasn't stable enough yet and she had a bad reaction.

"I looked into the supernaturals after that," Colt continued, his voice getting angrier by the second. "I saw the emblem on their jackets, and I knew something was suspicious about Harris Academy."

"You have to know that's not what happened to her, Colt," I stated. "We're healers. They were trying to *heal* her."

He scoffed. "If that were true, why isn't she here right now?"

"Sometimes we can't heal everything," I said regrettably.

"You're right," he sneered. "You can't heal everything. Maybe your kind needs a taste of what it feels like to have a soul taken from you."

Sarah pleaded in the background. "No, please, don't! I'm just—"

Bang!

Cries reached my ears through the phone, and my whole body stilled.

"*Go, go, go!*" I heard the sound of Chief Brown's orders from down the street.

I couldn't move. I couldn't breathe. The last gunshot felt so uncertain. This one needed no confirmation. I knew he'd shot her.

It felt like all my insides were being pushed up through my throat, and my knees buckled beneath me. Kellan grabbed me before I dropped to the pavement. The line had gone dead, and the phone dropped from my hands.

Above us, the dark storm clouds finally gave way, and rain began to fall around us. It was slow at first, just small drops tickling the back of my neck, but the rain quickly picked up speed, until it was pounding down on us. Wind whipped through the alleyway, and hail pummeled the pavement. It might've hurt—if I could feel anything at all. But I'd gone numb to everything but the heat.

There was so much heat—anger and grief all rolled into one. It started in my eyes as the tears spilled over, then spread through my whole body like a raging inferno. My element was rising to the surface, and I couldn't control it. Raindrops sizzled on my skin.

Kellan cradled me in his arms, rocking me back and forth as tears streamed down my face.

"Oh, God," I sobbed, my shoulders shaking. "He... he... because of me."

"No." Kellan ran his fingers through my wet hair. "This isn't your fault, Cora. This is his fault and his fault alone."

"But if I hadn't insisted we call—"

"Then things could've turned out worse," Kellan said. I couldn't tell if he meant it, or if he was just saying that to make me feel better.

Except nothing could make me feel better right now. This wasn't a *feel better* kind of situation.

This was a moment to grieve.

17

$\mathcal{A}$ darkness took over the academy the following week. I barely remembered how we'd gotten back to the academy after the gunshots. It felt like one minute I was sitting out in the rain, and the next I was being piled under a layer of warm blankets.

He shot Sarah. He killed her.

And it was my fault.

"There's nothing more we can do," Kellan assured me when I insisted we go back.

But I knew he was already forming some sort of plan in his mind.

Colt had escaped. It was all over the news. I didn't know how he'd done it—and the police were still baffled—but he managed an escape and hadn't been heard from since. The police caught his cronies and rescued our friends. I couldn't have been more relieved to see Travis, Caleb, and Laura after everything that happened, but things were different. When Laura and I were alone in our room, she barely spoke. I knew it had to be from the trauma she'd experienced, but I worried that on some level she blamed me like I blamed myself. Her parents had come to visit, but she assured them she wanted to finish the semester. I had a feeling that had something to do with staying close to Travis.

There'd been a memorial service for Sarah in the auditorium. Kellan held my hand the whole time, but he kept glancing around like he thought Colt might show up after what he did to her. Nothing happened during the memorial service, and it felt as if nothing happened the days following. No one really spoke, in my classes or in the common areas. It was like we all felt the weight of what happened to Sarah and knew it could've been any one of us.

"I had the opportunity to meet with the Alliance this past week, and they're doing the best they can," Kellan announced one afternoon when the Supernatural Cavalry got together in our dorm's rec room. There was something in his voice, however, that suggested the Alliance hadn't been doing enough.

I glanced to Kumar, who sat straight in one of the plush chairs and looked very interested in what Kellan had to say. Kumar hadn't said anything about the shooting to me, but I could see it in his eyes—he knew Annie had been close to meeting the same fate as Sarah. Annie had gone home in Colorado, but I could see the fight burning bright in Kumar's eyes.

Kumar's hands tightened into fists. "They haven't caught Colt yet."

"No," Kellan confirmed, his lips pressed into a thin line. "They got some names, but we have no way of knowing how many there are. They're spread everywhere, but it's almost like…"

"Like what?" I asked.

Kellan pressed his lips together. "Well, I don't know for sure, but my dad made it sound like things aren't adding up. Records have already gone missing."

"We better hope they caught enough of them," Travis growled. "Without his people, Colt's on his own."

"Does that make him less of a threat?" Laura asked, twisting her hands in her lap.

Kellan's jaw tensed. "I would think so. Luckily, finals week is upon us. We just have one week of protecting the students, then everyone will be back home for the summer. We can hope the Alliance will catch Colt before school starts up again."

Travis groaned and got to his feet. "Man, I don't know how you stay positive all the time."

Kellan wasn't being positive. I could see it in his eyes. He felt terrible about what had happened and was only saying what he had to because everyone looked up to him.

"We should be out there hunting this guy down," Travis said.

Caleb stood beside him and cracked his knuckles. "I'd like to break my knuckles on that fucker's face."

Shaylene pressed a hand to Caleb's chest and spoke gently. "Believe me, we all want to see Colt pay for what he did, but we can't stoop to his level. We're better than that."

"Yeah," Caleb agreed. "We *are* better than that. I'm not going to murder the bastard. I'll let the justice system take care of that."

"And we will," Kellan said. "In the meantime, we still have a school to protect until Colt is caught."

"I want to help," a female voice said in the doorway.

Everyone turned to see Celina standing there. I was so used to seeing Rhys at her side that I was kind of surprised to see her alone. On instinct, I stepped in front of Kellan, but he gently took my shoulder and pushed me aside.

"You what?" Kellan asked Celina.

"I want to help," she repeated.

Or you could go drown in a river, I thought. But instead, I said, "What makes you think we'd trust you?"

Celina stepped further into the room and crossed her arms.

"Because this isn't about me and Kellan. This is about all of us. I don't want anyone else getting hurt, either."

I eyed her up and down, feeling my fire warm my skin in disdain. "Why the sudden change of heart? You've hurt enough people."

Warner put his hand over his mouth. "Oooh…"

Celina shot him daggers. "Do you want more help, or do you want to fight a second war with me?"

Kellan narrowed his gaze at her. "You know what? I want to hear it. Why should we trust you?"

Celina's lips pressed into a thin line. "You shouldn't."

When she saw the look of shock on our faces—we never thought she'd admit it—she sighed and added, "I mean, you're right. I haven't given you a good reason in the past to trust me, and I don't have a good reason now. All I can ask is that you take a chance."

Kellan eyed her a moment longer, his eyes darkening with each passing second. "Sorry, Celina, but I can't do that."

Her eyebrows shot up. "You can't—?"

"I can't take a chance," he said, shocking me a little.

"But all I want to do is help!" Cora pointed out.

"We have enough people," Kellan said. "And I trust them."

He emphasized it like he didn't trust Celina—and never would.

"Kellan, come on," Celina begged. "My essence is really strong. I can help."

Kellan's fists tightened at his sides, but his expression read pain. "You want me to trust you, Celina? Then you're going to have to earn that trust back." He eyed her up and down before adding, "Good luck with that."

Celina's jaw dropped as Kellan turned away from her. "Kellan? Kellan!"

He ignored her, and she huffed and stomped away.

Kellan pressed his fingers to his eyes when she left the room, like he couldn't stand one more thing. He sighed, then turned back to the group. "Everyone's got this week's schedule, right?"

"Yep," Warner said, waving his phone with his email open.

"Okay," Kellan said, sounding defeated. "We'll meet again on Wednesday."

Everyone started gathering their things and left the room, until just Kellan and I were alone. He stood by the window and looked outside. The sun had dipped below the walls of the academy half an hour ago, and night was starting to settle over campus.

I wrapped my arms around him. "It's going to be okay," I whispered, though I didn't feel it myself.

With Colt still out there and his sights set on the academy, I was constantly alert. Until he was caught, I wouldn't feel safe. The only solace was knowing that by the end of this week, campus would be empty and our classmates would be back home. In the back of my mind, I knew that didn't mean anything for me—Colt had already attacked my family and could do it again. But at least everyone else would be out of his clutches.

Kellan ran a hand across mine, but he didn't say anything. I could sense the tension in his body.

"I'm sorry about Celina," I whispered. He didn't talk about it much, but I could tell he was still upset about it.

He turned around and took my hands. "Don't worry about her."

Kellan wrapped me in his arms, and I laid my head on his chest, enjoying the rise and fall of his chest.

"This past week has been…" I trailed off.

Kellan ran his hands up and down my back, and some of the tension eased from my shoulders. "Crazy. I know."

"We need a vacation," I teased.

Kellan chuckled lightly. "Believe me, I've been thinking about it."

"Well, maybe once this is all over, we'll take a trip this summer," I said.

Kellan stilled. It hit me only a moment later what I'd suggested. We hadn't even slept together yet, and already I was suggesting we take a vacation together.

I drew away from him. "I didn't mean—"

"No," he said with a shrug. "I think I'd like that."

My eyebrows shot up. "Really?"

He nodded and gave a shrug, as if to ask why not.

My heart lifted. "Where would you want to go?"

"Somewhere warm…" Kellan stared down at me with soft eyes, then pressed his lips to mine. The rec room spun around me. "And romantic."

"Mm…" I mused. "Romantic sounds nice. We've barely had a moment alone since we got together."

Kellan's lips twitched at the corners as his eyes roamed over my face. My chest warmed at the way he looked at me, and all I wanted to do was press my body closer to his.

"We need to do something about that," he suggested.

My eyes flickered down to his muscled chest. "Believe me, I want to. But you have Cavalry duty tonight."

Kellan frowned. "Damn… Do you want to join me?"

"Of course," I said, before I realized what his suggestion might mean. My heart beat wildly in my chest, because part of me wanted to take him up on the offer, while the other part reminded me nothing good could come from distracting him. "Wait. You don't mean…?"

Kellan laughed lightly and brushed my hair behind my ear. My skin tingled from where he touched me. "Is that what you want?"

My knees went weak when he suggested that. "Yes," I admitted. "But…"

"But…?" Kellan encouraged.

I sighed. "I thought things would be different, you know? That things wouldn't be all… crazy when we finally got together."

Kellan smirked. "That must be it."

"What?" I asked.

"We're cursed," he said simply.

I rolled my eyes. "You're right. That must be it."

Kellan's tone softened as he became serious again. "If that's what you want, Cora, then we'll wait."

"Hold on," I teased. "You, the *man*, are suggesting we wait?"

Kellan shrugged, but he looked uncomfortable, like what I said bothered him. "I just want it to be special for you… For both of us."

My heart melted. "I do, too. It almost seems… unfair, doesn't it?"

"What does?" he asked curiously, running his fingers across my collarbone as he stared down at me.

I dropped my head. "It's unfair that life keeps going on as normal for us after what happened. Sarah's gone, and Annie… well, she'll never be the same. Laura, either. She's been really quiet since it happened. I want to help, but I don't know how because she won't tell me how she feels."

Kellan pressed his lips together in thought. "You know what? You're right."

I raised an eyebrow. "That life's unfair? Yeah, I've kind of got the message since my mom was caught in an arson explosion."

Kellan's shoulders fell. "Exactly."

My stomach sank. "If you're trying to make me feel better, it's not working."

"No, I'm just saying… we don't really know what our friends went through in that bank," Kellan pointed out. "I think we should do something for them before the end of the semester."

The tension in my shoulders eased. "That's a really good

idea, Kellan. I think it would make us all feel better. It will help to focus on something else."

"So, what should we do?" Kellan asked.

I smiled for the first time all week. "You let me take care of that."

18

"There," I said, putting the finishing touches on the snacks I'd lain out on my study desk. I took one of the chips from the bag and scooped up some dip with it, then popped it in my mouth. I turned to Kaylee, who was lying on my bed. "Thanks for bringing all this."

Kaylee smiled. "What are friends for?"

I hadn't left the academy all week, but Kaylee had agreed to go shopping for me, and received clearance from campus security since she was a Davina.

I walked over to her and wrapped her in a hug. "I'm so glad you're back from Europe. I can't wait to hang out with you this summer."

"I know," she said. "It's been so long."

I plopped down on the bed beside her.

Kaylee sat up straight. "I have a surprise for you."

"You do?" I asked.

She beamed. "I didn't want to tell you over the phone."

"What is it?" I begged. It sounded like good news.

"I applied for next semester," Kaylee said. "I got in!"

"Oh my God!" I cried, squeezing her into another hug. "That's great."

"I know," she enthused. "Europe was *amazing*, but I'm ready to get back to my studies. And I missed you so much."

I nudged her in the side and teased, "You're just eager to meet all the hot guys who go here."

She chuckled. "Maybe…"

We shared a laugh, but it was short-lived. There was a coolness in the air that hadn't left for days. I had a feeling we could both sense it.

I sighed and leaned against her. "I really missed you, Kaylee. When you're here, it's like I can forget all the craziness that happened this semester."

Kaylee wrapped an arm around me. "Do you want to talk about it?"

I shook my head, but inside, my guts were twisting. "Not really. People will be here soon."

"Right," she said. "Well, if they're not here in the next ten minutes, I'm going to eat all those chips."

"Go ahead," I replied. "You're the one who bought them."

The sound of footsteps met my ears, and I sat up straight. Laura stopped in our open doorway and glanced around at all the food and the TV set up with video games. She furrowed her brow as she stepped inside.

I jumped to my feet. "Surprise!"

Laura's features softened. "We're having a party?"

"Yep," I said. "To celebrate the end of finals. I thought it'd be fun to play games and hang out before we all leave for the summer. Everyone else will be here soon."

For the first time all week, Laura cracked a smile. "I think that's a great idea, Cora."

Her eyes flickered to Kaylee on my bed, and I remembered the two had never met before.

"Laura, this is Kaylee, my friend from high school," I introduced. "Kaylee, this is Laura."

Kaylee stood and shook Laura's hand. "I've heard a lot about you."

"You, too," Laura said.

Kaylee's eyes lit up. "I hear you're the fashion expert around here. Do you think you could give me some pointers on my summer style?"

I'd told Kaylee my whole idea for the night was to get everyone's mind off what had happened. I had a feeling she made the suggestion to help Laura feel better, but I also knew the two would get along.

"Just summer?" Laura asked as she set her backpack at the foot of the bed. "We can come up with a plan for next fall, too."

"Really?" Kaylee seemed excited. "Fall's my favorite."

Laura reached for her stack of fashion magazines on her dresser. "Fall is gorgeous around here."

"Right?" Kaylee sat beside Laura on her bed, and the two started flipping through magazines.

Less than a minute later, Kumar stuck his head in the doorway. "I hear there's a party in here."

"Come in," I said, gesturing him inside.

"I brought the booze," he sang, holding two packs of beer above his head.

Kaylee lifted her head, and her gaze stopped dead on Kumar. He caught her eye and froze in place. Laura and I both chuckled, bringing them both back to reality.

Kumar set the beer on the floor and cleared his throat. "I don't believe we've met."

Kaylee giggled, like Kumar was being particularly charming. "I'm Kaylee, Cora's friend from high school."

"Well, hello, Kaylee, Cora's friend from high school. I'm Kumar, Cora's friend from college." He offered a light smile, which was promising, because I hadn't seen him smile at all after what happened to him and Annie.

To say that Kaylee fit in with my group at college was an understatement. As more people arrived, it was clear Kaylee was the missing puzzle piece in our whole gang. She got along with everyone great.

Everyone seemed to be having a great time hanging out, and it put me at ease. Laura and Shaylene leaned against a huge pile of pillows on Laura's bed and flipped through magazines together, while Kaylee and Kumar flirted in the corner and bonded over their love of snack food. Travis, Caleb, and Warner were laughing in front of the TV while they played a racing game on the video game console Kellan had loaned me. The rest of the guys—Drew, Miles, Everett, Jett, and Tucker—had set up their empty beer cans in the hall and were taking turns rolling a basketball at them.

Kellan and I sat on the bed and leaned against the wall. His arm wrapped around me, and my head lay on his chest.

"Why so glum?" he asked softly, so no one else could hear.

I looked up into his eyes. "I'm not glum."

"You're… quiet," he pointed out.

"I'm just enjoying seeing everyone having fun," I said.

He squeezed me tighter. "You did a good job. I think this is just what we all needed to end the semester with."

"How'd your finals go?" I asked.

Kellan smirked. "You're supposed to be taking your mind *off* things, Cora."

I chuckled lightly, but it felt forced. While I watched everyone enjoy their night, I was reminded of what had happened and everything that brought us to this moment.

"I'm trying," I told him honestly. "I just think… we all need more time."

"Agreed," Kellan said, running his fingers up and down my

arm. Tingles spread across my skin. "No matter how long it takes, Cora, I'll be here to help you through it."

My heart melted in my chest. It was obvious I was taking everything harder than him, but I stared into his eyes anyway and added, "I want to be there for you, too."

He brushed my hair out of my eyes and looked at me like I was the only girl in the room. The sounds of the guys playfully yelling at each other in front of the TV and the girls giggling at magazines across the room seemed to fade when he gazed at me like that. I relaxed into him.

"We will, Cora," he whispered. "We'll always be there, no matter what happens."

I forced the corners of my lips into a slight smile. "Because we're partners."

Kellan shook his head. "No. Because we love each other."

Then his lips came down to meet mine, and I was totally swept off my feet. The room spun around me, and the words he'd just said echoed in my mind.

We love each other.

In that moment, I actually thought everything would be okay from here on out.

I drew away from the gentle kiss, my heart beating rapidly against my rib cage. "I love you, too, Kellan," I whispered, running my hand across his chest. "No matter what."

Our beautiful moment came to a screeching halt when the sound of Celina's voice came from down the hall. "Thank God!" she cried. "You have to come quick."

The sound of beer cans knocking over met my ears, but it was followed by a moment of complete and utter silence. Travis pressed pause on the game, and everyone stilled.

"What's happened?" Drew demanded from out in the hall.

Kellan jumped to his feet and rushed outside the room, and I hurried behind him.

Celina sucked in a deep breath, like she'd been running. "I was leaving the Academy Center, and I swear I saw him."

Kellan stepped forward and spoke in a firm voice. "Saw who?"

Celina's face paled. "Colt."

My heart lurched in my chest, and a wave of heat washed over my skin. "He's on campus?"

"But how?" Drew asked.

Celina ignored his question and answered mine first. "I don't know for sure… He was wearing a hood, but I swear…"

She choked up a little. As much as I didn't like Celina—and didn't trust her—I had to believe she was telling the truth. She wasn't *that* good of an actress. By now, everyone else had come out of the room to see what was going on.

A muscle popped in Kellan's jaw, and he started down the hall without asking any further questions. "Come on, Cavalry. It's time to fight."

Kellan walked so fast that I had to take two steps for every one of his. My heart beat fast as I tried to keep up, and I felt as if a pile of bricks had just landed on me. This was bad. This was very bad.

But how did Colt get in? Security was all over the place.

"Wait," I said, turning to Celina, who had followed close behind. "Why'd you come to us first?"

"I didn't," she snapped. "I went straight to Chancellor Harris, *then* came here. If you think I'm lying—"

"It doesn't matter," Kellan said firmly. "We can't take any chances. But I swear on my very essence, Celina. If you're lying—"

"I'm not!" she insisted. "I told you the truth. I want to help."

Kellan eyed her a second longer, but must've decided there wasn't any time to waste, because he turned from her and said, "Fine. Let's go help security find this bastard."

Kellan took the steps at the end of the hall two times faster than I could. Everyone followed behind us, while Kellan barked orders. "Kumar, Caleb, Shaylene, and Everett, you take the West wing of the first floor. Miles, Tucker, Travis, and Laura, the East wing…"

His instructions faded as I raced out of the building behind him. I could hardly process what he said as my pulse pounded in my ears.

It's happening again. Colt's going to hurt somebody.

I wasn't going to let that happen.

It was dark outside, with nothing more than the streetlamps around campus to light our way. When we reached the Academy Building, there was already a large group forming outside the doors. People flooded out from all entrances.

"They're being evacuated," Kellan stated, but he didn't slow his step.

He pushed through the crowd, and we all followed behind.

"Rhys!" Celina shouted as she met up with him.

He wrapped her in his arms. "I'm so glad you're okay. Your message was terrifying."

We reached the front, where a group of security officers were pushing people back away from the doors. Two officers held up their hands when Kellan tried to get through.

"This building's on lockdown," one of them stated firmly.

"We're here to help," Kellan said. "We're an official student security group, approved by the Chancellor herself."

"I'm under strict orders not to let anyone pass," the officer emphasized. "I don't care who you are."

The officers pushed the group back further into the courtyard, until some were standing as far back as the Winged Fountain. Most people kept their distance, as they sensed something was wrong and dangerous.

Kellan's hands curled into fists. "We have to help! We can't just stand here."

The other officer stepped forward. "Standing back is the best help you can be right now."

I glanced through the glass doors, my heart pounding. I feared what I might see behind them. Instead of seeing Colt, though, I spotted Chancellor Harris standing beside her husband, Kane Harris, and a group of guys in fancy black suits. I recognized one of them as John Maddox, the public relations officer from the Alliance.

"What's the Alliance doing here?" I demanded.

I kept my eyes on Maddox. He took Chancellor Harris by the elbow and led her and the other Alliance members down the hall, toward one of the exits I couldn't see from here.

The officer ignored my question. "If you'll all please step back."

"What's the Alliance doing here?" I repeated, more firmly this time.

The officer pressed his lips together, looking displeased at my persistence. "It's nothing more than a regularly scheduled meeting with the school board," he answered, like that was supposed to ease my nerves about what was happening. "We're going to ask that you return to your dorms—"

Boom!

A deafening sound filled the air, so loud that it made my ears ring. I felt the shock wave move through my body, and I was thrust backward by the force of the blow. On instinct, my wings tore through my shirt, and I thrust them out on either side of me to slow my momentum. Still, I landed hard on the ground and gasped for breath.

I couldn't hear the screams over the sound of the crumbling building. My vision blurred, but it barely registered as reality came crashing down on me.

The academy center had just been bombed.

Colt Walter had just launched an attack on the school.

19

"Cora!"

Someone shouted my name, but I didn't hear who. My ears were still ringing, and when I tried to push myself to my feet, the world spun around me, and I was back on the ground again in less than a second.

"Cora!"

The voice came again, and I was suddenly aware of hands grasping my shoulders. I looked up into the face of the man shouting my name, but I couldn't focus on it. The streetlamps had flickered out above our heads, which left only the moonlight casting shadows across his face.

Essence whipped through my body, and my vision began to clear. Kellan's pale face swam in front of me, but I finally planted my feet firmly and saw him clearly. Color filled his cheeks as he drew more and more essence from me and into himself. Energy sizzled through me as I came back to reality, but my gut sank the moment everything came together.

"Oh my God!" I gasped.

The West wing of the Academy Center was in total shambles. It was nothing more than a pile of bricks. Parts of the East side still stood, but windows had been blasted out, and it looked like nothing more than a shell of the beautiful building that once stood there.

Screams filled the air around us, and I whirled around to assess the damage. Bricks and glass had been thrown into the crowd, and people were reeling on the ground in pain. Travis was knelt over Laura, who didn't look hurt but was a little out of it. Caleb had a huge gash on the side of his face from a shard of glass, and Shaylene was helping him heal it. Several of the guys had already jumped to their feet and were springing into action, while some of the crowd had scattered. Nearby, the blast had sent Warner into a tree, and he cradled his broken arm to his chest.

Panic hit me, but I pushed it aside. Now wasn't the time to get emotional. I knew that from my emergency training. Right now, I had to act.

I ran over to Warner and dropped to my knees beside him. "Kellan and I can help—"

"Forget about me!" Warner cried. "Help the people trapped in the building!"

He pointed toward the Academy Center.

Shit. He was right.

"We'll be back for you," Kellan told Warner.

"Go!" Warner shouted.

Kellan and I raced toward the Academy Center. The rubble was so thick that I didn't know how we were ever going to get down there.

"Shit!" Celina cried from beside me. I hadn't even noticed she and Rhys were behind us until she spoke. "We're going to need Earth Davina over here to move this stuff!"

Travis and Laura came up behind them. "We're right here," Travis said. "But it's going to take more—"

Boom!

We all jumped as a second explosion went off. It wasn't as

close this time, but it made my heart jump into my throat nonetheless. We all whirled in the direction of the deafening noise, only to see the white bricks of the campus boundary walls crumbling in on themselves. Before the smoke even cleared, hordes of shadows appeared through the wreckage. There must've been hundreds of people stepping over the rubble to get inside the school.

We all exchanged a look of utter shock. What the hell was going on here?

"This world is ours, demons!" one of the Infantry members shouted. "Go back to hell, bitches!"

Rhys cracked his knuckles. "Let's get those motherfu—"

Bang. Bang. Bang.

The sound of gunshots rang out over campus. It was so loud and constant that it sounded like a warzone. On instinct, we all ducked behind the rubble. Screams echoed off what remained of the boundary walls. I peeked over the top of the pile of bricks we hid behind, my heart racing. The gunfire was evident against the dark of night, and thick balls of essence, both light and dark, whizzed through the air. Supernaturals had taken to the sky to escape the attack, but the men with guns turned their aim skyward. Several Aedes and Davina spiraled out of the air. All around us, the ground began to shake, and whirlwinds stirred as Davina began to use their elements to fight back. But the Infantry retaliated so quickly and without regard that our fellow students and faculty members fell quickly.

"Oh, God!" Shaylene cried as she and Caleb ran over to us.

The rest of our group gathered around quickly and hid themselves with us in the rubble. Kaylee crouched beside me, with Kumar pressed up close next to her. Warner sucked a sharp breath through his teeth as he leaned up against a pile of bricks.

"Hey, dude," Miles said, shooting glances between Warner and the Infantry. "Can we help with that?"

"Help them!" Warner insisted.

Kellan jumped immediately into leader mode. "Davina, you're going to have to use your elements. Drew, see if you can knock some guns out of their hands with your air."

Rhys's features darkened as he glanced toward the advancing Infantry members. He nudged Celina in the side. "Let's burn these assholes."

"No!" Kellan barked.

Rhys looked him up and down. "Why not?"

Kellan took a few ragged breaths, and his eyes darted to Shaylene, then Laura, before finally falling on me. "Because if we aim to kill, it makes us no better than them."

"You're wasting time!" Rhys growled.

Kellan shook his head firmly. "This isn't the way supernaturals fight. We're healers."

I was shocked to hear him say it. He gave me this look like… I don't know… like something I'd said or done had changed his mind.

"Screw this," Rhys muttered, getting to his feet. "Let's go get them, Celina."

Celina hesitated and glanced between Rhys and the rest of us.

"You can't be serious!?" he roared.

Celina frowned. "I'm not a killer."

Rhys stared down at her a second longer, before scoffing and turning away. He jumped over the pile of rubble and raced away, dark essence forming in his palm. The tension in the air was palpable, but none of us had a moment to dwell on it. The Infantry were moving across campus quickly.

Celina pressed her lips into a thin line, as if trying to hide the way she felt about Rhys running off.

"You with us?" Kellan asked her.

She swallowed, then nodded firmly. "We stand together as one."

I never thought I'd ever see Celina take the school motto so seriously. She always seemed like the *I stand with you as long as you serve me* kind of girl. But she was serious about this. As Celina went silent, the obvious hurt on her face became evident. Rhys's departure was a betrayal—a clear end to their relationship. And yet, she chose standing beside us over him. She truly wanted to fight alongside us.

I held my hand out, palm to the ground. "We stand together as one," I repeated.

All hands came in to stack on top of mine, and the group repeated the school motto in unison. "We stand together as one."

"Let's do this," Kellan said in an encouraging tone. He turned to Kaylee. "You're water, right?"

"Yes," she answered breathlessly as the sound of gunshot continued to ring out, closer now more than ever.

"Make it rain to distort their vision." Kellan turned to me. "Celina, Cora, and Caleb, we need to create a barrier with your fire. Travis and Laura, we need you on the offense."

Travis gave him a salute. "On it, bro."

"Everyone else knows what to do." Kellan nodded toward the remaining guys, and they took off running. They zig-zagged between piles of rubble to get closer and start throwing their essence at the men across campus.

Kumar placed his hand on Kaylee's shoulder. "I'm on your team, okay?"

She nodded firmly. "Got it."

Kaylee aimed her hands at the sky, while Kumar opened her essence channel to make her stronger. Dark clouds swirled above us, blocking out the stars.

Celina looked over the rubble, her eyes darting every which way. I could tell what she was thinking immediately. There were Aedes and Davina running everywhere. Most of them were too distracted to use their elements, but I feared we'd hurt our own if we started firing at will.

"We need to get closer," I barked.

"I've got you!" Laura yelled. "Kellan, some help?"

Kellan took Laura's shoulder to power her up. She threw her hands up, and a wall of dirt rose out of the ground.

"Let's go!" she shouted.

Six of us ducked behind the earth shield she'd created—all three Fire Davina, our two partners, and Laura, who moved with us to keep us protected. We advanced forward, though the Infantry was only a hundred yards or so away from us now. Laura's shield hovered above the ground on her command.

"When you're ready, I'm going to create a break in the shield," Laura shouted. "Ready?"

Kellan glanced around the corner of the shield. "Go!"

Laura forced the dirt to part, and Celina, Caleb, and I all aimed our essence at the ground in front of the Infantry. Rain pounded down on them from above, but we created our fire just outside the range of Kaylee's storm.

The advancing men jumped back as fire ignited in a line in front of them. The flames were large at first, but quickly died down as they ate away at the manicured grass.

"Laura, we need more fuel!" I shouted.

She gritted her teeth and didn't tear her gaze from the dirt she was manipulating in the air in front of her. "I can't!"

Before anyone could give further instructions, the flames started growing higher. I glanced behind us to see Travis looking over one of the rubble piles and shooting me a thumbs-up. He was making the grass grow beneath our fire to fuel it.

Meanwhile, other Davina around the courtyard were flinging their elements at the men. Grass grew at their feet and tangled around their ankles, making them trip. Rocks flew through the air at speeds that could kill a person. Other Water Davina had joined in on Kaylee's storm, until the rain was pounding down so hard that we could hardly see the Infantry ourselves.

And still, gunfire rang through the air. I glanced around, and my stomach dropped when I saw how many people had fallen. There weren't many left standing.

"Where's everyone else!?" I yelled.

They should've been flooding out of their dorm rooms and trying to help, not hiding away like cowards.

Kellan ignored my question. "We've got this! As long as we—"

The sound of battle cries came from the other side of the crumbled building. The gunfire was deafening, and it hit me then that the Infantry had made it through the front gates of the academy. The huge group of men who'd come through the hole in the wall wasn't all of them—and they were still coming.

"Do we have enough elements to hold them off?" Shaylene asked. I was surprised at how level-headed she stayed.

Kellan shot a glance around the courtyard. "I don't know. There are too many people down."

"We have to get more Davina out here!" I shouted.

The earth began to shake more from the Davina controlling it. Ahead of us, a thick oak tree tipped over, making a loud smashing noise as it landed. Its roots tore up, leaving a huge hole in the ground.

Moments later, the horrible sound of cracking concrete met my ears. My eyes darted to the Winged Fountain not far from us, and my heart crumbled as the fountain split in two. The crack traveled all the way up from the base, until it reached the wings and one of them fell off and smashed into the pool below. Water sprayed everywhere, and it came pouring out of the broken base.

Someone somewhere began to control the excess water, and I watched wide-eyed as the water traveled in thick streams toward the new group of Infantry members. The water split in several directions and hit five of them in the face at once. Whoever was controlling it forced water up through their nostrils and down their throats. The five of them stopped in their tracks. Their mouths opened, like they were trying to scream, but nothing came out as water gurgled in their lungs.

I glanced back to my friends, taking my focus off my fire for a brief moment, to see that Everett was glaring at the incoming crowd with fury in his eyes. He twisted his hands, and the water followed his command. He ripped the water out of their mouths before they drowned, but it'd been enough to slow them down.

I was equally horrified as I was impressed.

"Watch out!" Kellan shouted.

From out of nowhere, a ball of glowing black Aedes essence whizzed toward us from the side. It was headed directly for Laura. She squealed and dropped her arms. Kellan jumped for her and tackled her to the ground. Laura narrowly missed being knocked out by the essence, but her shield had fallen. A cloud of dirt rose into the air, leaving us exposed. Bullets rained down around us, and the earth continued to shake.

Caleb let out a terrible cry and clutched his arm. Blood oozed between his fingers from where he'd been shot, but I barely had a chance to process the last second before Celina's hand was clutching my arm.

"This way!" she shouted, then dragged me and Shaylene behind the roots of the fallen tree.

"But Kellan!" I yelled.

I looked past the roots to see Kellan glancing around for me. He didn't see me, but it was obvious he didn't have time to waste. He threw his body in front of Laura and shielded her as they ran for cover behind the fountain. Caleb dove for cover beside them, and Laura threw up another earth shield.

Celina grabbed my arm before I could go run after them. She squeezed Shaylene's arm with her other hand and glanced between the two of us. "You run out there, you'll get yourself killed," she warned with an intense look in her eyes.

"But Caleb!" Shaylene protested.

"I know," Celina snapped. She took a breath to calm herself. "We'll find a way to get to him."

By now, the Infantry had swarmed all over campus. The three of us were crouched so low at the base of the rooted tree that no one noticed us. Yards in front of us, people ran across the courtyard, aiming weapons—both man-made and supernatural—at each other.

It was a freaking warzone! I didn't know how much longer we could hold out until the Alliance got here.

One of the Infantry spotted us. By the width of their shoulders and their hips, I'd guess it was a woman, but she was wearing a ski mask, so I couldn't see her face. She lifted her gun at the three of us, but we reacted quickly.

Three balls of essence whizzed through the air simultaneously—two white and one black. They slammed into her chest at the same time, and she went flying backward and landed hard on the ground. She'd been knocked out cold.

"We have to do something!" Shaylene cried, whirling back toward us.

I glanced between the two of them—a fellow Fire Davina, and an Aedes.

"All we've got is fire," I stated.

The girls shared a glance.

"Then if we're going to get back to our group, we know what we have to do," Celina said.

I nodded. Shaylene looked nervous, but after a moment of hesitation, she agreed. "Okay, I'll power you both up."

I already had enough power to sustain flames for days, but the extra boost would make me stronger.

Celina smirked. "Then let's light this place up, bitches."

Shaylene took a breath to steel her nerves, then held her

hands out to both of us. We each took one, and we jumped out from behind the tree. Celina aimed fire on the left side of Shaylene, while I lit the ground to my right. Red-hot flames streamed out of my palms, and the grass in front of me went ablaze. Raging flames licked high above my head, until we couldn't even see the fight going on around us.

"That's really hot!" Shaylene cried.

"Keep going!" I insisted.

Celina and I created a sort of fire ring around us, keeping back attackers and hiding ourselves from view. The flames followed us as we walked toward the fountain, creeping along the ground at our command.

When we reached the edge of the broken fountain, I breathed a sigh of relief and dropped my flames. I jumped over the edge of the fountain and into the dry base, where Kellan, Laura, and Caleb were hiding behind a mound of dirt Laura had created. She was hunched over Caleb and covered in blood.

"I can't..." she cried. "Kellan, I can't."

Caleb inhaled a sharp breath, but Kellan only reassured the two of them. "We'll find someone to help. You're going to make it, bro."

"We're here," I cried, coming to a halt as I landed on my knees. Blood dripped down Caleb's arm and pooled on the concrete below him. The bullet must've hit an artery for him to be losing blood so fast. His lips were void of color, and his eyes could barely focus on me.

"We have to stop the bleeding," Kellan demanded.

I didn't question it. I held my hand out to him, and he squeezed it tight. Essence poured through me, and I felt my healing magic well to the surface. I placed my hand on Caleb's wound, and warm, sticky blood coated my fingers.

But I didn't have a chance to heal him. A moment later, the sound of something metal clanging into the concrete fountain met my ears. I glanced to the side, and my stomach dropped out of my abdomen.

A grenade!

My friends and I leapt to our feet at the same time, all except Caleb, who could barely move from the blood loss.

"Run!" Shaylene shouted.

I barely had a moment to process what to do—because I knew Caleb wasn't going to make it to his feet in time. Shaylene shoved me out of the way as hard as she could, which sent me stumbling into Kellan. We both tripped over the side of the fountain. As we tumbled to the ground, the earth shot up around us, creating an instant hill. We couldn't control our momentum, and we went rolling down the hill and away from the fountain.

Boom!

The grenade went off before we'd stopped tumbling. Dirt went flying everywhere, and it was then that I realized the hill was another one of Laura's shields, but it was bigger than ever— at least ten feet tall, and it'd caused the sidewalk to heave up in all directions.

I lay on the ground beside Kellan, the two of us heaving and staring up at the shield Laura had made. It took a few moments for the shock to pass.

I looked upward to see Laura standing above us, her features strained and her hands held up to control the earth. She gritted her teeth a moment longer, before letting out a large sigh and dropping her hands to her side. The hill she'd created sagged a little, but it didn't go all the way back down to where it originally was.

Laura turned her head away, and Celina stepped forward. Gently, she pulled her into a hug. It was an unusual thing for Celina to do, but under the circumstances, it made sense.

Laura buried her face in Celina's shoulder. "I can't look," she whispered.

Kellen helped me to his feet. "Stay here."

The way he said it so firmly left my feet planted in the ground. It was like I couldn't move even if I wanted to.

Kellan stepped up the hill and peered over the side. I didn't need to see his face to notice his whole body sag at what he saw. Horrible images flickered through my imagination. Kellan turned to look at us, and all it took was a shake of his head for my heart to break into a million pieces.

"No!" I cried.

Kellan took several long strides over to me, until he wrapped me tight in his arms.

Beside me, Laura sobbed. "Oh, God. I didn't mean to leave them behind!"

"It's not your fault," Kellan told her while he rocked me back and forth.

I was shaking. Two of my best friends had just been killed. It wasn't real. It couldn't be. A wave of heavy emotions struck me all at once—denial, heartbreak, anger. I didn't know which one I felt more strongly at the moment, just that whatever it was made me ill beyond belief.

I lifted my head from Kellan's warm, comforting shoulder, to take in the chaos all around me. My friends had just been killed. Who knew how many other people had died tonight? And I literally didn't know how to stop it.

And then my eyes landed on *him*.

I didn't see his face, but I knew by the color of his hair and his build that it was him. Colt Walter slunk around the side of the Science Building.

"Kellan!" I cried, stiffening as my eyes locked on Colt in the distance. "It's him!"

Kellan glanced behind himself, but Colt was already gone. His eyes went wide. "You saw him? Colt?"

"Yes," I insisted. "We have to stop this."

I glanced to Celina and Laura. Laura's featured had quickly

turned to pure fury. "You go," she said. "Celina and I have some Infantry ass to kick."

Kellan grabbed my hand, but I couldn't force my feet to move. I *wanted* to go after Colt. I wanted him to pay for everything he'd done. But a heavy weight like bricks settled in my guts—

Fear.

I was afraid of facing Colt.

But I couldn't allow myself to stall. I formed my hands into fists and let my anger push me forward.

Kellan and I raced across the courtyard in the direction I saw Colt go. We were more alert than ever, and we each shot essence at every Infantry member we saw, weeding them out one by one. As a man lifted his gun to us, I shot flames straight out of my palm and landed them on his knuckles. It was so hot that he dropped his gun and screamed in pain.

I didn't know how we did it, but somehow, Kellan and I made it across the courtyard unscathed. As we rounded the Science Building and away from the fight, we spotted two dark figures. The first was obviously Colt, and the second I didn't make out before he stepped into the building. All I could tell was that he was male and was taller than Colt.

Kellan and I stopped in our tracks and ducked behind the bushes at the edge of the building. Colt glanced one way, then the other, but he didn't see us. He stepped into the building behind the other man.

"We have to get him to call off his men," I said to Kellan.

Kellan looked at me in a way he never had before. It was a warning—like I was about to make the biggest decision of my life. "Are you sure you want to do this? By any means necessary?"

I didn't know why, but in that moment, it was like I heard the words in my father's voice.

Are you sure you want to do this, Cora? What sort of legacy do you want to leave behind?

Legacy? I wondered. Right now, all I wanted was to prevent any more of my friends from being killed.

I wasn't my mother. Time and time again, she'd lectured me on sticking to my values, about doing the right thing. I knew that was how she won her battle twenty-five years ago, but it wasn't how I was going to win mine. Colt had too much blood on his hands—blood that I valued. And he was going to pay for that.

"Yes, Kellan," I said. "By any means necessary."

He squeezed my hand tightly. "Then stick close to me."

Kellan and I crept through the shadows, until we came to the door that Colt had entered. We quietly stepped into the building. A dark hall spanned in front of us, lit only by emergency lights every few yards. The hall was familiar, since this was where we had our Art of Healing labs every week. We could hear voices coming from down the hall, but it was hard to make them out.

"I think we can take them," I whispered to Kellan.

He nodded in agreement, then crept forward with me close at his heels.

"Why are you doing this!?" a woman cried.

My blood ran cold. It was Chancellor Harris!

Colt's evil laughter sounded down the hall. "To make an example out of the academy, of course."

Chancellor Harris scoffed. "I know why *you're* doing this," she sneered. "What I want to know is what's in it for *him*."

Kellan and I both exchanged a glance. Who was she talking about?

A familiar voice left me frozen on the spot. "It's just as he said, Casey," the man said smoothly. "I'm going to make an example out of you and your entire student body. No one will question keeping the supernaturals a secret again."

John Maddox!
I couldn't believe what I was hearing.
The Alliance was on Colt's side.

20

Something cold and hard pressed into my back between my shoulder blades. If I weren't already frozen in place, I'd have stopped dead in that moment. Instinctively, I knew it was a gun, and if I tried to fight back, I'd end up with a bullet straight through the heart. Kellan stiffened beside me, indicating he had the barrel of a gun pressed to his back as well. Slowly, we both lifted our hands in surrender.

"Move," a male voice demanded.

Kellan and I took a step forward. I tried to keep my knees from shaking, but I couldn't. I knew how to deal with injuries in a crisis. This was a whole other type of crisis. I didn't know whether I was supposed to fight back or stay calm.

The men behind us pushed us into the classroom where we studied Art of Healing. Chancellor Harris sat one of the chairs with her arms secured behind her back, while her husband lay unresponsive on the floor beside her. My guts twisted, and I hoped he'd only been knocked out. Three other men in suits stood in the shadows behind Maddox.

"We found these two lurking in the hall," one of the men said.

Maddox looked up from Chancellor Harris, the emergency lights casting deep shadows across his face. His features brightened when he saw the two of us enter the room. Colt wore a similar look of pleasure, but something about the way he was standing was strange. He stood to the side, like he was no longer the one in charge. It was actually a little terrifying.

The men holding guns to our backs stepped aside, and though the barrels were still trained on us, I felt like I could breathe now that it wasn't touching me. What I didn't expect was to see the men with the guns dressed in suits instead of ski masks. They were Alliance, not Infantry.

"Ah," Mister Maddox said brightly, opening his arms in a welcoming gesture. "Cora. Kellan. So nice of you to join us."

"Yeah, well, we couldn't miss the party," Kellan said coolly. "Mind telling us what's going on?"

Maddox eyed him up and down, as if deciding how much to tell him. Something in his features read amusement, like he wasn't at all offended by Kellan's demand for information.

"You realize you'll be dead before you have the chance to tell anyone," Maddox pointed out.

"Then we deserve to know what we're dying for," I stated simply, doing my best to keep my cool.

Maddox shrugged. "Very well. Secure them."

"What!?" I cried.

One of the men grabbed for my arms, while another shoved a gun in my face to make it clear not to struggle. I stilled and went with it, because I really didn't want to get shot in the face tonight.

The Alliance had come prepared. They didn't just find some old rope in the supply closet. They had handcuffs they secured behind mine and Kellan's backs before forcing us to sit in chairs they'd pulled up beside Chancellor Harris. I immediately glanced around, looking for a way out. We weren't exactly tied down to the chairs, but we'd never make it if we ran for the doors. My eyes landed upon a cart of dissection supplies a few feet behind me, not far from where Kane Harris lay on the floor. If I got my hands on a probe or even a sharp pair of tweezers, I might be able to pick my way out of the cuffs. But I couldn't get there from here.

"So, what is this?" Kellan demanded. "You've been working with the Infantry this whole time?"

Maddox began pacing in front of us. A hint of a smile touched his lips, like he was proud of how everything had played out and wanted to gloat about it. "No, Mister Greene. The Infantry was… convenient."

Kellan pressed his lips together. "Mighty convenient they attacked the same night you happened to be on campus."

Maddox chuckled in a way that made my skin crawl. "Oh, no, Mister Greene. *That* was no accident. You see, what you two did last semester has compromised all of us. You've made my job ten times harder trying to cover it up. Your stunt has sparked quite an uproar within the Alliance—some saying we can't keep hiding forever, while others believe repercussions for exposure should be punished more severely."

"And what do you think?" I challenged before I could stop myself.

Kellan shot me this look, like he was warning me away from danger territory. I knew I might be heading there, but it was hard not to snap at this asshole with the massacre going on outside. I didn't have the luxury of keeping a level head at the moment.

Maddox stopped pacing and looked straight at me. "If it were up to me, Miss Marek, you'd have received the death penalty the second you exposed yourself."

"That's what this is about?" I asked. "You want to kill us?"

"Oh, don't flatter yourself," Maddox scoffed. "This isn't about some petty revenge. This is a sacrifice necessary to maintain the security and privacy of the supernatural community. Once the

Alliance hears the death toll, they'll never consider letting our secret out again."

"There are people dying out there!" I exploded.

How could he not care? How could he justify the killing of his own people? People I loved had died tonight, and he was acting like that was some noble thing to be proud of.

"It's for the greater good!" Maddox roared, and I jumped in my seat. "The long-term benefits outweigh the short-term sacrifices."

"You call my friends' deaths *sacrifices*?" I snapped.

"Cora," Kellan hissed, warning me again that if I kept this up, I might get myself shot.

I pressed my lips firmly together.

Kellan looked to Maddox. "How'd the Infantry get involved?"

Maddox smiled, like he was proud of his mastermind plan. "The incident at the bank shook up a few Alliance supporters who believed it was time to expose ourselves, but it was clear they could not all be swayed. So I approached the Infantry myself and offered an exchange for their services."

"And what do they get out of this?" Kellan asked.

Colt got this crazy, blood-thirsty look in his eyes. "We get to kill your asses."

Maddox held up a commanding hand and spoke threateningly. "Mister Walter..."

Colt stepped back. It was amazing how much his demeanor changed when someone else was in charge. He was like a puppy bowing down to his master.

Maddox dropped his hand and crossed them both neatly in front of himself. "The deal was that I get Colt inside the school, and the Infantry goes hog-wild. They get the blood they've been looking for, and I get the assurance that the Alliance will continue to protect the supernatural race."

"How are you going to cover this up, though?" I demanded.

"It's one thing to persuade the Alliance. It's another to persuade all the witnesses."

An evil smile spread across Maddox's face. "If the Alliance wants it bad enough, they'll find a way to cover it up. And believe me, after tonight, they won't let anything slip through the cracks ever again."

"It doesn't have to be this way," Chancellor Harris argued. "Sharing the truth may just save us. Just like it did when the Alliance formed!"

Colt stared down at her with an expression of utter disgust. "Don't you get it, lady? No one wants you here!"

Chancellor Harris's jaw tensed, and her nostrils flared. "Tell that to all the people we've healed."

Colt laughed. "I'll be sure to do that, if I ever meet one of them."

Beside me, I heard the sound of Kane Harris stirring. He was coming to, but I didn't think anyone noticed. His eyes fluttered open and met mine. My gaze flickered from his to the lab equipment beside him. He took one look at my handcuffs and knew what I was getting at. Slowly, so no one else would see him in the darkness, he reached for one of the probes, then tossed it into my hands. By some sort of miracle, I caught it, and my heart leapt in relief.

Chancellor Harris looked to Mister Maddox, but she spoke to Colt. "You realize you've sold your soul to a devil."

Colt crossed his arms and smirked. "Don't think I know what you are—all of you. After tonight, you'll all go back into hiding and never bother us again."

There was something darker in his eyes. He acted like he was fine with us going into hiding, but something told me he had plans to continue hunting us down once this was all over. Acting was the only way to keep himself on Maddox's good side.

"You realize that will never happen," Chancellor Harris said coolly. "We're everywhere."

Colt's eyebrow twitched, another sign that he had further plans he wasn't sharing. "That's not what your Alliance tells me."

Maddox smirked.

"He's lying," Chancellor Harris said simply. "Don't you see you're a pawn?"

Colt's jaw tensed. A second later, he swung his arm out, and his fist connected with Chancellor Harris's jaw. Her head snapped to the side, her blonde hair covering her face, but she didn't make a sound.

Maddox's hand shot out to grab Colt's wrist. "Don't you dare touch her. She's mine."

Chancellor Harris took a deep breath and sat upright in her seat again, like the punch had barely fazed her. She wore a look of stone cold resolve on her face.

Colt shoved Maddox off of him. "What do you care? You're going to kill her anyway."

"You think that gives *you* the right to lay your hands on her?" Maddox sneered. "You're not in charge anymore, Colt."

"I thought you said we were partners," Colt growled.

Maddox chuckled, but he spoke in a smooth, condescending manner. "Unfortunately, Casey was right. You got your Infantry here. You're no use to me anymore, and I can't have you trying to expose us again."

Maddox raised his hand, and fire formed within his palm.

"We had a deal!" Colt shouted, backing up and looking terrified.

Maddox stepped toward him, the flames in his hands licking higher. "I'm afraid our deal has changed."

Maddox drew back his hand, aiming the fire at Colt. My stomach dropped, but he never got the chance to land the blow. The earth began to quake around us. Lab equipment rattled on the shelves, and beakers vibrated off the countertops and smashed to the floor. The cart of lab equipment rolled across the room, and the Alliance members all shot their hands out to the sides to help maintain their balance. The earth quaked so hard that I could hardly focus on anything.

Maddox whirled toward Chancellor Harris. "You think that's going to stop me!?" he roared, training his fire on her as she controlled the earth beneath us with her essence.

Chancellor Harris chuckled. "No, sir. If anything is going to stop you, it's my husband."

The handcuffs I'd been picking gave way, and Kane and I jumped to our feet at the same time. Dark essence shot out of his hands. One ball of essence landed square in one of the Alliance member's chest, while the other whizzed by Maddox's head as he ducked. Both of my shots of essence struck two other Alliance members, knocking them out.

Everything happened so fast that I could hardly process it. Kellan jumped up, but his hands were secured behind his back, so he couldn't fight with essence. Instead, he swung his leg around and kicked the gun out of the nearest Alliance member's hands.

Chancellor Harris made a similar, but much more impressive move. The rumors about her being highly trained in combat weren't exaggerations. When she stood, she kicked her chair so that it sailed through the air and landed square in the remaining Alliance member's face.

As Kane helped his wife undo her handcuffs, I whirled to help Kellan, and saw that the member he was fighting was twisting his hands to manipulate the air around him. Kellan gasped for air, and I knew the Davina was sucking the oxygen out of his lungs.

"Kellan, duck!" I shouted.

He followed my command, and my essence soared through the air and slammed into the Davina's chest, knocking him out.

Within moments, all of Maddox's backup were knocked out,

leaving us to fight only Maddox and Colt. Chancellor Harris and her husband lunged for Maddox at the same time. She landed a kick to the chest, and I heard the sound of several ribs crack. Kane aimed his essence, but before he could throw it, Maddox reached into his coat and pulled out a Glock.

Before I knew what was happening, a *bang* went off, and Kane Harris stumbled backward, clutching his stomach. Kellan and I both jumped.

The earth began to rumble more fiercely under Chancellor Harris's rage. She jumped on Maddox so fast that she was nothing more than a blur. I ran over to Kane and applied pressure to the wound, my heart racing. He gasped for breath as blood poured out of his stomach and onto the tile floor.

"Kellan!" I cried. "We have to heal him!"

"My hands," he replied in a rush.

I jumped to my feet and grabbed the dissecting probe I'd dropped on the ground, then quickly picked Kellan's handcuffs. His hands broke free, and we both knelt beside Kane.

So much was happening at once that I could hardly process it. Chancellor Harris had knocked the gun out of Maddox's hands, and the two were fighting hand-to-hand now with moves I'd only seen in martial arts movies before. It was obvious they had both been trained in combat. Each time one of them tried to knock the other out with essence, they dodged it and landed another punch or blocked the other's blow.

Colt seemed to have frozen still. The doorway was blocked by the fight, so he couldn't leave the room even if he wanted to.

I barely had two seconds to take it all in, because Kane Harris was still bleeding out beneath me. Kellan grabbed my shoulder firmly, while I pressed both hands to the wound in Kane's abdomen.

My essence channel opened like a floodgate, sending magic flowing through me. I guided it down my hands, and they glowed as I worked my magic to stop the bleeding and heal as much of the wound as I could.

Kane gasped, but his breathing slowed as my essence filled him. "Good enough," he breathed. "Help my wife!"

Kane wasn't taking no for an answer. He shoved my hands away from his stomach, though he still wasn't completely healed. There was nothing I could do but continue to fight.

Kellan and I jumped to our feet again. Everything happened in slow motion, a split second passing in what felt like a minute.

Colt held a gun and aimed it at Chancellor Harris and Maddox. It was clear he was aiming at Maddox—that he was furious about the betrayal. Maddox landed a blow to Chancellor Harris's face, and she went stumbling to the side. He whirled around and noticed the barrel trained on him and acted instinctively. He lunged to the floor where his gun lay and grabbed for it.

"No!" I screamed, jumping for Maddox.

To be honest, I didn't care if Colt lived or died, not after all the terrible things he'd done to my friends. But we still needed him to call off the attack. John Maddox may have had the upper hand, but as far as the Infantry was concerned, they still took their orders from Colt.

"Cora!" Kellan cried. Before I could reach Maddox, Kellan's arm grabbed me around the waist, and I sling-shotted back into his chest.

Another *bang* sounded through the room, and I flinched. When my eyes opened, time seemed to be standing still. I didn't know who had made the shot—or if they'd hit anyone. Then blood began to soak into Colt's shirt, and time started forward again.

I lunged for Colt and caught him before he hit the ground. At the same time, Chancellor Harris had gone for Maddox, but he anticipated it. Maddox aimed essence at her, and she went down like a rock. Kellan and I were the only two left standing against Maddox.

"Kellan!" I cried. "We need Colt!"

But Kellan wasn't listening. Maddox pushed himself to his feet, but he moved like he was in pain. His hair was tousled at the top of his head, and blood dripped down the side of his cheek. His nice suit was all tattered.

"You two have been nothing but trouble for me!" Maddox growled. "The Alliance will move on from this easier with the two of you gone."

Maddox raised his gun and pointed it at me. Utter dread dropped through my stomach, but I barely had a split second to react before Kellan jumped in front of me.

"We're not going anywhere," he growled.

Then Kellan reached back to grab my hand, and essence unlike I'd ever felt it swept through me. This wasn't like the floodgates he'd opened before. This was like the whole damn ocean pouring through me all at once. As Kellan siphoned my essence through himself, it was like his desperation had opened my connection to the max, giving the two of us complete access to all the essence that flowed through the earth. My entire body glowed with essence so bright that it was all I saw. Even when I closed my eyes to block out the blinding light, it was still there, swirling around me and holding tight like a warm hug.

No, wait... That was Kellan. Kellan's strong arms wrapped around me, and his face buried into my hair.

"Hold on, Cora," he whispered.

And I did. I wrapped my arms around him and held on for dear life.

And then...

Boom!

The essence that'd been filling our bodies exploded in one single blow. My eyes shot open, and all I saw was a huge ball of essence at least five feet wide spinning through the air at lightning speed, aimed straight toward the asshole with the gun on us.

He barely had time to react. All I saw were his eyes widening, then the essence blasted him back. Concrete went flying as the essence carried Maddox through the wall, blasting a hole straight through it and into the room across the hall. I'd never seen anything like it in my life.

I didn't need to see more to be sure—no one could survive that kind of blast. John Maddox was dead.

Complete silence fell over the room. I sank to my knees, my whole body quaking. Kellan wrapped me in his arms. I glanced below me to see that Colt had gone still. The life had left his eyes. And though I thought he deserved it, it was too much.

Tears poured over my lids and began streaming down my face. We'd lost our one chance at calling off the attack.

Maddox's men began to come to. But while I'd been crying, Kane had been limping his way around the room gathering all the guns. He stood in the middle of the room, black essence aimed at the Alliance members. As they all came to, it was the first thing they saw, and each of them stilled.

"I'm not going to kill you," Kane said through strained breath. "I want you to live with the regret of what you were a part of tonight. Now leave before I change my mind."

All five Alliance members glanced around. They saw the massive hole in the wall and must've thought better about sticking around, because they all scrambled to their feet and raced out of the room.

I sniffled into Kellan's arms. Moments of silence ticked by, but I still couldn't wrap my head around everything that happened tonight.

"How many do you think we lost?" I whispered into Kellan's shoulder.

Someone came up beside us, and I lifted my head to see it

was Chancellor Harris. I hadn't even realized she'd woken yet. She looked terrible, but at least she was alive.

She held out her hand. "I don't hear any more gunshots. Should we go out and see?"

I wiped the tears from my cheeks and swallowed the lump in my throat. If there ever was a time to be strong during a crisis, now was it.

I took her hand, but I shook my head as I got to my feet. My gaze flickered to Kellan, who kept an arm wrapped around me.

"I don't want to just see," I said. "I want to do what I've been preparing my whole life for—I want to heal."

21

When we stepped out of the Science Building, it was like stepping through a portal into a post-apocalyptic world. But somehow, I found that comforting. There were no more sounds of gunshots, and the earth was still beneath our feet. The rubble remained, and fires burned through the lawn. Several people shouted each other's names, and others ran across the lawn as they searched for each other in the aftermath. But the fight was over. No more people would die.

Chancellor Harris supported her husband's weight. "John was blocking all communication with the Alliance tonight. I need to get a message to them. And Kane, we need to get you proper medical care."

He clutched his stomach. "Yeah," he said through gritted teeth. "I'm going to need surgery."

"Cora, Kellan," Chancellor Harris instructed, "find as many healers as you can, and start with the worst injuries. You know what to do."

Chancellor Harris left us alone. It was obvious that she didn't think us incompetent, as most adults did. Instead, she trusted us, much like the vibe I'd gotten from her at the beginning of the semester.

I stood in place a moment longer, dreading what we might find. Would more of my friends be gone?

Kellan took my hand. "Come on, Cora. We have to help."

Kellan's words struck me. *Help.* That was all I ever wanted to do—help people. I could grieve for the friends I'd lost later. Right now, I had to help those who still had a chance.

I squeezed his hand back. "Let's go."

Kellan and I walked forward, assessing the damage as we moved. There were so many bodies on the ground. I didn't even know where to start.

And then I spotted three familiar female figures bent over a male form. One of them was siphoning essence from the other two, while the Davina girls pressed their glowing hands on the guy to heal him. I was struck by the oddness of it, since I'd never seen a group of three heal together.

Kellan and I rushed over to Laura, Kaylee, and Celina. My stomach dropped when I saw that the guy they were healing was Travis. He had a huge gash across his chest, but it knitted back together under the girls' touch.

"Oh my God, you guys!" I cried. "You're alive!"

The three of them glanced up to us as we approached, but they didn't move as they continued to heal Travis. Laura wiped the tears from her cheeks. "We're so glad to see you!"

Kellan furrowed his brow. "Wait. How are you two doing that?"

"Yeah," I agreed. "Kaylee, you haven't even studied healing."

"I don't know," she said. "Laura and I didn't even know we were compatible, but she touched me, and... it just came naturally."

"Same," Celina answered. "We didn't even mean to at first."

Travis stirred and inhaled a deep, refreshing breath. "I guess that makes me the lucky one tonight, huh?"

"Something's different," Laura pointed out. "I feel stronger."

"Me, too," Kaylee remarked.

My eyes widened, and Kellan and I exchanged a glance. We'd both experienced a huge surge of power back in the Science Building. Had the trauma we'd been through tonight built some kind of bond that strengthened our essence? I mean, Kaylee shouldn't have been able to heal without training. Yet here she was, healing with a total stranger.

I glanced around. There were so many bodies. Healing them could take hours—hours some of them might not have.

Kellan noticed the same thing I did. "You guys, how are we going to heal everyone?" he asked.

As I glanced down at Kaylee's glowing hands, something struck me.

"We need to get everyone we can together," I stated. "I have an idea."

Just as I said it, a group of guys came jogging over to us—Drew, Warner, Kumar, Miles, and Everett. Tucker and Jett were nowhere to be seen, and I worried we'd lost them, too. Warner was still favoring his broken arm, but it was clear he was going to make it.

"Everyone okay?" Drew asked breathlessly.

Laura swallowed, and her eyes darted in the direction of the fountain. She spoke in a small voice. "I think we're all that's left."

Travis sat up, his chest looking as good as new. "Cora says she has an idea."

Drew tilted his head to the side. "What kind of idea?"

I took a deep breath. "It's just a theory, but... do any of you feel a stronger connection with each other after tonight?"

Miles and Everett exchanged a glance, but it was Miles who spoke. "Everett and I just healed a girl's wing. We've never been able to heal together before."

The look in their eyes confirmed my suspicion. Tonight had

brought us all together in ways we never thought possible. Which made our essence more compatible.

I kept one hand in Kellan's and reached out with the other for Drew. "Everyone join hands."

Drew glanced down at my outstretched hand and hesitated.

"It's okay," I told him. "I don't hold anything against you anymore. We stand together as one, remember?"

He nodded firmly.

"Which is why I think we need to do just that," I said to the group. "Everyone join hands."

No one questioned what I was doing. They all just followed along, trusting that whatever I had in mind was worth it. Laura helped Travis to his feet, and we all joined hands in a circle—even Warner, whose arm must've hurt like a bitch when Celina took his hand.

"Aedes, you know what to do," I said. "Davina… let your essence flow. Don't hold back."

"Got it," Travis said.

Celina glanced around the circle. "We stand together as one."

I'd never understood the truth of that motto as much as I did in that moment. As the Aedes around our circle began to siphon our essence, magic began to glow white in all of our hands. We began one unit, growing and shaping our essence until beautiful wisps of light came off our skin and swirled into a ball in the middle of our circle.

"We stand together as one," the group repeated.

Each time we said it, the wisps of essence grew and grew, until streams were pouring out from the middle of our circle, reaching out like blessed hands all across the courtyard. Our essence was so bright and spanned so wide that it lit up campus like the morning sun.

Beside me, Kellan squeezed his eyes shut tightly, until moments later, feathery black wings erupted from his back. When it happened, I felt my essence channel open to mega proportions, and I followed his lead. I flexed my shoulders, and white wings grew out of my back. All around the circle, everyone had noticed, and they followed suit until each of us were standing in our full supernatural form, an even mix of white and black wings.

The ball of light between us grew bigger and bigger, until it was blinding to look at. Warm, calm essence unlike anything I'd ever felt swirled out of me. As it intermingled with my friends' essence, I could feel the warmth of their magic brushing up against mine, then twisting together like an embrace. I felt our essence swirl across campus and touch the injured. Somehow, without seeing it with my own eyes, I could *feel* it.

My essence was healing.

And with each person we healed, I felt their essence give something in return, something more warm and comforting than I could've ever dreamed. It didn't matter who we healed—Aedes, Davina, or human. They all gave something in return, which fueled even more healing power for everyone else.

I didn't know how long we stood there. It could've been minutes, or it could've been hours. But as we healed those who'd fallen during the battle, one thing became very clear.

Too many humans had witnessed our healing tonight—had been *part* of it. We couldn't hide the truth any longer.

We all shared this world together.

It was time *everyone* stood together as one.

EPILOGUE

"$\mathcal{A}$re you ready?" Kellan wrapped an arm around me and squeezed me close to him. It'd been days since the attack, but it felt like no time had passed at all.

I glanced to my friends and family surrounding me. Dad stood with his arm around Mom, who shot me an encouraging smile. She looked so vibrant and happy now that the restaurant had been rebuilt. Though she'd been severely burnt, there wasn't a scar left on her. It was great to see her back to her old self.

Kaylee stood beside me with a melancholy look on her face. Kumar had his arm wrapped around her shoulder. Next to them, Laura and Travis stood hand in hand. Beside them, Drew and Celina stood so close it should've bothered me, but it didn't. I actually thought those two would work well together.

The street was quiet as we stared up at the angel tree in front of the elementary school. It was summer now, so school wasn't in session. Some of the ornaments that had been placed there a few months ago had fallen off in the wind, but they'd been replaced. They sparkled in the sun just as beautifully as they had the first time I saw them, looking like diamonds swirling among the branches of the evergreen.

I took a deep breath and looked down to the ornament in my hand. Across the angel wings, Shaylene's name had been written in cursive. A lump rose to my throat as I thought about how we'd lost her—and so many others. She was so gentle and fun-loving. She would've been thrilled to see how we'd healed the entire courtyard with our essence.

Sometimes, I thought maybe she *did* see it—that her essence had combined with ours and she'd been with us to heal all those people.

She'd be proud of what happened afterward, how the Alliance had shown up to witness our healing, and how days later, after they had time to deliberate, they agreed that it was time to improve relations with humans, and not just those within government and special positions.

What came as the biggest shock was when Kellan's father, Ronan Greene, approached me himself and invited the two of us to serve on a new public relations council they were forming.

Kellan and I could hardly believe what we were being offered. It was what he always wanted—to serve on the Alliance and create policies that would make it easier for mixed families to assimilate into the supernatural world. This wasn't how he saw it happening, with us coming out in the open, but he would reach his goal nonetheless.

I took a deep breath and wiped a tear from my cheek. "Yeah," I said in an even voice. "I'm ready."

I stepped forward and hung Shaylene's ornament on the tree. Kellan placed the one with Caleb's name beside it, and the two clinked together. They started spinning until the strings were wound around one another. Each of my friends stepped forward and placed their own ornament on the tree, one for someone we'd lost.

My heart felt heavy, but as I stepped back and looked up at the sparkling tree, the weight began to lift.

It was far too quiet, but Celina took it upon herself to break the silence. She began to sing a melancholy tune, one that I knew her and Shaylene would've sounded perfect at in a duet. Normally, the sound of Celina's voice would've annoyed me, but it didn't. Right now, it was a comfort.

Laura reached her hand out to me, and I held on tight as we swayed back and forth to the sound of Celina's farewell song. Soon, everyone had joined hands and swayed to the same slow rhythm. Tears streaked my cheeks, and Laura sniffled from beside me. It was hard to say goodbye, but something about it was beautiful, too. I knew that wherever I went, the people I'd lost would be there with me, a part of my own essence. And their memory—their legacy—would live on.

Celina's voice faded, and everyone started pulling each other into hugs.

Mom and Dad wrapped me in their arms at the same time. Mom kissed the top of my head and said, "I'm so proud of you, Cora."

I drew away from her. "You are? But Mom, you never wanted me to fight like you did."

She swallowed, like she was on the verge of tears. "I didn't, but maybe you're not like me, Cora. There's a fire inside of you I never had."

I nudged her. "It comes from Dad."

My father chuckled, but his voice settled quickly. "Your mother's right, Cora. We're both very proud of you. You're going to do great things with the Alliance."

I smiled. "I hope so."

I glanced over to Kellan to see him and Celina exchanging a friendly hug. I knew he was deeply hurt by what she'd done to him, but he seemed like he was moving on from it now. Celina caught me eyeing her and walked over to me. My parents turned to Kellan, which left me and Celina alone.

"Hey, Cora," she said lightly. "I know we haven't always gotten along great, but after everything that happened… I just wanted to apologize."

Another few pounds seemed to lift off my shoulders.

"Look," she continued. "We're both really good at what we do, but I don't want to see you as competition. It got us nowhere during our final. I just don't want to be the bitch who ruins everything again."

I chuckled lightly. "Don't say that. You're not a… Well, you kind of were."

She crinkled her nose. "Yeah, I totally was."

"I want to put the past behind us, too," I said, but my eyes flickered toward Kellan. "I mean, as long as you don't consider us competition in *other* areas."

"Oh, God no," she laughed. "You don't still have eyes for Drew, do you?"

"He's all yours," I told her.

She smiled. "Good, because I was thinking of asking him out."

"Well, I guarantee he won't turn you down," I assured her.

"So, friends?" Celina asked.

I nodded. "Friends."

After Celina bounced away to go talk to Drew, Laura and Kaylee approached me again. The three of us shared a group hug. When we drew away from each other, Laura was the first to speak. "I'm so glad this is all over."

"Me, too," I said. "You went through so much."

Laura shrugged, but I could tell it bothered her. "Yeah, but it's finally over. I'll be in therapy for a while, but I know I'm going to get through this. I have you guys and Travis to help."

"And we will," I promised. "With anything you need."

She smiled. "Thanks."

"And I'll finally be at school with you guys," Kaylee said. "I'm sick of missing out."

Laura's eyebrows shot up. "Believe me, you should be glad you did."

Kaylee must've noticed the frown on Laura's face, because she quickly changed the subject. "Hey, what do you say we pamper ourselves later today? You deserve it."

"A mani-pedi?" Laura asked, her features brightening. "Are you a mind reader?"

The two of them walked off to talk about their plans for the day, and Kellan returned to my side.

"You were right," Kellan said as he draped his arm over my shoulder.

I looked up at him. "About what?"

"Hiding ourselves has only got us hurt," he clarified. "It's time to try something new and just… trust in the process."

"You're excited to be serving on the council, aren't you?" I asked.

"Do you even know me at all, Cora?" he teased, playing with a strand of my hair.

I pushed him lightly in the shoulder, but not enough to shove him away from me. "I'm glad you're looking forward to it."

He smiled lightly as he stared down at me with dreamy eyes. "I've been looking forward to it my whole life."

"I'll miss the academy," I said solemnly.

"Hey," Kellan said gently. "Joining the Alliance doesn't mean your studies are over."

"No," I agreed, "but I'm starting to think that maybe I'm not supposed to be a firefighter. Being on the Alliance *feels* right, but I'm going to have to change my whole course of study."

"As long as that's what you want," Kellan said. "You know you don't *have* to do this."

"I know," I said. "I want to."

"I'm glad to hear that. I get to do this with my girl at my side." He squeezed me harder, and my heart swooned.

"I'm glad, too," I whispered, before stepping up on my toes and planting a gentle kiss on his lips.

Kellan relaxed. "So, what do you want to do now? It sounds like Laura and Kaylee are leaving."

I glanced around, but no one was close enough to hear us. I lowered my voice to a whisper anyway. "To be honest, I'd rather be alone with you right now."

"Sure," Kellan said. "We could go grab a bite to eat or something—"

"No, Kellan," I chuckled. "I want to be *alone* with you."

I raised an eyebrow, and he quickly caught on. His mouth formed into a perfect O. His arms dropped from my shoulders, and he took my hands. "Well, that can be arranged."

"I should probably say goodbye to my parents first," I said.

Kellan's hungry eyes roamed over my body, and heat flared across the surface of my skin. "Hurry up, sweetheart."

My heart jumped when he called me that. He had no idea what sort of affect that had on me. He must've noticed my cheeks flush, because he asked, "You like that?"

I smirked. "A little."

"Hurry up, sweetheart," he teased.

I put my arms around his neck and pulled him closer, until his forehead was resting on mine. "The more you call me sweetheart, the more I want to stay right here in your arms."

He chuckled and pressed another kiss to my lips, then another, and another. A whirlwind of tingles spread throughout my abdomen and down between my thighs.

"Is that so, sweetheart?" Kellan teased.

"That's it," I said. "I'm never leaving."

Kellan's hands tangled in my hair, and he pulled me tight to him, until the side of my face was pressed tight to his chest. I could hear his heart beating, and it was the most wonderful sound in the world. Having him here in my arms eased the knot in my chest that'd been there for weeks.

"Then don't," Kellan whispered into my hair. "Don't ever leave."

"I won't," I promised.

And I meant it. Kellan and I had a future together. It wasn't the one I'd planned, but I guess sometimes life just surprised you. I never planned to fail my final exam our first semester. I never planned to expose ourselves as supernatural. I never planned to lose my friends like I had. Maybe the plan I had for myself wasn't the legacy I was meant to leave behind.

But one thing had never changed. All I ever wanted was to make a difference in this world.

Come hell or high water, I was making a damn good one.

THE END

This concludes Cora and Kellan's story, but the Davina have more adventures! Don't miss Cora's parents in the Divine Fate Trilogy.

ABOUT THE AUTHOR

Alicia Rades is a USA Today bestselling author of young adult and new adult paranormal fiction. When she's not dreaming up magical stories, she's either binge-watching paranormal shows, meditating, or spending time with her family. She has an unhealthy obsession with psychic characters and writes with a deck of tarot cards next to her computer.